The Naked Soul

Katherine Bennett

PublishAmerica
Baltimore

First printing

This is a work of fiction. Names, characters, places, and incidents either are the product of the author's imagination or are used fictitiously. Any resemblance to actual persons, living or dead, events, or locales is entirely coincidental.

ISBN: 1-4241-5625-4
PUBLISHED BY PUBLISHAMERICA, LLLP
www.publishamerica.com
Baltimore

Printed in the United States of America

 # INTRODUCTION

"We suffered, starved and triumphed, groveled down yet grasped at glory...we reached *the naked soul of man.*"

These words, written many years after the American Civil War by Sir Ernest Shackleton, the Antarctic Explorer, describe survival of the human spirit. They also paint a picture of the result of the Civil War or, as euphemistically described in the vernacular of the day, "The Late Unpleasantness." Former slaves, slave owners and many other people unfortunate enough to have lived in the south experienced the loss of homes, land and most of their possessions. Many were left with only the clothes on their backs. Whole towns and cities were put to the torch. Louisiana, once number two in wealth and prosperity in the United States prior to the war, became what Confederate Commander Kirby Smith described as "...a howling wilderness." No one escaped the horror. Slaves, though free, were left to flounder and starve along with their former masters. How a people beaten down to " ...the naked soul..." managed to rise again, is the story told in these pages.

Recently, a friend of mine, a Polish immigrant, was lamenting the loss of different parts of her country by various factions throughout several hundred years until the landmass was now only a portion of what it once was. I looked at her and smiled. "I know the feeling," I said. She expressed surprise. I explained to her about the Louisiana Purchase and how my small state once stretched all the way to Canada. I told her 10 flags of one sort or another had flown over my state from 1519 until 1812.

Then I told her of the devastation of the most "uncivil" of all wars.

As I researched the people and times in Louisiana prior to January 26, 1861, the date Louisiana seceded from the Union and joined the Confederacy, I was astonished to find stories so complete and detailed that the smell and flavor of people's lives seemed to leap from the pages. Louisiana women wrote two of the three most important Civil War diaries kept by southern women!

No story of the time could be complete without Fredrick Douglas's incredible perspective, but there were other slave narratives that rivaled the most horrendous accounts I had ever heard. As far as I know, many of these stories had not been in print for many years and certainly had not made it into the mainstream consciousness in my lifetime. I have taken the liberty of weaving these first-hand accounts into the lives of some of my black characters.

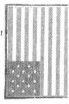

I also discovered there were slave owners who were 'relatively' kind and concerned about the welfare of their slaves. This in no way condones this hideous practice. However, it was the way life was lived at the time. I felt compelled to show both the less egregious as well as the more offensive, to give flesh and blood to this story.

In capturing the spirit and character of Louisiana, it was necessary to give voice to some of the dialects present during the period of the novel. I have tried to do this in a way that is not too distracting to the reader, and I have used phrases that can be easily interpreted.

The Author

3

Dedication

To my husband, Preston

His love, unwavering support,
and encouragement made it all possible.

Acknowledgements

I wish to thank the staff at the Gwinnett County Library, Five Forks Trickum Branch, Lawrenceville, Georgia. Without their help I could not have written the very first chapters of this book.

Dr. Ben Legendre, Agriculture Department, LSU, Baton Rouge, Louisiana, gave me a gold mine when he told me about David Stewart. David Stewart's family has owned Alma Plantation since before the Civil War. David spent hours answering my questions and showing me around Alma, explaining patiently and in detail the intricate workings of his huge sugarhouse. His generous loan of part of his collection of 19th century books and magazines was invaluable in helping me visualize and understand the sugar cane process from planting and harvesting to production. David's passion for the history of sugar cane was an inspiration and a validation of my choice of sugar cane over the usual cotton plantation as a more "typical" Louisiana plantation. Any mistakes in my descriptions of the processes involved in the running of a sugar cane plantation are my own and no reflection on my expert sources.

Heartfelt thanks to Dr. Daniel Dubovsky, doctor of Oncology, in Atlanta, Georgia, for his review of my description of untreated breast cancer in the 1860s.

Michael Hebert and Esther Blood of the Rapides Parish Library in Alexandria, Louisiana, were especially helpful in providing source material for Sugar Cane Production. Michael was instrumental in helping me find a copy of the definitive work for my purposes: "Green Fields—200 Years of Louisiana Sugar."

Mrs. Lucy Parlange was kind enough to give me a comprehensive tour of Parlange Plantation House and grounds. This was the model for River Rose and I will be forever grateful to her for her efforts in preserving this National Historic Landmark for all of us to enjoy. Parlange is a "living museum" of a gracious time long ago.

Special thanks to my two sons, Kerry and Mike Wolfe, and my husband, Preston Bennett, for their help in keeping my computer going, thus allowing me do much of my research from home.

Thanks to my brother-in-law, Jimmy Whittle, for the generous loan of his centennial copies of past newspapers from Alexandria, Louisiana. These included many first-hand accounts and a picture of the burning of Alexandria.

A salute to my "early readers" who provided great insight and suggestions to this novice writer: Kari Bennett, Preston Bennett, Kerry and Mike Wolfe, Mary Blalock, David Stewart, Johnnie and Clara Bennett, Krystyna Csuk, Kathryn Wolfe, Barbara Whittle, and retired editor David McCuen.

The Time Before

Chapter I

New Orleans, Louisiana—May 1838

"What will it feel like to slice through a man's flesh and bone and know his life is ending because of the thrust of your sword?" Zack McLoed posed this question softly, so softly that at first his friend was not sure he had heard correctly.

Pierre Beauregard shifted to a more comfortable position in the carriage.

"It will be different for each of us as it happens. But it will happen in war and we will be defending ourselves. We will not realize what has happened until it is over," Pierre said. He leaned forward in the carriage and watched Zack's face. "Are you having second thoughts, *mon ami?*"

"I know being a soldier is what I want. The adventure, the excitement, helping my country. But I wonder how I'll feel the first, second, or third time I see a man fall because of my shot or the thrust of my sword. Will it get easier? And if it does, will I have lost a part of my soul?"

"That will not happen to you. It will never be easy. But you will always do your duty, as will I," Pierre said.

"Duty…duty," Zack muttered. "It's ground into my bones."

Pierre stretched his legs to get more comfortable and unbuttoned his jacket. "We've been at West Point a long time. Things may look different when we see our families again. Duty may mean something else entirely when you see your father. Right now, I am just glad to stop feeling wobbly for the first time in days. New York to New Orleans was a long voyage. Sailing is not for me."

The coach plowed on, occasionally bobbing from side to side on New Orleans's uneven brick streets. Philosophical questions about life and death didn't deter the wheels from turning and the dogs from yapping as the coach rolled closer to each man's destination.

Soon Zack's thoughts turned inward again.

"I dread telling my father my plans. He thinks I'll be joining him in running River Rose," Zack said.

The men were anxious to see their families after their long time at school, but both were also dreading this reunion. The choice of a military career was not what owners of sugar cane plantations wanted for their sons.

Pierre frowned slightly and plucked absently at the pointed beard that along with his dark eyes and hair gave him a sleek, dandified appearance. Everything about him seemed precise. He was not tall but his personality gave people the impression he was larger.

"An engineering officer utilizes exact measurements and does careful planning. Every battle is different and requires total concentration. Running a plantation is the same day after day. It would not challenge me." Pierre paused. "I want to lead men into battle as did Napoleon." He settled back in the carriage. Pierre had studied every battle that the French general had fought.

His full name was Pierre Gustave Toutant-Beauregard, but because of the constant ragging from his schoolmates with names like Smith and Brown, he had dropped the hyphen and signed his name P.G.T. Beauregard.

Zackery Patrick McLoed was Irish, with sandy hair and blue eyes, of average height and stocky in build. He was fascinated with "soldiering" and had spent hours as a child moving his toy battlefield figures in intricate maneuvers. Battle strategy was what he loved and he studied history and battles to see what could have been done differently to affect the outcome of each. Pierre and Zack argued into the night on many occasions regarding strategy, luck, and whether careful planning really paid off. He wondered if it was true that all plans went out the window when the first shot was fired.

Only a month ago in the barracks they shared, the two men had been studying and arguing amiably as usual.

"A great commander has to have a certain 'battle sense' that takes over in the heat of battle. He has to know instinctively from his heart when to move each piece of equipment and regiment forward and when to fall back," said Pierre. "He cannot stop to *think* what to do. He must already know." Even after four years at the New York school, he still had the precise pronunciation of one whose first language was not English. He sat on one of the hard little chairs provided for their desks in the dormitory. As he talked he waved his hands and Zack could almost see him mounted on a great horse directing his men forward and calling up the cannon.

Zack walked over to the window that looked out over the Hudson River. It was a quieter river than the furious Red River back home. It was still dark and he could imagine for a moment he was looking at the unruly waterway that ruled the lives of plantation folk in his section of Louisiana.

Zack turned away from the window and said, "I want to be in a real battle that's planned out carefully, one where everyone knows his job and where he should be at every moment. I want to see what war is really like." He came back and sat down at his desk. "I want to see other places and have adventures before I settle down to plantation life." He was silent for a moment. "I have to see what else there is in the world," Zack said and his eyes sparkled. "I won't be a soldier forever, but I have to see what it's like in other places."

Pierre jumped up and began pacing with excitement. "I want to be a soldier forever. *Papá* will be furious with me but I have to do it. I will never settle down to plantation life. *Papá* sent me to this school to get my grand ideas of the pomp and ceremony of flags and parades drummed out of me by marching and the rigors of military life. Instead it has made me love it more! My brothers can continue the work of the plantation, not me." Pierre threw himself down on his bunk and put his hands behind his head. "I will always lead my men into battle. I will do my planning in a tent away from the main battle lines, but when the cannons roar, I will lead the charge!"

Zack could tell his friend was already envisioning himself in the throes of battle. Pierre was brilliant, and would graduate second in his class. He was totally devoted to the life of a warrior. Zack was not as passionate about soldiering as Pierre, but then nobody was as passionate about anything as Pierre. He admired his friend but they were totally different in many ways. The thing that drew them together was their love of Louisiana.

Outskirts of New Orleans

The coach drew up before Beauregard's aunt's house.

The two men looked at each other. They had been together for four years. Each was excited yet not sure of what his future would bring. A chance to soldier together might come, but it was more likely they might not meet again for years.

"Goodbye, my good friend." Pierre grasped Zack's hands warmly. "Until our paths cross again, may the gods smile on you."

Pierre sprang from the carriage and hurried up the steps of his aunt's home. His father would be arriving the next day to take him to Toutant, his family's plantation.

Zack didn't signal the driver right away. He wanted to remember this moment. The carriage with its brass and smell of leather, and the sight of his best friend striding away into the unknown future.

Finally, he tapped the ceiling of the coach with his stick, and the coachman gently pricked the horses with his whip.

On the road to River Rose, Zack settled back in the coach to think about what he would say to his father. Unlike Beaurgard, he had no brothers to take over the plantation. He was an only child. Somehow he must make his father see that the restlessness that had caused his father to agree to have Senator George Waggaman recommend him to the U. S. Military Academy had not been cured. It had only grown as he read of the great battles in his country and abroad. Would actual experience be enough to "settle him down" as his father put it? Zack didn't know.

He watched the landscape as the coach drove deeper into the Louisiana countryside. It was spring, the most beautiful time of the year, with sweet smells and an exhilarating feeling in the air. Not the stifling heat that would descend in a couple of months. He leaned back in the coach and let the familiar smells of home wash over him and began to doze.

He dreamed he was home. River Rose Plantation sat back from the riverbank and was hidden by magnolias, sweet gums, and water oaks so heavy with gray moss that it touched the ground in some places. In mid-summer the scent of the magnolias moved with the air in waves so that just when one thought it was too sweet, it was gone. Almost any time of day, squirrels could be seen scampering on the ground or climbing the huge oak trunks and leaping from branch to branch. A lawn of St. Augustine grass kept gardeners busy clipping the runners that seemed to grasp like fingers at the trimmed edges. The view of the river was breathtaking from the upper story of the planter's house but to the casual traveler on the road along the levee, the house itself was almost invisible. The lane that led to the big house passed wide steps leading up to the spacious galleries, curved and made a complete circle around Formosa and hedges and then kept on going back where it started, like it had better things to do than simply stop and deposit guests. Pea gravel was liberally scattered along the road to keep mud from bogging down the carriages. A tall, hipped roof supported by light wooden colonnettes gave the house its airy feel, like it was delicate and would disappear into the trees if you looked away for a moment. This was only an illusion, as it was a substantial building with a heavy cypress frame and bousillage construction. Two carriage dogs lay dozing on the wide veranda most days, but would come instantly alert at the first sound of hooves or wheels. Pigeonniers, painted white and made with bricks produced by slave artisans, soared elegantly on each side of the big house. Dove sounds could be heard in the evening, a soft counterpoint to the cacophony of the normal bayou sounds.

Zack roused from his nap for a moment and thought about how

disappointed his father would be that he wanted to stay in the army rather than settle down at River Rose.

River Rose's barking dogs startled Zack from his reverie as they came running to meet the carriage.

Patrick stood at the top of the porch stairs, shading his eyes. When the carriage came to a stop, he bounded down the steps and pulled open the coach door.

"Welcome home, Lieutenant!" Patrick grabbed his son in a bear hug and then stood back to admire him in his uniform. "What a fine-looking soldier you are, son! Come on in. Auralee's been cooking since sunup and everyone on the place is excited!"

"God, did I miss the best cook in Louisiana! It wasn't too bad at the academy but nothing like what Auralee conjures up."

Zack greeted several of the slaves that were shyly standing on the porch with broad smiles ready to welcome him home. Most of them had known Zack since he was a young boy and genuinely liked the planter's son.

Auralee padded onto the porch, her great bulk swaying. In her hands was a plate with his favorite dessert, pecan pie. "Heah you is all growed up. But I knowed you done miss my pie." Auralee beamed at Zack.

"Auralee, I have been dreaming of that pie since I left home." Zack accepted the plate with a grin. "Papa, we have to start eating on this right away."

"Come on in to the dining room and we'll have some coffee and pie. We have a lot to talk over. Let's have a late supper, Auralee," he said, nodding in her direction.

"Yasuh, I knowed ya'll want to talk. Couple hours I'll have you some suppah. Come on you gulls, we gots a lot to do." This was directed at two young girls following in her wake as she headed for the kitchen. The two black girls were learning to be "second" cooks and might someday rule kitchens of their own. They giggled as they watched Auralee negotiate her bulk through the swinging doors. She stopped and waved her finger. "You gulls can laugh, but ain't nevah been no good cook dat was skinny." Chastened they meekly followed Auralee out to the kitchen.

Zack followed his father into the house, the dogs at their heels.

Patrick and Zack settled down at the dining room table to the serious business of eating almost the whole pie. They sipped hot black coffee in silence for a few moments.

"How are things going?" Zack knew by this time of year the planting was done and the main activity was keeping the fields worked and free of weeds.

15

"We've had good weather," Patrick said. "We should have a bumper cane crop this year and now with you here I can expand the planting area. After you get cleaned up I want to show you some plans I've made." Patrick reached over and patted Zack on the arm. "It's exciting to have you back. We'll make a good team."

Zack stood up abruptly. "I won't be staying, Papa." The words hung in the air.

"What?" Patrick looked startled.

"Pierre and I will be leaving in a couple of months for our new assignments." Zack stood looking down at his father who had first turned white; now his face was suffused with anger.

"You've committed and plan to leave without even discussing it with me?" Patrick's voice was hoarse and shaking. Zack thought he might be having a stroke. He pulled up a chair and sat down next to his father.

"I have to, Papa! I can't stand not to go! I love you and River Rose, but I have to find my own way."

Patrick was breathing heavily. Then, all at once he slumped down in his chair. "I don't understand how you can give all this up. I came here because of the 40 free arpents the government was offering. This was a wilderness. Your mother and I put everything we owned in three wagons and brought our three slaves with us. You were just a baby."

Zack had heard this story years ago, but he didn't interrupt.

"We built two cabins and planted the first crop of sugar cane in this area the first year." Patrick's voice lowered. He was lost in another time and place. "Every penny I made I put back into more land and invested in more slaves. Then I built this house."

Zack thought his father had forgotten he was there.

Patrick wiped his face with his handkerchief and continued in a rambling soft monotone, as if to himself. "I called this house River Rose because that was your mother's favorite flower and…she loved the river so. This was the house of her dreams. She only lived a month after it was finished." Patrick seemed overcome at these sad thoughts. Then he looked at Zack. "They say the river killed her. Yellow fever does seem to come and go with its rising and falling."

Patrick seemed to come to himself. "How can you leave all of this? Everything I've worked for is yours. How can you do this to me?" Patrick looked shrunken and old like a rag doll with no energy left.

Zack felt guilty, but he could not bear not to go. Suddenly he said, "Papa, why did you leave Georgia? You had a farm. But you sold it and moved a long way away. Why?"

Patrick was silent for a while. Then he raised his head and looked at Zack. "I wanted to grow sugar cane. I saw a sugar cane plantation on the Georgia coast and I knew that's what I wanted to do." Patrick finished and wiped his face again with his handkerchief.

"I have to find out what I want to do, Papa. It will probably turn out that I want to grow sugar cane. But I haven't seen anything else. I have to see what else there is."

The room was heavy with silence that was full of disappointment and dashed dreams.

Patrick sighed and got up. "Do what you have to do, son. I only want what is the best for you." He walked slowly up the stairs leaving Zack staring after him.

Eight years later—the war between the United States and Mexico is on everyone's mind. Zack is home on leave and just for this May evening, such thoughts seem far way, at least for a while....

Zack rode down the path that led from River Rose to the road that wound along the plantation's lifeline to Red River, the main artery to market. Bayou Chatis with its blanket of delicate algae film curled its way around the entire back section of the cane fields like a pale green snake and barges loaded with hogsheads of sugar to be carried and loaded onto the steamer. It snuggled up to the levee two miles below the River Rose plantation house and allowed passage of smaller vessels for transport to New Orleans.

Zack turned his horse to the south as the setting sun spread pink and gold that seemed to melt into the river. For a few moments, even the muddy red water was transformed like shivery molten lava swirling against the green levee grasses. He slowed his horse for a moment and thought about River Rose: the layout of the buildings, fields, and waterways that seemed so perfect for the successful operation of a sugar cane plantation that now covered 2,000 acres. He knew someday he might be the "sugar boss" at River Rose, but after eight years in the military, his thoughts were those of a soldier. Now, this beautiful evening, he would think only of the present.

Zack approached the Delmonde Plantation house slowly, savoring the warm, sweet smell of the Louisiana spring. Though he had relished his time in different parts of the country, Louisiana was home. The horse kicked up the rich scent of the alluvial soil, and Zack felt Louisiana weaving her exotic magic once again. *You could never really leave this land,* Zack thought. *It seeped into the very marrow of your bones. Perhaps this was why his Irish father had settled here. Ireland was said to have the same effect on her native sons.*

Zack was in no hurry to join the throng of people he could hear laughing on the balcony of the house. Already, music was pouring out into the night, mixing with the soft bayou sounds. His uniform was pressed and sharply creased, and he should be looking forward to this first visit back into Louisiana society. Thoughts of the pending conflict with Mexico and eagerness to join Pierre and do some real soldiering made such partying seem banal. All the neighbors for miles around had been invited to this "Spring Planting" party. Creoles looked for any excuse to celebrate, and this was as good as any.

Patrick McLoed would have been with Zack except for a flair up of gout. He would miss the good food, and that was what he should miss. There would be a multi-course meal, dancing, and then midnight gumbo. Dawn would be streaking the sky before this house was quiet. Zack dismounted and strolled slowly toward the house, taking time to admire its beauty.

Delmonde was a classic example of Greek Revival architecture. A tall Doric portico extended completely across the front of the house and allowed the guests ample space and room to mingle outdoors on steamy evenings such as tonight. Zack had always thought that Delmonde was the most beautiful house in Louisiana, and having been away for several years he had not changed his opinion. The entryway glittered with lights refracted off the crystal chandeliers. Fingers of light streamed onto the lawn from the long windows that covered the front of the house. Ladies in spring gowns and gentlemen in fancy dress added to the lush feel of the parlor aglow with hundreds of candles. As the only one in uniform, Zack stood out among the more aesthetic-looking men. His ruddy complexion and husky build added to the impression of strength and rugged good looks. The dark blue jacket and light blue trousers brought out the blue eyes that were said by friends to be "piercing." A white shoulder strap embossed with the eagle plate and a white belt with "U.S.A." buckle completed the dress uniform. The yellow piping on the curved side-back seams of the cropped cavalry jacket gave it a jaunty look and matched the yellow stripes down the sides of the trousers. He didn't realize his life was about to change in ways he could have never imagined.

Chapter II

There are no little events with the heart. It magnifies everything; it places in the same scales the fall of an empire of fourteen years and the dropping of a woman's glove and almost always the glove weighs more than the empire.
Balzac

A tall, dark-haired girl spotted Zack's entrance and began to make her way to the receiving line. Lorraine Delmonde had been waiting for this moment. Her dark eyes were immense in her porcelain face. Black hair that was parted primly in the front and pulled back slightly gave way to a riot of curls that cascaded down her back. Her summer dress was a pale lavender silk taffeta, the waistline gently elongated in front in a soft point, emphasizing her tiny waist. The collar was of sheer lawn fabric trimmed in a lace border that hung over her shoulders, met in the front and clasped with a sprig of violets. Lorraine was a renowned beauty but those who knew her well were not deceived by her ladylike façade. Beneath the black curls were a sharp mind and a strong will. The planter's daughter had been looking for River Rose's only son all evening. Lorraine had set her heart on the young soldier years ago. She had graduated from finishing school in April and was ready to make sure no other eligible females tried to lay claim to this particular gentleman.

Especially her simpering cousin Clarisa, she thought. *If she thinks she can even get near him, she has another think coming.* Lorraine watched Clarisa as she began to move toward the receiving line. Abruptly changing direction to move past her, she jostled the girl's arm and primly apologized. Turning quickly, she moved ahead and was standing in front of Zack before Clarisa realized what had happened.

Gerald Delmonde and his wife were greeting arriving guests.

"Monsieur, Madame, thank you for inviting me." Zack bowed slightly to each. Gerald Delmonde gave Zack a warm handshake.

"It is our pleasure, Lt. McLoed. We are very proud that you are going off to engage the Mexicanos. Welcome home."

"Thank you, sir." Zack returned the handshake with equal warmth. He greatly admired the planter. Delmonde was considered one of the best managed and most profitable sugar cane plantations in the lower valley.

"Lieutenant, I know you remember our daughter Lorraine. She has just finished her studies and returned from Grande Coteau." Madame Delmonde spoke as she turned to the tall, slender girl who had just joined her.

Zack had to make a conscious effort to keep his mouth from dropping open. He was astonished!

"I used to know a Lori, but Mademoiselle, you have changed!" He bowed to the glorious girl smiling at him. "I would not have known you had we met somewhere else. How many years has it been?"

"Four years, Zack. I must say you look very different in your so-dignified uniform." Lorraine continued smiling.

Zack was still reeling. Could she have had those black eyes before and all those black curls?

She took his arm. "Mama is ready for us to begin supper. I want to make sure I have an interesting person to talk with. Come, Lt. Zack, we have a lot of catching up to do."

Lori led him to the long dining table lit with magnificent tapers standing elegantly in huge silver candelabra. Apparently there was assigned seating, as Lorraine headed immediately to the right of the head of the table. As he held her chair, he noticed the silver placard holders with names in curly script. He smiled to himself and thought, *Nothing left to chance. No boring dinner guests for the Delmonde family.* As he settled himself and lifted his napkin, he was immediately jabbed in the ribs by a thin, elderly man on his right.

"Well, son, I must say you look splendid in your uniform. You must be something special if Lorraine lets you sit by her." His voice dropped conspiratorially. "She is a tarter. My favorite niece, though. Never a dull moment." He resumed his normal conversational tone. "You look familiar. Did you grow up around here?"

Zack introduced himself.

Surprised, the old man slapped him on the back. "Of course! Patrick's boy. I do not know if you remember me. I have lived away for some time. You must have been about ten years old when I saw you last. I am Germiane Delmonde, Gerald's older brother."

Though Zack could not remember Lorraine's uncle, he recognized the family resemblance and the old fashioned French cadence of his speech.

"Do not worry. I will not require an inordinate amount of conversation, as I know it would irritate my Lorraine if I occupied too much of your time."

Lorraine made a small face at her uncle. "Oh *Oncle Germaine* makes me sound like such a bully person. Zack. It is not true."

Zack smiled and, following his hosts' lead, began to eat. Covertly stealing glances at Lorraine, he became fascinated with the delicate movements of spoon to mouth and her ability to carry on a conversation despite polishing off soup, sips of wine, and now a superb duck al' orange. Lorraine glanced his way and suddenly was convulsed with laughter. Not the suppressed giggles of some sophisticated young lady, but the robust, hardy joy of a child. Zack grinned. This was the girl he remembered.

"And what, may I ask, is so amusing, Lori?" he asked, brushing crumbs from his waistcoat.

"I was thinking of the time you fell off old Gypsy and rolled down the levee into the river." Lorraine was now holding her napkin over her mouth to stifle her choking mirth. "You were so mad and then embarrassed."

Zack smiled. "I was that. But you shouldn't have laughed. I could have drowned."

"Oh no, not in that section of the river. It was shallow, as you know." Lorraine dabbed at her eyes and continued to chuckle.

"I can see I will get no sympathy from my former shadow." Zack raised his wineglass as if to sip, then hesitated. A mischievous glint sparkled in his eyes, and he turned to his still laughing companion. "I seem to remember a young lady tumbling off her own horse at the last hedge in the lane and landing in the blackberry bracket. She screeched and cried, and her hair was wild as a little hedgehog when she finally got untangled."

"*Touché*, but that was not chivalrous of you to remember such a thing." Lorraine tried to look hurt, but the corners of her mouth kept twitching, and soon they were both laughing again. Several people at the table noticed their merriment and smiled.

Lorraine glanced at her cousin Clarisa and noticed her pointed face take on a resentful look and her eyes narrow with jealousy. Lorraine knew she was angry with her because she had reached Zack first. Clarisa was Lorraine's cousin on her mother's side and lived with her parents in New Orleans. She and Lorraine had never been close, but she was always invited to parties and celebrations. This gave Clarisa's mother a chance to visit with her sister. Clarisa was pretty in a delicate blond Dresden doll sort of way. But lacking the vitality that sparked Lorraine, she always seemed lackluster when around her dark-haired cousin.

This evening was not a total loss for Clarisa, however. Lorraine watched as she looked at the young man seated to her right. He was fairly handsome, and, more importantly, both women knew he was very rich. Lorraine smiled to herself as Clarisa flirted outrageously at the young man, tilting her head in the way Lorraine had seen her practice before a mirror. This caused a cascade of golden curls to fall gently over her shoulder and highlighted her large green eyes. The young man did not seem to mind the lack of depth in them and leaned closer to catch the scent of spring flowers surrounding this delectable girl.

When Zack thought he could not possibly eat another mouthful, Gerald Delmonde stood and announced that the first *contredanse* would begin.

Lorraine put her arm through Zack's, and they walked into the beautiful ballroom. The ornate pier mirrors glitteringly enhanced French wallpaper, blue with tiny bits of gold. Lace curtains hung at the floor-length plantation windows, set off to perfection by the Victorian furniture. Musicians began to play, and couples arranged themselves in four complex figures for the quadrille.

The couples finished the intricate movements in a blur of color and laughter. The night was warm and the music lilting and soon even the ladies with their light cotton frocks were begging for respite and a little fanning time.

Lorraine patted her face with a dainty handkerchief and said, "I am so warm, *mon Cheri*. Let us have some refreshment "

Zack was sweating heartily in his heavy uniform. "I'll bring some lemonade," he offered and headed toward the long buffet table covering the back of the room.

Returning, he was annoyed to find Lori surrounded by admirers. He was close enough to hear her say, "I have promised Lt. McLoed the first waltz, and here he is now." She graciously extricated herself from the group of disappointed men and took the cup Zack handed her. As the group turned to look at him, he noticed one dark-haired man actually glaring.

The strains of the beautiful Strauss waltz began softly. Lorraine looked into Zack's face and winked! *Outrageous!* Uncle Germaine was right. Lorraine was never dull.

Lorraine's eyes danced merrily. "A little white lie is sometimes better than hurting the feelings. Do you not think so?" she asked.

Zack grinned. "Especially if it means I get to waltz with such an unusual girl."

They continued their conversation during the elegant, slow steps of the waltz.

"How am I unusual?" Lorraine asked.

"You let nothing stand in your way, and yet no one minds. That is…" he hesitated.

"But why do you stop in saying no one minds?"

"That dark-haired gentleman seemed angry at my taking you away," Zack finished.

"Oh, Julien is just a grouch. He is much older than I and a widower. He thinks because he has such a fine house and so much land I should be impressed."

"Maybe you should be impressed," he teased.

"Those things mean nothing to me. It is the measure of the man I am interested in."

"Ah ha!" Zack exulted. "See, that is very unusual for a lot of girls."

Lori's eyes widened. "If that is the case, it is very sad. But then I cannot worry about anyone who is so stupid with her life."

The waltz came to an end. The room was hot and stuffy, and when Lorraine suggested they could do with some air, Zack readily agreed. *Could this really be Lori?* He thought, *The aggravating little girl who used to tag after me whenever our families visited together?*

"You are very quiet, Zack Mac." The old nickname slipped out.

"I'm still trying to get used to the idea that you have changed so much."

"You are behind the times, *Cheri.* I have already been introduced into New Orleans society." Lori fingered her long sash.

"Then surely you are spoken for?" Zack felt a sinking sensation.

She looked at him, smiling. "But of course. Four suitors have asked for permission to pay court. But I have not accepted anyone."

They walked the verandah as soft music filtered out of the open windows. Flickering candlelight played along the floor and occasionally overlapped the moon markings on the grounds below.

"How long will you be in Louisiana?" Lori stopped by one of the slender posts and leaned against its cool paleness.

"Our company leaves in three months," Zack replied. "I'll meet up with Pierre Beauregard and we'll leave from River Rose in mid August."

"That does not leave us much time." Lori looked at him.

"Time?" he asked.

"To get reacquainted. So that you know…." She hesitated and turned to look out over the fragrant darkness.

"So that I know what?" he asked.

Lorraine turned and smiled. "So that you know what you left behind. So that you think you will certainly die if you do not see me again. That way I can be sure you will see to it you do not die."

"You think I can have so strong a hand in my fate?"

"But of course. I will pray a novena so you will be certain to come back safely. That is, if you do not tarry. You must make up your mind." Lori looked at him without smiling

Zack followed Lori as she stepped down the south steps leading into the garden. The well-plotted life he had crafted for himself when he left the Point now seemed shifting and swirling, turning his mind into a cloudy fog. Trying to sort out feelings so powerful he could hardly breathe. Zack almost collided with Lorraine as she stopped suddenly.

"Let's sit here for awhile." She indicated the gazebo looming ghost like in the moonlight.

Lorraine settled her skirts around her and sat with hands folded looking expectantly at Zack. *Obviously she is accustomed to more sophisticated men than me*, Zack thought, feeling totally inadequate. Though experienced with the young ladies he encountered at the many parties officers were invited to, he admitted that Lorraine had a way of making him feel confused, like he was mired in quick sand.

Lorraine turned her head at a sound from the garden and for a moment he was mesmerized by the perfect white curve of her neck. He had to catch his breath as she turned back and looked at him. Zack reached down and took her hands in his. He gently kissed her fingers. Lorraine smiled at him and he realized he loved the beautiful girl looking steadily into his eyes.

"Zack, I have waited for you so long. Since I was a little girl. The time for waiting is over." Lorraine moved closer and he kissed her on the forehead.

"You are right, my darling," he whispered hoarsely, words tumbling out. "You have no objection to my speaking to your father?"

"How could I object when it is what I want most of all?" Lorraine's face glowed as she gently extricated her fingers from his grasp and touched his face for a moment. "Come, let us go find *Papá*. He is usually walking the porch by now to have a smoke."

Zack followed her as she walked back to the house. Gerald Delmonde was in fact making his way toward them as they ascended the steps. Lorraine gave a little wave of her fingers and walked back into the house.

Gerald Delmonde approached and greeted Zack heartily. Delmonde was smoking a panatela and offered one to Zack..

"These are from Cuba and the best my man has brought back in years." Delmonde was speaking of his Cuban "Sugar Tramp," the itinerant sugar-making expert that made the trip to Louisiana each year for the grinding season. "You might wish to save it for later. Lorraine and her mother both hate the smell."

Zack thanked him and pocketed the cigar.

"Lieutenant, I was hoping we could find some time together. I am anxious to hear your opinion on how the Mexican war is going."

When the young soldier hesitated, he added, "I would not expect you to betray any confidential information."

Zack grinned. "Sir, I do not even know any confidential information. What I can tell you is already known to all the troops and may even be old news to you. Although we had victories at Palo Alto and Resaca de la Palma, General Taylor and some 3,000 United States regulars are encamped opposite Matamoras." At the puzzled look on Delmonde's face, he explained.

"That's an area known as the Brazos. There is fear that a much larger force will attack him. General Winfield Scott is calling up 20,000 volunteers from the Mississippi Valley. Lt Pierre Beauregard, a friend from the Point, and I have already joined up and will leave in a couple of months."

The two men spent the next few minutes discussing the ramifications of the war on Louisiana.

As the discussion wound down, Zack turned to him. "Sir, I would like to make an appointment to see you as soon as possible. It is of the utmost importance."

Delmonde looked sharply at the young soldier. He sighed. "You, too?" He paused. "Come see me tomorrow afternoon. We can meet in my office around 3:00. I usually have a coffee then. That way we will have time to recover from tonight, or I should say, this morning."

The next afternoon Zack knocked on the door of Gerald Delmonde's office. It was situated toward the back of the plantation structure and was much cooler than the rest of the house.

Opening the door, Delmonde gestured. "Come in and sit down, Lieutenant. Have a coffee." He indicated a silver decanter on a small table next to a leather chair. Zack admired Delmonde's office. Walls of bookshelves were broken here and there by shutters that let in air but kept glare to a minimum.

"I very much enjoyed our discussion last night. But you have something else on your mind that you wish to talk about?" Delmonde asked. As he settled down in his comfortable leather chair across from the young soldier he thought, *I hate all of this. I like this young man and his whole family. To think Lorraine could be trifling with him as she has been doing all spring with her other suitors is too much.*

Of course, according to Lorraine, it was really her mother's fault for insisting on a "coming out" event. She personally did not even want a formal presentation to society. But her mother had insisted. "We would be shamed and shunned from society if we did not present our only daughter to the world. And how will she find a husband out here in the country if no one knows about her." He could still hear his wife's irrefutable logic. Still, you would think that with four suitors, at least one would have been acceptable.

"Sir, I would like to ask your permission to pay court to your daughter, Lorraine." Zack wondered if that sounded too formal. He had grown up with Lori but he certainly did not want to seem bold to this man he admired.

The planter sighed. He opened a handsome rosewood humidor on his desk, and removed two Cuban panatelas. Expertly he clipped the head of each cigar with a "V" cut in the European fashion to provide for proper air circulation, while keeping bitter tars down at the deep end of the "V" and away from the tongue. Lighting a match, Lorraine's father waited a moment to allow the head of the match to burn off first, avoiding a sulfur taste. Holding the cigar at a 45-degree angle with the open end down, he held the tip of the flame away from the foot without placing the cigar to his lips. After rotating the cigar slowly over the flame for a few seconds, he was finally ready to light the cigar. Zack gravely followed his lead and, after lighting up, sat back and slowly "sipped" the cigar as if it were a glass of fine wine. They both savored the rich tobacco flavor and began to relax.

"I give you my permission to call on Lorraine, Lieutenant. I know of no unreliable or bad reputation associated with either you or your family. You have been commissioned, so you can support a wife and will be heir to a fine home and land." He sighed again. "I will ask her permission. It's just…" he hesitated.

Zack raised his eyebrows. "What, Sir?"

"I will be honest with you, Zack." Delmonde had unconsciously slipped into a more informal tone of address. "There have been four others before you, one very rich young man from one of New Orleans' most distinguished families. And she said…" he hesitated again.

"What did she say?"

"Zack, she just laughed about each one and said 'Oh, *Papá*. You can not expect me to marry that man' and laughed some more. If you insist, I will ask her."

A knock sounded at the door. "Papa, are you in there?" It was Lorraine. Zack and Gerald looked at each other in panic.

"Yes, someone is just leaving. I will be out in a moment." Gerald Delmonde ushered Zack out of a side door. "I will send word as soon as I speak with her," he said, unable to meet Zack's eyes.

Zack slowly rode home. He thought about his father's reaction when he told him about his discussion with Gerald Delmonde and the visit this afternoon. Patrick McLoed was surprised.

"But she is quite a willful girl, I understand. You remember even when she was small, she always wanted to be doing things outdoors like riding and learning to shoot."

"I remember well, Papa. She was…is a most unusual girl. But she has grown up now." He stopped. "I knew at once when I saw her she was the one."

"Yes. It seems to be that way with us." Patrick thought back to the first time that he had seen Zack's mother. "Still, she is from a good family and will no doubt have a large dowry. I wish you well."

The courier came early the next morning to River Rose with a message. *"Monsieur Gerald Delmonde wishes to invite Lt. Zackery McLoed to dinner, in his private office at 1:00 o'clock."*

Once again Zack knocked on the door of Delmonde's office.

"Come in, Zack." Lorraine's father looked happy and his face betrayed an expansive mood. "Well, I don't know whether you are lucky or unlucky. But the news is, she did not laugh when I told her you wished to pay her court."

"What did she say?" Zack asked cautiously.

"She said, 'Of course, *Papá*, he is the one.' Then she waltzed out of here and said to tell you to meet her after lunch for a ride on the levee."

Zack beamed.

"You do understand, she is full of surprises." Lorraine's father cautioned Zack. "Despite the best efforts of the nuns, she is not your quiet, retiring Creole girl."

Though Delmonde did not share this with Zack, she had pressed her advantage when she gave her parent the good news that she finally would accept a suitor.

"Papa, can I have Nicholas for a wedding present?"

Nicholas was the new black horse her father had just purchased and which Lorraine had been begging for.

"Oh, yes. If it comes to that I will give you Nicholas. That is if you promise not to be vexing to Zack."

Lorraine threw her arms around her father's neck. "I promise. I will be an angel."

Two weeks earlier at Delmonde Plantation:

Lorraine finished "tying down" her clothes to make sure nothing could move in any wind that might come up. Joaquin had picked this day because it was overcast and nothing stirred in the trees or bushes. A windless day was crucial. Everything must be still. Lorraine moved as if in a dream, gently patting her hair that was pulled back firmly against her head. No wisps of black curls must mar the calm with which she had to surround herself.

Gerald Delmonde's equestrian master met her as she slipped quietly into the paddock. Joaquin Brevere was a small, wiry, dark man with an economy of movement. *He must be in his mid forties,* thought Lori, but he had the seamless features of a much younger man. He was a totally quiet being. This allowed him to move among the horses without disturbing them. His was a calming presence. Joaquin had been schooled in France and was truly a genius with horses.

Looking Lorraine over carefully, he nodded approval. She was ready. He handed her the special food the black horse loved, and she crumbled it gently in one hand. She had been dreaming of this moment for years, ever since she first saw Joaquin use his special technique.

"With these clouds there should be no shadow. But be watchful in any case. A shadow is frightening to a horse, especially when he is already worried about you. If you see any hint of it, slowly leave. Do not continue. Remember you are not finished until he comes to you and takes food," Joaquin said as he opened the paddock.

Lorraine nodded, her eyes fixed on the beautiful horse watching her warily.

She slowly entered the enclosure and carefully positioned herself as far from the horse as she could. Her admiration increased each time she looked at his perfect conformation. His shiny blackness rippled from the strong hindquarters over the sloped shoulders. Not only was he bred for beauty and speed, his stamina was also evident in the deep chest. He tossed his head and then became still, quietly watching her.

Her hand holding the special food was behind her. Joaquin's words hung in her mind. *"Don't move. Keep your feeding hand behind your back. Talk to him quietly and mention his name every so often. You may have to stand an hour or two, but eventually, if you have the patience, his curiosity will overcome his natural fear, and he will come to you. It is trust that you have to establish. When he comes to you, don't move. Let him nuzzle your arm, and then he will reach around to your hand. Let him open your hand. Then he will find the treat. After he eats, you may stroke his nose, then wait for him to leave. Talk quietly the entire time. He is imprinting your voice and your smell. It will be one small step. You will have to come each day to build trust and then love. He will let you know when he is ready for the bridle.*

It all happened exactly as Joaquin said. Lorraine stood for an hour as the horse first shied away, snorting with fear. After a few minutes he quieted and just watched her. He trotted around the paddock, seemingly oblivious. But Lorraine could see his ears begin to prick when she said his name.

Nicholas.

He slowed to a walk and began looking at her and tossing his head. The big horse edged closer. After a while he stopped and seemed to be listening as Lorraine continued her monologue. Once she was convinced he was listening, she lowered her voice so he would have to move ever closer. She looked into his beautiful eyes, so full of fiery intelligence, and saw the faintest stirrings of curiosity. Closer and closer he came, sidling up as if to say, *I'm just wondering. This is not a big thing. Just wondering what is in your hand.* His soft nose touched her arm. She ignored him. He nuzzled around to her hand. She gradually opened it and felt his breath as he greedily ate the food. Gently her fingers stroked his broad nose. He backed away and looked at her for a moment, then trotted off.

This scenario repeated itself every day for a week before Lorraine carried the bridle in and laid it at her feet. She made sure to handle it so that it was covered with her scent. When Nickolas approached, he stopped to sniff the bridle, and then accepted food again from her hand. This went on for a week until he ignored the bridle and came running to her as soon as she entered the pen. By this time she was touching him all over his head and ears and friendship was forming. The day came when she simply raised the bridle and slipped it over his head, talking the whole time and stroking him between the leather straps.

He snickered and pranced just to let her know he knew what she was doing but then let her lead him around the paddock.

Chapter III

Present....

"It's too dangerous to go that fast on the levee—your horse could stumble and you could end up in the river," Zack scolded an unrepentant Lori.

"Oh, do not admonish me so! Nicholas is very sure footed. Let us sit down and talk."

He helped Lori down from her horse, letting both horses' reins drop, allowing them to graze freely.

They sat on a grassy outcropping overlooking the river, and Lori wrapped her arms around her riding habit. She was dressed in yellow with white-trimmed silk draping gracefully from the fitted bodice. Her hat was a yellow silk covered with a yellow tulle chin wrap. Zack could not take his eyes off her.

She began trying to untie her hat's sheer ribbon. "Oh, this is so knotted, Zack. Can you help me?"

Zack's hands shook as he fiddled uselessly with the gauzy material that just kept slipping away.

"I think you are making it worse. Here, let me work on it again."

Finally the wrap came loose and her hat tumbled off. With relief Zack picked it up and laid it beside her.

The river lapped gently against the levee in a peaceful dance with the summer breeze. It was a beautiful summer day, not too hot, the trees gently waving their greenery like giant fans. It should have been a relaxing place, but Zack felt anything but calm. This was the first time he had been alone with Lori. He was still stunned that she would have allowed him to pay court after only three days. His throat was dry with nervousness, yet Lori seemed at ease. It wasn't that he had no experience with women, but this one caused him breathing difficulties. In desperation he plunged ahead with the questions pounding in his head.

"Lori, why didn't you laugh me off like your other suitors? I had only just met you again after four years." Zack had to know.

"Because…" Lori looked straight into his eyes, then smiled. "Zack, you were always my knight in shining armor. I came home to be here when you got back from your latest posting. And because you love me and will let me be free. I couldn't think of marrying anyone else. You do love me?" She touched his face. "*Papá* says you asked permission to pay court. Do you love me, *Chéri?*"

Zack took her in his arms and kissed her, at first in a very proper, gentlemanly way. Then feeling the rush of passion and knowing she obviously felt it too, he pulled away.

"Yes, Lori. Of course I love you," he said hoarsely. "But if you keep letting me kiss you like that, we'll have to be married tomorrow."

"But of course we will be married quickly, *mon Chéri!* Before you go off to war, and that will be soon!" Lori looked at him in such a way he again found it hard to breathe, much less think.

Zack released her and stood up. He walked a few steps and turned around. "Is it fair, my darling, for me to marry you before I go? I thought an engagement and then when my leave comes…."

Lori jumped to her feet and with hands on her hips actually yelled, "Zackery McLoed, if you think that for one minute that I would let you go off to fight in this stupid war without becoming your wife…." She stopped at the shocked look on his face. She remembered her promise to her father not to vex Zack. In a soft conciliatory tone she looked at him and said, "I could not bear to have you leave me otherwise." She wrapped her arms around his neck and continued quietly, "Let's just decide how quickly we can be married."

Zack and Lorraine spent as much time as possible together during the next few days and soon settled on a marriage date. Though committed to his enlistment, Zack realized his priorities now included settling down on River Rose and building a life with Lorraine. Over the next two years he would often wonder why seeing the world had seemed so important.

On July 10, 1846, Lt. Zackery Patrick McLoed and Mademoiselle Lorraine Marie Delmonde were married at St. Angeline's Church. Lt. Pierre Beauregard was Zack's best man.

In August 1846, Lt. Zackery McLoed and Lt. Pierre Beauregard left for assignment in Tampico as engineering officers under the command of General Winfield Scott. Both McLoed and Beauregard would be brevetted twice for exceptional bravery and promoted to captains.

Chapter IV

February 1848

End of Mexican War: On February 18, 1848, the official orders from Washington arrived relieving General Winnfield Scott of his command and naming General William O. Butler in his stead. On May 4, 1848 General Scott returned twelve-month volunteers to U.S. (Wounded were returned in February and March).

A gray swirling mist came toward her and grew darker as it approached. If it reached her she would not be able to breathe. She began to run. Cannon fire exploded all around her and whorls of red seemed to come through the air in pulsating waves. Turning to look back, she saw it was too late. The cloud, black with specks of gunpowder, began to smother her! Gulping for air she stumbled forward and then was falling....

Lorraine sat up in bed, shaking and drenched with sweat. Once again the nightmare had come to waken her just before dawn. Rising from bed, she walked over to the French doors leading to her balcony. Throwing them open, she felt a frigid blast of air. Even in Louisiana, February was cold this year. A few yellow and red streaks were beginning to show through the early morning mist. Something was wrong. Zack was on his way home from the war and was expected today or tomorrow. His letter indicated he could not be more specific because he would finish the last twenty miles on horseback. That was as close as the coach carried passengers from the steamboat. But ever since she had received his letter five days ago, she had been plagued with the same nightmare.

Lorraine slipped out of her bed wrap and nightgown. Bending over baby Jacob's crib, she marveled again at how much a son could look like his father at only nine months old.

Pulling the covers back over the sleeping form, she quickly began to put on her riding pants and shirt. Putting on her boots, Lorraine went back over Zack's last letter in her mind. He had been wounded, but seemed to make light of it. He said he had vowed he would beat Pierre Beauregard home. She could hardly believe he was coming home for good. After two years of seeing him only on occasional leaves, it would be heaven never to have to think of separation again. Somehow the fear of Zack's being killed had never entered her mind. He was so competent and strong. But now—she pulled on her warmest jacket and walked over to the little room next to hers. Lorraine tapped gently on the door and roused the baby's wet nurse, Jansie. For a few moments she spoke quietly to the young black woman, then made her way down the stairs.

Patrick McLoed was already downstairs and making headway with a plate of ham, eggs, and biscuits. He rose as she entered and touched his napkin to his mouth.

"Oh, Papa. I did not mean to disturb you."

"You did not, Mauvren," he slipped into the pet Irish name. "Zack's coming home has all of us too excited to sleep." Though Patrick was Lorraine's father-in-law, she had called him Papa even as a little girl because Zack called him that. Lorraine's father was *Papá* so there was no confusion. Patrick was a robust man with a mane of white hair and blue eyes that seemed to see into your soul.

He raised his eyebrows in a questioning look. "Why are you dressed for riding?"

"I have to go meet Zack. He's on his way," Lorraine hesitated, "on the road." She took a deep breath. "But I can't just sit and wait. I'm going to meet him. Jansie will look after Jacob until I return."

Auralee began setting out steaming scones on the sideboard near the table. The plantation's cook wore a big smile.

"You are up early too, Auralee," Lorraine said, gratefully putting one of the fragrant rolls on her plate and pouring a cup of hot, black coffee.

"We'uns all up, gettin' ready for Mastah Zack. I knows he'll need fatt'n up, and I's startin' cookin' now." She padded off, humming under her breath.

"Papa, I need Nicholas brought round along with a water flask." Lorraine would not meet Patrick's eyes.

"What is it, Lorraine? Why are you leaving so early? And why do you think you'll be gone so long?" Patrick was suspicious. Had Zack said something in his letter she had not told him?

"I have a feeling I might be gone awhile. I don't know, Papa. I feel like I have to go as soon as I can get away."

Rising at once, Patrick went out a side door and called for Henri, the groomsman, to bring Nicholas along with a saddle flask of water. He also added a small flacon of brandy. He knew his daughter-in-law well. More than once her resourcefulness and intuition had proven correct.

Later, mounting her horse, Lorraine paused and looked at Patrick.

"If I am not back by dark, you will come looking for us?" It was a question and a request. Then she was gone.

Patrick tried all day to pretend he was not worried. Going through the motions of preparing for his son's homecoming helped keep his mind occupied, but by mid-afternoon he could no longer concentrate.

Approaching the stables, he called out to his groomsman, "Henri, I need the carriage made ready. Put in a supply of blankets, brandy, and water."

"The carriage?" he repeated, a surprised look on his face.

"Yes, as soon as you can get it ready."

Shadows were beginning to stream across the road, and Nicholas was starting to tire. Lorraine stopped and drank from the water flask. Had she misread her premonition? It was getting late. Maybe Zack was coming tomorrow. She immediately knew this wasn't right. He was trying to get home now. She was sure of it.

Up ahead the road stretched—empty. Skinny branches of bare trees now tipped in silver drooped low over the ditches on each side of her path. No sound broke the stillness except the labored breathing of her horse. Nicholas' breath hung in little puffs, then disappeared in the air. Lorraine imagined for a moment she had left her homeland and was traveling in a dreamscape. (How could the land be so silent?) Cold was beginning to seep through her heavy clothes. (How long had she been on the road?) Nudging her horse, she continued, her concern growing.

A horse appeared in the distance. It looked like it was without a rider. Fear gripped her heart. A man could be killed or terribly injured by falling from a horse, even one going as slow as this one. She nudged Nicholas to a gallop. Coming closer, she could see the approaching horse did have a rider after all. A figure was hunched over the saddle. The horse was walking slowly, one of the reins hung down, almost dragging the ground. Pulling alongside Lorraine saw that the rider was Zack, his uniform hanging loosely over his thin frame.

"Oh, Zack! It's me, Lori!" Grabbing his horse's rains, she stopped him. Zack seemed to be barely conscious, and, touching his face, she realized he was burning with fever! Lorraine reached for her saddle rag and pouring water on it wiped his face. This roused him, and he seemed to sit straighter in the saddle. Somehow she had to get him to drink water. He would have a raging thirst with the fever. Maybe this would bring him fully awake.

Lorraine grasped the flask, put it to his mouth, and yelled loudly, "Zack, drink as much as you can." He gulped the water greedily and again seemed to come to his senses a little. Reaching around his horse, she brought the dangling reins up and wrapped them around the saddle horn. If only she had something stronger to give him. Lorraine then remembered the small flacon Patrick had put in her saddlebag.

The horses were moving restlessly, not liking the proximity of each other. Lorraine would have to be careful and not risk a sudden movement that could topple Zack from the saddle. Bringing the flacon up to Zack's lips, she forced his head back. He got a taste of the brandy and coughed. He was still barely hanging on to consciousness.

How had Zack come to be in this condition? He probably started home feeling weak but thought he could make it and illness overcame him, Lorraine thought. Tears stung her eyes as she realized how hard he was trying to get home.

A cold wind began to blow. Zack began to shiver with a chill. This increased his wobbliness in the saddle. If only she could somehow get him on Nickolas. Her horse was trained in the French art of "balance'ment," and would have had no trouble keeping Zack in the saddle. Sidling up to Zack's horse, she tried pulling him over toward her so that if he fell over she could brace him. The horses couldn't stand walking that close together and Lorraine could see the chances of his falling were greater than ever. There was only one thing left. Stopping both horses, she dismounted.

Snow began to fall, gently at first, and then the wind began to howl. Dusk was almost upon them. Lorraine's arms ached, and she was hoarse from her constant screaming at Zack to "Wake up!" She had managed to pull his left foot out of the stirrup and clambered up to sit in back of him. With her arms around him and holding the reins, she gently cantered the horses, terrified that at any moment they would both go tumbling to the ground. If they fell there was no way she could ever get Zack back on the horse even if they survived a fall. In desperation she reached out and reined Nickolas as close as possible. With a sob she brought the riding crop down hard on his right flank. Never had the big horse felt the sting of a crop. Nickolas screamed with pain and shock as he bolted and flew down the road. Lorraine hoped he could get someone's attention and bring help. She could not hold on much longer.

"Come on, Zack. No sleeping, darling. We are going home!" Lorraine urged hoarsely. She had hoped her body heat would reduce the chills shaking him, but they seemed to be getting worse.

"Papa, where are you?" she yelled desperately into the wind. Only the cold stillness of the normally vibrant landscape answered. Long fingers of branches, which were now covered in ice, bent over the road in spidery patterns. Breathing was difficult, and the air seemed to be heavier. Lori felt as though she was swallowing bits of ice with every gulp of air. Weariness enveloped her, and she strained to see. Trusting the horse to be sure footed, Lorraine buried her head in the back of Zack's coat, the frozen water crystals covering his back shocking her awake for a moment. Slowly her body began to relax again, and she was once more sliding into a frozen stupor.

A loud crack like a rifle shot jerked Lori awake. At first she was disoriented and then remembered she was trying to get Zack home. She looked around but could see no one. As the horse slowly turned a bend in the road, she saw a huge tree limb blocking it. The noise had been the limb, loaded with ice, separating from a huge water oak and crashing to the ground. Now the road was completely blocked.

Lori sat stunned. She stared for a moment before the hopelessness of her situation penetrated her mind. She started to cry but her tears began to freeze, and she wiped them away angrily with her sleeve. A rage she had never known welled up inside her and spilled over onto her face as she set her jaw. *There has got to be a way around this*, she thought. "I will get Zack home!" Lori shouted furiously at the empty road and the silent forest. Her anger spent, she began to survey her surroundings. The side of the road where the giant water oak stood was so heavily forested there was no way a horse could get through. A tiny offshoot of Indian Creek, now covered in ice, was on the other side. A small batture that crawled up from the main part of the creek just might give the horse enough purchase to go around the tree limb. Lori kicked Zack's foot out of the stirrup, and slipping her own foot in, got down from the horse. She grabbed the reins and cautiously began to lead the horse onto the tiny path alongside the road. Zack was still wobbly in the saddle. The least little jolt and he would go tumbling into the frigid water.

"Dear God, please help me!" Lori sobbed to herself. The horse was uneasy and Lori had to keep gently tugging on the reins. She talked soothingly and he seemed to calm down. With her understanding of horses, Lori was instilling confidence that he could trust her to lead him to safety. Slowly Lori led the horse and Zack along the little sandbar. When they were almost to the road, she noticed blood dripping onto the snow. The red seemed to glow on the pristine surface of the ground. Zack's leg wound had opened and was pouring blood! Frantically Lori pulled on the reins for the final push up to the road's surface. Taking one end of the reins, she fashioned a tourniquet around the upper part of Zack's leg. Climbing back on the horse, she once again headed for home.

Henri had not said a word since they left River Rose, despite Patrick's constant exhortations to go faster. He was caught up in the same dreadful imaginings as his master. The groomsman remembered Miss Lorraine's patience as she had carefully trained Nickolas. To this day she was the only one who ever rode the black horse. Henri could not imagine her falling from Nickolas.

Suddenly a frightening image came hurtling out of the gathering gloom. A huge, black riderless horse was bearing down on them, racing as though chased by demons.

"Oh my God, it's Nickolas!" Patrick yelled. "Turn the carriage. Block the road. We can't let him get by!"

Though he was an expert driver, Henri was barely able to turn the horses in time. The horse came to a halt, flicking foam from his mouth and shuddering with exhaustion.

Patrick turned to Henri. "I'll ride Nickolas back down the road. Lorraine may be lying hurt somewhere. Follow me with the carriage as fast as you can." Mounting the still-heaving horse, Patrick galloped into the blackness.

What could have happened to Lorraine? Patrick wondered. She was an expert horsewoman. He didn't think she could have fallen from the horse. Unless she was injured, had dismounted and sent the horse on ahead for help. Patrick decided this must be the case as he saw a single horse coming toward him barely moving. He pulled alongside and saw Zack and Lorraine.

"Papa, help us," Lorraine sobbed.

Patrick could see his son was barely in the saddle. "Henri's on his way with the carriage. What's the matter with Zack?"

"He is burning up with fever from wounds and is hardly conscious. I am so cold." Lorraine's voice was scarcely audible.

Henri thundered down the road. He saw the pair of horses and brought the carriage to a halt.

Patrick yelled at Henri as the cold wind caused his breath to come in gasps. "We have to get Master Zack and Miss Lorraine in the carriage at once and roll them up in the blankets." Patrick was already helping Lorraine down from the back of Zack's horse. It took both Henri and Patrick to lower Zack. Totally unconscious now, he was dead weight. Wrapping both of them in blankets, Patrick forced whiskey down their throats and took the reins from Henri.

"Tie Zack's horse to the back and take Nickolas. Doctor Bercoise's house is down the last turnoff we passed. Get him to come with you and catch up with us. Zack is pretty bad."

The groomsman was off like a shot. Patrick turned the horses around and started toward home.

Doctor Bercoise had just left the main road on his way home, when Henri skittered to a halt beside his carriage. The groomsman quickly explained what had happened. Turning his carriage around, the doctor followed Henri and soon caught up with Patrick. The doctor climbed aboard and began working on Zack as the carriage rumbled into the night. Sleety rain had begun to fall as temperatures dipped into the twenties and the coldest night of the winter settled over the land.

Doctor Bercoise sat down in the parlor after dressing Zack's wound and caring for Lorraine. He gratefully accepted the whisky Patrick offered him. "Your son would not have lived had he fallen off that horse and been exposed to this weather. Even if he could have stayed mounted he would not have gotten to shelter in time. Your daughter-in-law saved his life." The doctor stretched his legs out to the fire. "They are both suffering from exposure. Both of them must be watched carefully, especially through the rest of the night."

Patrick sat slumped in the chair next to the fire. "Henri's wife, Georgina, is going to be with them tonight and Martha will be here in the morning." He looked at the Doctor. "You trained them both as sick room aids. I know Zack and Lori are in good hands." Patrick turned a haggard face to the Doctor. "Do you think Zack will make it?"

"He is very thin. But he has youth on his side and was always healthy before. There is infection in his shoulder but not his chest. His leg wound bled so much it is very clean. No infection at all." Dr. Bercoise rubbed his hands over the stubble beginning on his chin. "Yes, I think he will recover. You must make sure he gets nourishing soups, and with Auralee around, I know that will happen."

Dusk crept into the corners of the room, giving it a yellowish glow. In the huge canopy bed, two figures lay side by side. One began to move slightly.

Zack opened his eyes and was startled to see his wife lying next to him quietly sleeping. He lay on his side, and she faced him with both hands tucked under her face. (How did he get home?) Then he remembered, in a hazy way, saddling up and starting down the road as dawn was just breaking. Though Zack had felt sick and knew the fever was upon him, he could not delay starting for home. Surely he could manage to ride twenty miles and then recuperate at home with Lori. Oh how he had missed her! As the horse galloped along, Zack floated. He remembered Lori calling to him to do something and then…nothing. Deciding he would leave the questions until later, Zack went back to looking at the face he had dreamed about all these months. Pale skin, so clear, and dark eyelashes that fanned out in waves over her cheeks. Then a heavy weariness overcame him, and he slept.

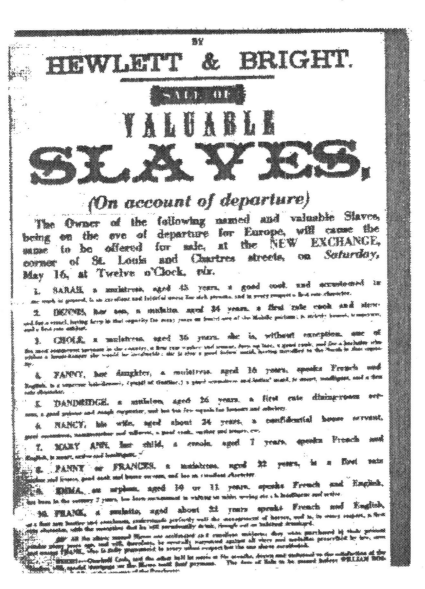

Chapter V

Evening shadows completed their journey through the bedroom. The silence was broken only by the soft, barely discernable whispers of exhausted breathing, with an occasional rasp.

A young black woman named Martha entered the room quietly and rearranged covers over the sleeping pair. She was concerned about their not eating, but the doctor had been definite. Rest and warmth were more important now. The woman settled back in her chair to continue her quiet vigil and thought about how she came to be in this room, in this place, at this time. She was only eighteen years old and proud to have been given the responsibility of caring for the mastah's son and his wife.

Her mind went back to the first time she had seen the mastah. *It was a cold blustery day in Charleston. The slave traders were busy as always regardless of the weather. Word came that a large plantation owner would be bringing in a number of slaves to sell, and a crude slave stand had been hastily erected. Martha was barely seven years old and clung to her mahme's ragged, damp skirts in terror as the noisy crowd surged forward and jostled the shaky stand. Her mahme swayed weakly, and Martha was afraid she would topple over. Mahme had been sick for what seemed to the little girl like a long time. When Martha's da died from a beating by the plantation's overseer, her mahme seemed to grow even weaker and now was slack jawed and listless with despair. A red-faced burly man grabbed at her mahme and yelled something that Martha could not understand, and soon several people yelled out at once. Then her mahme was snatched away, and thrown off the stand into the arms of a hulking man who was then swallowed up by the surging crowd. Martha cried frantically, "Mahme, Mahme!" No one noticed her small figure, and she was roughly pushed aside as another group of slaves was brought forward. All at once, a man tossed some money at the slave trader, and she felt herself being lifted down. The man, who now owned her, held her gently against his coat, and she could smell the wet wool of his jacket. He talked quietly, trying to calm the sobbing child. She remembered* *being wrapped in a blanket and placed in a carriage. Martha huddled in fear as the carriage rumbled up to the train depot. She was carried onboard by the man and given over to a sweet-smelling lady who made distressed noises that sounded to Martha like she **need not be afraid.*** Most of the children sold that day were without a mother or a father. Slavers found they could get more money for children unencumbered by parents. The large sugar cane plantation owners especially prized children, as they were ideally suited to the harvesting of the delicate sugar cane stalks. Though her new owner also had a sugar cane plantation, Martha was soon to learn that Mastah Mac never bought children "away" from their parents.

Louisiana was the only state that had a law expressly forbidding such practices. *Missus Mac told her later that Mastah Mac bought her because his own sister, Maureen, was about the same age, and he couldn't leave Martha to the merciless slave traders. She was one of the fortunate few children that would not be a field worker at all.*

Some slight movement of the bedclothes interrupted Martha's memories. She quickly left the room to alert Mastah Patrick that Miz Lorraine was waking up.

Lorraine gradually came awake, and as consciousness slowly returned, a wave of terror swept over her! She remembered. Zack was hurt! Lorraine then realized she was in bed and he lay beside her, his breath rasping but steady. Zack's bandaged chest was clear of blood and he seemed free of pain. She relaxed against the downy pillow and looked at him. His light brown hair was long and the loss of weight caused his naturally angular features to stand out in sharp relief. Sleeping dropped years from his face and he looked very young. She reached out and gently traced his cheek with her finger. The rhythm of his breathing changed slightly but then resumed its steady cadence. Lorraine couldn't guess what time it was, but she knew she must get up. So much needed to be done! *My hair must be like a bird's nest, and I need to wash up,* she thought.

A firm pressure to lie back down came from Martha who suddenly materialized.

"Mastah Patrick say you to stay in bed, Miz Lorraine, no mattah what."

"But I am fine! I just slept too long," Lorraine assured her. "I am in dire need of my toilet and food. I'm very hungry!"

Martha's face brightened.

"If you's hongrey, you gwoin to be fine. I will go get your suppah and be right back to help you."

Lorraine sat quietly on the edge of the huge four-poster. Though she still felt tired, having Zack safely home invigorated her. Reaching for her wrap, she put her foot down on the bed steps and suddenly realized she was a little shaky.

Several hours later, a groggy Zack rolled over on his back and groaned at the sharp pain in his shoulder and leg. Then he remembered. A blow from a saber, though deflected by his own, knifed through a considerable portion of his right chest and upper thigh.

Zack opened his eyes and saw Lori leaning over him.

She was a strong woman, but when she saw Zack in pain, her heart seemed to dissolve. "Darling let me give you some laudanum." Her voice quavered slightly.

Martha hurried over with the bottle of easement medicine and Lorraine carefully measured out the right number of drops. It took both her and Martha to hold Zack so he could swallow the mixture. He grimaced and lay back down.

"Whisky would be better, I think," he said weakly.

Both women smiled.

Chapter VI

December 1848
"Grinding"

It was a cold, crisp morning, and the shock of going from the chilly December air to the warmth of the sugarhouse was like a comforting blanket. Zack entered by the side door, not wanting to distract from the intricate process going on near the front of the huge structure.

The sugarhouse was filled with smoke and noise and the sweet fumes of sugar that swirled around men, kettles, and hogshead barrels day and night during the grinding season. Some described the fumes as a sickly, sweet smell, but Zack loved every aspect of the sugar-making process, especially the fumes. Dr. Bercoise had even been known to advise his patients recovering from illness to bed down on the top floor of the sugarhouse, where the scent was the heaviest. Many doctors were convinced the fumes had rejuvenating properties.

Passing the train of kettles, Zack watched the workers expertly leading the squeezed juice that had been chewed into pulp by the teeth of the big iron rollers on the cane-carrier. The juice was led first from the biggest kettle, or "grande," to the next, known as the "flambeau." As the juice concentrated by evaporation, it was transferred from kettle to kettle, the workers waving the long poles with buckets attached, called "swords." The rowing motion, though fast, was done with such precision that hardly any splashing occurred. At the same time the juice was clarified, or skimmed of impurities, as it boiled. The sugar maker would add lime to help the process along. The juice made its way to a third kettle called the "sirop" and finally to the "batteire," the smallest kettle. At a certain point the sugar maker, a specialist brought to River Rose from Cuba just for the "grinding" season, would decide that he had allowed the exact amount of boiling and would make a "strike."

A "strike" had just been called and Zack's sugar maker stepped back to allow the other workers to begin ladling the masscuite of crystals and molasses into cooling troughs where it would continue to crystallize, the grains growing bigger as they cooled

Zack took this opportunity to take the man aside and compliment him on the success of the production so far.

Zack had brought Juan DeArgo to River Rose to supervise grinding five years ago. Both Zack and Patrick were so impressed with his skill that they had asked him back every year since. This time Juan brought his wife Mariabella. Zack sampled her cooking and decided it would be a good idea to have her help Auralee during the grinding season when the numbers of hands was the greatest.

"Juan, have you had a chance to think over what we talked about last week?" Zack asked.

"*Si Señor*. I thing I would like to do eet, but Mariabella does not wan to leeve her *madre*. She very old and sick. Wen she no longer weeth us," Juan unconsciously made the sign of the cross, "we weel come. There would be nothing to hold us anymore."

Zack knew Juan and Mariabella's only son was working in New Orleans and their daughter had married and moved to the Florida Keys. Zack shook his hand. "Whenever you're ready, let me know."

Zack moved away smiling to himself. The competition for excellent "sugar tramps," as the itinerant sugar makers were called, was often fierce. These specialists traveled from Cuba around the Caribbean following the trail of sugar. Patrick and Zack had decided on a bold move to assure they had the best man for this critical position. They had offered Juan DeArgo a year-round job if he would relocate to River Rose permanently. There was always work to be done, and it would be worth the cost always to have the best sugar maker ready for the grinding every fall.

Zack climbed to each level of the huge structure, savoring the different sounds and textures of smells. Looking out one of the small windows, he saw the long building known as the "purgery." Even after all of the boiling and cooling, Zack knew some of the syrup would fail to crystallize, and the sticky residue that remained with the crystals had to be separated. Hanging from the rafters in the purgery were rows and rows of perforated barrels with the molasses residue dripping slowly into larger hogshead barrels.

Zack reached the top and looked down, marveling once again at the beehive of activity that had a rhythm unlike any other. The pace would reach frenzy as January approached, though this year the balmy weather was holding, and he had not even bothered to "mattress" any cane. This would be a banner year, and he estimated a production of over 700 hogsheads of sugar. They would be carried by wagon to Bayou Chatis to be loaded on to barges for the trip to Red River, and then on to New Orleans, where his factor would secure the best price possible.

His reverie was interrupted by one of his workers who appeared breathless at the top of the stairs. "Belray say you to come quick, suh. Miz Mac is fixin to birth!"

Belray was the plantation's black midwife and all-around medicine woman. She had made the trip from Georgia with Zack and his father and was trusted as much as any doctor.

Zack hurried down the four flights of stairs and galloped to the house on his horse. His mind whirled with excitement and fear! Lori was strong and healthy, but childbirth was always risky.

Dr. Bercoise thought the baby would not come for several days. Belray had a different opinion. "Dis secon baby gwon to come early and fast. Miz Mac is ready, and she gwon to have anudder big boy," the old woman had declared last night.

Lori had given birth to their first son, Jacob, a year and a half ago with no problems, but the birth process could be dangerous. Had something gone wrong? Zack had hoped for another boy. They had decided he would be named Jon Rue after Lori's uncle in France.

Now he begged God, *Just let Lori be safe. Just let her be her usual brave, unmanageable, wonderful self...please, God.*

Jumping from his horse, Zack cleared the front steps in long strides and ran up the stairs toward the master bedchamber. A loud scream tore through the hall and stopped him in his tracks. Martha came out of the room and beckoned him in. He hesitated and then slowly entered. Several black women were hovering over Lori, and he couldn't see her at first. Belray turned and with a triumphant smile said, "I tole dat doctah dis baby wudn gwon to wait no moah days. Miz Mac such a tall lady, she not have no trouble birthin babies. You has a fine son, Mastah Mac!"

At that moment a loud wail tore from the infant and Belray cackled with satisfaction. "He's a big ole strong boy, suh." The old woman handed the wriggling baby to the wet nurse.

Zack glimpsed a fat, red bundle with light fuzz of hair. He bent over Lori who was covered in sweat and gasping in pain.

"Don't you worry non, Mastah Mac, I gave her some laudanum. She be alrit soon." Belray straightened the bedclothes and made soothing noises. She wiped Lori's face and Zack could see the medicine begin to work as his wife's eyelids began to droop.

"Is he not beautiful, *Cheri*?" Lori asked sleepily, reaching for Zack's hand.

He leaned over and kissed her on the cheek. "Most beautiful boy I ever saw," Zack lied

Chapter VII

December 1848

Iffen you was caught, they whipped you till you said, "Oh, pray, Master!"
One day a man was saying, "Oh, pray, Master! Lord, have mercy!" They'd
say "Keep whipping that nigger, goddam him." He was whipped till he said,
"Oh, pray, Master! I got enough." Then they said, "let him up now, 'cause
he's praying to the right man."

Excerpt from Slave Diary contained in
"Lay My Burden Down"
B. A. Botkin

A bloody hand reached the bottom step, and then the thing's other hand scratched weakly for the next. Then the hands were still.

Auralee had heard the hounds, and she shivered. Another slave was being hunted. She opened the back door to look out toward the woods to see if she could see the hunters. That was when she noticed the bloody creature with its clawing hands now moving again, trying to climb the steps.

"Oh Lawdy, help me!" she screamed and ran to the big house. "Mastah Mac, Mastah Zack, come see dis at the bac doh." Despite her great bulk, the "best cook in Louisiana," according to anyone who had ever graced her table, fairly flew the short distance to Patrick McLoed's office.

"What in the world?" Patrick said. Zack and Boliver, the overseer, turned to look at the frantic figure.

"It's somthin' all mashed and bloody, maybe a haint!"

The three men ran toward the kitchen door and paused only long enough to realize what lay at the bottom of the stairs, still clawing futilely. Patrick and Zack grabbed the mangled man and carried him into the kitchen.

"Auralee, get some grease blankets! Hurry," barked Zack.

The sounds of the hounds were louder now.

Boliver ran back into the house, shouting over his shoulder, "I'll get the guns!"

Patrick and Zack laid the mutilated black man on his stomach and turned back to the door. The thud of horses' hooves and scuffling of dogs swirled around in the dirt at the bottom of the steps. The dogs were going wild at the scent of the blood.

"I know ya'll got that no count niggah in thah and I want him out now!" Kirby the Winter Wind overseer yelled belligerently.

Boliver returned to the kitchen with the guns, and the three men moved toward the door.

Patrick stood in the door, Zack, and Boliver glaring over his shoulder.

"Been trying to kill your hands again, Kirby?" Patrick's voice was ice cold.

"It shore ain't no concern of yourn, Mr. McLoed." Kirby was surprised to see the plantation owner himself and his well-armed son and overseer. He shifted uneasily in the saddle. He had not counted on this.

"We jes need to take that niggah back whah he b'longs and no hard feelins." His tone was now decidedly conciliatory.

"You tell your boss to come see me tomorrow, and we'll talk about it. Our talking for today is over. Take your men and dogs and clear off River Rose land. Right now you're trespassing." Patrick stood solid as a rock in the door.

"Whatever you say, Mr. McLoed. I shore will tell Mr. Descant." The overseer turned his horse, and the men followed him, calling the dogs as they went. Kirby could feel the men cutting their eyes to try and see his reaction. "Boy, Mr. Descant will shore be mad over this here. I don't know what'll happen. It won't be a purty thang." Kirby pulled his jacket closer as the evening chill descended. "It shore won't be purty."

As the three men reentered the kitchen a loud groan escaped from the man lying on the floor.

"He's still alive," said Patrick. "We need to send for Doctor Bercoise. He may not make it through the night."

"I'll send someone to get him and have old Belray come on up and start tendin' to him," Zack said. "We need to move him to the 'sick' cabin and get him wrapped."

The "sick cabin" was one of the many outbuildings located at the back of the big house. To the right of the "sick cabin" stood a privy. Several yards away, a small schoolhouse stood empty in the gathering dusk. Tomorrow all the children that lived in or around River Rose would come tumbling into the tiny structure. This included slave children whose parents wanted them to have "book sense" as they called it. Some slaves wanted their children to learn trades instead, so that they could be considered valuable additions to the plantation. There were not a lot of jobs open to an "educated" slave. A huge blacksmith shop was situated farther back, almost to the tree line. With a hundred mules and thirty horses to keep shod, it was one of the busiest places on the plantation. A few yards past the smithy was the smokehouse. River Rose was a self-contained mini-village in most aspects, and the smokehouse accounted for part of that self-sustaining ability.

Patrick and Zack wrapped the injured man in a greased cloth and carried him out to the cabin, struggling to keep from reopening his wounds.

Patrick and Zack carefully eased the unconscious man onto one of the four beds similar to what the slaves had in their regular cabins. The beds were supported on puncheons that were fitted into holes bored in the walls. The puncheons were planks laid across these poles. Mattresses made of ticking had been filled with corn shucks and moss to make up the rest of the bed. The sick or injured were cared for in the "sick" cabin by one of the oldest slaves on the place, named Belray. Old Belray knew everything about healing, as she said, in the "old folks" way. Normally she would handle any illness without calling the doctor. But this would be beyond anything she had ever seen.

Belray came after them into the room and stifled a cry as the grease cloth was carefully removed.

"Lawd, dis is da wost I evah seed, and…" She hesitated. "I knows dis boy. He Theesus. He from Winter Wind place, ain't he?"

"That's where he's from alright," Zack agreed.

"He runned away?" Belray asked in disbelief. Slaves never ran away. That guaranteed a certain beating, maybe death.

"We don't know the details yet," Patrick said. "Maybe he can tell us if he lives."

"I'll shore need ease medicine, Mastah Mac," Belray muttered, still looking in awe at the man lying now unwrapped from the greased cloth.

"Boliver sent for the doctor. He'll give you everything you need," Zack assured her.

The two men left the cabin and walked slowly toward the big house.

"There'll be hell to pay over this, Papa," Zack said.

"I know. Descant is a bastard at the best of times. He'll be furious that we saw what happened on his place and even angrier that we now have his property," Patrick agreed. "Tomorrow will be an interesting day."

The next day...

The sheriff rode slowly from Alexandria down to River Rose Plantation. Sheriff Antonio Dickerson was tall, lanky, and dark-haired. Spanish ancestry on his mother's side and Dutch on his father's had produced a handsome man whose dark eyes hid a pragmatic nature. All during the ride, he pondered the unusual situation he saw unfolding. A runaway slave taken in by another plantation owner! Dickerson had never heard of such a thing. The most amazing part was the fact that all of this had happened at River Rose. Patrick McLoed was one of Tony Dickerson's oldest friends and a most sensible man. As an experienced lawman, Dickerson knew there must be a lot more to the story than Descant's overseer had told him. Kirby had been pounding on his office door at daybreak, frothing at the mouth over some wild tale about Patrick McLoed harboring a runaway slave and ordering him and his men off the plantation.

"Mr. Descant said he wanted you to move quick on this, else all the slaves in the parish'll be runnin' off to River Rose ever time they have a toe ache." This last was delivered in the pompous way of an underling not used to being in the position of representing a powerful man.

"Just calm down, Kirby. I'll ride over and see what this is all about," Dickerson said, in tones meant to soothe the man's anger.

"Well, I jes hop'en you know how serious this here is." The overseer had little flecks of spittle clinging to his scraggly mustache as he puffed himself up.

"I expect I can judge what is serious after I interview all the folks involved. Tell Mr. Descant I will be by to see him after I talk with McLoed."

The overseer stalked out of the sheriff's office and said, still blustering, "I'll tell Mr. Descant to expect you and that runaway slave later today."

As River Rose came into view, Dickerson sighed. He had the feeling there would be no winners by this day's end.

"Good to see you, Tony." Patrick shook hands with the sheriff and led him into the plantation office. "I've asked Zack and Boliver to be here, as they were witnesses to this whole sorry business."

"I appreciate your cooperation, Patrick. I know there must be quite a story behind all this," Dickerson replied as he accepted one of the comfortable leather chairs in the sitting area of the office.

Morning sunlight streamed through the shutters and striped the surface of the plantation owner's cluttered desk and large swivel chair. Zack and

Boliver followed Dickerson's example and settled into the chairs surrounding the sofa.

"Ready for some coffee?" Patrick picked up a steaming pot from a small table next to his elbow.

"Thank you, yes," the sheriff accepted gratefully.

Patrick filled the men's cups and then sat back rubbing his hands across his eyes.

"One of Descant's slaves showed up here yesterday. He had been beaten within an inch of his life and was barely alive. Belray recognized him. Said his name is Theesus. He's in the worst shape I have ever seen a person to still be alive. I'm sure they intended to kill him. Somehow he got away and started running. He ended up here."

"What is the condition of the slave now?" Tony asked.

"Doctor Bercoise saw him last night and left this for you. I guessed that you would be visiting me today." McLoed handed Dickerson the physician's official report.

Dickerson read quickly and whistled under his breath.

"He's still alive?" The sheriff looked shocked.

"I think it would be a good idea for you to see for yourself," replied Patrick.

"Might as well see him now," Tony said, finishing off his coffee.

As they walked toward the "sick" cabin, the sheriff continued, "If he ever regains consciousness, then we'll find out what really happened. Otherwise it will just be Descant's word."

Belray was unwrapping Theesus as they entered the cool, dim structure. The doctor had instructed her to sprinkle a special liquid over his back, arms, neck, and head. This area was now oozing pus from open wounds.

At the sight of the wounds, Dickerson let out his breath. "Damn that overseer! I'd like to take a whip to him myself!"

The wounded man seemed to be totally unaware of his surroundings, until the old woman began her ministrations. Pain from his wounds caused him to rouse up and cry out.

Patrick hurried to his side.

"Theesus, can you hear me? It's McLoed. I have the sheriff here. Can you tell us what happened?"

Dickerson and McLoed both bent down as close to the suffering man as they could get.

"My sister. The master hurt my sister bad. I think she's dead...." This last was very low and then he fainted.

"Belray, call me if he rouses up again," McLoed said. "Take note of anything he says. Even better have one of the children that can write come stay with you, and write down anything you hear out of this man's mouth. If he says anything about what happened, come and get me at once."

As he issued orders, Patrick covered his astonishment over the very literate words coming out of this slave's mouth. *Where had Theesus been educated?* he wondered. Only in the last few years had Patrick McLoed made the controversial decision to allow slave children admittance to the little schoolhouse on his property. Controversial, because the prevailing opinion was that an "educated slave" was a dangerous slave. In Louisiana, it was against the law to educate slaves. No one had complained, so the sheriff had pretended he didn't know about Zack allowing his slaves' children to be schooled. But Theesus was a grown man. He was educated long ago.

The men walked slowly back to the house.

Dickerson looked at Patrick. "Very surprising young man," he said. "Wonder where he was before Winter Wind?"

"I don't know his history, but obviously he lived a different life than now," Patrick commented sadly.

"I promised I would go by Winter Wind after I saw you. I doubt if I'll find out anything near the truth. Do you have any of your hands that can find out what really happened?"

Patrick thought for a moment. "Yes, I think I know of someone. Can you stop back by here after your visit with Descant?"

"Certainly. I might even get back in time for supper." The sheriff was of the same opinion as everyone else regarding the excellence of Auralee's cooking skills.

"That would be fine. We'll look for you then." Patrick shook hands with his friend and walked him to his horse.

Later that day…

The old wagon bumped along with its load of trinket jewelry, knives, looking glasses, tobacco, salt bags, musket powder, axes, pots, pans, and just about anything else an Indian, slave, or country folk might need. It was a familiar sight, and nobody paid any attention. Sometimes the old tinker man used his pirogue, and pushed up and down the bayou to reach outlying areas. In his wagon he made his way through paths that were hardly there. His best customers were the slaves and Indians. Sometimes the slaves would actually have a few coins, but mainly they just traded. Some of the women slaves were wonderful weavers, producing beautiful cloth that they bartered for ribbon and beads. The men occasionally produced excellent woodcarvings. This allowed them to trade for extra tobacco. Indians traded furs and pottery. Some were skilled at basket weaving and used this as their currency.

The old man stopped his wagon at the east section of Winter Wind, just where the woods started. A small figure crept out from under the tarp the old man always spread over his "goods." Unless one happened to be looking exactly at that place, at that moment, no one would have seen the figure enter the woods. The tinker clucked to his ancient mules. They plodded forward to the edge of the slave quarters and stopped to conduct business and deliver a message. If any one had been watching, he would have seen a figure with an ax go toward the woods, looking industrious. Later the wagon returned to the woods, and the small figure crept back under the tarp. Starting up his mules, the tinker went back the way he came. He was smiling to himself, as he thought, *Descant is such a jackass. Serves him right to be in trouble!*

Patrick and Zack were so horrified by what the trinket man's spy came back and told them, they decided they would just have a light supper in the office with the sheriff when he arrived. Lorraine was still recovering from the birth of Jon Rue, and had been having her meals in her little sitting room upstairs. Zack told her they had some pressing business to discuss, and he would come up to see her after supper.

Zack kept pacing the office and simply could not settle down after the news from Winter Wind.

Patrick answered the knock at the door and welcomed Dickerson.

"I assume you were successful in getting information for me. Auralee says we're eating in here," the sheriff said, removing his hat.

"Yes. Have a seat. We've got a cold supper tonight. After what we heard, we didn't have the heart for a big meal." Patrick sat down and passed a dish to his friend.

"That bad?" Dickerson said softly. He settled in his chair. "Let's hear it."

"Julien Descant, as you may have heard, has an affinity for young slave girls. He has been able to pretty much do what he wanted, because there really is no recourse for the slaves, and the girls and women, except to go along to…get along."

"And he wonders why his slaves are always running away, and why they don't produce like River Rose." This from Zack who was still unreconciled to what he had heard.

"This time he chose Theesus' younger sister, who was only 12, and made his move while her brother was in the fields. The little girl was terrified, and he had to beat her. In the process, he choked her hard…and he killed her. When Theesus came in from the fields and found out, he went into a rage and attacked Descant. Of course he was beaten mercilessly, and it was intended that he would die. But somehow he managed to escape, started running, and ended up here."

The sheriff put down his bread and shook his head.

"I see what you mean about not being hungry," he said.

The room was filled with the images of a little slave girl, and the abomination inflicted on her. The dreadful sight of Theesus and his wounds intruded. An anguished silence filled every corner of the room and hung like a dark cloud over the men.

Two months later…

Belray did her usual amazing job of nursing and utilizing what seemed like miraculous curative powers. Despite all odds, Theesus began to heal and with Belray's constant urging and cajoling went through the painful process of exercising his arms.

Theesus jerked awake and then groaned as the movement pulled at the buildup of scar tissue covering his mutilated back and shoulders. Gingerly, he raised himself to a sitting position and saw the watery sunlight barely tracing itself on the beams of the cabin. Despite the mud stuck between the logs, little flecks of daylight penetrated here and there. Putting his head in his hands he thought of what lay ahead. *More shouts of "move those ams and shoulders" as Belray coaxed and pleaded and him trying not to cry and scream. He knew it had to be done. The doctor said otherwise he would be like a frozen statue. "Like dem pillahs of salt at Sodum and Gomorah" according to Belray. Would it ever end? What if he just went down to the river and jumped in? Yesterday he had stopped on the levee with some slaves coming back from the field and looked at the roiling water. He knew it would be cold at first but then he could close his eyes and just float away and join his mama and sister. Bertie, another slave, saw what was in his face and drug him away. "Come on, Theesus, you is too smart foh dat. You is goin to get ovah dis. Come on." Bertie kept on pulling at him, and he finally walked away from the relief of sweet death. What if he did get well? He was still a slave. Even if Mastah McLoed was a kind man and not like Descant at all.* Theesus went to the door of the cabin and looked out on a cold but bright morning. *If there was just something to hope for. Would there ever be anything to hope for?* He shook his head trying to clear the despair in his mind.

By February, Theesus was able to wear light clothes for part of the day and take short jogs around the place. He belonged to River Rose legally now. Armed with the doctor's damming certificate of "purpose inflicted injury," Sheriff Dickerson advised Descant to agree to sell the mutilated slave to Patrick McLoed. There really was no legal recourse to keep Theesus from being returned to what would be certain death since he was still the property of Descant. However, it was pointed out that since he was not expected to live, it would be less trouble to sell him than have the medical document published as would be required by law. This was a stretch and the sheriff had great latitude in these matters. Dickerson made it plain to the plantation owner that he would see that it was widely circulated if he did not agree to allow Theesus to remain at River Rose. The sum suggested was much below the normal value of a young, strong, male slave. However, no one really expected the man to live. Descant was able to convince himself and those around him that he got the better of the bargain.

Chapter VIII

The pale winter sunlight was flickering toward early dusk. Martha had timed her journey to the cabin she shared with three other slaves to coincide with Theesus' early evening exercise. She had heard the stories about Theesus from Belray and others who had witnessed his courage as he tried to recover from his hideous ordeal. His back would always bear the terrible tracking scars interlaced with deep pocks where the stubby nails at the ends of the whip had bitten into his flesh. Still, he was an attractive man. Despite his eyes. His unusual gray eyes were the saddest Martha thought she had ever seen. The most amazing thing about him was that he spoke like an educated man!

Theesus jogged to a stop near the water pump, Martha handed him the dipper.

"Have some good cold water and rest foh a minute." Martha smiled at Theesus. When Martha smiled it was as if heaven opened up. She did not smile often. She still carried a little girl melancholy from her early years. But it was worth the wait when it happened.

"Thank you, I will," he answered.

After a few drinks he wiped his mouth on his shirtsleeve and replaced the dipper.

The sun had given up its weak assault on winter, and deep shadows covered both of them. Martha could just see his outline against the corncrib.

"My name is Martha," she said, and realized she sounded timid.

"I know," replied Theesus as he looked at her slender, shadowy form.

In the days and weeks that followed, Martha and Theesus met at the end of the day at the well and often shared supper in Martha's cabin.

Sometimes they would time it just right and manage to be alone. It was during one of these occasions when they shared their past histories. Theesus' name was actually Theseus. He printed it out for her on a scrap of paper that he had saved from supplies brought from town. Martha noticed he saved any paper he could get and supposed he wrote things down when he was in his own cabin at night. He shared quarters with six other single men slaves. She was amazed when she learned he could read and write. He explained how his mother had been an "inside" slave to a rich white plantation owner near New Orleans. The plantation owner's wife died and about a year later Thesues was born. He was raised up right along with the owner's white children, and taught by the same tutor in the upstairs schoolroom. Thesues even had a few books of his own. Everything changed when the planter died. The children he had grown up with decided they no longer wanted "black kin." They sold Thesues, his little sister and mother to Descant's factor. At Martha's puzzled look he explained.

"A factor is someone who takes care of plantation business away from the place, buying and selling slaves and supplies." Theseus shifted as his still sore back demanded attention.

In a more comfortable position, he continued.

"*Mama* died of yellow fever the first year we lived at Winter Wind. Kirby put her to work in the field. She wasn't used to being out in bad weather and had gotten weak during the coffles from New Orleans to Winter Wind."

Martha knew about coffles. These were the forced marches to the plantations from wherever the slave trading took place. Men, women, and children were shackled by their necks, and then chained together, usually barefoot and with minimal clothing. They walked in all kinds of weather until they reached their destination. If they fell and could not continue they were shot. Thesues' precious last three books that he had so carefully hidden were lost crossing a stream that turned out to be deep. As the books floated away, he managed to snatch a few pages from one and stuffed them in his pants pocket without the guards seeing him. As it was, he was beaten because slaves were not allowed to have books. He still had those few tattered pages that he always kept with him. One time when he and Martha were alone and there was still enough daylight left to see he read her part of one page.

> Out of this wood do not desire to go:
> Thou shalt remain here, whether thou wilt or no.
> I am a spirit of no common rate,
> The summer still doth tend upon my state;
> And I do love thee: therefore, go with me;
> I'll give thee fairies to attend on thee;
> And they shall fetch thee jewels from the deep,

And sing, while thou on pressed flowers dost sleep;
And I will purge they mortal grossness so,
That thou shalt like an airy spirit go.
Peas-blossom! Cobweb! Moth! and Mustard-seed!

He finished and looking distant said, "This was Hermia's, my little sister's, favorite. She did not really understand it all, but she loved the woods and said it made her feel safe when I read it to her."

Martha did not understand it all either, but she knew he had never shared his secret pages with anyone before, and tears of joy stood in her eyes.

In April, a black Jesuit priest from New Orleans came to the plantation and presided over Theseus and Martha McLoed "jumping the broom" in the customary marriage ceremony. They pledged to each other the traditional slave marriage vow, "until death or distance do us part." Their names were entered in the marriage book kept by the plantation. As was also the custom, Theseus became a McLoed, as Patrick was now his owner. He was not sorry to shed the Descant name.

As the months passed, Theseus made remarkable progress in overcoming his terrible wounds. He would never be capable of the hard physical labor required of the typical field hand, and this preyed on his mind. Though the other slaves assured him Mastah Patrick never separated families, Theseus worried about the possibility of the mastah selling him and Martha. This fear was laid to rest one afternoon in summer, when Miss Lorraine called him into the house and showed him the extensive library that Patrick and Zack had accumulated over the years. Theseus stared in awe at the four walls lined with bookcases and filled to capacity with volumes from all over the world.

"Zack and Patrick have been collecting books for years and ordering them from booksellers both here and abroad," Lorraine said. "There never seems to be enough time to sort and organize the collection. The books need to be catalogued by title, author, and subject for reference. As it is now, unless someone remembers a book they have used recently, we have to search forever." Lorraine stopped. She knew Theseus could read, but she did not know whether he could write legibly.

As if reading her mind, Theseus spoke up. "I would love to work on the library, Miss Lorraine. At my other place, not Winter Wind, but before, I took care of all the books and kept them in order. My penmanship is something I have worked hard on. Even now I practice..." he hesitated, "whenever I have some paper scraps."

"That sounds wonderful. Let us discuss where we should start," Lorraine said. She handed Theseus some writing paper. "Draw up a plan for the library and bring it to me at supper. I will show it to Mr. Patrick and Mr. Zack and see if they approve."

Hope swelled in Theseus' heart. This was a way out of despair. To be allowed to work around books again—maybe even be allowed to read some of them! He rushed to his cabin and began work on the library plan.

Theseus presented his ideas as to how to organize the library to Miss Lorraine at supper. She thanked him and promised they would speak of the project as soon as Mr. Zack and Mr. Patrick had a chance to look at his work.

Zack and Patrick were amazed at how well Theseus presented his thoughts and gave their approval for the plan to go forward. Zack was especially impressed with Theseus' beautiful penmanship.

Theseus began work on creating the new library system.

Watching his careful work and seeing his great knowledge of books gave Lorraine another idea. Miss Jacobs, the teacher Zack employed to teach in the little plantation school, was becoming increasingly frail with age. Even starting up the wood-burning fireplace and sweeping out the schoolhouse was sometimes too much for her, and she would often ask for help. Lorraine knew she would have to be careful, as it was against the law to allow slave children to go to school. It would really be unusual to have a slave as a teacher. *But if he started helping out with chores and gradually assumed more and more responsibilities….* Lorraine thought this to herself, smiling at her own deviousness.

Soon, Theseus was not only working in the library but helping the elderly teacher. He was also observing her ways of teaching. Each child was taught at his or her level of understanding.

Sometimes she would let him listen to the reading assignments for one group while she helped another. Within six months Theseus and Miss Jacobs were sharing the teaching responsibilities. Theseus had great patience with the children and would read to them for hours. He was especially helpful with the slower children and had the ability to make them feel at ease. Theseus was never referred to as a teacher. He was still Theseus. But he was working with books, and Miss Lorraine encouraged him to read whatever books from the library he wished. He was the happiest he had been since before his mother died. He only wished his little sister could have shared this new life.

Chapter IX

Now, drawn near the shelving rim,
Bird-like shadows suddenly rise;
Shapes of mist and phantoms dim
Baffle the gazer's straining eyes.
Walt Whitman

June 1853

Jon Rue McLoed kicked at his blocks and sent the carefully constructed building tumbling to the ground in brightly colored disarray. Hot tears of frustration replaced his momentary five-year-old rage. Nobody had time for him anymore. Not even his mama. He would show her! He would show everybody! He would leave and then they would be sorry! Jon Rue looked around the nursery for anything to take with him. His old bear only had one eye left and almost all the stuffing was gone, not fit for a boy leaving home. He stomped loudly down the stairs. Everyone seemed to be occupied somewhere else and no one even heard the loud slam of the door at the back of the house.

Jon Rue didn't know where he was going but it was away from all the people who no longer noticed him. Taking an overgrown, little used path on the side of field near Bayou Chatis, he saw some slaves a few fields over, just as outlines against the sun. The afternoon was hot and dry and even the insects were quiet. The small boy kicked up puffs of dust as he trudged along. After a while his feet began to drag with tiredness. In the distance he saw the purgery. He would stop there and rest.

Jon Rue's eyes took a moment to adjust to the semi-darkness. Walking slowly up and down the long structure, he craned his neck to see the dark shapes of the huge barrels hanging from the rafters. The soft drip, drip of the molasses was soothing, and the smell enfolded him in a blanket of sweetness. It was as if he had crawled into one of the big magnolia blossoms that hung in soft petals from the trees near the front of the house. He could imagine his mama holding him and singing songs that he could vaguely remember from some other time. But his mama had no time for him now. All she did was lie in bed like she was waiting for something, he was not sure what.

Jon Rue could hear his mama saying it would all be over soon, and she could play with him again. He crawled to the back of one of the drip pans and lay down on a soft pile of rags stacked against the wall. Wiping his face with a grubby hand, he cried, deep, gulping sobs that finally ended in sniffling hiccups. He was glad his brother couldn't see him now. Jacob always wanted to run off and play with his friend Benny, Martha's boy. Jacob thought Jon Rue was too young for his big adventures. Drip, drip. The sound was soothing. Sleepily he turned on his side and closed his eyes. He would rest for a minute and quit thinking about his mama and brother and think about his papa.

Jon Rue knew his papa was gone on the river to another town. He couldn't remember the name of the town but knew papa was coming home tonight. Papa always had time for him. He would see him soon.

Zack stepped off the barge and greeted his overseer, Boliver, who was standing with their horses at the dock. Boliver towered over all the other people milling around the barge. He had an imposing presence and booming voice that assured his orders to the hands were always taken seriously. Boliver had a bull neck, a large head, and a well-muscled body. Black hair and eyes and sun-darkened skin gave an impression of mystery and power. The people who worked under this massive man knew him to be fair and never cruel. Zack trusted him completely and never worried about leaving the plantation in his capable hands.

"How are things going?" he asked, grasping Boliver's hand.

"Jist fine, Mistah Mac. The plantin' on Borge Isle is finished, and there is a good stand o' young cane in Midway Fort and Thro-set."

Zack knew exactly what parts of the plantation Boliver was describing without even needing a map because all the areas of the fields had names.

Zack and Boliver mounted their horses and headed to River Rose, continuing their discussion.

"Are the quarter drains all clear?" At Boliver's nod Zack continued, "What about the split ditches in the Thro-set?" Zack was talking about the complex drainage system necessary to all sugar cane plantations.

By the time they reached River Rose, they had covered every aspect of the running of the plantation. Zack was confident everything had been handled satisfactorily, and now he turned his attention to his family.

Dismounting, Zack entered the house and quickly ascended the long staircase to the main bedchamber. Lori had been confined to her bed during these last three weeks of a difficult pregnancy.

"Zack! I am so glad you're home." Lori reached out for him as he entered the room.

"My darling, I'm glad to be home. You know I wouldn't have left if I'd any other choice." He held her in his arms and kissed her gently, the smell of her hair and skin enveloping him. "How are you feeling?" he asked, stepping back to look at his wife.

Other than tired, she looked beautiful as usual. "I am fine, *cheri.* I think it will be soon now. Then I can quit neglecting you and our sons."

"You haven't neglected anyone. Just rest. This'll soon be over. This will be the last time. I can't stand the worry over you." Zack put his arms around Lori, and she laid her head on his chest.

"Do not worry, my Zack. Belray says I will be fine. She says this one will be a daughter." Lori raised her head and looked at her husband. "What would you think about naming her after my little sister?"

Zack looked into his wife's face. "Emmageline is a beautiful name, and I'd be honored to have a daughter named after such a wonderful person."

Lorraine's sister had died in a yellow fever epidemic when she was fifteen. Zack could still remember her sweet disposition, and a face that was the image of Lori's.

"Oh, thank you." Lori looked up into Zack's face with shining eyes.

He bent down and kissed her again. "I could never refuse you anything when you look at me that way," he said softly.

Releasing her, he stepped down from the bed. "Where are the boys? It seems quiet around here."

"Jake and Benny have gone fishing and…" she hesitated, "Jon Rue wandered out several hours ago in a pout because I could not take him to the sugarhouse. It is very hard on him. He is so young. He cannot understand why I am unable to play with him like always."

"Well I'll see if I can find something to do with him for the rest of the afternoon. Do you need anything?" Zack asked from the door.

"No, I will just rest awhile before dinner. I can be easy now that you are here."

Zack entered the playroom expecting to see Jon Rue building one of his many blockhouses, but there was no sign of him. He spoke to several of the house servants. No one seemed to have seen the boy. He headed for the stables thinking perhaps his youngest son had prevailed on Henri to take him out in the carriage.

Henri was grooming one of the horses, and said he had not seen Jon Rue all day.

Puzzled, Zack headed back to the house. He met Jake and Benny at the back of the kitchen. Each held a stringer with several fat fish, which Jake almost dropped in his excitement over his father's return. They had not seen Jon Rue either.

Twilight shadows lengthened with no sign of Jon Rue. Lori would have to be told he was missing when Martha brought up supper. Both boys and Zack always joined her in the little sitting room off the main bedroom when she could not come down to the big dinning room.

Patrick took several men and rode off to check along the bayou. Though Jon Rue could swim, there were snakes and alligators all along the water. When the hands came in from the field and sugarhouse, they were questioned. No one had seen Jon Rue all day.

The old building was dark. Clouds covered the pitiful sliver of a quarter moon. No light filtered through the few small windows. The little boy sat up suddenly as a screeching owl complained loudly. Confused at first, he could not understand where he was. Then he remembered running off to the purgery because his mother wouldn't take him to the sugarhouse. He heard a skittering noise, and two rats scurried out from under a nearby pan. Jon Rue jumped up quickly and realized he was all stiff and sticky. One of the pans had run over, and his arms and legs were covered with molasses. Stumbling into the main room, he made his way to the door. Pushing it open he peered out into darkness. Looking around, Jon Rue realized he didn't know which way to go. He had never been in this area at night. Everything looked different.

Walking out to the path in front of the building, Jon Rue couldn't decide whether to go left or right. He jumped as the owl screeched again.

Something was moving in back of him! He could hear the rustling! Jon Rue began to run. The rutted old road was difficult to navigate, and he fell hard on his left knee. He wanted to cry out but was afraid whatever was chasing him would hear him. He got up and started to limp down the road as quietly as he could, glancing over his shoulder constantly. It seemed like he had walked for hours, but still he saw nothing that looked familiar.

He started to cry, little gasping child gulps of fear. Through the shrubs and trees, he saw lights and voices floated out on the still night air. Creeping up under some bushes, he looked in on a scene that filled him with terror! Several men were holding chickens that were gutted and bleeding. Men were dancing around with blood forming ever-expanding circles on the ground. Shirtless, their bodies were shiny with sweat and streaked with blood. They writhed in a sinewy beat to the sounds of women who formed a ring and sang strange words over and over, words Jon Rue could not understand merged with the chant and began to pound in his head. One of the dancing figures dropped to his knees wrapped his arms around his body and began to sway. A low moan came from his mouth. It was almost a guttural sound but higher pitched. Jon Rue gasped! The man's eyes were completely white and he began to fall sideways. Another figure reached out and helped him gently to the ground. The figures converged on the prone form. Strange sounds came from the prostrate man. Jon Rue could not understand what he said. The women began a keening, then everyone drew back, and the women's voices got louder. The chanting sound seemed to float in the air. Jon Rue felt a dizzy, floating sensation. His eyelids felt heavy, and his head began to droop.

Suddenly his neck was seized in a fierce grip, and he could not move or even breathe. He tried to scream but the sounds would not come. Then something came down over his head, and everything became dark, and he knew no more.

Evening descended and there was still no sign of the missing boy. Zack and Patrick rode over to the sugarhouse, but no one there had seen Jon Rue. Trying to imagine where a small boy would go who was "running away from home," they stopped at the purgery and dismounted.

Patrick found the pile of rags and the pan that had overflowed. Molasses footprints looked the right size for Jon Rue but ended just before the door leading out of the purgery.

Zack and his father used lanterns to try and see footprints on the old road leading away from the plantation. They were finally able to make out scuff marks that lead to some bushes near the side of the old path.

"It looks like he stumbled onto a Santerian bloodletting,'" Patrick said. Senteria was a religion practiced by slaves from the Caribbean. No one knew much about its tenets, except that it was very secretive and that the offering of a blood sacrifice pleased the Orisha, or saints.

Zack looked closely at the ground. "The tracks end here. It looks like he just vanished."

"Everyone knows Jon Rue. They wouldn't hurt him," Patrick muttered under his breath, more to encourage himself than with any sense of reassurance.

"Son, outsiders are not allowed to observe their ceremonies. You know that. But we'll keep searching. He may have gotten frightened and run away before they noticed him. He could be lost, still wandering around out here," Zack said.

By this time all the hands had been called in to help with the search. Men moved out in a long line with lanterns. Some were on foot, some on horseback. A moaning noise swelled through the foggy night. "Jon Ruuu...Jon Ruuuu..." they called. The last syllable was drawn out and sounded like an ancient chant.

Patrick and Zack were on horseback, and led two of the groups.

Dawn was almost breaking when Boliver came riding up to the line that Zack led.

"He's home. Someone or something brought him home, Mistah Mac!" Boliver shouted. The men raised a loud hurrah, and everyone turned and ran and galloped back to the house.

Jon Rue had arrived at the kitchen door dazed and covered with dirt and molasses. He didn't know how he got home. He was taken to his mother who grabbed him up, sticky stuff and all. She sobbed into his hair and kissed him all over his face, calling him her precious baby. Martha took him away and cleaned him up. By the time Zack got home, Jon Rue was snuggled up in the bed with his mother sound asleep.

An ancient Cajun named Etienne folded a sack and put it away, smiling to himself. He walked out onto his front porch and looked at the sky turning pink and blue. Someday he would tell the little one about this adventure. And then...maybe not.

Chapter X

June 1853

Out of the cradle endlessly rocking,
Out of the mocking-bird's throat, the musical shuttle,
Out of the Ninth-month midnight,
Over the sterile sands and the fields beyond, where the child
leaving his bed wander'd alone, bareheaded, barefoot...
Walt Whitman

The rain had been falling for a week. Roads were mere ruts and the fledgling sugar cane was bowing and in some rows falling over into the mud like vanquished warriors. Patrick, Zack, and Boliver rode dispiritedly past a section of the field known as Midway Fort. The split drainage ditches that normally carried water to the "cross" ditches towards the back of the fields had overflowed early this morning after the main drainage canals backed up.

"If the rain doesn't slacken soon, we'll loose this whole stand," Patrick said. He eased his horse under a large oak that offered some protection from the relentless pouring rain.

The three men looked out over the rapidly deteriorating crop. A storm rider from New Orleans had stopped at River Rose late last night. The news was devastating. A hurricane was now pounding the Gulf and expected to hit New Orleans by nightfall. Though details of the storm were unknown to the McLoeds, this was a huge storm that spread out over 100 miles and was moving excruciatingly slowly. Normally the hurricane season didn't even begin until July, but this storm was a renegade in the true sense of the word. It was too early in the year and moved much slower than usual. It had moved through the Lesser Antilles and was heading for landfall near the mouth of the Mississippi by tonight. This could mean storm surges of 8 to 10 feet. By the time it reached River Rose, the flooding from the continual rains would be more than any of the elaborate ditches and canals could contain.

"Our only hope is that it turns before it gets to the Mississippi. We could salvage some of the crop if the rain lets up by tomorrow," Zack muttered bleakly.

Patrick turned his horse toward the house. "We aren't doing any good out here. Might as well go back and see how Lori's doing. I know you're anxious to get back, Zack."

Zack nodded. Lori was due to deliver at any time, and he was loath to leave the house for even a short period of time.

Early the next morning, a small figure crept into Zack & Lori's bedchamber. Since his experience in the purgery, Jon Rue would sometimes wake in the night in the throes of a nightmare. He would feel the strange sensation around his throat that he had experienced just before he lost consciousness. He would sit up with a start, and then coming fully awake, run to his parents' bed. But this time he hesitated before climbing the bed steps. There was now a smaller bed in the room, and Jansie, the wet nurse, was dozing in a rocker next to it. He tiptoed over and looked inside. Amazed, he stood transfixed. There was a tiny person lying among the coverlets. It was a quiet little being that looked steadily at him with dark eyes just like his mama's. Jon reached out and touched its head and smoothed the silken black curls. It curled its tiny mouth and smiled at him. Something inside him seemed to melt and flow through him. He reached out his finger to one of the tiny, flailing hands. It grasped his finger tightly and, looking up at him, smiled again.

Jansie roused up, looked at him, and grinned. "This yoh baby sistah, Mastah Jon Rue. Huh name is Emmageline. She was bon last night in dat bad stohm. Maybe she bring us some good luck." Jansie nodded toward the window. "Looks lak I see some little bit'o sun."

Jon Rue scarcely heard anything Jansie said. The baby mesmerized him. "I'll take care of you and make sure nothing hurts you…Emma gulene," he stumbled over the long name. "Can I call her Emma?" he asked to no one in particular.

"Yes, Jon, Emma will be fine," his mother said. She was now awake and looking down at him from her high bed.

Jon Rue scrambled up the bed stairs and into his mother's arms. Looking up he said, "Can we keep her? I promise I'll help look after her."

Lorraine looked into his earnest little boy face. "Of course we will keep her, and I will need your help. She is a brand new baby and cannot do anything for herself."

At this point the baby began to make little mewling noises, and her face started to get red.

"I think she is missing you already, Jon," his mother said with a smile.

For the rest of their lives there would always be a special bond between Jon Rue and Emma. True to his word, Jon Rue was always protective toward his sister. As they got older, though Emma was motherly toward both Jacob and Jon Rue, she always felt a special need to watch over Jon Rue. He was never as practical as his older brother and seemed to possess an edge of recklessness that worried Emma.

Jansie had been right in saying the new baby brought good luck. The hurricane had turned just before it hit New Orleans and swept up the Gulf Coast, not striking land until it hit the Florida panhandle. The sun almost immediately brought back all of the bowed cane. Within three days the land had dried out enough that even some of the stalks that looked broken were struggling upright. A collective sigh of relief went up all along the lower valley as most of the crops were saved.

Chapter XI

Summer 1853

Child of the pure, unclouded brow
And dreaming eyes of wonder!
Though time be fleet and I and thou
Are half a life asunder,
They loving smile will surely hail
the love-gift of a fairy tale.
Through the Looking-Glass
(1872) introduction, st.1
Lewis Carroll
(Charles Lutwidge Dodgson)

The small child turned his hand this way and that, letting the sunlight settle first on the back of his brown hand and then on his pink palm. He looked curiously at the other small boy playing nearby. Puzzled, he walked over and put his hand next to his playmate's light colored hand.

His parents watched from the window of their little house in the slave quarters at River Rose.

"He is becoming aware of himself," said his father.

The child's mother looked sadly out at her bright, beautiful brown son. "He sees he a different culah," said his mother. "Foh long he'll come to know what dat mean."

As they watched the two boys laughing and playing, the brown boy's father remembered exactly the day he realized he was not only a different color but that he was a "slave."

Theseus lived in the big house on a large cotton plantation with his mahme and little sister, Hermie. The same governess that instructed the mastah's children taught him. The governess was kind and treated Thesues and his little sister, the same as the plantation owner's children.

At days end, however, everything changed. Thesues and his sister went out to the small, shabby slave quarter house they shared with their mama.

69

For supper they had whatever food she had grown in her small garden and leftovers from the big house kitchen. Usually it was plentiful, and his mama was a good cook. Once when he was very small he had followed her into the big dining room to help her serve when another slave was sick. He saw what the big house children ate. Cakes and pies and candy were on the sideboard and the children were allowed as much as they wanted after they finished their main meal. Thesues' mouth watered when he thought of all the sweets. In the kitchen when cook spilled sugar and flour on the table while she was baking, the slaves were allowed to scoop it up for their own use. Sometimes his mama could save enough for a cake, and he loved her sugar icing. He asked his mama why they couldn't have cake every day like the children of the big house. His mama sat him down and explained that he was a slave, bought and paid for by the mastah. Mama said he would always eat leftovers and wear worn out clothes that others had worn before. He would get his first pair of shoes when he was old enough to work in the fields. She would try to keep him working in the house as long as she could, but someday the field would be where he would work from sunup to sundown. His mama cried for awhile and then drew him close. She said the only thing he owned was the thoughts in his head, and he had to learn as much as he could from the governess. He could see the words she spoke hurt her. He never asked questions about being a slave again. The only other time he had seen her cry was when he asked where his da lived. The other slave children lived with their mama and da, sometimes two families to a house. His mama said his da lived in a place he could never go, and tears ran down her face. He never asked about his da again. But he wondered why they had a house to themselves when there were only the three of them. When he was very young he thought that being a slave made his skin dark. But later he realized he was a slave because his skin was dark. Once he tried to cut off the brown skin from his arm, but it hurt and his mama cried again and said there was no way to get rid of the dark skin. Someday he would have the same discussions with Benny.

One day Benny's mama made a cake and told him it was his birthday cake. Benny and Da and Mama celebrated in the little house and he received a present. Benny's da had carved a little carriage pulled by a prancing horse. Benny could not contain his joy and wanted to immediately show it to Jake. His da looked at him and said, "Benny, we are not allowed to celebrate birthdays. This is just for our family."

"But Jake had a party for his birthday and a cake and presents and everything," Benny protested.

"That's just the way it is for us, Benny. Mastah Zack is a good mastah but he is still our mastah. You are getting an education and maybe someday," Thesues paused, "maybe someday things will be different."

"Why do we live in a little old rundown house and Jake and the others live in a big house? Why are we left out? Is it because we are dark?"

"It's because we is slaves," his mother explained. "Bought and owned by Mastah Zack." Martha finished with a sigh.

"Will I always be a slave?" Benny asked.

"I don't know, son," his father said.

Jake finished up treacle custard and sighed happily as he wiped his mouth with a fine linen napkin.

"Can Benny come with us to New Orleans?" Jake asked his mother and father as they finished supper.

Zack sat back in his chair and looked at his oldest son. He realized it was time to explain about Benny's situation.

"Benny's a slave, Jake. He can only travel with us as a valet and he's not old enough to be in that position."

"But why? We play together all the time and go to school together," Jake persisted.

"There are laws that we have to go by or Sheriff Dickerson will come put me in jail. One of those laws concerns where and how slaves travel. Because I own Benny, I have to make sure I abide by those laws."

"It doesn't seem right that you can own a person," Jake muttered.

"Someday it may be different, son," Zack said.

"Everything is always someday. I want someday to be today," Jake said.

Chapter XII

Spring 1858

"He who knows what sweets and virtues are in the ground, the waters, the plants, the heavens, and how to come at these enchantments, is the rich and royal man."

Ralph Waldo Emerson

The two boys crept through the woods toward the bayou as quietly as they could. This meant they sounded, as one of their papas was wont to say, like 'stampeding horses.' The older of the two was Zack's son, a stocky 11-year-old with sandy hair and ruddy complexion, named Jacob, but called Jake. Jake's very best friend in the whole world was Thesues' son, Benjamin, always called Benny. He was only 10 "going on 11" but was almost as tall as Jake. Stopping to listen and survey their surroundings, they heard a whistle, and both boys grinned. Sure enough Ettienne was out and about as they had hoped.

Ettienne Berzac was an Acadian of indeterminate age. Jake guessed he was 120 but Benny was sure he was older. The old man was so wrinkled his eyes seemed closed except when he laughed or told scary stories to the wide-eyed boys. His hair stood at attention in wisps all over his head. Though short in stature, to Jake and Benny he seemed large. After listening to their stories about him, Jake's mother decided he must have what she called 'presence.'

"It's my turn to answer," Benny whispered loudly.

"Okay, but it sure seems like it's always your turn," grumbled Jake.

Benny carefully spread his first two fingers between his teeth and softly answered Etienne in the one, two notes he had been taught.

Silence. A deep silence. Even the insects, birds, and small animals were quiet. The boys were not sure why this special whistle caused the strange silence. But it always did. They had been cautioned never to teach the secret whistle to anyone else. They had promised they never would. Etienne was very shy and would not answer or show himself to just anyone. It had taken a long time for the old man to come to trust the two young boys, and they would never betray him.

As they waited, the warm, moist air of the bayou caused sweat beads to form, even in their light shirts. Benny looked up at a sound overhead but it was only one of the many egrets teeming in a large cypress. They stood quietly by the old cypress tree where they usually met their friend. It had been burned by lightening many times, had several knees, and was easy to find.

Jake reached out and touched Benny lightly on the arm. An old oak tree to their left completely wrapped in gray moss that swayed in the slight breeze had now sprouted what looked like an arm. Sure enough, the Acadian cautiously began to show himself. Etienne always wore a gray sweat rag around his scraggly black hair. His shirt was homespun and a color that blended perfectly with the trees and foliage. A Choctaw friend of his, whose wife was expert at weaving, furnished him with his shirts and long trousers that came down over his leather 'booties.' The Indian called Light Moon traded with Etienne for furs that he expertly trapped in large numbers. Though Light Moon was adept at trapping himself, Etienne always managed to catch the most desirable pelts, such as nutria and muskrat, in his particular part of the woods. The traders in Baton Rouge especially prized them for their more wealthy clients. They were fashioned into lush capes, bonnets, and carriage blankets.

The "booties" were especially fascinating to the boys. They knew better than to go outside without high boots during this time of year, much less stomp around in the snake-infested swamp. Snakes were waking up and hiding under and hanging from almost anything. Benny's father had been heard to declare the two boys could scare off all the snakes in a whole parish, as noisy as they were. Nevertheless, boots were a necessity. But Etienne's footwear seemed surprisingly flimsy. That is until one day he took one of the booties off and let the boys inspect the inside. They were amazed. The bootie looked like regular leather until you touched it. It was incredibly soft and pliant. The old man handed them his knife.

"Try and cut it, *mon ami*," he said in his soft voice.

"But it will ruin it. It'll cut it like butter," protested Jake.

"Go on. You cannot hurt it, no," Etienne insisted.

Jake set the point of his knife and expected it to go straight through the boot. He tried harder.

"Here let me try. You're not pushing hard enough," said Benny.

Jake handed the boot to his friend and shook his head. *Benny was sometimes a pain,* he thought.

However, he had no better luck than Jake did, even though he jabbed with all his 10- "going on 11-" year-old strength.

The most curious thing about the booties was the lining of straw. Etienne explained that even when they became full of water almost at once they became warm and comfortable. "Thees is because thees hay is full of the holes of air and that is warming to the feet."

The boys watched in wonder as their friend pulled his bootie as he called it, back on his foot.

Soft boots that were strong as the toughest leather were only one of the mysteries surrounding the small, wizened man. True to his Acadian heritage, he had learned to derive his sustenance of and from the land, and kept his own council. He appreciated his friendship with young Jake and Benny but never let it cause him to drop his guard. As a people, his ancestors had become outcasts in Canada. Forced to flee in boats, they settled on the lush Louisiana coast and eventually found their way up as far as the bayou country surrounding River Rose. Etienne knew all Americans except Indians were from other lands. But immigrants had *chosen* to come here. The slaves of course were a different matter. Theirs had been a cruel, forced entry into the country. He often wondered if they longed for their lost homeland. He never did. His homeland was here and now. There were even times when he forgot about ever having a Canadian history. Louisiana suited the Acadian temperament. Sometimes when he was feeling especially full of *jhwa da veev* or the "joy of living," he even allowed himself to think that his people's exile was part of a master plan. Perhaps after all the Acadians were a favored people and had been led to Louisiana. He thought the swamp was like a cradle, teeming with animals for food and warm fur for trading; the bayous and small streams filled with catfish and bream were magical as they wound through the woods acting as a flood barrier when it rained too much. Over thousands of years the overflow had produced a rich alluvial soil that would grow anything.

Jake and Benny had learned early in their friendship never to question Etienne. He would look at them in his quizzical way and just smile.

"Today we weel set a trap for the muskrat. Dey still in full fur but not for vury long. Be sure and follow me and…be quiet," he admonished the boys. "Put your feet just so."

Each boy tried to move just as Etienne and place his feet noiselessly, but invariably they made a small sound in the mushy ground.

"If we had booties like yours we could be quiet too," Benny complained.

"My booties are not what make me quiet," Etienne replied. "I have quieted my mind and you must learn to do the same."

"How do you make your mind quiet," wondered Jake out loud. "Whenever I want my mind to be quiet it just goes on thinking, louder and louder."

If they had not been following Etienne and concentrating on where they placed their feet, they would have seen him smile.

"Listen to the bayou. Listen. Clear your mind and you can become quiet." Etienne stopped. "Close your eyes and let the stillness speak to you."

Both boys stood perfectly still with their eyes tightly shut. Jake had to rub his nose and got momentarily distracted.

"Can you hear her talking to you?" asked their friend.

Benny opened one of his unusual gray eyes.

"You cannot quiet your mind with one of your doors open." He touched Benny's head lightly. "You must practice, and it will come to you."

They had reached the place Etienne wanted to set his trap. He showed them how to set it. It was different than any trap they had ever seen. He explained this was so the muskrat would be killed at once and not suffer.

Benny had a soft heart, and it hurt him to think of killing anything.

"Don't you feel bad killing that poor little muskrat?" he asked, his voice quavering.

Jake looked at him in disgust. That was the only thing wrong with having a friend that was still a baby.

For a moment the little man was silent. Then he looked at Benny and said gently, "It is good to feel dat way for all living tings. But my Indian friends need da warm Muskrat fur. When I trade with dem, I get dese booties only de know how to make. I think dat is da way it supposed to be. Like cutting a tree for a house, or killing da pig for da meat. It da natural way."

Etienne finished the trap and covered it lightly with swampy grass and leaves.

"Are you hongry?" he asked. "I have something vury special for our dinner today."

He motioned for the boys to follow him through some hanging vines to a clearing near a stream.

"I was up early thees morning and caught me some fish. Dey are cooling in da stream." Reaching the water he held up the stringer with pride. Three copper-nosed bream dangled enticingly.

"We weel cook our dinner right here." He began to scale the fish with his knife that hooked just for that purpose. "Find some stones, and we will dry out some groun foh cooking."

The boys gathered stones quickly, as they were beginning to feel dinner time pangs. Suddenly they both stopped where they stood as if frozen.

"Etienne," Jake's voice started out strong and then became wobbly.

"What is eet?" The old man noticed the change in tone. Laying his fish aside, he walked over to where the boys stood paralyzed. He looked down. His sharp intake of breath was not lost on the boys. Three people saw the small pile of bones and the skeleton head of a small child. Fish, dinner, everything flew out of their minds.

"You must go git da people who weel know about dees tings. I weel stay here. Jake, go find your papa. Benny, go with him. I weel wait for you."

"Do you know whose bones they are?" Benny asked softly.

"Yes," said their friend. "Jake, tell your papa we have found *la petite* Rosemarie."

Chapter XIII

Winter Wind Plantation
Five years earlier…

Chubby hands reached up for Adine. Her headache had started in the early morning. Julien's sister had listened to him go on and on about how he had been over charged for his last six slaves, and what a crook his current factor had turned out to be. The pain was now a throbbing mass and as was sometimes the case with her headaches seemed to take on a life of its own. She looked wearily at her small daughter.

Rosemary dropped her arms. Even at four years old she knew the look. Mama had her "head hurt" again. There would be no playing with mama now. Everyone else had gone for the afternoon. Mama and *Oncle* were the only ones left around the tea table that had been set up on the front lawn.

Descant had observed his sister's distress and said in a surprisingly solicitous tone, "Why don't you go upstairs and lie down. We have an excellent new girl, Oleane. She has a soothing way about her. She can rub your head and put a cloth on your eyes. You will feel better by supper."

Adine felt great relief, and tears of gratitude sprang to her eyes. Normally Julien was disdainful of ladies' "aches and pains," as he called them, and very unsympathetic.

"But what about Rosemary? You know you find small children a terrible trial." This last was said out of the little girl's hearing.

"It's time I took more of an interest in my only niece," Julien said. He had taken note of the fact that Rosemary was an adorable little girl. She had only been a babe in arms the last time his sister had visited from Memphis. Rosemary had dark curls and even at four, dancing black eyes that captivated all who saw her. Now he thought the time had come that they should become better acquainted. But he would have to careful. Sometimes Julien was visited by his *demone* as he thought of her. She caused feelings that seem to come unbidden. As long as it concerned one of his slave girls, it did not matter. Deep in his soul he sometimes thought what if…but no, he could control the *demone*. He had her well under control.

"Come, *ma cher.*" Julien took Rosemary by the hand. "We will go for a ride in the carriage with the white horse that you like so well."

Adine watched as the two walked toward the carriage house. Maybe Julien had changed. She had dreaded this trip. Her husband, a doctor in Memphis, was going to New Orleans for a medical meeting. He had suggested she stop off and stay with her brother, as he was sure it would be difficult to be in a hotel for a week with a small child. Though Julien still seemed full of complaints, this kindness toward her was unusual. She sighed and slowly made her way to the house. It would be wonderful to lie down in the beautiful room that used to be hers and be ministered to by one of Julien's many slaves.

Rosemary was brimming with excitement! A carriage ride with *Oncle* Julien and the beautiful white horse! She still felt shy around her uncle, as this was the first time she had been to his house that she could remember. She had been told that she had been born in the bedroom that she and Mama shared the last few nights. Try as she might, Rosemary could not remember this.

Descant lifted his small niece into the open carriage. Climbing in, he gave a flick of his whip, and the white horse lunged forward.

Out of earshot, his groomsman swore under his breath. *I told him never to use the whip on the carriage horses,* he thought resentfully. *Just the reins. They know how to trot. He just likes to beat these horses and show them he is boss.* The groomsman detested his master, as did most of the slaves on the place. But the master was boss, and, if he wanted to avoid a brutal beating, he kept his thoughts to himself.

Descant had managed to settle the horse down after the first bolt, and was just holding the reins loosely and giving the horse his head. He saw a little-used path leading off into the more densely forested area.

The little girl's cheeks were rosy not only with the warmth of the day but the excitement of adventure.

Descant felt a sharp pang of alarm. He had begun to sweat. He unbuttoned his collar and loosened his jacket. A hazy feeling enveloped him and his breath came in gasps. He turned the carriage onto the woodsy path. Relief, he had to get some relief. And there was only one way.

Adine lazily pulled back the netting that covered all the beds during the summer. Julien was right. Oleane was truly expert with her soothing touch and special herb-soaked cloth. Her headache was gone and she was truly hungry for supper! It was already growing dark. Julien must have really been patient to entertain her little girl this long.

Suddenly she heard someone running up the stairs, and her brother burst into the room.

"She ran away, and I can't find her! We must get word to everyone to search before dark!" her brother fairly screamed. Adine stared at him, unable to comprehend what he was saying. She had never seen him so distraught and disheveled.

"Where is my baby?" she screamed, suddenly coming to herself. "What do you mean? Have you lost my baby?"

Sheriff Tony Dickerson, his two deputies, and ten men from neighboring farms and plantations, along with twenty slaves, scoured the countryside using torches until well after midnight.

After a rattlesnake in the treacherous swamp bit one of the men, the sheriff called off the search until daylight. One of slaves was able to tie a rag around the man's leg and draw out the venom, so the man would live. But he would nurse a swollen, sore leg for some weeks.

The men gathered in the large dining room of Winter Wind for drinks and cold soup. Several began to nod off in their chairs. The sheriff finally sent everyone home, asking them to return at first light.

As the last weary man stumbled out of the room, the sheriff looked at Dickerson and suggested they needed to have some time to talk through their plans for resuming the search. What the sheriff really wanted, was privately to hear Descant's version of the "disappearance" of his little niece.

The sheriff had been watching the plantation owner ever since he arrived in late afternoon in answer to a desperate summons by Kirby the overseer. As he expected, Descant gave every appearance of a distraught uncle. But there was something not quite right. A jarring note. Something fluttered around the edges of Dickerson's consciousness. He told himself he was being judgmental because he personally detested the man. Yet, his years in dealing with all kinds of people told him it was more that that.

The two men settled themselves in Descant's office at the back of the main house.

"Tell me again what happened. When did you first notice your niece was gone?" Dickerson spoke in his deceptively soft drawl.

Descant tossed back a shot of whiskey and rubbed his hands over his eyes and face. The years had not been kind to him. Dissipation was the word that came to mind when one looked at the man. His eyes were blood-shot, and large pockets of fatty tissue under his eyes bagged and now almost met the beginnings of his jowls. His black hair hung in several strings around his ears. A potbelly that he no longer attempted to hide marred his waistline.

"It is like I have already told you! One minute she is there and the next she is gone. Poof!" He made a gesture like a magician. "My sister is going mad upstairs. She blames me for everything and has sent for the child's father! She says he will kill me!"

"Give me a description again of what she was wearing. Any jewelry? What kind of shoes?" Dickerson continued.

"What difference does it make? She is the only four-year-old running loose in this whole parish. I am sure there are no others that age wandering in the woods and swamps." Descant was sputtering now with rage and something else. Fear! What was he afraid of? The sheriff was sure it was not that he was afraid the little girl's father would actually kill him. Unless…there was more to it than carelessness.

"You were tying your carriage horse to a branch, only looked away for a moment and…." The lawman reiterated what Descant had told him when he arrived.

"And when I turned around she was gone. I called and called, and searched all over until I realized I needed help." Descant ended his recitation and slumped down in the large leather swivel chair behind his desk. He fingered a letter opener, set it down, and picked it up again.

Dickerson watched the letter opener now moving slowly across the smooth, polished surface of the desk. A large scratch appeared in its wake. Suddenly realizing what he was doing, Julien dropped the knife and clasped both hands in front of him on the desk.

"Is there some place in or around the house where she might be hiding and have fallen asleep? Some special place where she likes to play?" Tony Dickerson watched as pallor came over the other man's face.

"No, no! She has only been here for three days and stays close by her mother. She would not even know any places to go," this last was barely audible.

"Still, I would like to have a few men search the house and outbuildings," he paused, "with your permission of course."

"Of course, we must search everywhere," Descante agreed.

"We will begin again first thing in the morning." The sheriff rose slowly and started toward the door.

"Oh, Sheriff. Tell the men we will have breakfast for them here when they arrive."

"Thanks, Mr. Descant. I will."

After the sheriff left, Descant slipped out the side door of his office and walked to the stables. The carriage was still parked where he had left it. He had instructed his groomsman to just look after the horse and leave the wagon so he could get an early start in the morning. The wagon had a hidden storage area in the undercarriage where Descant carried valuables when he was traveling. He kept it locked. No one even knew about the lockbox, as he did not trust anyone. They might tell someone who might decide to rob him on a lonely country road.

Now the moon was hardly visible, and late night sounds were masters of the dark landscape. Only an owl saw a figure take a small bundle from under the wagon and move toward one of the outbuildings that had already been searched. A hush settled over the grounds, that short time between night and the first faint stirrings of the day. The time when life hangs suspended, waiting for a breath to whisper secrets not able to be told in the light.

The search went on for three more days. The men, who soon became exhausted in the heat and dangerous terrain, were replaced by others at the end of each day. One of the horses fell, broke his leg in the marshy outcropping of a ravine, and rolled over the deputy riding him. Though the man's ribs were bruised he would recover. The horse had to be shot. Finally the sheriff called off the search. He sent information by telegraph to Baton Rouge and New Orleans describing the little girl. Descant suggested she must have been kidnapped and might be sold into white slavery. Dickerson did not believe this was even a remote possibility, but this would allow him to call off what he had begun to regard as a futile search.

Adine's husband, Dr. Dumaine Rabouin, had arrived. He spent most of his time caring for his distraught wife and the rest arguing with his brother-in-law. Like Dickerson, he could not see how a small girl could have simply vanished in so short a time. By the end of the week, all concerned were spent, physically and emotionally. Dr. Rabouin asked for a conference with Sheriff Dickerson.

The sheriff promised to stay in touch with the Rabouins and to continue to follow up on anything he could find. He agreed with the Doctor that it would be best for Adine to return to Memphis with her husband for rest.

The case haunted the lawman for months, and even after several years, whenever he saw Descant or heard the name "Winter Wind," he felt a great sadness. In his heart he knew little Rosemary was dead. He was sure he knew who killed her. Since no trace had ever been found there was nothing he could do. But sometimes the swamp is not good at keeping secrets.

Present day...

Both boys ran as fast as they could, ignoring underbrush and low hanging vines. They splashed through boggy water and were soon covered with mud. Scratches went unnoticed in their headlong flight. It was almost as if the tiny corpse was at their heels shouting, "Tell someone I am here!"

Finally, reaching the clearing that faced the back of the truck gardens behind the slave quarters; they collapsed on the cool grass gasping for air. Benny glimpsed his mother picking peas and yelled with all his might. He was so out of breath, only an ineffectual little squeak came out. At that moment she looked up and saw both boys floundering on the ground and ran toward them in alarm.

"Whachu boys got into now?" she demanded drawing close enough to see their panic and state of disarray. They looked up at Martha, faces scratched, clothes torn, eyes wide with excitement.

"We found bones of a little child. Etienne says it's somebody named Rosemarie," gasped Jake, who was finally able to make his mouth work in between breaths.

"Lawd," Martha put her hand over her mouth. "You boys come with me," she said, helping them to their feet.

The group of men, including Sheriff Dickerson, two of his deputies, Zack, Theseus, and the two boys, moved quickly through the swamp. They found it easy to follow the trail left by the frantic boys.

"It looks like two elephants scrambled through here," Zack observed

"We never saw any bones of a person before," Jacob said. "It was scary."

Sheriff Dickerson said, "It's scary to me anytime I find human bones, and I have unfortunately seen things like that many times. But you did the right thing getting to me as quickly as you did."

Jacob felt better. "We're almost there. It wasn't too far from the stream."

Etienne came into view, still standing guard over the little pile of bones.

The men and boys stood and looked sadly at the pitifully small remainder of a life that had ended so young. Sheriff Dickerson and his deputies, though accustomed to such sights, were stricken at the sight of the tiny remains. Zack and Theseus could hardly bear to look at the now flooded gravesite. Zack could not help but think of Emma at the age of four, and sudden moisture caused him to rub his eyes. The two boys were once more overcome with fear and stood slightly behind their parents.

"Are the remains exactly the way you found them?" Dickerson asked Etienne.

"Yes. I have touched nothing," he assured him.

"Well, let's get to work, men," the sheriff said.

The lawmen began carefully digging around the site and laid each section of bones with sod attached on a large piece of waxed canvas. Soon every remnant was encased and firmly tied. The two deputies hoisted their small burden and began the trek back to the wagon for the trip to Alexandria where everything would be examined.

Though Tony Dickerson had been saddened by finding the small child, he was hopeful that now he would be able to prove what he had always known. Descant had killed his niece. He was sure of it! But with no body, he had been unable to charge him. First he would have to have a positive identification.

While Doctor Bercoise examined the body, Dickerson went through his file containing the interviews with the mother and Descant. There was no fabric remaining on the body, but part of one shoe with an unusual buckle and a gold necklace, had been discovered in the dirt surrounding the body. Looking carefully through his meticulous notes he found what he was looking for. He had carefully saved two drawings: one depicting a silver buckle, and one of a gold necklace, with a locket. Dickerson placed the two pieces found at the gravesite next to the drawings. They matched perfectly!

Next he sent word to Dr. Dumaine Rabouin that his daughter had been found and that he could claim her remains whenever he wished.

He then wrote a letter to circuit Judge John Noble, informing him that he would need to schedule a trial date for a defendant to be charged with murder.

Now he goes along the dark road,
thither whence they say no one returns.
CARMINA III I.

Winter Wind—the next day...

The middle aged slave carefully poured the swamp water from an old jar over a certain place on the carpet and dragged a portion of the coverlet on the bed through the dank liquid. It stained the bed covering a dark brown and had the musty, rank smell of the bayou from which it came. Solena smiling faintly, slipped the jar back into the large pocket of her skirt, and glided from the room without detection. She knew Mastah Descant was in a drunken slumber from which he would not awaken until midday. She only wished she could see and hear his reaction when he saw the "gris-gris" was creeping up into his bed. Having escaped the house, she now allowed herself a cackle of glee. Another slave passed by and shivered as she gave her a wide birth. Solena was known to possess "devil powers" and when she had the look on her as she had now, it usually meant she had put a curse on some unlucky soul. Everyone on the place had seen the look on her for months now. Something bad would soon happen.

As Solena had predicted, it was almost noon before Descant managed to drag himself out of bed. He missed the top step of his bed stairs and fell heavily to the floor cursing. He lay there, not wanting to be awake and yet not wanting to go back to sleep. The nightmare had come again. This time it was more vivid and louder than ever! He thought he could still hear the screams. Putting his hands over his ears did no good. The nightmares first came after the "incident" with his little niece several years ago. Then, for a while he was able to put it out of his mind. He was a strong-minded man, after all. Not like his ninny of a sister who had killed herself last year. And left a letter blaming *him*! Remembering how angry he was, he sat up, gripped the side post of the bed, and got to his feet. As he rose, he realized his feet felt wet. Not again! For the last few weeks every morning he found a larger and larger wet spot on his bedroom rug. Shouting and yelling at his roofer about a leak did no good. He glanced at the ceiling. As the workman had pointed out, there was no stain on the pure white ceiling cloth that soared above. Suddenly the coverlet caught his eye. It was wet and stained brown! The carpet spot had grown bigger each day and was now crawling into his bed!

"Henry! Come in here right now!" he yelled to his personal slave, who sat outside his door waiting for his call each day and who had been dozing peacefully.

"Yassuh, Mastah, what you need?" Henry stumbled through the door.

"You can tell me how this water keeps getting on this rug, and how it's now on my bed!" Descant's voice was hoarse with sleep and remnants of last night's liquor.

The slave looked fearfully at the rug, and his eyes widened as he saw the trail up on the bed.

"Well, don't just stand there. How did it get there?" Descant was yelling again.

"Suh, it sho looks like…" he hesitated. The mastah hated it when his slaves mentioned anything of an unnatural occurrence.

"What does it look like? Tell me at once, or you'll have a beating you won't forget!"

"Suh, it look like duh 'gris-gris'!" Henry said in a shaky voice. Shaky not just because of the threat of the beating, but also because it was unlucky to say "gris-gris" out loud. People had been known to assume the curse themselves by voicing it.

Descant was taken aback. Anyone who lived in Louisiana knew what that meant.

"Who does 'gris-gris' around here Henry?" He grabbed the trembling man by the neck. "Tell me or by God I'll whip you myself until you're dead!"

Solena heard the mastah coming before she saw him through her window. She slipped out of the back of her cabin and melted into the tall corn in her back garden. In a moment she was in the woods. He would never find her in here.

A small black child made his way into the woods and called to Solena.

"Mastah say he going to beat a niggah a day till he kill us all, ifn you don come to him." He finished his message, turned, and went back to his mother standing at the edge of the woods.

Solena did her incantations, and put herself in the trance that would allow her to minimize the agony she knew was coming. She walked slowly to the big house. All the slaves stood in a row and watched her go in. Calmly Solena entered the mastah's office. She looked at the now drunk, dirty, unshaven man before her. He smelled terrible.

"So, you think you can put your nigger curses on me, do you?" He grabbed her arm and pulled her right up to his face.

Her eyes were blank. She was somewhere else.

"Take it off! Take the curse off, do you hear me, or I'll kill you!" Descant was screaming now.

Solena looked at him with her blank eyes. She smiled a slow dreamy smile. She was in the bayou now fishing for bass. Sunlight dappled the little stream, and the cicadas were calling. Moss was swaying in the trees. The smell of the first spring violets was in the air. Bending over she put her face in the purple flowers growing on the riverbank by her arm. Everything was so peaceful. She didn't feel the vicious blows to her head or the mastah's cruel fingers tightening around her throat. Solena would not know how her eyes bulged, and she gasped involuntarily at the end, her body desperately seeking air. She shivered once and dropped gracefully to the floor.

The man stood looking down at her and for a moment saw once again the beautiful young girl she had been. She had fought him at first, but soon came to understand life was much less painful if you were the mastah's favorite. For five years she had been his favorite, until another, younger slave had taken her place. During this time, Solena learned about trances. Other places occupied her mind during the time she spent in the mastah's bedroom. Becoming expert at detaching herself from the horrors of her real world had led her to other abilities, and ultimately saved her the anguish of suffering the final terror.

Descant shook his head. *How had he come to kill her? It was another unfortunate incident. She would not lift the curse! What could he do?* He thought frantically! Suddenly he noticed the room had darkened. The rain was pounding on the windows. It had rained off and on for days now. The streams were overflowing everywhere. A shot of fear went through him! What if the grave gave up it grisly contents? He sank down on the settee and leaned back.

A pounding headache was starting again. Another drink might help. He drank straight from the bottle in gulps and felt the soothing warmth of the fiery liquid flow through him. He fell back over the chaise lounge and sank into a stupor. A grave overflowing with water and tiny bones swirled in a whirlpool and came closer and closer. It seemed like tiny arms and hands were reaching for him, and he heard screams that got louder and louder! And the pounding...someone was hammering on his door and calling him. He jerked awake and looked at Solena still slumped on the floor. The pounding continued. A rifle lay in a satiny teakwood case by his desk. He took it out and caressed it lovingly. A beautiful weapon. The rain had stopped, and the room was almost dark. Some light filtered through the shutters that were partially open to let in the last bit of breeze. This was his favorite time of day, and this was his favorite room. The bookshelves were filled with books that he had never read, but it comforted him to know that others did not know that. His office had the personality of the man he wished he were. People were invariably impressed with his office. Slaves kept everything polished and shining. What had happened to the man that he had planned to be years ago?

Wealthy and thought of as handsome by some, he had married a beautiful young Creole from a good New Orleans family. His wife died trying to have their first child, and then he had met Lorraine. Now he heard more pounding outside his door…years ago he would have paid his weight in gold to marry Lorraine. But even she would not have been able to satisfy his desires, whereas the young slave girls…he paused. If only he had not made the mistake with his niece so long ago.

The shouting seemed to continue, and one of the voices sounded like that idiot Dickerson. It wouldn't surprise him if Solena had led him to the grave. But how would she know where it was? Solena knew things. He was tired of it all. He could not bear to hear the screams anymore…he lifted the rifle to his mouth and fired.

Chapter XIV

Summer 1858

*O the joy of the strong-brawn'd fighter, towering in the arena in
perfect condition, conscious of power, thirsting to meet his opponent.*
**A Song of Joys, Leaves of Grass,
Walt Whitman**

The huge, dark skinned man looked up through the coils of moss and low hanging vines. What he could see of the sky told him it was a good day for hunting. He carefully laid the rock in the knob hole of one of the rotted knees in an old cypress at the back of the slaves' garden patches. He knew it would not be long before it would be gone, and the boys would be ready to meet him at the *batture* on the inward side of the river bend. Jon Rue would be especially eager, as he had missed out on the big adventure with his brother and the slave boy in the spring.

The big man smeared bear grease, diluted with the herb spikenard, over the exposed parts of his body to keep the mosquitoes away. The herb helped to mask the unpleasant smell of the potion. Crouching low by the riverbank, he began to sharpen his hatchet. Baptiste thought about the young Jon Rue, the one he called *Fiñe*. *Fiñe* was the best he had ever seen at navigating the *prairie tremblante*. Even better than Etienne. It was not just that he was slight of build; the boy was one with the swampy, quivering portion of the land where Baptiste did not dare walk. Not because of his enormous bulk but because he was *not* one with the peculiar, always wet mud that made up most of the land. Baptiste would have sunk up to his ankles and maybe fallen into one of the fearsome "sandy suck" holes that lurked beneath the mossy substructure. *Fiñe* could skim over mush without leaving a sign and not sink. Some said it was 'Creole' power inherited from his mother. Suddenly he listened.

" Baptiste, are you there?" Jake whispered unnecessarily. He was so used to the quietness of Etienne he could never quite get used to Batiste's rough and tumble approach to hunting.

"You don't have to whisper to Baptiste." Jon Rue admonished his brother.

As Baptiste immerged from the underbrush, both boys were struck with admiration at the sheer bulk of the man.

"Are we going to finally get to see you hunt?" Jon Rue demanded impatiently.

"*Fiñe*. It good to see you an' youh brother." The giant man shook hands solemnly with Jon Rue and Jacob McLoed. Both boys stood a little taller. They were really men now, going hunting for the swamps' most ferocious killer.

Their mother had been hard to convince that it would be safe for the two boys to accompany Baptiste on this hunt. Zack interceded pointing out that Baptiste was so big and experienced in the ways of the land that they were probably safer with him than racing horses up and down soggy terrain, their favorite pastime. What really made her decide was Jon Rue's bitter disappointment in having been at his *grampapá's* when Jake and Benny discovered the grave in the spring.

Finally, she grudgingly gave her permission.

"Today, we follow tracks to da nest and den I call." Baptiste put his hatchet back in a bag that hung from the vast expanse that was his waist. He picked up a long pole and a coil of rope that had been leaning against a gnarled water oak.

"Be veery carful with dat musket Jacob. I can see yoh not use to eet," he said. "It is loaded? A gun is no use if it is not loaded."

"Papa showed me exactly how to load it," Jake assured the man. He thought he would never forget the vision of his father pouring powder into the barrel of his very own musket; then showing him how the oil-soaked wadding should be tamped down with the ramrod; loading the shot and the most exciting but scary part of all, placing a percussion cap on the nipple and then, oh, so slowly lowering the hammer.

Jacob now carefully shouldered his new possession making sure the musket was pointed back over his shoulder. Hard hanging vines and branches that reached all the way to the ground made up the swamp and could easily coil themselves around the hammer like a person's finger. His gun could be shot accidentally by the foliage itself and injure or maim someone.

Jacob and Jon Rue followed Baptiste along the more solid land that ran alongside the slippery, peaty soil.

"Where are the tracks, *mon sour*?" Jon Rue asked anxiously. He did not want anything to go wrong on this day. Missing out on his brother's great adventure had made him determined this would be the one they remembered instead. Jacob's younger brother was slight and gave no hint of the height he would attain, surpassing Jacob finally, but always having a lighter build. Jon Rue could feel the atmosphere in the woods taking over his body and mind. The light-headed feeling he had come to expect somehow was associated with his ability to move *over* the marshes rather than *on* the ground.

"See dis paw prints, with a leetl' bit of space beteen? Dat whe' she puts her feets." Baptiste smiled in satisfaction. "It gots a leetl' watah stil', so has not been so long ago."

Suddenly a loud roar pierced the quiet. Both boys jumped nervously. Jake held on to his musket as though it was a rope thrown to a drowning man.

Baptiste put his head back and roared with laughter. He sounded a little like the loud beasts' thunder himself.

"Is only big papa tak'n the sun on a log and enjoy hisself." Baptiste continued down the trail of more solid ground. Then he pointed to a cone shaped mound of mashed green and brown leaves, and cattail stems. It sat near the edge of a stream that was almost dried up, with a small amount of muddy water near the base.

"Deh it is, de nest. She gwon' to be close by, I garon'tee you." As he said this, he blew through his lips.

Probingly, he began to push the pole, hook end foremost, into the puddle at the bottom of the nest. Moving this way and that, the pole followed the tunnel that led from it. The sound of the iron hook grating along the horny-ridged hide of the beast caused Jon Rue an involuntary shiver.

Squatting down by the bank, the man began to make grunting noises, higher pitched than that of the bull they had just heard. Everything was quiet for several minutes. The invisible end of the pole continued to move, Baptiste manipulating it along the rough hide. Surging violently, the outer end of the pole suddenly flew to one side, as if it had a life of its own. Powerful though he was, Baptiste had to struggle mightily to keep his grip. Still skillfully manipulating and removing the pole from the bindings that held it, he twisted the rope around his hands and began to pull, a tiny bit at a time, each hand covering the thumb of the other to double their strength. The muddy water swirled, and the beast thrashed to the top of the pool with a blast of a huge tail. The pocked crater of flesh came crashing out of the hole the creature had dug for itself. Its noisy roar was deafening as it swept Baptiste over into the mushy swamp, the iron hook still imbedded in its mouth. Both boys screamed as their friend floundered in the gooey marsh still holding fast to the rope. Loud curses came from the big man as he fought the giant reptile. Jacob and Jon

Rue were backed against a water oak whose gnarled roots were more above than below the ground. They kept halfway falling and grabbing the slippery bark, Jacob still holding fast to his musket. His musket! Jacob raised his gun. He dare not miss! Firing at the black, green, roiling mass, he watched as the alligator's head split and blood flew threw the air and down the creature's back. The thing kept moving and slashing and thrashing. Jon Rue and Jacob fell back onto the mess in the muddy water, scrambling to gain purchase on the other side, anything to escape the monster!

As quickly as it began, everything was over. Silence descended. Jacob and Jon Rue still scrabbled with broken nails and bloodied fingers, trying to climb up the side of the stream. They looked at each other. Both were covered in equal parts mud and blood. The terrible musky smell of the dead alligator swirled around them. Then they heard Baptiste's scream.

"Help! I in sinkn' hol'!"

Jacob managed to get shakily to his feet using his musket as a crutch. Jon Rue was close behind. In his struggles with the alligator, Baptiste had lost his hold on the rope and could no longer reach it. The sandy soil was gradually sucking the large man down. In his rising panic, he was finding it difficult to control his primal need to thrash. He knew he must be still, but the inching, suffocating soil terrified even his courageous soul.

"I'll get the hook out. Jon Rue, you will have to 'skim' the marsh and get the rope back around him," Jacob yelled, already tugging on the slippery bloody thing that had penetrated the alligator's mouth.

Jon Rue nodded and began his light steps across the ground. He reached Baptiste and pulled the rope tight around his huge shoulders, then slipped it under each arm, all the time watching the inexorable approach of the soil.

Meanwhile, Jacob secured the hook into the sturdy root base of the oak.

"We can't pull him in ourselves. This will hold for awhile. Jon Rue, you have to go for help!" Jacob yelled.

Jon Rue's swift feet floated over the ground to clear land.

Later, Patrick and Zack helped Baptiste to solid ground. He was covered with mud and sweat and leaned back against the water oak gratefully accepting the water pouch Patrick handed him. Thirstily he drank and then lay back again.

"She is dah biggest 'gator I evah see in mah whole life," he said between gasps of breath. "I will have a time skinnin' that one."

The two men and boys stared at the beast that now lay sprawled halfway out of the water. Insects were beginning their work on the ragged green flesh that once was the head. Turkey vultures could be seen through the canopy of moss and trees circling in anticipation.

"You'll have to get started pretty quick. Can you do it on your own?" Patrick thought Baptiste look pretty well done in.

"Oh, yah. Dis one will bring a big price. I can do dis in a leetl time," he rose and pulled his hatchet out of his pouch. "Because you boys sav mah lif, you can hav each a egg foh yoself."

Eagerly the boys approached the nest. The eggs were brown and had a leathery feel. Jon Rue almost dropped the one he was holding in excitement.

"It moved," he shouted excitedly

"Oh, dey is ready to hatch yeh," Baptiste said as he began swiftly to skin the alligator. "Leev me a few to take bac to sell to Yankees. Dey buy dem to take up noth."

Soon Patrick and Zack, with two boys who would not soon forget this day, were making their way back home.

"We saved Baptiste's life, killed the biggest alligator ever and have two gators of our very own," Jon Rue exclaimed running ahead of the group. "This is the greatest day, isn't it, Papa?"

Zack grinned.

"I have to agree. My only question is what will your mamma say about two baby alligators?"

Chapter XV

Two centuries ago, Edmund Burke said, "There is no safety for honest men except by believing all possible evil of evil men."

Emmagaline and her mother looked up as the noise and activity of the sugarhouse reached their ears. Their farm carriage was passing this beehive of activity on the way to the slave quarters. Fall was one of the busiest times of the year. Slaves and hired Irish immigrants made a constant trek, both day and night, to the large complex with their two-wheeled carts loaded with sugar cane stalks.

The mistress of the plantation and her young daughter had been looking over the stops they needed to make around the slave quarters. A new baby had been born and three more were due in a few weeks. Josie, one of their oldest slaves was declining and not expected to live for many more days. Dr. Bercoise had seen him the last time he was through and said there was nothing more he could do. Age was simply taking its toll. As with most slaves, no one knew for sure how old Josie was, but it was estimated he was ninety.

"I think he is a hundred," was Emma's guess that morning as she and Lorraine shared a breakfast of coffee and baguettes. She stirred her "coffee milk" as she made this solemn pronouncement. Coffee milk was her mother's concession to coffee for six-year-olds; it was made up of equal parts milk and coffee laced with two teaspoons of sugar.

Lorraine smiled at her small daughter. Emma could act so old for her age, as she did then with her grave expression.

Emma looked at her mother.

"Why don't slaves ever know their age for sure, Mama?" she asked.

"Some do. Those born here at River Rose know their ages, because their parents are here. Your papa keeps a record in the plantation book. Not all slave owners keep these records, however, so if a slave is sold and his family broken up, or members of the family die or are separated, he can loose track of his birth date."

"Is that why they don't have birthday parties?" Emma asked.

Her mother nodded absently as they finished their breakfast and made their way to the carriage.

Later, Lorraine would realize with a jolt that she had never thought of birthday parties for slaves. She thought about young Benny. Maybe Martha and Theseus did some kind of birthday celebration in private. This was not something she had ever heard mentioned. What a sad thought. Maybe Zack knew something about this. She would speak to him tonight.

The slave quarters came into view, and Lorraine began to gather up her papers with her notes about each family.

She turned to her daughter. "We have some new slaves that you will meet today from Winter Wind. Your papa bought several from the estate." Lorraine said this last softly. She was thinking of all the damage Julien Descant had visited on the world during his life. A shudder went through her body.

"Are you cold, Mama?" asked Emma, observing her mother's spasm.

"No. Just thinking about sad things. Emma, these new people may not be as strong and healthy as you are used to seeing. Please do not make comments until we are back in the carriage and you can talk to me in private. Do you understand?"

"Of course, Mama," Emma replied. Did her mama think she was a child? She knew how to act in front of strangers.

The carriage came to a stop in front of the "baby" cabin, Emma's favorite place. All the babies and toddlers were watched over here by two elderly slaves named Hona and Bess. Emma loved the smell of the freshly bathed babies, their chubby sweet faces and arms that reached up to be held and cuddled.

Lorraine had a basket of special baby lotions and powders, some that were prepared right on the plantation and some that had been ordered from Doctor Bercoise. As she and Emma entered the cabin they noticed an unusual amount of noise. Three babies and one toddler, apparently the newcomers to River Rose, were crying and whining. Normally Hona and Bess had children so placated and content there was hardly ever any crying or 'baby fussing' as Bess called it. As they moved to the area set-aside for the dressing and feeding, Lorraine and Emma got a better look at the crying children. The toddler was having trouble standing. At a look from Lorraine, Hona whispered in her ear.

"It's duh shaky leg sickness. She get bettah wif food." Hona reached out and picked up the tiny girl.

"How old do you think she is?" asked Lorraine.

"About three, so her mammy say. But I tink older. She have her teeth, but dey bad."

Lorraine could see stubs of blackened teeth as the girl smiled shyly.

"I think dey been feedin huh ash cake," Hone said sadly. "But we get huh bac with some good food."

Lorraine looked shocked.

"Ash cake. That awful stuff," she murmured under her breath.

"Dahs' right, Miz Mac, even grown peoples can't hardly abide it, but little uns deh don do well atall."

"Mama, what's ash cake?" Emma was especially fond of cake and wondered if some children were allowed to live on it.

"I don't know exactly, but Hona can tell you while I look at these other children."

Hona drew Emma close to the hearth in the middle of the large room. "Miss Emma," the old slave began. "You see deez coals and ashes? Ashcake is a little cohn meal mixed wif watah and meat if dey is some. Deh mix it so dis spoon would stan up in it like dis." Hona made a corn meal paste dry enough to demonstrate how the spoon would stand up by itself. "Wen day make dis it means dey have no oven. Aftah duh wood dun burn away, dey takes dah coals and ashes dat are left from dey fires and completely covah dis cake about dis deep." Hone showed Emma a finger spread of about a sixteenth of an inch. "Aftah it stays long enuff with des ashes, den it baked. And some peoples has to eat dis. It bad foh teef and belly, but ifen dat all you got, it bettah dan nothin."

"But how could you eat that?" Emma asked wonderingly.

Hona shrugged.

"I has to get back to my churin." She turned and walked away, leaving Emma staring after her.

Suddenly Lorraine was at Emma's side. She suggested that she take a ride in the carriage to join papa and her brothers at the sugarhouse.

"But, Mamma, I want to see the new babies," Emma pleaded.

"Later. Not today. They need tending to. They are not used to this strange place," her mother explained, hurrying Emma out of the door.

As Lorraine returned to the cabin, she tried to compose herself. She could not let Emma see the new babies. Not in their condition! She came and stood beside Bess as she tried to sooth one of the wailing infants. The baby no more than two months old was swollen with insect bites and apparently had been out in the sun too long. His face and tiny hands were peeling and looked raw. Bess was attempting to change his bottom cloth and when she removed the cloth, Lorraine almost fainted at the hideous red sores that were open and bleeding.

"Dear Lord, Bess! Do you have anything to ease his pain?"

"Yesum, Belray done send oveah huh pain mixtuh for babies skin and ease drops. Can you hep me hole him?"

"Of course." Lorraine gingerly lifted the now screaming child so Bess could drop the ease medicine drop by drop into his mouth.

"How do you know how much to give?" Lorraine asked.

"We has to treat dat bad skin, so we has to neah bout put him out. I drops it in until he rests." Bess expertly continued to drop tiny bits of the liquid onto the baby's tongue until he finally sighed deeply and was quiet.

She took him from Lorraine and laid him on a greased cloth and began gently applying the baby skin grease. The child moved only slightly, but then was perfectly still as Bess continued her ministrations.

"How did this happen?" Lorraine asked.

"What dey tells me is dat little chiluns at Wintah Win had no safe place like River Rose with peoples lookin aftah 'em." Bess's sweeping gesture took in the entire cozy cabin; its big hearth with it's wire screen so tiny hands were unable to touch the flames; the walls that were left open in spring and summer for air and now had already been filled with mud and made snug for the chilly weather to come; all the baby bottom cloths stacked in neat piles on the turning table along with clean blankets and shirts; modest wooden toys and beads in a special play area covered in a huge cloth that was cleaned daily.

But most important, thought Lorraine, *were Hona and Bess, with their loving care and attention.*

"Dis baby was lef undah a tree wif a little five yeah boy, and he fohgot him and went off playing. When he got bac, da ants had got to him. He even got soos in his mout." At this even Bess shuddered. "But we fix him up, you see," she assured a distraught Lorraine.

"Where are the other two?" she asked shakily.

Bess hesitated. "Is you shu you wants to see dem?"

Lorraine took a deep breath.

"Yes. I'm sure," she said firmly.

Bess guided her over to two cribs. They were beautifully carved of natural pine, handmade by one of the slaves over 20 years before. Worn but soft blankets peeked out around the edges. The two babies were awake and now quiet. At first Lorraine could not tell that anything was unusual about them.

But when Bess pulled back the blanket of the first one, she gasped. One of the little ones' legs was twice the size of the other. She pulled the blanket back on the other baby to reveal an infant whose head was slightly larger than normal and limbs that were like a rag doll, flaccid and limp.

"Tell me their stories," Lorraine said faintly.

"Dis fust one was in a baby basket at de end of a cotton row."

Lorraine understood. On plantations where there was no one to care for small children and babies, slaves took them into the fields. The mothers would then leave them in a big basket at the end of the row they were working and move them as they completed the row.

"Huh mama was almos finish wit da row. Den she saw dis big cotton mout moc'sin come sliding in dah basket. Befoh she could get der it don bit dat baby and got away. She tie a rag aroun dah leg and suck out da poson, but dat leg nevah go bac down."

The little baby looked up at the two women and smiled, waving her tiny arms.

"She vere sweet gul, don cry much but I don kno if dat leg evah be right," Bess finished sadly.

"Dis little boy was bon like dis," Bess continued on to the next baby. "His mama tinks she was hut bad from a beatin she had."

Bess reached down and picked up the small bundle. The boy had a head that was too large for his frail body and spindly arms and legs that flailed with a gripping, curling motion like he was under water and trying to keep from drowning.

"But surely even Descant would not beat a woman with child?" Lorraine looked her horror.

"Dey didn even take de 'precahshun,'" Bess said, "just beat her lik regulah."

Lorraine looked puzzled.

"Duh 'precahshun' is when dey wants to beats a woman fixin to hav a baby. Dey lays her down on boards wif a hole wher hur belly can hang down and beats her dat way. But 'ole devil man,' he beat her reg'lar." Bess stopped suddenly, realizing what she had called a white man.

Lorraine did not seem to have noticed. She just sat and wiped her face and took deep breaths.

Chapter XVI

December 1860

...What is it that the gentlemen wish? What would they have? Is life so dear or peace so sweet as to be purchased at the price of chains and slavery? Forbid it, Almighty God. I know not what course others may take, but as for me, give me liberty or give me death!

Patrick Henry
Speech in Virginia Convention,
Richmond (March 23, 1775)

Christmas Eve at River Rose

Everyone joined in the trimming of the giant Christmas tree that stood at one end of the double parlor. The scent from the loblolly pine permeated the entire house and to the McLoed family was the smell of Christmas as much as the fruitcake and pecan pie smells from the dining room. On Christmas morning, one hundred candles would be ablaze as people opened their gifts amid shouts of laughter and the odor of melted wax. The candles would be carefully snuffed afterwards to ensure there was no chance of fire. Now Lorraine finished hanging the last of the popcorn strings and joined Zack on the settee near the fireplace.

Both parents looked with pride at their three children. Jacob and Jon Rue, though excited over the prospect of gifts on Christmas morning, considered themselves almost grown and tried to display a calmer attitude than Emma. At seven years old, she was unrestrained in her joy about everything Christmas. Her white silk frock had lace rushing at the neck, and her black hair was tied back with a matching grosgrain ribbon.

Zack and Lorraine watched as the children carefully placed all of the family ornaments on the branches, stopping to hand some to Henri. During the Christmas tree trimming, Henri was the official 'top of the tree' man, balancing on a ladder to reach the top-most branches.

Glancing at the ormolu clock on the mantel, Zack noticed that it was getting late and that Patrick had not come down for dinner.

"I am going to see about papa. He is never this late," said Zack to Lori. He rose and went up the stairs now festooned with greenery from the many pine trees at River Rose. The delicate green needles were interlaced with red velvet ribbon and sprigs of holly berries. He knocked softly on his father's door but, getting no response, he entered.

Patrick was sitting in his rocker looking out of the window that faced the river.

"Papa, are you not feeling well?" Zack crossed the room and looked down into his father's face.

Patrick sighed, "I'm just tired and not really very hungry. But I will come down now. I want to see the children trim the tree."

As they walked down the stairs, Zack noticed his father was moving slower than normal and did seem very tired.

"Dr. Bercoise will be coming for dinner tomorrow. I think you should have him look at you," Zack commented as they stopped for a moment before entering the parlor.

"I really am fine. Just tired. I will get a good rest tonight. That's all I need." Patrick entered the festive room with Zack following.

Later, after the children had been sent off to bed, Patrick, Zack, and Lorraine sat before the fire. They discussed the unrest that had gripped the nation and Louisiana in the last few months.

"I wonder if this will be the last Christmas we will all be together," Patrick said in a melancholy tone.

"What do you mean, Papa? Are you not well?" Lorraine's face mirrored her concern. Her own beloved *papá* had passed away last summer, and she and Zack's father had become even closer than before.

"No. I'm thinking about how things might change if we have war. That is a distinct possibility, my dear. There is talk of forming a provisional government in Montgomery." Patrick sipped his brandy and continued. "Ever since Harper's Ferry, I've thought there will be either civil war or a terrible insurrection that could culminate in war."

"Papa, our slaves would never do what John Brown and his men did." Lorraine paled at the thought.

"We're not the only slave owners in Louisiana. Think about Winter Wind. Some of those slaves probably have built up enough hate to do anything."

"You are right. Those poor little children we brought over and some of the grown slaves like Theseus…." She shuddered.

"I've always been determined to treat my hands kindly, but slavery is such an evil proposition, well, it's bound to end, either through insurrection or bloody conflict."

"The North is so self-righteous when they speak of freeing the slaves. They don't care about our slaves personally. They are angry about the competition for crops," Zack muttered angrily.

"That is true, Zack. But it doesn't change the fact that slavery goes against everything our country stands for." Patrick pulled out a cigar and handed one to Zack. "We must find a way out of this dependency. But it can't be done overnight. It has to be gradual. That means we may have to secede from the Union while we settle on some reasonable alternative."

"But what is a reasonable alternative? I thought Popular Sovereignty was reasonable as a transition, but look what happened in Kansas four years ago. Or I should say what happened in 'bloody Kansas.'" Zack stared into the fire. "What happens if we declare secession? Will we be allowed to?"

"We certainly have the right. Even the *New York Tribune* pointed out that we have as much right to secede as the colonies had to secede from Great Britain." Patrick pulled his chair closer to the fire. "In the meantime, I have decided I am going to go ahead and do something I have thought about for a few years. When Armand Decuir comes tomorrow for our Christmas dinner, I plan to discuss some changes in my will regarding the slaves." Decuir was the lawyer and old friend that guided Patrick in all things legal. Patrick looked at his son and daughter-in-law for their reaction.

"What do you plan to do, Papa?" asked Zack, though he thought he knew the answer as he and his father had talked about this many times.

"As of January 1, 1861, all children born at River Rose will be free. And all River Rose slaves will have their freedom three years from that date."

Zack reached over and took Lorraine's hand. "We totally agree with your plan. We have spoken of something like this to each other. But why free the children now? You know the law in Louisiana will not allow children to be sold away from their parents. In fact we are the only state that has such a law."

"One never knows when laws might change. But this is more than that. I have come to a point in my life when I never want another child born into slavery at River Rose."

"Three years will give us time to transition to hired labor. We will have to make some changes," Zack was thinking out loud now. "It can be done, and it will be done!" Zack pounded the arm of his chair for emphasis. "Then this terrible yoke will be lifted from all our necks. The yoke of slavery and the yoke of guilt will be lifted. When will you tell our people?"

"I plan on announcing this on New Year's Day after the final cane cut." Patrick looked at Zack and Lorraine. "I've never been prouder of both of you than I am now."

Christmas Day dinner

"Auralee, you have outdone yourself." Patrick led the applause for the kitchen staff as they came forward for their special Christmas gifts. The remnants of the huge feast spread out before him attested to the enjoyment of his guests. The gumbo, roast chicken stuffed with chestnut dressing, roast beef, sweet yams, pecan and fruit pies, and cake had everyone stuffed and feeling pleasantly drowsy.

"Here's to Auralee and Charlotte, Julie, Sophie, and Martice from the kitchen and our servers, JohnDee, Oren and Percy," he said raising his glass in *salut*.

After much bowing and thanking everyone for the traditional Christmas gift of new clothing and small personal gifts, the kitchen and serving crew departed, congratulating each other in soft whispers of excitement.

"Now it's time for some brandy." Patrick stood and led the men to his study while Lori and her friends and children gathered around the tree to open some more small presents. The main gifts had been exchanged earlier in the day. Jacob was beside himself over his new saddle and could hardly wait until morning to try it out. Jon Rue had received his first musket and though it was unloaded it never left his side. Emma's new doll and baby carriage were constantly trundled up and down the entrance hall for all to admire. The women and children now exchanged small gifts of sweets and hand-made scarves and handkerchiefs. Afterwards, Lori would lead the singing of carols as she played the harpsichord.

In his study, Patrick settled the men down with fine cigars and brandy. These were his best friends and included his son and a young nephew who had come from Georgia to visit for the holidays. He excused himself and stepped into a smaller section of his study that afforded privacy and motioned for his lawyer, Armand Decuir, to join him.

Patrick explained he wanted to change his will and his intentions regarding his slaves. His friend looked at him in astonishment. "Are you sure you want to do this, Patrick? Can River Rose show a profit without slave labor?" Decuir looked genuinely distressed.

"There must be a way to raise a profitable sugar cane crop without slavery. Zack and I are committed to finding a way," Patrick insisted.

"You will alienate some of your friends by this decision. The whole slavery issue is extremely sensitive right now. We may be at war by this time next year over this very issue." Decuir tried to make Patrick see the dangers involved.

"I know some people will not understand. I simply will not have another child born into slavery on my place. Things are changing. There are already some machines I have heard about that can reduce the necessity for so much manual labor. Some slaves already are farming small tracts of land and paying fees based on their crop production. There are ways to make this work."

Decuir could see that his friend had thought this through and would not change his mind.

"I plan to tell my people on New Year's Day after the final cane cut." Patrick turned and reentered the main part of his study. Decuir followed, but his concern for his friend consumed his thoughts for the rest of the evening. He was afraid Patrick did not appreciate the controversy that would ensue when his plan was made known. The lawyer settled into one of the comfortable leather chairs around the fireplace, accepted a cigar, and watched Patrick talking amiably with the other men. Nodding and smiling with Tony Dickerson he seemed the epitome of a true southern gentleman. And he was. However, his idealism was always rearing its aggravating head and stirring up trouble. Decuir remembered when Patrick decided he wanted the children of his slaves admitted to the same little school his own children attended on the plantation. Sheriff Dickerson simply looked the other way, and, since no one formally complained, Patrick got away with essentially breaking the law. While he would not be breaking the law in choosing manumission for his slaves, he would invoke enmity from some of his planter friends. Decuir decided he would speak with Patrick again and try to persuade him to rethink this whole idea. But Decuir realized it would be unlikely that he would be able to change his friend's mind.

New Year's Day

The final cane cut was always the start of a great celebration on sugar cane plantations. It was an eagerly anticipated event both for the field workers and the planters' family. As the final row was reached, Boliver looked for the tallest stalk left standing and tied a brightly colored ribbon around it. The workers finished the row in frenzy of chopping machetes, and then all work stopped just short of the beribboned cane. Now was the time when the worker who had worked the hardest and produced the most cut cane would be recognized as the *meilleur couteau* for the year. Boliver put his hand on a short stocky man's shoulder. The winner, Ezralee, bowed to the remaining sugar cane stalk and then twirling three times with his machete raised high in the air, on the fourth turn struck the cane to the ground. At this a loud cheer rose from everyone and the women ran forward and carried the "slain cane" over their heads singing joyfully. The men followed, joining in the singing. This great parade ended at the big house, where a huge spread of food and drink awaited one and all. Large plank tables were set up just outside the porches that surrounded the front of the house. Gaily colored lanterns had been strung from all the trees, and, weather permitting, the celebration would continue into the night.

This year was a little different. Patrick ascended the front steps leading up to the galleries that circled the house and raised his hands for everyone's attention. As the laughter and singing subsided, he looked out over the upturned black faces, some old, some only children, and some poor, ruddy-faced Irish immigrants that were hoping someday to buy small plots of land of their own. He looked at his own family standing just to his right, especially Zack and Lorraine. Slowly they both walked over and stood one on each side of him.

"We want everyone to know this is what we all want papa," Zack whispered.

"I want to make a special announcement to start off this New Year." Patrick stepped forward and the crowd gathered closer. "This affects you and all children born to you from this day forward."

Families gathered close together with mothers clinging to children's small hands or holding babies tight to their breasts fearfully. Their thoughts were reflected in worried faces. *Mastah Mac wouldn't separate them, they knew that, but what if some were going to be sold off to another plantation? Each slave on the place had heard horror stories of things that happened on some plantations. Winter Wind's people were fresh in their minds.* There was not a sound now. It was as if all were holding their breath.

"Any child born at River Rose from now on will be born free." Patrick paused and looked at the crowd. Each face a vivid memory: Old Belray, who had made the trip from Georgia with him so long ago, now aged, leaning on a cane; Auralee, the best cook in the world, standing beside her husband and two young daughters; Martha, the little girl, he had bought at one of the awful slave auctions in Charleston. Martha was now grown and had her arm around her young son Benny, a brilliant child who was being educated right along with Zack's children, and her husband Theseus, one of Winter Winds' tragic slaves. It had gotten colder and as they breathed, little puffs of smoky air billowed up from the crowd.

Patrick continued. "Three years from today, on January 1, 1864, all River Rose slaves will be free!"

Free!

The word seemed to hang in the crisp air. Four letters in a word wrapped itself around all who stood there in a breathless grasp. No one stirred. It was as if they were afraid any movement would cause the word to crumble and fall away and it would be a dream. Then a great roar came soaring up from the crowd. It was somehow a combination of cheering and singing. Women stood and sobbed and hugged their children. Grown men unashamedly wept. All at once, everyone came together and held hands and sang:

No one knows de trouble I seen...

The moon shown down just as it had before the word "free" rang out, but the earth in one small place had been forever changed.

In that place, on January 1, 1861, freedom had won. It would continue to be won in small increments, bathed in blood, over the next four tumultuous years.

On January 26, 1861, Louisiana seceded from the Union.

On February 10, 1861 Jefferson Davis was elected provisional president of the Confederacy.

Chapter XVII

January 10, 1861

Can a man take fire in his bosom, and his clothes not be burned? Can one go upon hot coals, and his feet not be burned?
Proverbs 6:27–28

Trees sparkled with branches of icy jewels as a tiny burst of moonlight shone through the heavy cloud cover. Three men dismounted in the woods bordering the back of River Rose Plantation, an area known as Borge Isle. Tethering their horses, they reached down by one of the cross ditches that funneled water to the main drainage canal. Each man grabbed a handful of mud and smeared it over his face. They wore dark clothing and carried long sticks with rags wrapped tightly at one end. There was only stubble in this particular section, so they crouched low, taking advantage of the dark shadows cast by the nearby trees. The cane had already been cut, and there was not a good place to slip across the field undetected at this time of year. Frost had silenced the insects. The only sound was the wind that wrapped around the naked trees making a ghostly scraping noise as the branches rubbed together.

"Would a' been safer ifn we had a done all this afore da cane was cut," one man whispered.

"Well, Mista Dupre´ didn't know McLoed was about to free his slaves den, did he? Now shut up," the tallest of the three hissed. He was a thin, bearded man with black brows that grew together and gave him a perpetual scowl. This gaunt figure was the leader of the group.

He waved the other two men to slink lower. They were now crawling on their bellies, and the other two men grumbled softly to themselves. Moist dirt began to cake their clothes and hands.

The sugarhouse loomed like a sleepy giant, with eyes blinking occasionally, as flames from the kettles leaped up high enough for the tiny windows to catch their glow.

"Now member. We go in da back door and stay up agin da wall till we get to dat area near da sugah train." The tall man spoke softly. "Dah men on da train changes shifts at midnight. Everone 'ov um clears out. Thass when we has to be ready. We git it goin' and in da con-fusion we git out up against da walls like we come in." He looked at the other two men.

They nodded their understanding.

The three figures moved silently to the back of the structure and slipped in the back door. Clinging to the shadows afforded by the walls, the men slowly made their way around the ground floor. The light was dim until they got closer to the sugar train. Fire curled up from the round bottoms of the large iron kettles and threw out light and heat. Melodic Spanish voices rose and fell with the rhythmic swish of the sugar swords as they waved back and forth over the steaming kettles.

A gong sounded somewhere. The workers laid their sugar nets carefully across the kettles and walked toward the front of the sugarhouse.

Quickly the three men reached out from the their hiding place in the shadows and set their torches in the fire under the kettles. At the moment the torches became fully engulfed in flames, someone yelled, "Hey, whatchall think youah doing?"

Startled, the men grabbed their torches and tried to run. Cut off on two sides by approaching sugarhouse workers, they turned and fled the only other way open. It led to some stairs, and they immediately began climbing as fast as they could. Halfway up, they saw other workers coming down the stairs toward them.

"Jump! Is duh only way out," the bearded man yelled. The light was dimmer up high. The men dropped their torches and jumped blindly from the stairs. An agonizing cry went up as one of them landed on the rim of a boiling sugar kettle and bounced off into the fire. His two companions landed outside the sugar train but were surrounded by angry workers.

At that moment one of the torches made contact with a side beam near the stairs. The fire quickly ignited the dry cypress beams of the lower structure and began creeping up the sides of the sugarhouse. Tongues of flame spread toward the overhead beams, suddenly filling the structure with light. Sugarhouse workers ran for empty water buckets and sent men up to the higher levels where large barrels of water were stationed. Forgotten in the ensuing confusion, two of the intruders ran for the back door and escaped into the cold black night. The third man lay writhing on the ground, screaming in pain.

Shouts went up all over the plantation as the bright lights of the fire in the sugarhouse illuminated the countryside. Zack and Patrick raced to the flaming structure with every able- bodied man on the place following close behind.

Inside, the heat and shouting of the men was a pulsating caldron of sound and fury.

Water buckets passed from man to man. Every sugarhouse worker knew where his place was on the bucket line, and water constantly streamed down the walls near stairs where workers could stand and pour. The long cotton sheets that were kept soaking in brine for just such an emergency were thrown up to catch on the hooks lining the walls. Covering the walls with the wet salty mixture helped smother any flames that the water from the buckets was unable to reach.

Gradually the flames were contained, but smoke hung heavy in the damp air. Burned areas were scraped to make sure no dying embers were left to ignite later.

Zack and Patrick stood on the top level and surveyed the destruction below. "It could have been worse." Zack said.

Patrick wiped his steamy face—smearing soot and sweat. "Let's go talk to the man that fell on the sugar train. See what he has to say about this devil business."

There was weariness about Patrick that Zack had never seen in his father before. Something in his eyes.

"Yes. I have some questions for those two that got away. I've already sent for Dickerson," Patrick said.

Hours later...

Patrick, Zack, and Boliver rode slowly back to the big house, exhaustion competing with soot etched their faces with lines. The damage to the sugarhouse was extensive, but as Zack said, "It could have been a disaster. We could have lost it all."

Grinding had been underway since October and was almost complete. Patrick estimated they could be up and running again in two weeks. He thought they could finish the remaining sugar cane by the end of the month. What really bothered Patrick and Zack, even more than the results of the fire, was finding out that one of their neighbors was responsible for hiring the men who started the fire.

Patrick sent a courier to Alexandria to get the sheriff as soon as he heard the hysterical ravings of the injured man left behind by the other two thugs. He would give the sheriff the names of the two escaped men when he arrived. Dr Bercoise did not think the burned man would live and had transported him to the hospital in Alexandria.

The men dismounted at the stables, and walked slowly toward the house, Boliver breaking off to go to his small house in back.

Lori and the children were at breakfast and looked shocked when they saw the two blackened faces emerge from the doorway leading from the detached kitchen.

Lori ran to the men. "Are you hurt in any way?" she asked. She looked from one to the other of their dirty faces, clothes, and tired eyes.

"No, we're fine." Zack bent down and kissed her cheek, trying to avoid smearing her with soot. "Just hungry, tired, and discouraged that one of our own neighbors would try to sabotage our grinding."

"Sit down and eat. Then you can get cleaned up and rest." Lori indicated two places waiting for them.

"I don't know about rest." Patrick said. He ran one grimy hand over his eyes. "Dickerson should be here at any time. We need to make arrangements to make sure we have some plan to guard the plantation in case someone else gets the idea to retaliate." Patrick sat down slowly at the table.

"Retaliate?" Lori asked.

"Doran Dupre´ thinks I'm some sort of traitor to the south because I'm freeing my slaves. He was trying to teach me a lesson and discourage other planters from doing the same, or so his hired fire starter says."

"He is not a leader in our community. No one will pay any attention to what he thinks," Lori declared angrily. She thought about how she had always tried to help Dupre´ and his pitiful little wife. They had five children and were always in need of clothing and shoes. When their house had burned down, she and Zack had given them household goods to start over.

Patrick looked around the table at his family. "A thing like this can sometimes take on a life of its own. Everyone needs to be careful until this blows over. Children," he looked at his three grandchildren watching him with wide eyes. "Stay near the house for a few days. Let us know if you see anything unusual." He stood up. "I think I'll go up and rest for a bit. I'm kind of shaky." As he turned to walk away, Patrick stumbled and fell forward.

Dr. Bercoise came out of the bedroom and paused to turn and look at the sad tableaux around Patrick's bed. Zack and Lorraine held each other and cried. Jacob and Jon Rue stood like statues as tears coursed down their cheeks. Emma had climbed on the bed and lay in a sobbing heap next to her beloved 'papa.' Lori bent over and gently smoothed back the white hair and kissed Patrick's forehead.

"He was my second papa, Zack," she sobbed brokenly.

The doctor slowly descended the stairs. Unshed tears burned his eyes. Patrick had been more than a patient. He was a lifelong friend. The doctor had been summoned from the hospital at Alexandria, where he had taken the burned and dying fire starter. Somehow he knew it would be like this. Patrick had seemed so tired lately. And sure enough he was too late.

"He was gone when he hit the floor. A massive heart attack," Dr Bercoise told Zack and Lori. "There is nothing anyone could have done." *But it was precipitated by the despicable actions of Dupre,* he thought resentfully.

Getting in his carriage, he paused again and looked back at River Rose. *Everything is changing,* he thought. *War may be coming and now Patrick is gone. A new generation will take over. A new way of life is coming. There are new waves pulsing through my profession, too.* Dr. Bercoise clucked to his horse and slowly took the winding lane back to the main road, the bare branches of the trees waving a cold goodbye.

KATHERINE BENNETT

THE EMANCIPATION PROCLAMATION:

By the President of the United States of America:

A PROCLAMATION

Whereas on the 22nd day of September, A.D. 1862, a proclamation was issued by the President of the United States, containing, among other things, the following, to wit:

"That on the 1st day of January, A.D. 1863, all persons held as slaves within any State or designated part of a State the people whereof shall then be in rebellion against the United States shall be then, thenceforward, and forever free; and the executive government of the United States, including the military and naval authority thereof, will recognize and maintain the freedom of such persons and will do no act or acts to repress such persons, or any of them, in any efforts they may make for their actual freedom.

"That the executive will on the 1st day of January aforesaid, by proclamation, designate the States and parts of States, if any, in which the people thereof, respectively, shall then be in rebellion against the United States; and the fact that any State or the people thereof shall on that day be in good faith represented in the Congress of the United States by members chosen thereto at elections wherein a majority of the qualified voters of such States shall have participated shall, in the absence of strong countervailing testimony, be deemed conclusive evidence that such State and the people thereof are not then in rebellion against the United States."

Now, therefore, I, Abraham Lincoln, President of the United States, by virtue of the power in me vested as Commander-In-Chief of the Army and Navy of the United States in time of actual armed rebellion against the authority and government of the United States, and as a fit and necessary war measure for supressing said rebellion, do, on this 1st day of January, A.D. 1863, and in accordance with my purpose so to do, publicly proclaimed for the full period of one hundred days from the first day above mentioned, order and designate as the States and parts of States wherein the people thereof, respectively, are this day in rebellion against the United States the following, to wit:

Arkansas, Texas, Louisiana (except the parishes of St. Bernard, Palquemines, Jefferson, St. John, St. Charles, St. James, Ascension, Assumption, Terrebone, Lafourche, St. Mary, St. Martin, and Orleans, including the city of New Orleans), Mississippi, Alabama, Florida, Georgia, South Carolina, North Carolina, and Virginia (except the forty-eight counties designated as West Virginia, and also the counties of Berkeley, Accomac, Morthhampton, Elizabeth City, York, Princess Anne, and Norfolk, including the cities of Norfolk and Portsmouth), and which excepted parts are for the present left precisely as if this proclamation were not issued.

And by virtue of the power and for the purpose aforesaid, I do order and declare that all persons held as slaves within said designated States and parts of States are, and henceforward shall be, free; and that the Executive Government of the United States, including the military and naval authorities thereof, will recognize and maintain the freedom of said persons.

And I hereby enjoin upon the people so declared to be free to abstain from all violence, unless in necessary self-defence; and I recommend to them that, in all case when allowed, they labor faithfully for reasonable wages.

And I further declare and make known that such persons of suitable condition will be received into the armed service of the United States to garrison forts, positions, stations, and other places, and to man vessels of all sorts in said service.

And upon this act, sincerely believed to be an act of justice, warranted by the Constitution upon military necessity, I invoke the considerate judgment of mankind and the gracious favor of Almighty God.

Chapter XVIII

April 1861

Good-bye my Fancy!
Farewell dear mate, dear love!
I'm going away, I know not where,
Or to what fortune, or whether I may ever see you again,
So Good-bye my Fancy.
"Good-Bye My Fancy!"
Leaves of Grass
Walt Whitman

Spring came to River Rose as a bittersweet accompaniment to grief and worry over the impending war. The loss of Patrick still seemed unreal to his family and friends.

Sheriff Dickerson paused for a moment at the entrance to River Rose's path. He was on his way to another plantation but the pull of old memory held him for a moment. Planning to retire, he had been urged to reconsider, as there would be no one to take his place. Every able-bodied younger man was heading for Virginia to join up with Louisiana's General Beauregard. Zack McLoed was planning to leave in a week. Sighing, he continued on his way, vowing to stop on his way back.

River Rose was in turmoil because Zack was leaving. Boliver and Zack's nephew Seth would be left in charge of the plantation. Jacob was only 14, and, though large for his age and dependable by nature, he was still too young to be responsible for the day-to-day business of running an enterprise as large as River Rose. Seth, though only 20, was a hard worker and anxious to learn the sugar cane business. He was born with a clubfoot and was not able to go to war. This responsibility assuaged his guilt because, as Zack pointed out, he could not go himself without someone like Seth to head up the family interests.

Lorraine could hardly bear the thought of Zack going to war again, but there seemed to be no alternative. Louisiana had seceded from the Union in January and the newly formed Confederacy was calling all her young men to service. *If he had to be at war, she would rather have him with Pierre than anyone else. They had fought side by side in Mexico and returned safely.* She finished sewing the last of the buttons on Zack's new gray jacket. Sewing his Captain's bars to the shoulders, she thought back to the first time she had seen him in a uniform. *It was spring and she had just come home from school. He had recently graduated from West Point. He looked down at her in the receiving line with the blue eyes she remembered and the shock on his face still made her smile.*

Zack stood in the door watching his wife holding his uniform jacket and smiling in some sort of reverie. He never tired of looking at her, and catching her unaware was delightful.

Stepping into the room, he spoke softly so as not to startle her. "What deep thoughts are going through your mind that makes you smile so?" he asked.

Lori jumped up and threw her arms around his neck. "Darling, I was thinking of the first time I saw you after I graduated from school. Remember the dinner dance at Delmonde before we were married?"

"Of course! I was surprised to see you had changed. In looks that is," he amended. "You were the same unpredictable, unusual girl I knew from the past. But all grown up." He kissed her lightly on the nose, and arm in arm they walked to the small settee near the window.

Looking out, they could just see the river swirling, red and angry after a spring storm the night before.

"The river never changes, just keeps rolling down to the Mississippi. No matter what happens to us. It's always ready to carry us away and bring us home." Zack eyes held a great sadness.

"*Cheri,* it will bring you home to us again. Just like before." Lorraine spoke softly and laid her head on Zack's shoulder.

"Mama, Papa, Jake, and Jon Rue are going fishing and will not take me!" Emma burst into the room, a determined look on her face.

"It's too late to go fishing. They are only teasing you." Lorraine soothed the agitated girl. She drew Emma into the circle they made by the window.

"What are you looking at, and why does Papa look so sad?" As usual Emma asked two questions at once.

"We are just looking at the river and thinking about how soon it will bring me back to all of you." Zack looked down at his small daughter who looked so much like Lori.

"Will you be gone a very long time, Papa?" Emma absently twisted her skirt between two fingers.

"I don't know. Probably not too long. Everyone seems to think we will send those Yankees packing in a couple of months."

"What are Yankees?"

"Yankees are folks who live in another part of our country," Zack explained patiently.

"Why do we have to have a war anyway?" Emma grumbled.

Jacob and Jon Rue suddenly came tumbling into the room and interrupted Zack before he had to answer a question he asked himself nightly.

Emma was affected deeply by the departure of her father. The concept of war was alien to her young mind and she felt as if she had been abandoned. Lorraine decided to try and distract her by giving her a favorite treat, a ride on her Connemara pony. Buttermilk, so named because of his milky white color, was small even for a Connemara and Emma loved the little animal with all her heart. When Lorraine mentioned the ride, she saw happiness for the first time in several days, in her little daughter's eyes. Normally the children were not allowed to ride until dryer weather because of the danger of horses becoming mired in mud and breaking their legs. Lorraine decided this was a different time and emergency measures were in order. They set out in early afternoon. The sun had dried the moisture from the grass and the ground seemed firm. Nickolas was leading the way, carefully skirting the stones and making slow progress up a gently sloping hill that was a favorite lookout point over the plantation. Buttermilk followed the big horse with Emma gently holding the reins as she had been taught.

The little pony seemed to stumble, right himself, and then stumble again. Emma felt herself falling helplessly through the air into a nearby ravine. She rolled over several times and finally came to a stop with a sickening thud and knew no more.

As she became aware of her surroundings, she heard two gunshots in rapid succession. This was the plantation's signal for help. In the distance she heard two answering shots. Emma tried to raise her head but a wave of dizziness swept over her and she put her head back down. After a few moments she gingerly tried to sit up. Her left ankle hurt and she began to cry. Then she thought of Buttermilk. Turning over, she could see her pony lying on his side not far away. But why? She had never seen him lying down and was immediately alarmed. *Maybe he had a broken leg. I will nurse him back to health. I won't let anyone shoot him,* she thought. She crawled over to the prone form. His legs looked okay. Emma put her hand up to his muzzle. She loved to feel his soft breath as he nuzzled her hand for treats. But no familiar nuzzle was there. Buttermilk's eyes were open but Emma realized he didn't see her. He would never see her again or nuzzle her hand or run up to her when she called him. She reached over and closed his eyes and began to sob. Not little girl sobs, but deep down sobs, from her very soul. Emma lay with her hand stroking the little pony's face until she heard a yell and noise from up above the now crumbling ledge.

"Emma! We're coming for you. Don't move!" Boliver was sliding down the rope that had been anchored to a sturdy tree. He waved and called to her again.

"I won't move," Emma screamed through her tears.

Later, as Emma rode home in the carriage with her leg propped up she couldn't stop crying.

"I killed Buttermilk, Mama!" she kept repeating over and over.

Lorraine gathered her daughter in her arms, being careful not to twist her sore ankle.

"You have had a bad fright and are in pain and not thinking clearly," she said.

"I am, Mama. I killed him," Emma repeated

"If you had been killed in the fall, would Buttermilk have killed you because you fell in the ravine?" Lorraine asked, looking intently into the small child's tear-stained face.

Emma stopped crying and just made snuffling sounds for a moment.

"No! But this is different!"

"How is it different?" her mother asked.

Again, silence except for snuffling and heaving of the small chest.

"I guess it was a accident after all," Emma admitted. "I guess it was a accident."

"Yes. A terrible accident, but nobody's fault." Lorraine pushed back the wet curls from her daughter's face and kissed her forehead. You will see Buttermilk in heaven someday and he will still be looking for treats," she said.

"Like always?" Emma asked.

"Like always," her mother said.

War

Chapter XIX

June 2, 1861
First Manassas

Simple and fresh and fair from winter's close emerging,
As if no artifice of fashion, business, politics, had ever been,
Forth from its sunny nook of shelter'd grass innocent, golden,
calm as the dawn,
The spring's first dandelion shows its trustful face.
The First Dandelion
Walt Whitman
Manassas, Virginia

Rolling hills greening up from spring rains painted a pastoral beauty with blue tinged mountains in the background. Sweltering heat was felt during the middle of the day, but nights were still cool. Only the signs of bivouac belied the calm. Rows and rows of square tents and the more comfortable Sibley tents lined the countryside near the Alexandria Road.

Headquarters, Brigadier General P. G. T. Beauregard, Alexandria Road

The small farmhouse that housed General P.G.T. Beauregard's headquarters sat back off the Alexandria Road. It was orderly, though crowded. General Beauregard himself was occupied with maps and studying every conceivable plan that the enemy could execute. The pine table in his upstairs office was laden with folded dockets and other documents precisely placed for immediate reference. The lower part of the farmhouse was filled with desks occupied by clerks. Constant streams of orderlies and dispatch riders came through, but because of Beauregard, there remained an air of cool confidence and precision.

Pierre Beauregard was not a tall man. At only 5'8", he nevertheless seemed larger than life. His personality and air of assurance gave him a commanding presence. His Cajun ancestry showed in his black hair and eyes and an occasional twinkle even in the direst circumstances. Though some thought he projected an air of bravado, he always "led" his men into battle,

Beauregard raised his eyes from a map he was studying as his friend Colonel Zackery McLoed came clumping up the stairs. Zack had recently been promoted to Colonel and was now constantly working with Beauregard, especially in the area of planning maneuvers. This was Zack's greatest strength. His great strategic ability coupled with the General's genius for "battle sense" made them a formidable pair.

Beauregard leaned back in his chair.

"At ease, Zack. Have a seat and tell me what you have to report."

Zack spread out several sheets of drawing paper with precise lines and sketches of each placement. "I finished looking at the earthworks, and they are totally inadequate, as you surmised. We'll have to build these as quickly as possible. I spoke with some of the other officers and they said the men are complaining they are gentlemen and didn't enter the war to dig ditches."

"They have a different point of view than the Charlestonians who were willing to do anything to help with fortifications," Beauregard commented.

Zack nodded and wiped his forehead with his handkerchief. Summer had come to Virginia with a vengeance.

"That's very disappointing. What do you recommend?" The General knew Zack never posed a problem without having given some thought to a solution.

"There is a possibility the locals would let us use their slaves. It's the only thing I can think would give us enough hands for what we need."

"That of course is not our only problem." The General rose from his chair and began his characteristic pacing. "We need many more men to defend Manassass. There is a small stream called Bull Run." He stopped in front of one of the many maps hanging on the walls of the little room. He pointed to a place on the map, and Zack rose and crossed the room to join him.

"My line should be behind it. It has a devilish number of fords in it." He traced a line with his finger to show how the water ran north and east of Manassas Junction. "I've already written the president asking for more men, and they should start arriving tomorrow."

"What about supplies and food? We're running low," Zack said. He resumed his seat as Beauregard settled back in his chair. "There's plenty available from the locals if we need it."

"I've been ordered to only use supplies sent from Richmond. I cannot get around that because the Army Commissary General, Northrop, has caused some difficulty. But keep me apprised of the situation. If things get critical,

I will just have to pursue other avenues. There is another matter that no one else seems to think is important, but I do. The color of the men's uniforms concerns me. The experienced men seem to have mainly old blue army coats," he looked at Zack, "not like what you have."

"That would be what I would be wearing too if Lori had not outfitted me before I left," Zack agreed. "Many just came with what they had or have no uniforms at all unless their wives or mothers managed to sew for them before they left home."

"I have suggested to the president that maybe some group of the ladies of the Confederacy could make scarves for us, red on one side and yellow on the other. President Davis decided that would be too large and has directed that we should wear small rosettes instead." He pushed a pouch across the table. "What do you think?"

Zack opened the packet and a tumble of rosettes scattered over the plain surface. "They're mighty small, sir," he said, fingering several. "Only about the size of a button."

"That's what I think. But, we shall see," he sighed and walked to one of the small windows overlooking the encampment. "What I'm afraid of is that we will be mistaking each other for Union soldiers and start shooting our own men."

Mid June 1861

Reinforcements began to arrive around the middle of June, and part of General Beauregard's concerns about his troops being mistaken for Union soldiers was allayed, with the arrival of the flamboyant Louisiana Tiger Rifles of Major Roberdeau Wheat's 1st Special Infantry Battalion. Though their flag pictured a lamb with the legend *'As Gentle As'*, they were truly as fierce as tigers. Fighting was the same as breathing to these eager warriors, and their very presence raised everyone's spirits. They would fight to the death using knives if necessary. Their nickname, 'Gentle Tigers,' was simply a tribute to their utter fearlessness. Their uniforms were as flamboyant as their fighting style and were patterned after French Algerian Military wear. They consisted of red shirts under short brown jackets. Baggy trousers of blue and white striped bed ticking material tucked into white leggings were topped off by bright red skullcaps with long tassels. Their mettle would be tested severely on a beautiful Sunday morning in July.

General Beauregard now had reinforcements that brought his army up to about 15,000. He had also devised a battle plan that he was convinced would drive the Federals from Virginia.

The Federals were not standing idly by. General Irvin McDowell, who had been a classmate of Beauregard's at West Point, had been strengthening his position and troop strength.

Washington—Early July 1861

Mrs. Rose Greenhow was a Washington insider but also a confederate sympathizer and someone privy to advance information. The day she observed from her window was gray with clouds scudding across a slate colored sky. She began pacing her little sitting room. Her beautiful Federal-style home looked out on the busy street, and from her window she could see anyone coming or going for a block in either direction. Bettie Duval should have been here by now. Miss Duvall was fearless and still young enough to be reckless at times. Rose constantly worried that she might inadvertently give something away. Turning to continue her journey back and forth, she caught a glimpse of a bonnet and gave a sigh of relief. She had a moment to study the trim figure as it approached her door. The cheap homespun dress was perfect for a farm girl, which would be the role Bettie had to play for the next few hours.

"I'm sorry I'm late," Bettie said breathlessly as she was shown in to Mrs.Greenshaw's sitting room. She waited until the aged butler quietly closed the door, then continued. "I had to wait until papa left so I would not have to answer a lot of questions. Everyone is so suspicious and nervy right now."

Rose gave her a hug and indicated she should join her on the settee by the window. "It is a most unsettled time. Would you care for some tea?"

"I really would rather be on my way," said the young girl.

Rose noticed she was twisting her hands in nervousness. Bettie had beautiful white hands. Not the hands of a farm girl.

"You will probably need to keep your hands covered. Do you have some gloves?" Rose asked.

"I did not think to bring any, but they would not have been right in any case. Not for a farm girl." Bettie looked worried.

"Here. Try these." Mrs. Greenshaw handed Bettie a pair of gloves with the tips of the fingers cut out. "They have been transformed into work gloves. I think they will do."

"Truly, Madam, you think of everything." Bettie looked admiringly at the older woman.

"I also thought we should darken your face a little. I have a mixture here that I think will do nicely." With her finger she tilted the girl's face up and applied a rosy brown cream from a tiny jar. She sat back and smiled with satisfaction. "Ah, yes. A true farm lass you are now."

Handing Bettie a hand mirror, she smiled at the reaction.

"It's amazing. I don't look the same at all." She looked at Mrs. Greenshaw. "I know I shall be able to fool anybody now. I think I am ready."

"One last thing. The note for General Bonham. Do you have a secure place to carry it?"

"A most secure place indeed."

Rose smiled as Bettie showed her the hiding place for the note.

"You have the address and know where to wait for the wagon that will be going to the country?" She asked.

Rose went over the details one last time.

"Oh, yes, mum." Bettie smiled. "Do I sound right?"

"You sound just like an uneducated country girl."

It was easy to get a ride in a farm wagon all the way to Bettie's friend's house in Virginia. Bettie quickly changed into a riding habit, borrowed a horse, and raced to Fairfax Courthouse, General Bonham's headquarters. Dismounting, she ran inside. A young soldier stopped her at the door to the General's office.

"I have an urgent message for the General," she said removing her bonnet.

"Better let me see that message, Miss," The young Lieutenant said importantly.

"Tis for his eyes only, sir. Tell him it's a rose. He will understand." Bettie Duvall looked steadily into the soldier's face. He turned and with an irritated look knocked on the door.

"Enter," the General's voice boomed out.

"I have a young lady says she has a message about a rose sir." The soldier announced with as much dignity as he could muster for such a silly message. To the young man's surprise, the General bounded out of his chair and swept past him into the entryway.

"Come in, m'dear. I have been expecting word." The General took Bettie's arm and led her into his office. "What have you got for me?"

Bettie looked questioningly at the soldier still standing with the door open and his mouth agape with astonishment.

"Close the door, Mister." The soldier quickly scurried out, and the general looked expectantly at the girl before him.

"One moment, sir." She laid her bonnet on his desk and began to uncoil her long hair. A white paper fluttered to the ground. The General overcame his surprise quickly and retrieved the note. He read: *General McDowell will advance to Manassas, July 16.*"

"That's exactly what that soldier's information said," Colonial McLoed murmured, reading the note in Beauregard's headquarters that night. On July 4, a soldier who was also a clerk in the adjutant general's office of General McDowell had been captured by one of the confederate pickets. He had the responsibility of compiling returns of the army, which he had just completed. The papers showed the numbers of soldiers under McDowell as of 1 July.

Beauregard nodded. "Yes, Colonel, and it also exactly mirrors what two other sources have indicated.

"If my tally is correct, Arlington will be at 50,000 strong with all forms of artillery. The most I can be sure of, with small reinforcements from other areas, will be 18,000 men with 29 guns." The General paced back and forth. "Our only hope of an early victory is to overwhelm the enemy. We will need every Confederate we possess, even if that means drawing men away from other conflicts. Colonel, take this message and have it sent at once to the president. I need General Johnston right away."

The light from the tents cast faint yellow droplets down the rolling hills, and then became flat as the land broadened into a dark meadow. Sweat and dirt turning to dried mud caked the little scout with the bad leg. He wriggled over the top of a hill as the moon slid behind a cloud. Even though he knew this was a confederate camp, he cautiously made his way in a running crouch to the picket line. A large gray uniform moved toward him and a bayonet pointed at his heart.

"Halt, you there!" he whispered.

"Esra of the green valley," the scout murmured. The big soldier waited.

"And west is gone." The last of the passwords fell from his lips, and the gray hulk grabbed his arm and began hustling him toward a tent hidden behind earthworks.

General Beauregard looked up as the strange apparition entered his tent. His best scout never failed to surprise him with how disreputable he always looked. *Did the man ever bathe or wear clean clothes*? The fastidious commander recoiled at the idea. *His scout would have plenty of time to bathe after the war*, he thought. Ever the pragmatist, he added to himself, if he lived. Scouts had even shorter life spans than the infantry did in most wars. But Tib was very good.

The General roused from his contemplation and asked, "What do you have for me, Tib?"

"Warrenton Turnpike is where they be gathering, sir." The small figure breathed excitedly.

Sunday morning, July 21, dawned, hot and humid. The rolling green hills with the backdrop of mountains hid an army. For some it would be their last day on earth. In one tent two farm boys pulled on their boots and checked their 58-caliber Mississippi rifles one last time. One looked in a cracked mirror.

"You think lookin in that mirror goin to make some hair grow on yowr face?" The older of the two brothers, Maurice, grinned at the younger boy's discomfort.

"I guess it don't matter how young you arn, you can die jest as easy as olduns," said Robbie, the younger one. He pulled back the tent flap and gazed out at the mountains in the distance. "Never seen mountains like that." he mused. Both soldiers bore the unmistakable uniforms of the Louisiana Tigers. "I hate lookin at them mountains. Makes me feel all smothered like. I shore don't wanta die lookin at them mountains.

"As long as Major Wheat's leadin us weuns got a betteh chance than any Yankee, that's for sure. Bring um on. Let um see what Louisiana's got waitin for um," Maurice said. Both men strode confidently into the early morning mist.

General Irving McDowell had been on the move since three in the morning, and his men had had little or no sleep. As usual McDowell had overindulged the night before and was wracked with stomach pains, but he ignored these as the column trudged forward. *We're five days behind schedule because of supply delays. But it couldn't be helped. They were ready for anything now,* he thought.

Like a drunken caterpillar, the line stopped and started in the darkness and uncertain terrain. Men swore softly under their breath at the rocks and stumps looming up suddenly in the early morning darkness. If they weren't falling over obstacles, their ill-fitting uniforms that were too long caused many to stumble on flat land. Memories of their drillmaster's shouts of "right face," "left wheel," and "right, oblique, march," faded and seemed like words from another life. By dawn they had stripped down to basics: blankets, haversacks, canteens, muskets, and cartridge boxes.

General McDowell set his teeth as his "green" troops tried to march through Centreville on the turnpike road. At daylight, near Cub Run, buggies and all sorts of wagons with ladies accompanying congressmen and the cream of Washington society began tagging along. His column frayed, with men stopping to accept baskets of food from giggling girls out for a Sunday lark to see the "war." Expecting to be home before dusk, they began to set up picnics, distracting the soldiers even more. Everyone imagined how he or she would spend the rest of the summer recounting what it was like to be there when the Union fought back those "dreadful southerners" and put them in their place. Some of the soldiers had eaten all their rations before the fighting started.

The fledging Confederacy faced its first real test that beautiful morning. General Johnston was the ranking officer at this battlefield. But because Beauregard had occupied the area since June and was totally familiar with the terrain, and knowing the seriousness of the situation, the General decided not to assume command, but to assist Beauregard.

General Johnston's army of the Shenandoah had arrived the afternoon of the 20th, bringing 8,340 men with 20 guns. Thus the total forces mustered, including General Holmes and Beaurgard's Army of the Potomac, now stood at 29,188 rank and file with 55 guns. Beaurgard's confidence soared. Even after reports of McDowell's strength of 50,000 troops, the Creole's carefully thought out plans and extensive knowledge of the battlefield made him feel he was on equal footing with McDowell.

By nine o'clock, Generals Johnston and Beauregard had positioned themselves on a hill in the rear of Mitchell's Ford, waiting for the opening of an anticipated attack.

A column of 18,000 Union army troops with 24 pieces of artillery, lead by Burnside's Brigade, crossed Bull Run. The Second Rhode Island regiment with its battery of 6 rifled guns was immediately engaged by Major Wheat's Louisiana Tigers, backed up by Colonel Evans' South Carolinians' two howitzers. The Federals attacking line was soon shattered and driven back into the woods. Major Wheat was severely wounded in the lungs and when told by the doctor there had never been a recovery from his kind of wound he whispered, "There will be now."

Several hours of fierce battles raged back and forth. The noise of the shells and shouts of commanders mingled, and confusion began to be the worst enemy. Smoke made it almost impossible to see the advancing line of Federals. Occasionally a breeze would clear the air and the line could be seen slowly advancing.

General Bee looked up in admiration at General Jackson's brigade and exclaimed, "It looks like a stone wall!"

Smoke was so thick, soldiers strayed into other regiments, the lines in disarray.

General Beauregard sent word that the Regimental colors should be carried out to the front for the men to rally around. This was speedily accomplished, and the men now could see where their commanders were and receive their orders. They began to advance..

One of the howitzers blasted close to the Louisiana Tigers and Maurice was blown back against one of the breastworks. He lay dazed as thumping noises raged around him. At first he thought it was mini-balls, then realized it was big clumps of dirt. The smell of the earth took him out of himself for a moment. He was back home, plowing the fertile, black Louisiana soil. His sister was coming toward him with the water bucket. The good cold water from the well...Maurice came back to himself and looked over the embankment. The noise was deafening and he couldn't see anything but dust and smoke. All at once the soldier saw the union flags. Again the howitzer blasted and he saw the line falter.

Maurice roused himself and looked for Robbie. His younger brother came over the top of the ditch. His eyes were round with fear and excitement.

"We's gotum on the run, we has," Robbie shouted. "Let's finish um off."

Maurice grabbed his rifle and the two brothers charged into the smoke. It was like dropping off into an unknown world. Maurice felt like he was underwater. Everything moved so slowly. Time was suspended and then the thunderous noise returned. The confederate line held. General Jackson's brigade was performing like a "stone wall" again. Beauregard rode over to have a word with the General, and at the same moment the commander's horse was shot out from under him, the bullet taking part of his boot heel. Beauregard would loose four horses that way before the day was finished.

It was noon, and the sun beat down mercilessly on the men in blue cautiously making their way down the road. An eerie quiet settled over the smoldering landscape. Smoke still hung in the hot air. The soldiers came upon a little house on the hill to the left of the road. Later it was told, an aged, bedridden, widow, Mrs. Judith Henry was killed in her bed during the furious fighting before their passing.

Now everything was quiet. Young soldiers began to chant, "We've whupped um, we have, the war is over!" A fence was pulled down at the foot of the hill to let Griffin and Ricketts's batteries through to the Henry plateau. They stopped in an open field next to the road. Men stood wiping their foreheads and setting up their guns. All was peaceful.

Without warning, a massive volley came pouring into the battery. Gray-coated soldiers were everywhere, shouting the Rebel yell! Bleeding Union soldiers fell over their caissons. Horses screamed in pain and terror as they, too, were ripped with musket fire. Wounded horses began to gallop off, trailing blood in the dust. Cannoniers fell with their rammers still in their hands. The battery was annihilated in a flash. Those who could get away ran. Most did not get away. A moment before, a green meadow was spread out at the foot of the hill. Now it was littered with broken cannon, dead men and horses and the sounds of moaning wounded. Their cries mingled with the screams of the still living horses. Smoke hung once more in the air. Orderlies began to tend to the few living wounded Union soldiers.

Robbie lay sprawled under a tree. His brother, Maurice, had seen him fall and dragged him to the shade. His attempts to staunch the blood from the terrible wound in his brother's chest were futile. Finally he just covered him with his jacket. The wounded soldier seemed to rouse up.

"I don't want to die lookin at no mountains," Robbie whispered.

Maurice gently pulled his brother around to the other side of the tree. "Look, Robbie. The mountains are gone," Maurice said.

Robbie looked out of eyes that were glazed. "Yeah, they is. And Moyra has a cool rag…." His words seemed to trail off.

A cold knot of fear settled in Maurice's stomach. Moyra was their sister and she sure wasn't on this battlefield. He looked into Robbie's eyes and knew he was gone. His gaze traveled the length of his brother's prone form. Robbie was a lanky kid. His Zouave pantaloons stopped at mid-knee instead of the traditional calf-length to the leggings. *He must've grown an inch in the last month,* Maurice thought. *He'll never have to worry about outgrowing pants any more.* He reached over and closed his brother's eyes. Maurice bowed his head. He thought about the years that his brother had followed him around the farm place trying to imitate everything he did. Somehow he would have to get word to his sister, Moyra. Their parents had died during the yellow fever epidemic in '58 and Moyra had been like a mama to both boys ever since. He dreaded thinking about writing a letter. Robbie was better at his letters than Maurice. He always let Robbie do any letter writing or reading. Maurice didn't begrudge his younger brother his skill at letters. Maurice was the better hunter. Maurice was good at big things. Robbie was good at little things. Together they were a team. Maurice wiped his eyes.

A wagon, piled high with bodies, rolled to a stop near where he sat.

"We needs to bury as many as we can as soon as we can," the young private driving the wagon said.

Maurice looked up and nodded. "Jest don't bury him face'in no mountains."

General Beauregard came through and saw the Union's Captain Ricketts, who was badly wounded in the leg. He had known him in the old army and asked him if there was anything he could do for him.

"Sir, I just wish to be returned to Washington," Ricketts replied, gasping in pain.

"It shall be done. I'll send my own surgeon over." Beauregard motioned to one of his officers. "Colonel Jordon, please accompany Captain Ricketts and see that everything possible is done for him."

General McDowell tried to salvage what he could. He withdrew two brigades and a reserve along with some regiments that had just come on the scene from Alexandria. Putting these together, he attempted to form a force and have his retreating right flank join up to make a stand at Centreville. The men were now fleeing in panic and only wanted to make their way back up the road they had marched down so confidently before. Ironically the wagons and buggies of politicians and civilians who had come out to enjoy the "show," again impeded them.

Long twisting shadows began to cover the landscape. The unseeing eyes and open mouths that were already beginning to fill with flies were unbearable for daylight to show. Scavenger birds circled overhead, piercing the air with their hideous screeching. An occasional pistol shot rang out as soldiers found still living and injured horses. Finally a soft darkness covered the battlefield with one army rushing away and the other falling into exhausted sleep.

Look down fair moon and bathe this scene,
Pour softly down night's numbus floods on faces ghastly swollen, purple,
On the dead on their backs with arms toss'd wide,
Pour down your unstinted nimbus sacred moon.
Drum-Taps,
Look Down Fair Moon,
Walt Whitman

Message to General P.G. Beauregard:
Manassas, VA., July 21ˢᵗ, 1861
Sir, --Appreciating your services in the battle of Manassas and on several other occasions during the existing war, as affording the highest evidence of your skill as a commander, your gallantry as a soldier, and your zeal as a patriot, you are appointed to be "General" in the army of the Confederate States of American, and, with the consent of the congress, will be duly commissioned accordingly. Yours, etc.,
Jefferson Davis

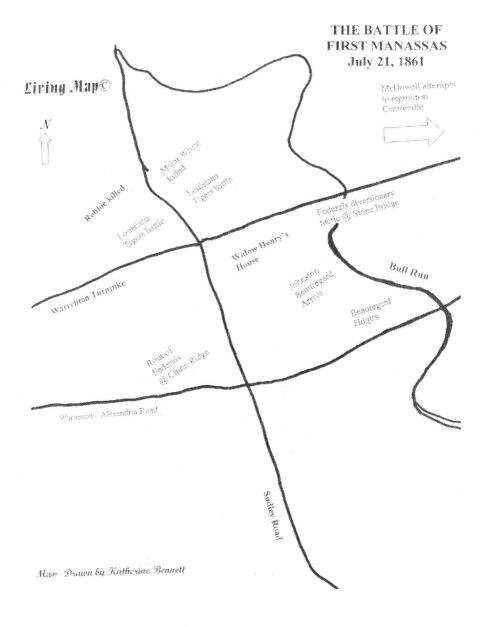

THE BATTLE OF FIRST MANASSAS
July 21, 1861

Liring Map©

N

McDowell attempts to regroup at Centreville

Major Wheat killed

Robbie killed

Louisiana Tigers battle

Louisiana Tigers battle

Federals diversionary tactic @ Stone Bridge

Widow Henry's House

Bull Run

Johnston Beauregard Arrive

Warrenton Turnpike

Beauregard Hdqtrs

Rout of Federals @ Chinn Ridge

Warrenton – Alexandria Road

Sudley Road

Map Drawn by Katherine Bennett

Louisiana Battalion on Manassas Battlefield

Widow Judith Henry's House

Chapter XX

Fall 1861

Long have we lived, joy'd, caress'd together;
Delightful!-now separation-Good-bye my Fancy.
Good-bye My Fancy,
Leaves of Grass
Walt Whitman

Lorraine halted at the edge of the tree line near the part of the plantation named Midway Fort. As the name implied, she was now halfway across the area where sugar cane waved gently in the soft breeze. Her field of vision swept the cane field and came to rest back at the forest, ablaze with October colors. Nickolas, now an aging horse, was content to simply nibble the grass along the tree-shaded edge near the stand. Lorraine dismounted, let her reins fall to the ground, and removed her wide-brimmed hat. The trees beckoned with their shady, strangely calming presence. She still had not accustomed herself to Zack's absence. It had been six months since he rode away in the Confederate Uniform she had so carefully stitched. She could still see him turning at the river road and waving his cap. Raising her hand to her lips she had blown him a kiss. Jacob and Jon Rue had run down to the edge of the house road hoping to catch a last glimpse of their father. Emma stood still grasping Lorraine's hand, while tears trickled down her face.

Lorraine found a mound of leaves and settled down cautiously. She rested her back against a tall skinny pine that allowed her to observe Nickolas. But that was only out of habit. Her old horse would not stray. When he finished eating, he would just sway and nap in the soft autumn sun. Leaning her head back, she carefully moved her fingers over her bodice, holding her breath, hoping she would not feel the knots again. But no, there they were, even larger than the last time she had summoned the courage to check. Lorraine sobbed and in this private place away from maids and children she let the tears and wracking, mournful sounds flow unabated. Finally spent, she wiped her eyes with the clean handkerchief she always tucked under her waistband.

Lorraine remembered the days and nights spent nursing her mother when she had the "knotting sickness." An old woman named Gainya came every day near the end. She spread her soothing poultices over *Mamá's* chest, trying to ease the pain. Lorraine thought back to the day her mother died. It was late winter. The bare tree branches still scraped like skeleton fingers across the windows in the wind. The huge mound on her mother's chest had opened the evening before. Lorraine stayed up all night giving her laudanum and wiping the awful drainage from her chest. Near morning, Janine Delmonde passed away quietly while her daughter was dozing. It was as if her mother passed her hands over Lorraine's forehead, but when she jerked awake it was only a breeze from the window. Or was it? The sun streamed into the bedchamber and Lorraine felt a sense of release for her mother.

The old woman thought all day there was a sad time coming. She fingered her tiny pots of herbs and little jars of measurings. These "sad times" feelings depressed her but also sharpened her already heightened powers of perception. Over the years she had come to accept this as the burden she paid for her gift of healing. She knew from long experience that someone would be coming to consult with her soon. It could be anyone from any part of the Louisiana bayou, rich or poor. Though 1861 was an enlightened time, there were still many things that caused women, especially, to seek out old Ganiya, as she was called, especially private "women things."

Gainya carefully pulled out her big drawer with all the drawings she had done over the years. She was a natural scientist and kept careful records of all her patients' ailments, treatments she had recommended, and the courses of their diseases. She had done so from the beginning. Measurements were her keys to tracking progress or decline. Initially, scales were beyond her means. This turned out to be a blessing as it led to her discovery of her table of measurements for all parts of the human body. She had compiled hundreds of sketches showing normal and abnormal dimensions expressed in terms of diameter. Gainya thought of her initial concern because she could not weigh her patients. Now she would never think of doing such a thing. She considered scales totally unreliable. After all, weight included growths and knots. How many times had she seen apparently hale and hearty people working in the field fall dead on the spot while their skinny counterparts lived to great ages? Measurements, on the other hand, did not lie.

Lost in her thoughts, she had not heard the carriage until it was almost at her door. She watched as a beautiful, dark-haired woman walked up to her house. There was something vaguely familiar about her.

"Entrée, Madam," Gainya said bowing slightly. She waved to a small settee in one corner. "Please to make yourself comfortable."

"Thank you" replied the woman.

Though still lovely, the women was not as young as Gainya originally thought, and again she had the feeling she had seen her before.

"May I presume to offer Madam some coffee?" Gainya held up a demitasse.

"Thank you that would be wonderful. I seem to get so tired in the afternoon," the woman replied softly as she settled herself comfortably.

She took a few sips, then looked directly at Gainya. "I am Lorraine McLoed. My mother was Janine Delmonde of the Delmonde Plantation. You helped her with her illness. I was only just married then. It was during the Mexican War."

"Of course, Madame." The old woman looked sadly at Lorraine. "I remember her. She was very beautiful and very brave. She had the 'knotting' sickness."

"I fear I have the same," Lorraine looked at Gainya with unflinching eyes. "I need to know if it is the same, and how long before it will take me."

Gainya sighed. "I will have to examine you. It is an unusual sickness, not often seen or at least told about." This last was said softly. Gainya had her own opinion about the prevalence of the 'knotting' sickness. She had only seen four cases in her years of treating women. She felt there were probably many that were simply unknown. And it seemed to be an older woman's sickness. So many women died in childbirth. Gainya guessed there would be a lot more of this sickness if women lived longer.

Leading her patient into a small room next to the sitting area, she began to take her crucial measurements. First with clothes on, then without.

"You have lost weight lately, yes?" she queried.

"About 10 pounds in the last few months," Lorraine replied.

Gainya knew this already from the way the women's clothes no longer fit.

"Show me where the knots are and which are new ones," the old healer said as she began the tedious examination of the woman's breasts.

Lorraine was dressed now and quietly sipping another cup of coffee in Gainya's little parlor. Though she had cried softly as Gainya found three small knots and heard the old woman's sharp intake of breath when she saw the large lumpiness in her left breast, Lori was now composed. She watched as Gainya finished her meticulous notations on her sketch and consulted her myriad charts filled with tiny numbers.

Gainya hesitated, "I cannot say for sure. I need to see you again in two weeks. I can give you a more sure time."

"But what do you think now?" the woman asked calmly.

"You have lost 1 inch in your clothes. That is much." Gainya knew the McLoed's were wealthy, and Madam would not be wearing clothes that did not fit perfectly. She continued. "The big knot has been there a while and does not move. It will not be long. Maybe two or three months. I am so sorry, Madam." Gainya's head hung low.

There was silence in the room. Then the rustling of skirts as her visitor stood.

"I will be back in two weeks. This is for your time and skill. Pray for me." Lorraine pressed bills into the old woman's hand and was gone.

The carriage pulled up in front of River Rose and the mistress of the house disembarked and walked slowly up the wide front steps. Lorraine turned and looked out at the trees now turning red and gold and the bright blue of the autumn sky. Why did the sky always look so vivid in the fall, she wondered? Was it the contrast of the brightly colored trees? Or the last splash before the cold dreariness of winter? She turned and entered the house. It seemed cold. Lorraine realized she had been cold all day.

"Martha, please have Jonnie lay a fire in the parlor. I am chilled to the bone," she said as she saw Martha coming down the stairs.

Martha looked surprised. The weather had been unseasonably warm for the last few days. But she noticed a slight shiver go over Miz Mac's slender form and hurried away to call the parlor boy. Coming back to check on her mistress, she wondered why she had not noticed how thin Miz Mac had become. As Martha entered the parlor, Lorraine drew her chair close to the fire. Martha had gotten one of Lorraine's shawls from the bedroom and now gently put it around her mistress' shoulders.

"Oh, thank you, Martha," Lorraine said. "You always know exactly what I need."

"Does you want yoah suppah brought in here?" Martha asked.

"Is it time for supper already?" Lorraine didn't wait for Martha's answer. "I will just have tea and a biscuit," she said. "I'm not hungry. Just a little refreshment is all I want right now. Maybe something else later."

Lorraine wrapped the shawl tighter around her shoulders and gazed into the fire that was now beginning to catch from the kindling. She watched the first tentative flames and then basked in the warmth as the fire grew bigger and brighter. Like my life, she thought. Marrying Zack was the beginning of a great fire and the warmth of his love had carried through their whole time together. In a few months, just like this roaring fire, everything would be just embers and then ashes. She shook her head to rid herself of these morbid imaginings. But unlike the fire, Zack and her children would carry on with parts of her always with them.

Rising, she started toward the stairs, leaving her tea untouched.

"I must write Mr. Zack a letter," she said to Martha. "Please warm up my tea and maybe Auralee could heat some soup to go with it." She walked toward the staircase and then slowly fell in a faint. Martha caught her before she hit the floor.

Two days later

Jon Rue knew his mama was sick. She hadn't ridden Nickolas in three days and now she lay propped up in bed.

She smiled at him and motioned for him to come sit on the big bed. Lorraine thought about how many times he had come running into the room to share one of his great adventures or come to have her soothe a hurt when he was small. He was a big boy now, thirteen, and taller than Jake.

Jon Rue heard his mama's words but somehow couldn't take them in. It seemed like she said she was going to die. How could that be? He was proud of his mama; she was so pretty and young looking. How could she be going to die? He started shaking his head, screaming, "No! No! No!"

Jon Rue ran from the room and down the stairs into the morning sunlight. He kept running until his breath was gone. The levee loomed ahead. The boy lay down on the levee path, panting, and looked at the river swirling and tossing sticks and debris from upriver. A great stone was pressing on his chest or was it his heart. He wondered if his heart was breaking. How could you live without your mama?

October 1961—Confederate soldiers somewhere…

Rain fell in great whooshes, like a waterfall, filling all the holes and crevices in the ground and ditches. The horses slogged onward, water sliding off their bodies in a constant flow, so that after a while they became mesmerized with the constant splat, splat and walked in a dream like state. The soldiers didn't even have to use their quirts. Riders and horses moved as one, with just the slosh and splat drumming in their ears.

Zack checked his pouch to make sure the letter was still dry and wondered how he would tell Jake about his mother. Jon Rue was still at home. Lori said she had told him and explained to him that he would be joining his father when it was over.

When it was over! The words were seared in his brain. How could he go on without Lori? Maybe the old healer was wrong, maybe…. He pulled himself up mentally. He knew it was true. But how to tell Jake?

They bivouacked at the base of a hill. Zack and Jake sat in their tent listening to the relentless pouring rain. Zack had said the words but Jake didn't seem to understand. He sat and looked at his father blankly.

Finally he dropped his head and said thickly, "But mama is not an old lady. How can she die? It isn't right."

Zack sat down next to his son and put his arm around him. He had not done that since Jake was a small boy. But Lori was always hugging her older boy. When he protested she would laugh and hug him more. Who would hug him now?

"I know it isn't right. Her mama had the same sickness when she was your mother's age." Zack said.

Once again it was quiet, just the sound of the rain hitting the tent and splashing away onto the ground.

Then great sobs tore through Jake's body and Zack put his head down on his son's shoulder and let his own tears flow.

Springfield, Ohio—October 1861…

Emma looked at her cousin's tear stained face as she put down the letter. "Is it bad news, Mary?" She asked.

Mary was Lori's second cousin on her mother's side. When war came to Louisiana she had offered to take Emma for a few months until everything settled down. She was stunned at the news from River Rose. In the few months Emma had been with her family she found herself wishing Emma could stay forever. Emma lit up their house and lives with her young energy and enthusiasm. Mary and her husband had no children and almost thought of Emma as their own daughter. Now it looked like she would be with them for at least a year or more. The war couldn't last much longer than that. But how to tell Emma that she would never see her mama again? With the blockade, travel to Louisiana was impossible.

"Yes, Emma, it is bad news. It's bad news from River Rose."

Emma settled herself down on the settee by her cousin and waited anxiously.

"It's your mama, Emma. She is very sick. And we can't get you home because of the war."

Emma watched Mary's face closely.

"How sick is Mama?" Emma asked.

"She is sick like her mother was many years ago. Before you were born. Your mama will not get well, Emma." Mary put her arms around the small girl.

Emma's fists were tightly curled in her lap.

"I will never see Mama again?" Emma's voice was low and tight.

"No, Emma, you will see her in heaven." Mary tried her best to soften the blow.

"That's what Mama said about Buttermilk. But I have a big hole where he used to fit. And it stays empty. Heaven is a long time to be empty, Cousin Mary."

December 1861…

Martha's head drooped and then she jerked awake. The breathing sounds of her Mistress had changed. She watched as the slight figure in the huge bed hardly moved the covers. But there was still breath there. The blanket moved up and down. Was there a longer time in between the up and down? If only Mastah Mac could make it before death claimed Miz Mac! Martha stood and walked to the window, then walked back to the bed. How many times in the last few hours had she made the journey? Each time she returned to the bed she was terrified that the covers would have ceased their gentle movement. Martha wiped away the fluid that soaked through everything she and Belray had used to try and staunch the dreadful flood. How could one small body contain so much poison? That's what Martha thought was eating away at Miz Mac. Somehow some poison had invaded her mistress's chest and was taking over her body. Martha tried to remember Dr. Bercoise's words describing the awful thing in Miz Mac's chest. He had written it down for her to show Mastah Mac. She looked at the piece of paper the doctor had left on the little table by Miz Mac's bed. "…growth, causing a fungating, weeping wound." Martha was not sure what it said or even what it meant. Maybe it was the name of the poison. She sat down next to the bed to continue her vigil. Would it ever be over?

Zack knew he was driving his horse to the limit. He had been riding for two days, only stopping a few hours for rest and to feed and water his horse, then pushing on. The big roan stumbled and righted himself and plowed doggedly forward. The horse seemed to know there was no stopping now. Ahead, Zack saw the turn-off to the river road and urged his horse on. He finally drew up in front of River Rose and breathed a sigh of relief. There was no wreath of mourning on the door! He had made it!

Jumping down from his horse he thundered up the stairs and into the master bedchamber. Martha moved away from the bed and eased out of the room. This was the time for privacy between lovers.

Zack's heart broke as he saw how slight the form was under the coverlet.

"Lori, can you hear me, darling?" He pushed damp curls back from her face. Her eyes fluttered open and she smiled weakly.

"My Zack. You are here at last." Lori's voice was soft and weary.

Zack lay down and cradled her in his arms.

"You won't leave me again will you?" she pleaded softly.

"No, my darling I will never leave you again," Zack whispered.

Christmas 1861

"...I WILL COMMENCE THIS HOLY DAY by writing to you. My heart is filled with gratitude to Almighty God for His unspeakable mercies with which He has blessed us in this day, for those He has granted us from the beginning of life, and particularly for those He has vouchsafed us during the past year. What should have become of us without His crowning help and protection? Oh, if our people would only recognize it and cease from vain self-boasting and adulation, how strong would be my belief in final success and happiness to our country! But what a cruel thing is war, to separate and destroy families and friends, and mar the purest joys and happiness God has granted us in this world; to fill our hearts with hatred instead of love for our neighbors, and to devastate the fair face of this beautiful world! I pray that, on this day when only peace and good-will are preached to mankind, better thoughts may fill the hearts of our enemies and turn them to peace."

General Robert E. Lee

Chapter XXI

"A Place of Peace"
Shiloh, Tennessee
The "Sunken Road" or "Hornet's Nest"

From the stump of the arm, the amputated hand,
I undo the clotted lint, remove the slough, wash off the matter and blood,
Back on his pillow the soldier bends with curv'd neck
and side-falling head,
His eyes are closed, his face is
page, he dares not look on the bloody stump,
And has not yet look'd on it.
Walt Whitman

Early evening—April 6, 1862

The "sunken road" was quiet now. Smoke still hung in a haze over the small dirt path where so many now lay dead. This small insignificant place would forever be called "the hornet's nest." Rain began at dusk, a cold springtime rain that clung determinedly to winter's memory. Whenever it touched the men's skin it felt like tiny prickles of glass and would rouse them for a moment from their exhausted stupor. They would nod off again wherever they happened to have fallen. Images hammered at their exhausted brains. Friends' faces floated by and were gone to be replaced by other images; all of death, fire, smoke, and blood until an unconscious blackness mercifully claimed them. A few crawled into captured enemy tents that now lay abandoned with openings flapping in the wind. Another group stumbled and fell onward to a small pond. Their thirst was overwhelming. If they could just put their head in the cool water. As they fell forward into the icy coldness, some were shocked awake and pulled themselves up and after a few gulps lay back on the ground gasping. But some never raised their heads. Several of the men had been bleeding for hours and the last of their strength was spent. Their heads dropped lower and lower and lay still. Their comrades would not realize they were drowning until it was too late. By daylight the small body of water not far from the 'hornet's nest' would have acquired a gruesome nickname, 'the bloody pond', because of the many men who drank their last from its seductive waters.

Colonel Zack Jacob McLoed of the 10th Louisiana had followed one of his young privates to the pond and pulled him out when he seemed to be submerged too long. The soldier came up sputtering and coughing. Zack hauled him back to one of the tents and bundled him in a blanket left behind by the former occupant. Though he was no longer gasping for air, the sputtering was now accompanied by convulsive sobs that racked his skinny frame.

Zack removed his flask and forced the fiery liquid down the man's throat. He guessed the age of the soldier as 17 or younger.

"Private, you almost drowned back there, but you'll be okay now as soon as you get warm," Zack said trying to calm him.

"But sir. I'm so skeered and I know now I'm nutin' but a coward," he stuttered slightly. He began to regain control of his voice and with one last shuddering gulp was still.

"What makes you say such a thing, son?" Zack asked. The Colonel had noticed that the man's sleeves were much too short for his long arms with their bony wrists and big hands. His jacket was too light for the cold weather and was almost threadbare. *Probably had joined up to escape poverty and had not the faintest notion of what fighting was all about*, he thought.

"I know it be a fact sir, cause I tole you I was" he corrected himself, "am, so skeered. Them cannons are still booming through my head. I shot a man today. Killed a man…" his voice trailed off and he put both hands over his eyes.

"Private you are not a coward. I know that for a fact!" Zack's voice boomed out and startled the prone figure. He was still for a moment and then sat up.

"Why do you say that sir? How can that be?"

"Because I have proof." Zack knelt down in front of the man's cot. "I can prove that you are not a coward!" Zack looked steadily into the young face streaked with dirt and tears. "What is your name private and where are you from?"

"I'm Private Jeb Henshaw, sir." He added, "From Marksville, Louisiana." The eyes had lost some of their despair. "Tell me how you have proof, sir."

"You are still here, aren't you?"

"Yesire I surely am," Private Henshaw responded softly.

"Well then that proves it. If you were a coward you would be ten miles up the road heading back home like some of the other deserters, now wouldn't you?" Zack challenged.

"Beg'in your pardon, sir, that don't prove nothin'. I couldn't go back till I paid my debt."

"What debt is that Private," Zack's eyebrows raised in a puzzled look.

"The boots, sir." The soldier brought his legs back over the cot and put his feet on the ground, feet shod in army boots that were now caked with mud. "These are the first real shoes I ever had. I owe the army for three more months. That's what my enlist is for. I reckon I can't leave no matter how skeered I get till I pay for these boots."

Zack sat down next to Private Henshaw on the rickety cot.

"Let me tell you what bravery is. Cowardice is being scared and running. Brave is being scared and staying. Not being scared out here is plain stupid. You, young man, are not stupid. So you must be brave."

The Colonel stood and looked down at the soldier.

"Now I order you to get some sleep. I will have need of you in the morning," he turned then and left the tent, closing the flap against the cold wind.

Private Jeb Henshaw pulled his blanket around him and stared up at the pointed top of the tent until it became blurry and sleep overcame him.

A faint light shown in the small window of Shiloh Church next to Sherman's abandoned tent, where Brigadier General P.G.T. Beauregard had his headquarters. Plans were being discussed and discarded, with talk always coming back to the tragedy of General Johnston's death that day from a leg wound. Despite this blow to morale, the Confederacy had prevailed this day and not only beaten back but also captured General Prentiss and 2,100 of his men.

Colonel McLoed entered the cabin and saluted the officers surrounding his commander's table. The kerosene light flickered and cast shadows up the sloping walls of the tent and emphasized the tired lines and hollows in the officer's faces.

McLoed wondered at the stamina of Beauregard who he knew never slept at times like these. He still looked alert, but for the first time he noticed streaks of white in the jet-black hair.

"What say you, Colonel?" Beauregard gestured to one of the straight back chairs that normally held the little church's worshipers.

And now we come to worship the God of war, thought McLoed.

Zack, wet from exposure and sore from being in the saddle for almost 24 hours, gratefully eased into the chair

"We've at last rounded up all the Union prisoners and confiscated all armaments. Our wounded have been moved to as much shelter as can be afforded by the Union tents."

"What are our estimated casualties?" Beaurgard asked.

Zack reported the horrific numbers then paused, "Twenty were lost at the pond."

"What do you mean? What pond?" the Creole General demanded.

"The men call it 'bloody pond'. Some of the men that were wounded dragged themselves over to drink and couldn't summon the strength to pull themselves up after they drank. I've posted guards to keep anyone else away."

There was silence in the room. Officers held their dreadful thoughts to themselves. As bloody as today had been, tomorrow held even more opportunity for lives lost. Especially with rumors of the massive reinforcements making their way up the Tennessee River under the command of General Carlos Buell.

"Have you had any word from the 'Watcher'?" Beauregard used the code name for McLoed's young son who was also one of his main couriers.

"No, but he would come here straight away in any case, sir," McLoed assured his commander.

Colonel McLoed finished his report to the officers and left the cabin as sleet began to cover the camp. He entered his own cold, confiscated Union tent, and sat down heavily on his cot. Pulling off his boots he sat staring off in the darkness not bothering to light the lamp. After a while the chilly night began to seep into his clothes and even through his heavy long johns. Stretching out on the flimsy bed he pulled up the blanket and lay thinking about Jon Rue and what could have delayed him. Since Lorraine died, he had come to realize unthinkable things could happen even to a McLoed. But Jon Rue was cagey. He would make it through. He had to believe that. His other children peopled his thoughts. Jake was here in this very camp. Emma was safe up north with relatives, but he missed her terribly. It had been over six months since he had watched her small figure climbing the steps to the train, looking back with tears streaming down her face. "It will only be a few months," he had promised her.

River Rose filled Zack's mind. It was a sunny day and Lorraine came riding up on Nicholas, scattering dust, and laughing at his admonition to slow down. She jumped from the big black horse and ran to him as he waited on the wide verandah.

"*Mon Cheri*, but you worry too much," she said kissing his cheek.

Suddenly he jerked awake as a terrific gust of wind caught the loose flap on the front of the tent, and a blast of frigid air poured in. Zack fastened the tent more securely and settled back on the cot, colder than ever.

Night before:

Twenty miles up river, the "Watcher" stood in the shadows of a huge water oak and watched the last of the passengers climb aboard the steamer. He moved toward the group, stooped in his old man's clothes and unkempt beard. Blending in the shadows of the moonless night, he moved with the group onto the boat. No one noticed anything or anyone as the chilly rain increased, and the wind picked up. He settled into a corner of the seat in the darkest part of the main cabin, now lit by pale kerosene lanterns swaying with the movement of the river. Pretending to doze, he listened to the quiet murmuring of the people around him. The information he had was correct regarding the movement of Buell's Army of the Ohio. Now he had to manage to get to Shiloh in time to report it.

Before dawn, the steamer slid alongside the dock at Pittsburgh Landing, and the group of passengers began streaming off into the misty countryside. The 'Watcher' was careful to seem to associate himself with a small contingent that headed toward one of the waiting carriages. His shadowy form disengaged just before the group reached their destination and was swallowed up by the darkness.

The "Watcher" sensed the presence just before the rifle butt came down on his head. Another man, who inhabited the same twilight world as the "Watcher" was also disguised as a civilian. "Slipper" as he was called had decided this "old man" could not be allowed to continue on his way. He would have quietly killed him, but he could not be totally sure he was not what he seemed. "Watcher" was very good and had only made one mistake. "Slipper" had nudged him as they entered the steamer, and unconsciously the "old man" briefly glanced up and allowed his young eyes to meet his. It was hard to disguise young eyes. But still…he could not be sure. He finished tying the "old man" to the tree. Whatever words this courier needed to repeat to a confederate general would not be heard anytime soon. The 'old man' would never leave this tree unless he had help. Whether he lived or died would now be up to fate. 'Slipper' soundlessly vanished into the woods to continue his own work.

When the "Watcher" came to, both his hands and feet were tied to the tree, and dawn was breaking. The rest of the day he heard cannons and guns raging only a few yards away from his forest prison. Though he scraped the ropes until his hands and wrists were bleeding, he could not get free. Whoever had harnessed him had done a thorough job of it. By the time a Confederate soldier found him the day's battle was already engaged. He was freed just in time to join Beauregard on the retreat to Corinth, after the mammoth reinforcements of 50,000 troops under General Buell overwhelmed the smaller Confederate force.

Because of the heat and massive death toll, Union Soldiers buried 750 Confederate Soldiers in a large pit the next day. Union soldiers that could be identified were buried in private graves, but hundreds more were buried in a mass grave as well.

Jon Rue never knew who kept him from alerting Beauregard to the menace, but the resulting carnage, over 3,400 men dead and over 20,000 missing or wounded would rank as the largest loss of life in any battle fought in America to that date.

May 10, 1862

Union ships sailed up the Mississippi River and fired a broadside into Will Pinkney's regiment, the 8th Louisiana Infantry Battalion. Confederates set their gunboats afire and floated them down to meet them wrapped in flame, twenty thousand bales of cotton blazing in a single pile, molasses and sugar spread over everything.

June 18, 1862

Governor Thomas Overton Moore of Louisiana issued the following order: "Let every citizen be an armed sentinel. Let all our river-banks swarm with armed patriots to teach the hated invader that the rifle will be his only welcome on his errands of plunder and destruction."

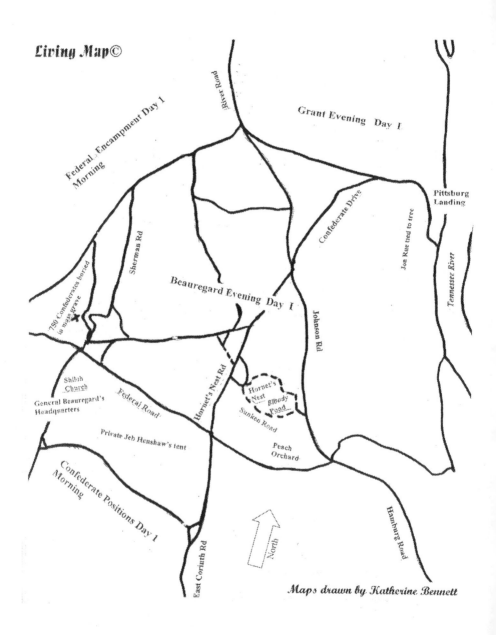

Living Map©

Living Map©

River Road

Grant Evening Day 1

Federal Encampment Day 1
Morning

Pittsburg
Landing

Sherman Rd

Confederate Drive

Jon Rae tied to tree

Tennessee River

Beauregard Evening Day 1

Johnson Rd

750 Confederates buried
in mass grave

Shiloh
Church

General Beauregard's
Headquarters

Federal Road

Hornet's Nest Rd

Hornet's
Nest

Bloody
Pond

Sunken Road

Private Jeb Henshaw's tent

Peach
Orchard

Confederate Positions Day 1
Morning

Hamburg Road

East Corinth Rd

North

Maps drawn by Katherine Bennett

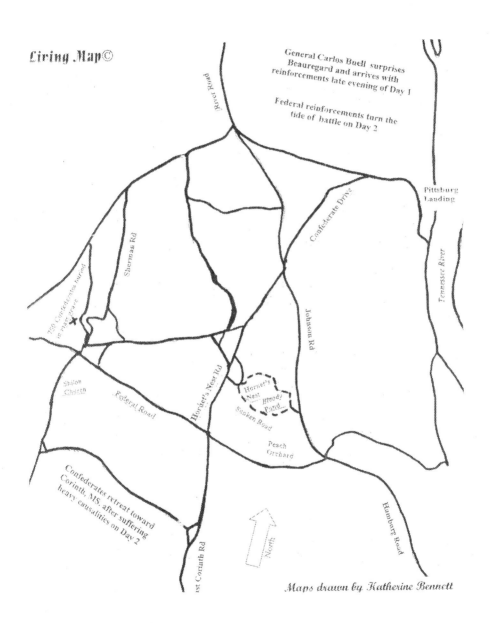

Living Map©

General Carlos Buell surprises Beauregard and arrives with reinforcements late evening of Day 1

Federal reinforcements turn the tide of battle on Day 2

River Road

Pittsburg Landing

Confederate Drive

Sherman Rd

Tennessee River

750 Confederates buried in mass grave

✗

Johnson Rd

Shiloh Church

Hornet's Nest Rd

Federal Road

Hornet's Nest

Bloody Pond

Sunken Road

Peach Orchard

Confederates retreat toward Corinth, MS. after suffering heavy causalities on Day 2

North

1st Corinth Rd

Hamburg Road

Maps drawn by Katherine Bennett

147

Shiloh Log Church—General Beauregard's Headquarters

Mass Grave of 750 Confederate Soldiers

Chapter XXII

May 14, 1864

Fellow citizens, we cannot escape history. We...will be remembered in spite of ourselves. No personal significance or insignificance can spare one or another of us. The fiery trial through which we pass will light us down, in honor or dishonor, to the latest generation.

Abraham Lincoln

River Rose Plantation—20 miles south of Alexandria

The tall woman moved slowly among the lines of sick and wounded men lying in the long double parlor of the plantation house. The furniture and carpets and their accruements had been moved to other areas of the house and out buildings. Twenty makeshift pallets had turned the River Rose plantation house into a gray army hospital.

Since the house sat back from the river amidst a thick grove of trees and hanging mosses, Zack's nephew Seth and now Zack's sister, Maureen, and the remaining black plantation workers had been able to disguise their existence. Rains had washed out the roads leading to and around the plantation, and unless you knew exactly where the house was you would not notice it. Since River Rose was not a cotton-producing plantation, it was not marked on any of the Union maps for stealing this most valuable commodity. A rumor was circulated that yellow fever was raging in the area, and this also helped to discourage any curiosity seeker. The surreptitious dwellers in this house never used lamps at night and thus far had avoided detection.

Maureen Jamison wearily eased herself into one of the few pieces of furniture left in the big room. A rocker that used to reside in the nursery felt wonderful to her aching back. Seeing the suffering that surrounded her day after day was as wearing as the actual work in nursing the men.

It was now dusk, and her meager supply of laudanum had been doled out to the most horribly wounded. The room was quiet for a while, but she knew the quiet would not last.

Leaning her head back, she prayed silently for her brother Zack and her nephews Jake and Jon Rue. War had taken them far away from the local fighting, to fight with Beaurgard in the "big" battles. A tear found its way down one cheek as she thought of the "big" battles everyone here in Louisiana fought daily. Half dozing, Maureen remembered the Alexandria battle and how she came to be here in this secret place of suffering and death. It began over two years ago.

Lorraine had managed to send her daughter Emma to friends in the north when war seemed inevitable. Though the young girl protested, both her mother and Maureen had assured her it would only be a few months. Lorraine had died shortly after she waved goodbye to Emma from the train platform.

Maureen, her stepson Seth and her elderly Aunt Sosie, had joined Zack in Louisiana when Maureen's husband Jeb, was killed at Shiloh. Jeb was quite a bit older than Maureen. He was forty-seven when he died in one of the bloodiest battles of the war. Jeb's first wife, Seth's mother, had died of yellow fever when he was twelve. Jeb and Maureen had married three years later. Seth had taken over the day-to-day running of River Rose when Zack left to fight with Beauregard. Maureen had settled in Alexandria, feeling safer in town than in an out-of-the-way plantation house down river.

In January 1864, Maureen moved to River Rose to help nurse wounded soldiers that sought shelter there. The secluded plantation house soon became a secret field hospital.

Maureen's aunt was too feeble to move and stayed in Alexandria with Maylee, a sick room helper that Maureen retained. As often as she could, Maureen made the trip to Alexandria to check on her aunt. She managed to get to Alexandria just before General Bank's troops arrived. Maureen closed the windows in the small house and did everything she could to make it look deserted. It was not on the main street and she hoped the soldiers would pass on through and they would be safe.

The One Hundred Thirteenth New York Regiment "faithfully and efficiently" guarded Alexandria for two days and nights. Then policing the town was turned over to the cavalry. They were to prevent any hint of fire, which would give notice to the Confederate Army that they were abandoning the area. The departure began early on the morning of May 13th, with the 16th and 17th Corps under General A. J. Smith bringing up the rear. Despite General Bank's orders, that's when the burning and plundering began.

On May 13, under a gloomy sky, all thought of safety vanished as soldiers came down the narrow streets of the small town with kerosene-soaked torches, buckets of camphrene, and mops. Maureen could still hear the slap, slap on the sides of the houses. She walked to her window and at first could not understand what they were doing as they hit the sides of structures.

Then she smelled smoke and realized they were setting the buildings on fire!

"Maylee! Help me get Aunt Sosie down!" Maureen screamed for her maid. Aunt Sosie, who had been suffering from the hectic, was in the upstairs bedroom. It was all she and Maylee could do just to clamber down the stairs with the elderly woman.

When they reached the street, two neighbor children came to help as they desperately ran and fell and stumbled toward the river. It was a hellish scene in the street. The smell of fire and camphrene and burning animals was a tangible thing that she could feel as she groped through smoke. The fiery air pressed down by the damp overhanging clouds, made breathing agony. And the noise! Wood crackled and exploded. Houses fell in on themselves and made great whooshing noises. Worst of all were the screams of terror from the horses still trapped in carriage houses. One of the horses had kicked out of its fiery prison and was now fleeing wildly down the street, mane, and tail blazing. Chickens and animals hit by fireballs from houses and burning trees ran past in a rising frenzy of pain and fear, their pitiful yowls and screeches a crescendo of noise that was deafening.

The old men who now made up the fire brigade had made a valiant effort with their buckets but had only succeeded in making the brick streets slippery with water. They abandoned all efforts when Union soldiers shot both of the fire house horses and threatened to do the same to them unless they went into the river with the other townsfolk.

Maureen almost tripped over a dog that had been trampled by the horseman. As she rounded the corner onto Front Street, she stopped at a sound that rose above the melee. In the old stable yard she was sure she heard screams. Leaving her aunt with Maylee and the two children, she slipped into the small shed, one of the few structures not ablaze. A soldier was tearing the blouse from a young girl. Maureen suddenly recalled Zack's voice as he demonstrated to her how to use the small pistol he insisted she purchase when her husband died several years ago.

"You may never have to use it, but it is peace of mind for me to know you can. However, no matter how well I teach you, the only thing that is important is what's in your mind. Make up your mind now that if the situation calls for it, to save your life or protect another, that you will use it. No wavering."

Maureen had thought about this for several weeks and then bought the gun he recommended. A few days later, when visiting River Rose for a few days, he had taught her how to use the gun. She discovered she was an excellent shot. In fact, he commented, she was a much better shot then any of the men in the family. Her little gun was sewn to fit in her reticule so that all she had to do was raise and fire.

"Leave her alone!" She now screamed at the lunging soldier.

The man turned briefly and, laughing, said, " Well come on in darling. We can have a party!"

"No! Stop now!" Maureen took a step toward the struggling pair.

"Well now, let's jest see what you're like with that pretty red hair," he said as he roughly grabbed her arm.

Maureen could smell his hot, rancid breath and see in his eyes no mercy for man or beast. She raised her small purse and fired. A small neat hole appeared over his heart. A surprised look came over his face before he fell back into the hay that was now beginning to smolder. Maureen ran to the hysterical girl and wrapped her own shawl around the girl's shoulders. She threw a covering of hay over the soldier's body. Making sure some of the burning embers were included under the top layer would guarantee that all evidence of this man's cruel life would soon be over. She helped the quietly sobbing girl to the street and rejoined her aunt and Maylee struggling toward the river.

Now shaking, Maureen had no time to reflect on the killing. She heard a high-pitched, keening sound as she and her little retinue came closer to the river. The women, children, and elderly were raising their cries in one loud skyward chorus of despair. They stood in the muddy river; some with hair singed and burned clothes hanging in rags from their swaying figures. Waving their arms ceaselessly in a dreadful dance of horror that was like a hypnotic vision, Maureen felt for a moment she was in a trance. The whole world seemed to be an inferno. Cold water jerked her back to reality. The exposure was dangerous for her old aunt, but they had to wet themselves in the river water to keep the flames at bay. Finally a space opened up near the bank, and Maureen and Maylee were able to drag her aunt's poor spent body up on land.

Maureen turned in time to see the marauding fire starters descend on the only building left standing. St. Francis Xavier Catholic Church would be the last to go as it was nearest the river. She watched in dread as the group of mounted demons approached the small structure. With a sharp intake of breath she saw the skinny, black-clad figure of the priest come out of the front door with a large rifle in his hand. Father John Belie had been in the French Army before becoming a priest and knew how to handle a gun.

The group of men stopped.

"The first one that torches this church will be shot, and you will have to shoot me to get to it." The priest uttered the threatening words in a calm but strong voice belying his small stature.

An odd silence fell on the group. General Smith looked at the priest, and the priest returned his gaze. A steady look, a resigned type of fear, but there was no doubt he meant what he said.

The General edged his horse closer to the church. It wasn't a very grand church; just a small building made of piney wood. It would be gone in a minute. Flames danced closer, and the priest and his church were silhouetted in red. *This is what hell looks like*, Smith thought. Sweat poured from the priest's face, the heat now palpable. The renegade General admired courage no matter where he found it.

"I guess I won't kill any priests today," Smith muttered. His men looked at him in astonishment. Smith said nothing, just turned, and led his men out of town.

The people in the river who heard the exchange and saw the men ride away said little prayers of thanksgiving, since they knew about the priest's big gun. For one thing, it didn't work. It hung in a rack over his desk, and it was his favorite joke that he had it "just in case the devil comes calling." Father also had no bullets for his gun. All munitions had been donated to their soldiers. The devil had "come calling" today, and the gun had done its work.

Maureen's old aunt roused up, as the noise from the people in the river seemed to reverberate through the stifling air.

"I'm so thirsty," she moaned in her quivery old lady voice.

A young girl with a water bag edged up to Maureen.

"We have some water left, mam. Just please leave us some. I have a little brother," she spoke softly. Maureen looked at her benefactor. Her face was black with soot, except for the tearstains. She had what used to be blonde braids, now gray and singed on the ends. The little brother clutched his sister's burned skirts, his eyes round with fear in his small-blackened face.

"Thank you. She just needs a little." Maureen turned back to her aunt. Her heart broke at that moment she saw that Aunt Sosie would not need water ever again.

"She done gone to the Lawd, Miss Maury," Maylee said and began to cry.

"...did not see any necessity for firing the town. I knew there were a good many Union people there and I gave instructions to General C. C. Grover to provide a guard for its protection,..which he did."
**General Banks testimony before the
Joint Committee on the conduct of the war**

Just as twilight was descending over these terrible scenes, some bluecoats, lagging behind, found a small boy wandering in the street. The group of soldiers surrounded the little boy who had become separated from his mother in the mad dash to the river.

"Well, what have we got here, a pint-sized Rebel devil?" One of the men yelled.

The boy looked up at the men who now formed a circle, jeering at him.

"This boy needs to give the pledge to the union or we'll just hang his worthless neck. Well, boy? What's it goin' to be?" A burly sergeant jerked the boy up and wound a rope around his neck.

"Let's hear you shout it out like you really mean it!"

"No!" the boy said stoutly.

The men were startled. The sergeant pulled on the rope and dragged the boy to a nearby tree. He threw the rope over a limb and began to hoist the child. Choking and struggling the boy flailed in terror. The sergeant pulled out a knife and cut the boy down. He lay gasping on the ground.

"Let's hear the pledge now!" The sergeant yelled. Tears streamed down the boy's face, and he wiped them away with a chubby fist.

"No!" He croaked. The group of men stirred uneasily. They had not planned on hanging children when they joined up.

"Damn you! You will take the pledge!" The sergeant's face was red with anger. He would not let a child humiliate him in front of his men. Pulling the boy up, he wound the rest of the rope around his neck and began to hoist him again. The boy's fingers grasped frantically at the rope biting into his flesh, his little legs wildly thrusting. Suddenly he sagged and was still.

"Well, Sarge, I guess you done kilt him," one of the soldiers said reaching out and cutting the rope. The child's body hit the ground and dust flew up and then everything was still. Just a small sprawling corpse, face up in the dirt. The horses kicked up more dirt as they trotted by. The boy's purplish face and bulging eyes were the only testament to the evil done that day.

Daylight brought little relief to the ragged inhabitants of Alexandria. A smoky haze blotted out the sun and created an eerie gray landscape. To a people used to vividly sub-tropical colors even in winter, this simply confirmed in their minds and souls the hopelessness of their situation.

Maureen managed to find one of the few wagons left intact and with her last money secured a place for herself and Maylee heading south. They would get off before they reached River Rose and walk the rest of the way so as not to give away its location. Father John, the stalwart little priest, promised he would see to a proper burial for her aunt.

The wagon bumped along the rutted road. Even calling it a road was an exaggeration. No repair work had been done since the war started. Rain and constant use from the armies and wagons had rendered the pitiful path almost impassable. If it began to rain the wagon would have to move to higher ground or risk becoming mired until everything dried out. Five other people shared the wagon, all in various stages of shock. Their faces were blackened by smoke, and they all coughed constantly, their lungs still burning.

After only a few miles, the wagon rounded a curve and came upon a woman and two children by the side of the road. Back in the trees were the smoldering remains of a shack. Several slaughtered chickens lay in small, bloody piles around the now crumbling steps. A pig lay sliced open under a scrub tree. Turkey vultures were already circling. A butchered mule was stuffed feet down in a now shattered well box. Black horseflies were already descending in clouds over the carcasses.

"Could we please git a ride, wherever yalls goin?" begged the woman. "We is burned out. No clothes or food, nuthin left," the woman gulped back tears. She was probably no more than thirty years old but already had the tired, 'war lines' around her eyes. Her threadbare dress was faded from too much washing, and her sandals were coming apart. A tiny girl, no more than four, looked at them with pleading dark eyes. Her little dress was too short even as small as she was. She was barefoot. But a boy of about ten seemed to be apart from these two. He sat on a stump with a dog in his lap. The dog was a non-descript yellow creature with only part of its head left. Blood had dried on the boy's hands and patched overalls.

"This here's my boy. Them Yankees done kilt his dog. Said they had orders to kill bloodhounds. Them kind that tracks niggers. We told 'em, he ain't no bloodhound. He just a cur, and my boy cried and begged, but they shot him anyways. The lead man said if he couldn't kill no priests he could sure kill a dog."

Maureen got down off the wagon and went to the motionless figure sitting with his pitiful burden.

"What's your name, boy?" she asked softly.

Some of the blankness went out of his eyes as he looked at her and said, "Percy, mam. My dog's name is Goldie cause of his color. He's a good'n. Best dog ever."

"How about riding with us for a spell, Percy, and when we get where we're going, we'll see about what to do with Goldie." Maureen started to help the boy to his feet. Moving slowly like a sleepwalker, he followed her to the wagon and clambered aboard still clutching, 'the best dog ever'.

By dusk, they reached River Rose. They had walked from the road through a roundabout trail dragging a cloth for the last two miles, to ensure no one would follow them. Maureen and her little maid were exhausted, and the woman and her children were scarcely able to stand. The children's feet were bloody, and all of them were desperately thirsty. Maureen had only brought a small pouch of water, which was soon consumed by the extra travelers. The small boy had continued to drag the now dirty carcass of his dog despite his obvious tiredness. As they reached the back of River Rose's kitchen outbuilding, Maureen motioned to one of the hands to come to her side. She whispered something and the man took Percy's hand and led him away to a small grove of trees where all the River Rose pets were buried. She left them talking quietly as they moved among the little markers showing each pet's name. Tomorrow she would make sure he acquired a new puppy.

"Louisiana, from Natchitoches to the Gulf, is a howling wilderness and her people are starving."
General Kirby Smith, Confederate Commander

The Burning of Alexandria, Louisiana

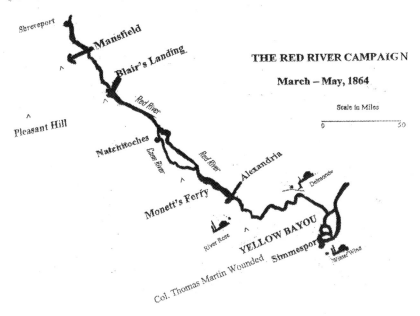

Living Map ©

Shreveport

Mansfield

Blair's Landing

Pleasant Hill

Red River

THE RED RIVER CAMPAIGN

March – May, 1864

Scale in Miles

0   50

Natchitoches

Cane River

Red River

Alexandria

Delmonde

Monett's Ferry

River Rose

YELLOW BAYOU

Col. Thomas Martin Wounded   Simmesport

Winter Wind

SUGARHOUSES

BATTLE ^

Maps drawn by Katherine Bennett

Chapter XXIII

May 14, 1864
Delmonde Plantation

An early spring rain had begun to fall, making a soft pattering sound on the blanket of leaves where the two women huddled. It was chilly, as the feeble rays of the early spring sun slowly began to fade. Smoke filled the air, and an occasional crackling noise let the women know the impossible had happened. Delmonde plantation was almost gone. The big house would soon be a sodden pile of ashes.

One of the women, a former slave, removed her own shawl and wrapped it around the small, shivering blonde woman who sat beside her. Esta knew Miss Clarisa was shaking more from fear than cold. She wondered if this frail woman would survive this latest ordeal. Miss Clarisa's husband had been killed at Shiloh, and as she had no other relatives, she had lived at Delmonde ever since. Her cousin, Miss Lorraine, had died several years ago, and she was the only Delmonde left.

Esta stared at the smoldering ruins. Were those forms twisting and rising up from the ashes ghosts of all the Delmondes and slaves who had lived and worked within the walls, or were they just shadows of the coming darkness? Was the mist playing tricks on her old eyes?

A Union soldier came walking toward the woods, and Esta came back to reality in time to pull Clarisa back into the little hiding place they had made for themselves.

"I don't see 'em anywhere!" the soldier yelled. "They must have got clean away." With a perfunctory glance at the stand of woods, he returned to the group of soldiers surveying their handiwork.

The women let out a sigh. Then Esta turned to Clarisa.

"Miss Clarisa, we needs to start walk'in to River Rose. It'll be dauk soon. Dat da safis time to try and get thru."

Clarisa looked at Esta in the vague way she had and nodded. "How far is it, Esta?"

"Miss Clarisa I don know foh shu. I tink it take us about one or two days cause we has to walk at night."

The impossibility of walking two days with no food or water did not seem to register with Clarisa.

She nodded and rose shakily to her feet. "May I lean on your arm, Esta?" she asked.

The two women started to walk through the tangle of forest. They had to step over limbs and watch carefully not to twist their ankles in the many holes, dug by forest animals that were covered with leaves. Esta knew they had to walk under cover of the forest as long as the Federals were in the area. Almost at once, their flimsy slippers were wet. After a while, Esta discarded hers and rolled up her skirt, as it was sodden too. Clairsa lost one of her shoes right away but didn't seem to notice. Esta stopped and helped her roll up her skirts and secure them to her waistband.

"Oh, Esta! I've lost one of my shoes," Clarisa said in alarm.

Esta looked at Clarisa's poor white feet and legs. Scratches and bug whelps were already covering the tender skin.

"Miss Clarisa, it don't matter. Just trow de udur one away."

Clarisa obediently discarded her remaining shoe as tears came to her eyes. "We're in a lot of trouble, aren't we, Esta?"

Esta took the small woman's arm, and as they trudged off, said, "Yes, Miss, we is. A lot of trouble."

Morning sunlight was watery, and the sky looked like it couldn't make up its mind whether to rain or clear. The two exhausted women sank down beneath a large water oak. Esta and Clarisa tore strips from their petticoats and bandaged their bloody feet. They lay back against the tree and fell instantly asleep.

Late afternoon shadows were creeping along the ground when Esta jerked awake. She couldn't tell where she was at first. Then she remembered. Delmonde had been burned to the ground, and she and Miss Clarisa were walking to River Rose. Esta was thirsty. Her lips were cracked, and her throat was dry. She ran her tongue along the cracked ridges of her mouth. Grabbing a few wet leaves from the side of a puddle of water, she pressed them to her lips and sighed. Esta was careful not to swallow any of the water because some people thought you could get typhoid fever from bad water. She looked at the sleeping form beside her. Poor thing. It was just as well that Miss Clarisa didn't fully realize the hopelessness of their situation. Clarisa was sleeping peacefully, her arms and hands lying loosely in her lap. *What will become of her?* Esta wondered. The old woman had looked after Clarisa all her life, from the time she was a baby. Esta was getting old. *Who will look after her after I'm gone?*

Esta looked out of the copse at a narrow trail. An old black man was coming toward them on an ancient mule. *That was why the mule is still here,* she thought. The mule was so old he swayed when he walked. Any mules that were any good at all had been taken by the Federals. Esta stood up and left the shelter of the trees.

"Hey old man," she called softly. She didn't know who might be around.

The stooped figure looked up and waved. He slowly made his way toward her.

"Whachu doin out hea in dees woods?" he asked.

"Da Federals don bun us out and wes tryin to make it to River Rose." Esta's voice was raspy from her dry throat.

"Y'all gots a long way to go." The old man came closer and saw the sleeping white woman. "Who else is witcha?" the old man asked.

"It's a lady what lived at Delmon. She not strong and huh nuves is bad."

"My name is Mota. I try to hep if I can. Maybe she could ride a spell on ole Judas." He patted the mule. "Da Federals peah to uv' done cleaed out dees pahts."

Esta looked doubtfully at the ancient mule.

"We can try," she said. Turning, she began to rouse Clarisa.

"I has some watah and cohn cake." The old man pulled out a water pouch and some corn cakes from a pack hanging from the mule. "Not much, but I spec you is hongry."

"Mainly we needs watah," Esta said hoarsely.

Clarisa was now sitting up, and Esta put the water pouch to her lips. She drank greedily. Esta then took her turn and swallowed. The water was sour from the old pouch but it slaked her thirst.

Esta and Mota managed to get Clarisa on the mule and the strange little procession wound its way through the woods and along one of the paths that old Mota knew about. By daylight the next day they had reached Bayou Chatis.

A young black man stepped out of the woods in their path. "Esta, what in the world are you doing over here?" Benny noticed the small form slumped over the mule's back. "It's Miss Clairsa isn't it?" Benny asked.

"We don got burned out and tryin' to git to Riva Rose. We don gots nowhere else to go," Esta said. She was limping badly by now. Blood had soaked through the bandage strips, and she moaned at every step. "Dis man, Mota, came along and is hepin' us."

"Your feet are bad. Wait here. I'll go get a horse. Miss Clairsa, come on with me," he said pulling on Judas' halter. "Mota, you stay with Esta. I'll be back as quick as I can."

By late evening Esta and Clarisa were each on a cot in the mansion turned field hospital. Their feet were bandaged, and they were given water and Auralee's stout vegetable soup. Maureen had given them some laudanum, and both women soon drifted off to sleep. Esta awoke toward daybreak, soaked in sweat. All night her dreams were filled with the ghostly forms rising from the ashes of Delmonde. Clarisa slept soundly but roused up when Esta sat up in bed.

"Esta, why are you sleeping in the room with me? Have I been sick?" Clarisa said looking around the small upstairs room. "This doesn't even look like my room! What has happened, Esta?"

Esta looked sadly at Clarisa.

"Miss Clarisa, Delmon got burned, and we is at Rivah Rose. Member, dos soldiers burnt us out?"

"Well that can't be right Esta. Come, help me get dressed and we'll see about this."

Esta realized Clarisa had no memory of what had happened the last few days. It was probably a blessing. She watched as Clarisa looked at her bandaged feet that were now seeping blood. Clarisa began to scream.

Chapter XXIV

The Battle of Yellow Bayou
Simmesport, Louisiana

Twice or Thrice had I loved thee,
Before I knew thy face or name.
Air and Angels, st. 1
John Donne

Afternoon—May 18, 1864

Colonel Thomas Martin shifted in the saddle as William Parson's 12th Texas Cavalry prepared to confront the Federals immerging from the thicket onto the open field. The several ditches in front of this wide-open space would allow the infantry to support them if needed. The Federals continued to move forward about 200 yards then availed themselves of one of the ditches to reform behind the barrier. Confederate artillery pounded the positions and then subsided. General Wharton ordered Parsons to attack. They surged forward, and the Union forces began to fall back. Colonel Martin knew Parsons expected a huge casualty count and had argued against this particular battle in this area. Now, watching the retreat of the enemy he was loath to sacrifice any more men. General Wharton's harsh words, relayed to Parson rang in his ears: "Tell Parsons to charge the enemy at once, or I will prefer charges for disobeying orders."

"If I must, I must," Parsons muttered, gave the order, and led the army as the Rebels charged forward into a hail of enemy bullets and cannon fire. Union forces continued to fall back. Colonel Martin urged his men forward until he felt a hot burning in his side and arm and was suddenly lifted out of the saddle by another blast. Clinging to his horse's saddle horn, he lost the bridle but his horse kept charging. Heat came over him in waves and he seemed to be choking. Then he knew no more.

A week earlier…

Thomas hated to face his mama this morning,

She would look at him with reproach in her eyes. "Why do you have only three days? Margaret's boy has a week's leave." She would turn and gaze out the window, her back stiff with emotion, whether sorrow or anger he could never be sure.

"I'm an officer mama, and there aren't too many of us left." No, he couldn't say that. She already knew the casualty count.

"This war's almost over. All the young men are dead, and most of the old ones are wounded. You've given enough. Stay and look after granny and me." Jane Martin had said the same thing every day since he had been home. Yesterday his granny had motioned to him after this exchange and led him out on the porch.

Musidora Martin was his granny on his daddy's side and as different from his mama as night and day. She was 90 years old with snow-white hair and the bluest eyes he had ever seen. They weren't old eyes either. This was what disconcerted people meeting her for the first time. Musidora looks "all the way through a person" was the way his mama put it. Thomas loved to look in her eyes. They were clear and you almost felt like you were falling…somewhere. He supposed she had seen everything there was to see. Yet she was still eager to see something new.

"Sit down here beside me Thomas." Musidora settled herself in the wooden swing. "Don't mind Jane. She's just being your mama."

"We don't have many men left, granny. Most are just boys. Our seasoned soldiers are 16 and 17. My Captain is only 17 and he's brevetted. All of his training has been on the battlefield in the line of fire. I'm considered an old man at 24."

"I know, son." His grandmother looked at the sun slowly sinking behind the stand of trees by the barn. You could never tell what she was feeling. The lines in her face were etched so deeply, fleeting expressions had no chance to make an impression. "You will come back, I know that."

"How do you know that, granny?" Thomas stood and walked the length of the porch, stopping near the water bucket. "That's what you always say. My men are dying all around me every day, and I keep hearing your voice saying, 'Thomas will come back'." He drank his fill from the dipper. The cool water soothed his feverish mind as well as his throat.

"Calm yourself, Thomas. I just know these things. Go kiss your mama and tell her you will be back soon. And you will. I promise." Musidora looked at her grandson and smiled. "Everything will be different soon. You'll see."

"How soon, Granny? How long can we hold out?" Thomas lowered his head and tried not to think of all the young men whose blood drenched the Louisiana soil.

"Not much longer, Thomas. Not much longer."

Present...

Two of Martin's men carried their Colonel back to one of the thickets. His horse had been shot out from under him before anyone realized he was wounded.

As darkness came, both sides fell back, and Martin's men were able to get him to one of the tents where they had water and some medical supplies.

"I thought you said I would come back, Granny," said Thomas as he came to consciousness and looked at the man bending over him. Then he slipped away into a dark quietness.

"We have to git him better help than this. Some real doctorin' somewhere," the youngest soldier said.

"Old Jeff knows his way aroun this area purty well. I'll go ask him." The sergeant made his way around the piles of sleeping men to a small form huddled next to an old log.

"Jeff. It's me, Sergeant Pike. I need your help."

The elderly black man raised his grizzled head and patted the ground beside him. "Have a seat, Sergeant. I'll shore hep if I can."

The big soldier settled himself on the ground and ran his hands over his eyes. He was bone tired. No, soul tired. The kind of tiredness that would take a year of sun and his wife's lovin' to relieve. If he ever saw his wife again...

"You know Colonel Martin is bad."

"Yessir, I knows dat." Jeff said. Jeff admired Colonel Martin. He had rescued Jeff and his family from a fire several years' back. When the war broke out and the Colonel's Regiment came through his town, Jeff had volunteered to join him as a cook.

"We can't tend him good enough. He needs doctorin' bad. I know you know this here land pretty well. Is there any place we can git hep?"

"Does you have a map I can look at?"

"Sure. It's jest a scrap, but it's a cohrec scrap." Pike removed a ragged paper from under his shirt. "Let's go back to the tent. I have a lantern we can use."

Pike smoothed out the crumpled paper and set a rock on one end and the lantern on the other end. The two soldiers watched as Jeff's gnarled fingers traced an indistinct line across the page. "Dey is a secret place. No one knows about it. Duh McLoed plantation. It's a hospital now. Has a lady dere. She nurses good. I don know about no doctor."

"How far away?" Pike asked.

"Two days. Maybe more. It's some bad sinky land to covah. Snakes everweah. I has to show you. It's no road lef now. Das why dey been safe."

Sergeant Pike, Private Orin Blake, and old Jeff set out as soon as they had foodstuffs packed. They traveled slowly carrying Colonel Martin between them. Creeping through the swamp at night was treacherous, but they knew time was short for the Colonel. They had tied rags around his leg, but the blood seeped through and insects clustered around the makeshift bandage. At first the men tried to swat them away, but soon realized they had to save their strength for the ordeal ahead. Though it was evening, it seemed as hot as midday. The swampy air was heavy and made it hard to breathe. Pike finally called a halt to rest just before morning. Jeff took out his tobacco pouch and handed it around.

"Da tobaccy'll help keep da bugs away. When it gits in yoh skin dey don't like it."

Private Blake was fair-skinned and so covered with insect bites his eyes were almost swollen shut.

"Any thang to keep them bugs off, thas what I want." He grabbed a chaw and put it in is cheek.

"Put some wet mud on yoh face. That'll help dem bites," offered Jeff.

All three men began to smear the sticky wet dirt on their faces so that just their eyes were uncovered.

Pike looked over at the Colonel. Blood was pooling around his leg.

"Come on. Let's get started again."

The onslaught of insects abated after the sun came out, but the heat, even in the swampy shade was intense.

Each man took turns tearing up their shirts to make tourniquets for the Colonel.

"I nevah knew a man had that much blood in 'em." Private Blake was rewrapping Colonel Martin's leg where they had stopped to drink and rest.

"Son, you'll find out a man's got a lot'blood in 'em fore this war is ovah." Sergeant Pike said. He was trying to estimate how much longer it would take to get to River Rose. At least another day he thought. Jeff seemed to read his mind.

"We'll git there tomorrow evein' I spect."

"I hope he lasts that long." Sergeant Pike said softly.

166

The next evening these same three men stumbled up to River Rose Plantation. Colonel Martin was delirious and weak from loss of blood. His men sadly gave him over to the woman who seemed to be in charge. The Rebels and old Jeff rejoined the 12th Texas just above Mansura, Louisiana. Neither man expected to ever see their Colonel again.

Maureen thought the Colonel wouldn't make it through the first night. He called to his mama and granny over and over, promising them he would come back. Toward daybreak he was very low, sunk in a stupor. She thought the end was near. Leaning over to change a bandage she heard a man's boots coming toward her. Maureen turned in alarm and then breathed a thankful sigh.

"Benny, can it really be you?"

Jake's 'best friend in the whole world' grinned down at her. "Yes it's really me. Dr Moreau and I thought you might need a little help doctoring."

"Oh, Dr. Moreau. This poor soldier is so bad. It may be too late. He's very weak."

Dr. Belier Moreau looked down at the soldier in the blood soaked gray uniform. "I have my best helper with me." He nodded to Benny. "Let's see what we can do for him. "

Thomas Martin heard noises, muffled and smelled the scent of flowers. A dark shape loomed over him, and then there was some redness and gentle fingers on his face. He tried to open his eyes, but everything swam in a filmy haze. Then the pain came, for an instant so searing he knew nothing.

"He's fainted; that's good. By tonight I should have morphine. I'll have to finish surgery then. I've managed to stop the bleeding for now." The doctor pulled a paper from his bag. "Have Auralee make up this mixture for me. It's a blood builder. You must somehow get it down him every three hours for the next few days."

The sun was well up and Dr. Moreau and Benjamin McLoed had ridden all night. Dr. Moreau knew there were others waiting for him, but he needed food. "Do you think Auralee has anything in her kitchen for a starving Doctor?" he asked Maureen as he pulled the covers over a now sleeping Colonel Martin.

It was raining. He heard the splat of rain on the window. Then the smell of Jasmine or something like Jasmine. Something kept pressing his mouth until he opened and swallowed a bitter tasting liquid. There was a rhythm. First the flower smell, then the pressing and swallowing. Sometime he could hear the murmur of voices. At other times he heard groans. Once it sounded like someone yelled. Now everything was quiet. There was a breeze and it was hot. He could hear cicadas and knew it must be dusk. A rustling startled him and he opened his eyes. At first everything was blurry and dark. He blinked his eyes and someone leaned over him. The flower smell and the red…she had red hair.

"Colonel Martin, can you hear me?" The woman said.

"Ye, yes." He struggled to clear his throat.

"I'm Maureen Jamison. You are in a plantation house that's a field hospital. How do you feel?" The woman moved to help him sit up slightly, supported by pillows.

"Very sore and…" he panted a moment. "Painful to move." He could feel sweat soaking his clothes.

"Let me give you some of this. We do want you to sit up as long as you can to clear your chest." She gave him some liquid in a spoon. It was not the bitter taste he remembered, but rather sweet.

"How…?" His throat betrayed him again and he coughed uncontrollably.

"That's good Colonel. Cough as much as you can." A tall young black man now loomed over his cot. "I'm Benjamin McLoed. Dr. Moreau and I have fought a tough battle the last few days."

Seeing the surprise on his face, the doctor smiled.

"I know you never expected to see a black man in a suit, much less working with a doctor. I was raised here. Mr. Zack McLoed took my father in years ago. He gave us all our freedom and sent me to school in New Orleans. I come back here to help out whenever I can get away. I am in preceptorhip training with Dr. Moreau. Someday I hope to be a doctor. Mr. Zack's son Jake McLoed and I were raised together."

"Jake is a Captain in my regiment. He came over last year from General Beauregard's command." Thomas was breathing heavily now. Talking had exhausted him.

"Just lie back and rest a while."

"But I have questions…" Thomas said.

"Maureen will sit with you a while. Just rest. She can answer your questions." The doctor moved on down the line of cots.

"How long have I been here. What day is it?" he asked.

"It's Wednesday. You've been here three days." Maureen settled down beside his cot. She squeezed out a rag in a basin and wiped his face. It was cool and soothing. The medicine began to ease his pain. As long as he did not breathe too deeply he was comfortable. He realized he no longer wore his uniform.

"What about my clothes?" Thomas asked.

"Your clothes were ruined. They were soaked in blood, and we had to cut them off so Doctor Moreau could operate."

"Operate, what kind of operation?" The panic in his eyes reflected a soldier's greatest fear.

"No limbs are gone," she reassured him. "Doctor Moreau removed a bullet from your side and one from your thigh. Apparently another one grazed your arm. You bled so much the wounds were all clean. Our biggest worry has been to keep you from bleeding to death and now to get your strength back. Rest now. I'll be back soon. I think you may want me to get word to your family so they know you are alive and where you are." She moved away to another figure down the long row of cots.

Maureen was surprised to see Colonel Martin sitting up the next morning. His head hung low, and as she moved closer she could see he was in pain.

"Let me give you some easement medicine." She poured some of the liquid into a spoon and carefully lifted it to the suffering man's mouth. "Why didn't you call me sooner?"

"I'm trying to see how long I can go without the medicine. It makes me sleepy, and I need to get back to my men."

Maureen eased Thomas back down on the bed as the medicine began to work.

"Colonel, you don't need to worry about getting back to your men."

She gently wiped his haggard face. As he fell asleep the lines in his face seemed to fade away and for the first time she saw how young he was. Probably about her age she thought. In some ways Thomas reminded her of her dead husband. But more alive and eager to stand up to life. She stood and looked down at him. I could love this man she thought.

Maureen had not bothered explaining why he didn't need to worry about getting back to his men. She would have to tell him soon enough that the war in Louisiana was over. The last remaining bands of Confederate soldiers in the area had been killed, captured, wounded, gone back home or scattered to Texas, where a few hold-outs still swore to battle on.

Chapter XXV

Colonel Martin opened his eyes and tried to think where he was. He tried to remember what day it was. For some reason he was disoriented and couldn't place himself in time or place. It was evening of some day. The shadows were long, and night noises came in through the long windows on either side of his cot. He could hear vague murmuring and an occasional raspy cough. Then he smelled a memory. The smell got closer, and she sat down on the edge of his cot.

"How are you feeling?" The red-haired woman asked.

"Better. I'm not sure where I am or how I got here. What happened to me?"

"Your men brought you here five days ago. You were badly wounded and had lost a lot of blood. If Doctor Moreau and Benny hadn't shown up, I don't think you would have made it." Maureen looked closely at the man's face. He seemed coherent and looked good considering what he had been through. Colonel Martin moved to a less painful position in the bed.

"I know your nursing must have had a lot to do with it," he said. "I remember glimpses of you during the last few days. It seemed like you were here day and night. You smell so good, like flowers." He began to cough then and grimaced.

"Let's prop you up, if you can stand it." She helped him up on the pillow.

He looked at her, really looked at her for the first time.

"What is your name?" he asked.

"Maureen Jamison. My brother Zack McLoed owns this house and plantation, or what's left of it."

"Jacob McLoed is my Captain. At least he was when I left. Have you heard anything about my men?" Colonel Martin looked at her anxiously.

"Jacob is on his way home. No one is sure where my other nephew is right now. He's a courier." She stood and walked wearily to the window and looked out at the gathering dusk. "I haven't heard from Zack. He usually stays pretty close to General Beauregard and I know he's been sick. If the General can't go on, Zack may be coming home, too." She came and sat back down on the cot. "Most of the fighting is over around here. Any that aren't wounded or captured have either gone home or back to Texas."

Colonel Martin put his head back and closed his eyes. He thought of all the young men who had died and bled and lost limbs and for what? The land around him was a wasteland. There had been hardly any food for his men. There must be terrible food shortages in the civilian population.

"I have to see if I can get up." He tried to struggle to his feet. A terrible weakness overcame him and he slumped back down.

"It will be a while, Colonel. Lie back and just rest."

"My name is Thomas. Just Thomas now." He closed his eyes and slept.

The sun was hot and it felt good to perspire from exertion after so many days of pain sweating. *Not that I've exerted myself much*, Thomas thought wryly. He had offered to help Seth mend some harnesses and though he had to stop every few minutes to rest, he had finished the most damaged one. Holding it out for Seth's inspection, he grinned as the young man admired his handiwork.

"I would have thought that harness was worn out. But it looks like new, except for the worn places." Seth fingered the fine leather stitching and said, "You must have a lot of experience with farming."

Thomas nodded. "Until the war, that's all I did. We have a farm and run a few cattle on a spread just outside of Woodville, north of Beaumont. My mother and granny have been struggling to keep it together, but they have only two hands left and they're old fellows. I need to get back as soon as I can travel."

"Come on in you two, and get some lunch." Maureen called to the men.

Lunch was fried chicken, turnips, and corn bread. Potatoes would not be ready for a few more weeks. The cornmeal was running low, but they did have enough flour to last a while. After they finished, Thomas helped clear up and take the dishes out to the kitchen.

"Thank you, Mistah Mahtin. You shoh is good help," said Auralee. The old cook could work only part of the day because, as she said, "dese old feets and legs has stood too long wit too much weight." Auralee was close to eighty and had fed two generations of McLoeds. A younger version of Auralee named Ceil took over the main cooking duties after the noon meal. Supper was usually leftovers with dessert.

"It's not much, but I have to keep moving around as much as I can to try and get my strength back," said Thomas.

"We need to change some of the beds. I could use some help with that, Thomas." Maureen said.

Thomas followed her into the large room that was now a field hospital.

"That's something useful I learned in the army. I can make up a cot." Thomas proceeded expertly, though slowly, to strip a cot and remake it with tightly tucked clean sheets. He sat down to catch his breath for a moment and then limped over to the next cot.

Maureen watched as Thomas dutifully made up each cot. She wished there was something she could do to ease his pain. Not just the pain in his leg but the pain in his soul. She knew he agonized over the loss of so many of the young soldiers under his command. Now that the war was over, the land and property destroyed, survivors seemed adrift. Maureen thought it was almost as if they all moved in slow motion, in a gray mist. The only time Maureen felt alive was when she was with Thomas. Had she fallen in love with the handsome colonel?

Thomas looked up from the cot he was finishing and grinned. "I know I'm slow as molasses, but I eventually get the job done." He said.

"You're getting faster every day. I don't know what I would do without you." Maureen smiled.

There were fifteen soldiers left in the hospital. Some would be able to leave on their own soon, and a few were waiting for their families to come take them home.

A waif-like creature seemed to hover just outside the room, and Thomas noticed she occasionally could be seen drifting down the halls or wandering the outside galleries. Maureen introduced him one morning.

"Thomas, this is Clarisa, the daughter of Zack's wife's sister. Clarisa, this is Thomas, one of our patients who's still recovering."

"Good morning, mam." Thomas nodded his head.

Clarisa just looked at him and said nothing. After a moment, she smiled slightly and walked away in a strange floating motion that made you think she had not been there at all.

"Clarisa has not adjusted to her husband being killed and the plantation house burning. She seems to be still in shock," Maureen explained.

"It takes some people a long time to get over war. Some never do." Thomas watched Clarisa's ethereal progress until she disappeared around a corner.

After a couple of weeks, Thomas was able to help in the garden, which was the main source of food for the assorted people who had arrived at River Rose seeking shelter.

A young mother and her two children, a boy and a girl, worked every day on the place. The mother tended the garden, and the two children helped to feed the chickens, the one hog still remaining, and two old mules.

Seth worked with the fifty hands that had chosen to stay at River Rose after the Emancipation Proclamation. Patrick had freed the children of his slaves three years before and all of his slaves were to be freed on January 1, 1864. The date the proclamation came into effect, he promised his former slaves that they could stay in the same houses as before and of course utilize their gardens. He agreed to pay them as contract labor as long as he was able to sell sugar cane. That ability had stopped when the Federals seized control of the river. Seth was hoping that now he could get sugar to New Orleans for payment in U. S. Dollars from the plantation's factor. The factor had a contact at The Old Bank of New Orleans and could move produce for U. S currency. Seth could pay back at least a part of what was owed the help and have enough left for desperately needed supplies. Though Seth was crippled, he had done a yeoman's job keeping River Rose intact.

Each afternoon, as the remaining patients slept, Maureen and Thomas would walk along Bayou Catis and talk about what was going to happen when everyone returned and whether things would ever be normal again.

It was late on one such afternoon when Maureen and Thomas decided to tackle a long line of blackberry bushes that crawled along the bayou. The berries looked just about right for picking, and the promise of their succulent sweetness beckoned them in the soft gathering twilight. They picked enough to fill the basket Maureen had used for their lunch and were just turning back to go home, when Maureen slipped on a patch of damp grass. Thomas tried to catch her but missed, and she twisted her ankle.

"Oh!" She gasped in pain.

"Darling, are you all right?" The term of endearment slipped out unconsciously as Thomas knelt down to help her.

Maureen began to cry, and Thomas was terrified! He couldn't imagine this strong woman weeping. She must be terribly hurt to be crying. He struggled with his bad leg to pick her up, scattering the basket of blackberries everywhere. Finally managing to get to his feet he began to limp as fast as he could toward the house.

"We'll get you help right away!" He assured her. Then he stopped as he looked down into her face. Maureen was smiling up at him through her tears.

Thomas slowed his panicked rush to the house and looked at her in amazement.

"Oh, Thomas. My ankle does hurt, but I'm crying because I'm so happy!"

"What do you mean?"

"You called me darling." She said this so softly he had to stop and put his head down to hear. Then he found himself kissing her. He laid her gently on the ground and held her close while he told her how he had loved her from the first moment he saw her and felt her gentle hands on his face.

The world slipped away and the rest of the evening was spent in a sweet recounting to each other of how and when they felt the first twinges of love.

Maureen's ankle was sprained, but with rest and the doting attention of Thomas, it was quickly as good as new.

Thomas kept hearing about the battles still being fought in Texas and worried that somehow the war would spill over onto his part of the state. Word from his mama told of an outbreak of yellow fever in Galveston and that most of the war skirmishes were taking place at or near Brownsville. She had heard from riders coming through that the Federals seemed to be occupied with the Gulf of Galveston and the Brazos Santiago. Everyone who showed up at River Rose was sure the Red River Campaign, as it was being called, was the last gasp for Louisiana and the section of Texas bordering the Sabine River. He still felt the urgent need to get home. He wondered what Maureen would think of his place. It was a little run down since he had been gone and was by no means as grand as River Rose was and might be again. But it was good land and Texas would need cattle to rebuild from the war.

Two months later...

Maureen looked at the empty cots and thought of all the young men she had nursed. Her beloved Thomas was the only soldier left in what had been a room full of wounded men. At times there had even been pallets on the floor. Thomas was sitting on his cot reading a letter. He had received several letters from his family in the past few weeks. Thomas was the only man she had loved since her husband had died. The first time she had seen his face, something in her heart had turned over, even before she had heard him speak. In the past two months she had come to know his courage and character and gentle ways and loved him even more. They had had long conversations about what would happen now that it seemed certain General Lee would eventually surrender. Maureen knew he was devoted to his family back in Texas and already could feel that same devotion lavished on her in the brief time they had been in love.

He looked up and rose to greet her. The smile on his face let her know he had received good news.

"Maureen! My family is coming for me next week! They're bringing a wagon. I can make it in a wagon." Thomas was jubilant.

"Yes. You can make it in a wagon. I'll make sure you have a good mattress, so the bumps won't be too bad. I'll take good care of you."

"I can't wait to have you meet my family. They will love you Maureen. I just hope you won't be too disappointed in our place. It's not very fancy. But with you by my side, I'll make it into something good."

Maureen just looked at him and smiled. He put his arm around her.

"Oh, Thomas. What your house looks like doesn't matter. What matters is what you look like, inside and out."

Thomas held Maureen close and said, "You are so beautiful, inside and out, in every way. Especially your red hair. You always smell so good, like flowers."

Maureen and Thomas planned to get married at his home. Thomas had written his mother and she had said their itinerant preacher would be arriving in a couple of weeks.

For the rest of his life, Thomas would always say there was one great thing about the war, Maureen.

Chapter XXVI

1864

I sit beside my lonely fire
and pray for wisdom yet
For calmness to remember
Or courage to forget
Charles Hamilton Aïd

The watcher quietly slithered up a slight rise and slowly raised his head just so he could see over the tall grass. The picket he saw appeared to be asleep but he couldn't take a chance. The butt of his rifle came down hard on the soldier's head, toppling him over. The shadowy figure still had a day's travel ahead of him to get his pouch to Beauregard at Petersburg.

Slipping undetected around the bivouac at the bottom of the hill, the watcher made good progress on his journey. He traveled without stopping for the rest of the day. He planned to stop at a cave he knew and rest at dusk. Just as he was approaching the hiding place he stopped. Out of the corner of his eye he detected a slight movement that caught his attention. He dropped to the ground. The vernal soil felt warm to his face.

He watched a dark figure as it skillfully maneuvered across the pony truss bridge over the small stream.

The creature crouched low and actually seemed to slip between the wood beams, moving silkily along the side beam of the bridge, so that unless you had noticed him before you would have thought he was part of the structure. This was something or someone who knew about being hunted. He was a small stooped figure but did not appear to be old.

The watcher recognized the signs of mistreatment rather than age.

As the creature crawled down to the muddy land the moon sent a sliver of light over his head giving a brief glimpse of a brown face. A runaway slave. He was coming toward him and could not help but see him. But now he posed a problem to the watcher. Kill or be killed: This was the credo of the watcher.

Something about the figure made him hesitate. Curiosity overcame caution: He could always kill him later. He moved back into the cover of a low hanging tree.

He saw the strange figure slip into what looked like a cove of bushes. It was the entrance to a cave that was invisible to anyone who did not know where it was. He soundlessly followed the man into the cave. The man turned when he sensed the watcher looming over him. The watcher put up his hand and said. "You have nothing to fear from me."

Bowing his head the man nodded his understanding. He still had not spoken a word. No sound, even when he was startled to see a stranger in his hiding place. The watcher knew the kind of discipline it took to stay absolutely quiet. He motioned to the fugitive to sit.

The two men settled into the cave and pulled the thicket cover over the opening. They knew from experience there was no longer evidence of a cave entrance. The interior of the cave was pitch dark, but they lived in darkness as much as light, so this was not a problem. The watcher preferred it this way, as he could tell more about the small man without light.

"I is John Bone," the runaway said softly.

"I am no man," said the watcher. He used the special wadding in his mouth, so his accent could not be detected.

"We is da same den. I is no man in dis land," John Bone replied.

"Why're you running away? It's a hanging offence if you're caught." The watcher shifted his position to lean back more comfortably against the rocks. "How did you know about the cave?"

"I run away befo, but dey always ketched me." John Bone settled in cautiously as he began to think he might trust this strange man.

"Dey wants me bac caus of the exp'ments."

"Experiments?" queried the watcher.

"My masta lended me to a docta foh his exp'ments. Dey bout tru now. Maybe dey leav me alon."

"More than likely they'll hang you this time." The watcher's eyes had grown accustomed to the dark, and he could faintly see the man's battered and broken face. One of his eyes was not right. It protruded and was off center. "What did they do to your eye?"

"Dat wern't no exp'ment. I was kicked by dah oveasea. He say I not move quick. It took a long time git ova dat. My eye still hurts." John Bone rubbed his hand over his head near his eye. He didn't touch his eye, just rubbed around it. The battered slave shook slightly and continued. "Da exp'ments was about how much heat a man can take and how fah dwn in skin da blac goes."

The watcher lay back against the flowstone cave formations. He knew the rocky sides and walls of the cave were made by tiny wind currents and evaporation rates peculiar to this area of Virginia. John Bone's awful words now lay along the cave ridges and seemed to sink into every crevice so that the cave seemed to become part of this small, brown man. He took some hardtack from his pack. He had refilled his own water bottle from a nearby spring before he spotted John Bone.

"Do you have any food or water?" he asked as he finished spreading the food on a small square of cloth.

"I has some wata and some cohn meel, sagamite, and beah greese. But we needs a fiah fo dat."

"I have enough for both of us for tonight. We can't be starting any fires at night. Tell me about these experiments while we eat."

The two men ate in silence for a while, then John Bone seemed to gather himself in and settled down in a small crouching position. The watcher noted the typical slave posture for beatings that he had seen during the war.

"My masta loan me to Docta Matews cause I was one o' his strongest men. I was curus, but afrad too. He had 'em dig a hole in da ground about tree steps deep, tree steps long, and two steps wide. Lot a dried out red oak bak was throw'd in, den set afiah. Dat bun'd for longest, til it was like a oven in dat pit. Da embahs was taked out and a plank was laid cross da bottom of da pit and dey put a stool deah. Docta den test it with a thah-a-meta, he call it, to see what it said. Den I had to take ofen my clothes and git in with jes my haed up out of groun. He give me some med'cine and when I were in dis hole he covah it wit wet blankets wit scantlings laid across. Dis was to keep in da heat. I soon felt da heat bad. I tried to keep up again it, but afta while I loose my sense. I was took out and brought to mysef. Docta made a note of what numba da thah-a-meta said. I were put in tween daylit and dahk, afta I don finish my work. Masta don like to loose no field time. Afta three or four days the exp'ments was don again and foh six mo times. Duh docta want to see which med'cine let me stan da heat da best. He say da cayon peppa tea was best and he sole dat as heat stroke med'cine. Made a lot of money, day say." John Bone shifted his position and leaned back against a stone outcropping.

The cave was filled with a dark silence. It was so heavy the watcher thought it would crush them both. Little lacy moon drawings crawled through the bushes covering the entrance to the cave. An owl complained, and the last

178

part of his voice seemed to fade into a windy nether world. The watcher wondered what terrors were being visited on other powerless people right at this moment.

John Bone sighed and opened his water bag. He drank his fill and resumed his resting position. He looked at the shadowy figure that now seemed to be a part of the cave except for his legs that lay in the path of the moon writing.

"Doctah Matews want to know how fah down dis black go." He pulled back a sleeve of his ragged shirt. "He put blisters on my hands and legs and feet. He kep on till he drawed up da dauk skin from tween uppa and lowa. He did dis about evry two weeks."

John Bone thrust his arm between the moon shadows, and the watcher could see the blistery scars. The words of torment and torture clung to the sides of the cave and seemed to become part of the uneven surface of the walls.

"Dey was wus udder tings but I can't tell em." The black man seemed to choke and hid his head in his hands.

The watcher again felt the smothering blackness of evil that seemed to encompass the cave. Then he recognized it! He had felt it before, coming from an incredibly evil man. Now it emanated from a natural structure. Was the evil a live thing or the miasma of evil thoughts?

"We have to move now!" Gathering up the remnants of their meal and hurriedly thrusting his eating materials into his backpack, the watcher whispered urgently, "Follow me." He quietly removed the covering of the cave, looked around, and motioned John Bone to follow. They slipped through the woods silently until morning.

By daybreak, the watcher had reached another shelter. Not a cave but a secure out- cropping over a ledge. It could only be reached one way, and once you were in the shelter of the tree branches and bushes, you were invisible. The two men were exhausted and needed to rest.

As they two men settled themselves, the daylight emphasized their contrast. One bent and old beyond years, the other young, strong but wary in the ways of elusiveness.

John Bone looked at his young companion now in the light of day.

"You a young man. You not a soldier?"

"I cannot tell you how I serve." The watcher pulled his blanket around his shoulders.

"Why we leave da cave so hurry like?" John Bone knew the answer but did the young man?

"You know why. It was covering us. We couldn't stay there and let our guard down by sleeping." The watcher lay back in the bed of leaves.

John Bone smiled to himself. He also took precautions. He spread a special mixture around the entrance to their den. Then and only then did he lie back and close his eyes. They slept dreamlessly.

Late in the day the two men parted. John Bone on his way to meet up with a man who helped runaway slaves and Jon Rue McLoed to deliver his courier pouch to General Beauregard.

The cave they had abandoned earlier was filled with a smell. A putrid smell that whorled up out of the blackness—you could smell and feel it pulsing—but you couldn't see it. It crept into every hole and fissure and the side of the hill began to shake and then flames leaped up and around the trees and bushes. It was not a red flame, but light blue and wherever it burned it smelled of the blackness. After there was nothing left, a dripping, shiny liquid poured into the nearby stream, carrying with it the thoughts and words of an abomination inflicted on one small, brown man. Soon the stream ran clear. But the place would always be cacodemonic. Nothing ever grew there again.

Chapter XXVII

Summer 1864

When thou and I first one another saw:
All other things, to their destruction draw,
Only our love hath no decay;
This, no tomorrow hath, nor yesterday,
Running it never runs from us away,
But truly keepes his first, last, everlasting day.
The Aniversarie, 1. 5-10
John Donne

A butterfly landed on her arm and she felt it. The yellow and black wings beat back and forth in a slow, lazy wave. She watched it intently. The colors were so bright, like they were brand new. And perhaps they were. A brand new butterfly! Clarisa knew this moment was special. This was the first time she had felt anything in a long time. She had been living in some half world; like her head was covered in gauze…she corrected herself, lace. Flimsy, but every now and then with a hole to see clearly through. But now she saw everything clearly. She felt as though she had been sleeping and was now fully awake.

She had felt different from the first moment she woke up this morning. Tingly and alive. Clarisa walked down the verandah steps to the lawn. She would test her newfound self. She reached down and plucked some clover and bit down on the stems. The juice was tart just like she remembered! Passing a cluster of wild violets she sat down on the grass and bent to inhale. The sweet aroma filled her with joy! All day she drank in the pleasures of being alive again. The touch of a gentle breeze that riffled her hair and the look of the fluffy clouds against the bright blue sky enveloped her in joy. Even when the clouds scudded along before a summer shower, she enjoyed their very unruliness. Later, the exquisite touch of gentle rain drops on her skin made her almost unbearably happy.

The next morning she made lemonade and took it to Seth in the barn. The weather was hot even this early, and as she walked up she noticed the sweat marks on the back of his shirt. He had broad, thick shoulders and his arms moved slowly as he lifted the pitchfork up and then over the stall to the waiting horse. Clairsa stood for a few moments watching him work. Seth always looked straight in her eyes, not off to the side as many had done since she first came back to Delmonde and then to River Rose. She looked at his deformed foot that caused him to lean to the side as he did his chores. Clarisa called his name.

"Seth, can you stop for a minute and rest? I brought you something to drink."

Seth turned and smiled.

"Why thank you, Clarisa. I am mighty thirsty." He came toward her wiping his hands on his pants. "What are you doing out so early?"

"I thought you might like something to drink." Her voice was soft and tentative.

Their hands touched briefly and then Seth took the glass and drank deeply.

Seth looked at Clarisa and smiled again. Her eyes were different. Aware. Her beautiful face was now animated in a way he had never seen.

"Have a seat." He motioned to one of the barn stools and he pulled up one beside it.

I just wondered," she hesitated, "if later we could go on a picnic, or something. After you finish your chores."

Seth was silent for a moment trying to regain his equilibrium. This lovely girl/woman had seemed so out of touch to anything or anyone, he had been content to admire her from a distance. Most of the women he met were not interested in a crippled man and over the years he had given up the thought of normal man/woman things like picnics. He avoided social gatherings and contented himself with learning as much about growing sugar cane as he could and saving River Rose.

"That would be fine. I'll be finished up here around noon," Seth said.

Clarisa nodded. "I'll ask Ceil to make up a basket for us. We can meet on the veranda."

Seth and Clairsa walked slowly in the midday heat to a grove of shade trees not far from the house. Ceil had put a cloth over the picnic basket which they now spread on the ground, and Clarisa began to set out plates and knives and forks. Seth lifted out the fried chicken and cornbread. He poured water into their tin picnic cups from the water pouch.

"I think you're feeling much better," Seth commented.

"Yes," said Clarisa. "I feel like my old self again. It's like I have been away."

"Sometimes people have to go away to find their way back, especially during war," Seth said and started eating a piece of chicken.

Clarisa put a piece of cornbread on her napkin and picked at it absently.

"You could always see I was here, even when I wasn't sure myself." Clarisa looked at Seth. "You never looked away."

His gray eyes looked darker for a moment and he said, "I have a lot of experience with people looking away." He gestured to his foot.

Clarisa looked at his foot.

"What does your foot look like without your boot?"

Seth was startled.

"I don't think you want to see my foot. It's bent and deformed." Seth stood up dropping the remains of his chicken on the ground. He felt hot and humiliated. He should have known better. She was only curious about his deformity!

Clarisa jumped up and ran to his side and took his hand.

"Seth, please don't be hurt. I just wanted you to know that I don't care what your foot looks like. I want to be friends with you. I don't care about your foot. Just like you wanted to be my friend when I was not even able to know you. Please Seth. Let's be friends. I need a friend."

Clarisa clasped Seth's hand to her face.

"I don't think I can just be your friend Clarisa." Seth withdrew his hand and limped back to the house.

Seth and the overseer left early the next morning for New Orleans to meet with the plantation's factor. They were gone before Clarisa came down to breakfast. Seth had not been at supper last night either and she was desperate to talk with him. She wished Maureen were still here. She could have talked things over and asked for advice.

Somehow she had to make Seth understand. Clarisa wasn't even sure she understood what was happening herself.

Seth was gone for a week. Clarisa had everything sorted out in her mind. She now knew what she had to tell Seth. She must make him understand how she loved him. Even when her mind was wandering in the mist of unawareness these last few months, she was aware of him. It was as if she were blind. Until she emerged from her blankness, she didn't even know what his physical self looked like. Clarisa knew and had fallen in love with his soul. What he looked like on the outside simply had no meaning for her. Could she make him understand?

Seth had not sorted anything out. He was miserable. Up until now he had thought, though not really a happy man, that he was at least content. Until Clarisa had brought lemonade and invited him to the picnic! That's when it all started. He dreaded the return to River Rose. He dreaded the idea of seeing Clarisa again. Zack and Jacob had given him free rain to manage River Rose and promised him they would allow him some land when they returned. He felt his future was secure. But he couldn't stay here now. Not and see Clarisa every day and be her friend!

When Seth was a small boy, life had been wonderful. His mother loved him, cared for him and never let him know he was different. He learned to run in a hobbling, swaying way that was pretty fast and allowed him to keep up with the few small children with whom he came in contact at family and church gatherings. It was not until he got older that he realized his "difference" set him apart from other boys his age. The rough and tumble of games was not a problem, as he was a sturdy and determined boy. It was when it came to girls that he became aware that he was not the "perfect" specimen some girls seemed to prefer. He did have a close girl friend named Mary, in the "friend" sense, but neither Seth nor Mary ever thought of themselves as more than friends. Later Seth would realize part of his difficulty was probably his own fault. As soon as he realized that, because of his deformity, he did not always appeal to every girl, he withdrew from any opportunities that would have caused him embarrassment. He never went to socials. When he and his family attended church, he always drove the wagon, and under the pretext of tending to the horse, managed to slip in at the last minute and sit in the back pew. This allowed him to leave quickly, reach the wagon, and hide his foot before most people made their leisurely way outside. He sat in the driver's seat and chatted amiably with people as they came by. Newer people in the area were not even aware he was crippled. Some assumed he was shy. But now his heart was actually hurting in his chest as he thought of Clarisa. Terrified, he realized the unthinkable had happened. He had fallen in love.

The carriage came up to the house at dusk. Clarisa had been listening for the sound of the wheels and ran out on the veranda. Seth gritted his teeth as he saw her standing there in some pink something that fluttered around her. She looked lovelier than ever.

He took his bag from the back of the carriage and started up the stairs.

"I'm so glad you're back Seth. I've missed you. Ceil has some tea things out now. Come on in and refresh yourself."

Clarisa led a silent Seth into the dim coolness of the front parlor to the little tea table.

"Clarisa, I really need to wash up." Seth had a frown between his eyes. Not a frown of concentration, but of tenseness, almost fear. He wanted to get away and began to move toward the stairs.

"But Seth, I have to talk to you now. It can't wait. Please!" Clarisa pleaded with tears in her eyes.

Seth walked back to the parlor and sat down across from Clarisa.

"You didn't understand the other day. I don't want to be your friend either, Seth. I want more than that." She had said the words now. Clarisa hoped she had not misunderstood his feelings.

Seth was stunned. Could he be hearing right?

"You're just getting well. Maybe you won't feel this way later," he said cautiously.

I'll always feel this way. As soon as I came to myself I knew. Because you have been loving me all along. Haven't you Seth?"

The little tea table was too large an expanse of space between them.

Seth pulled Clarisa to her feet and cupped her face in his hands.

"I have always loved you. I never thought you could love me."

Seth kissed her gently and they clung together. A summer breeze blew the curtains slightly and a brand new butterfly settled on the tea table.

The next day word was sent to Father Belier in Alexandria that River Rose would be having a small wedding as soon as he could arrange his schedule.

Martha and Esta talked it over in the way of women. Though Mistah Seth was a lot younger than Miss Clarisa, she was still beautiful, and besides there were hardly any men left, young or old. And who knew when any of the men would ever come home again?

"Happiness is somethin' yuh has to grab foh when you can git it." Martha allowed.

1865–6

Word over all, beautiful as the sky,
Beautiful that war and all its deeds of carnage must in
time be utterly lost,
that the hands of the sisters Death and Night
incessantly softly wash again, and ever again, this
soil'd world;
For my enemy is dead, a man divine as myself is dead,
I look where he lies white-faced and still in the coffin-
I draw near,
Bend down and touch lightly with my lips the white
face in the coffin.
"Reconciliation"
Walt Whitman 1865–6

Aftermath

Chapter XXVIII

Spring—1868—New Orleans, Louisiana
Forsythe Classic Finishing School for Young Ladies

"Everyone in my family is just absolutely thrilled that you're coming for the summer! I still can't believe it," Emma gushed for a least the tenth time in the last hour.

Anne Leyton looked fondly at her favorite pupil. "I am absolutely thrilled that you were kind enough to ask me. I'll try not be too much of a damper on your spirit."

"You could not be a damper if you tried," Emma replied. "You just need a little change of scene. A few walks on a Louisiana riverbank, a harmless flirtation or two with Jon Rue and his friends, and you'll be your old self."

Anne finished packing and looked around her small bedroom. She would miss her flat provided by the school. These little rooms had shared her day to day challenges and successes with her pupils for the last three years. After the war, when her emotions were as ragged as the gray uniforms of the soldiers she had cared for, these little rooms were her haven. When her father had died suddenly, these were the rooms that provided refuge as she struggled with the aftermath. The small legacy he had left her had given her unexpected financial independence. Somehow it made her know she needed to start over somewhere else. A close friend had just done that very thing. Plagued with war memories, he had packed up last week and headed west. The war. It still colored every aspect of life in the south. Could it have been over three years? It seemed longer.

It was professionally acceptable to spend some time with Emma McLoed's family. Emma had graduated two days ago with honors and was no longer her pupil. If Emma was to be believed there was nothing more wonderful than her home 'by the river'. A full history of how an Irish family had come to inhabit a Louisiana Plantation, when most, but not all of the area was peopled with French and Spanish, had been provided by Emma. 'Grandpa came with his family from Georgia 30 years ago. He had heard that anything would grow in the "blackest of the black soil" and he wanted to grow sugar cane,' Emma had finished this proudly. "He and papa were very successful."

Anne finished replaying this conversation in her head as Emma broke in, "There you go, daydreaming," she chided. "We have to go or we'll miss the boat."

Anne good-naturedly allowed herself to be pulled along toward the hansom waiting to take them to the pier.

The carriage rolled bumpily along New Orleans' brick streets. Anne took a farewell look at the city that had been her home for so many years. Summer always came early in this coastal city. Already the azaleas were in bloom. An esplanade mule car passed and Anne marveled as she usually did at the unique streetcars. They were coming into the city proper now and she felt the pang of loss. Many buildings still showed reminders of the war; fire and shelling had left many in rubble. But people were rebuilding. She knew rural areas of the south were not coming back to life as quickly. Between here and Baton Rouge it was said there were miles of ruin, even the fields had not yet been reclaimed. Most farms were wiped out. Many of the great plantation homes were burned or wrecked. Emma said the only reason their home was spared was General Bank's impatience to reach New Orleans. It was also not a cotton plantation. This meant that it was not on the target list for cotton raiding. Sugar cane was not an easily traded commodity. Being an avid student of history, Anne knew that since 1519, when the Spanish explorer Alonso Alverez de Pineda first glimpsed the gulf shore, New Orleans had reigned as the Crown Jewel of the coast. Anne had no doubt its reign had only been temporarily interrupted.

Later in the day...

The boat steamed up the river, the sound of the paddle wheel soothing in the monotonous slap, slap of water. Emma and Anne were settled conformably in their sleeping quarters. In fact Emma was already dozing.

Finally giving up trying to read her book, Anne closed her eyes and allowed herself to think of the past few months. Her father's sudden death had devastated her. They had quarreled and parted with bitter words, and then in three days he was dead. She never thought her father would die. Her mother had died years ago when she was so young she could hardly remember her. But her father, so strong and sure of himself, he could not die. Now that she knew of his illness, she wondered if the strain of his keeping it a secret had caused him to be more irritable than usual. Their argument was really over nothing. She had planned to visit him that weekend, thinking they would picnic and make up and everything would be fine. But it wasn't fine. And she couldn't shake the sadness that seemed to envelop her. Even Emma had noticed and insisted she come stay with her for the summer. Tears streamed down her face. The day was late, and she hid her face in the shadows of the window's tight little curtain. If she could only tell him she didn't mean it, that it would be all right.

Then the other memories crowded in. She had to get some air. She stumbled over Emma's sleeping form and weaved her way up to the observation deck. Anne watched the receding sun's purple haze almost obscuring the dense forest along the bank. Dusk brought some relief from recriminations as the soothing blackness of night closed in.

Heat shimmered in moist waves and mixed with the dust from the horse's swift passage over the "River Road" as Emma called it. Though there had been some improvement since the war, one Union commander's assessment of Louisiana's roads as "almost but not quite impracticable" was not far from the truth. Anne had fallen in love with the river on the boat, but the levee now obscured it. Emma assured her there were wonderful walking paths along the river and an inspiring view from the "special" room Anne would be using. "Everyone is so thrilled" had been repeated so many times this morning that Anne was beginning to look forward to time alone in her "special" room. Then she chided herself. Her little friend was so devoted and only trying to help. Still a little peace and quiet would be welcome. Am I getting old? she wondered. Though only twenty-two, to Emma's 17, she knew many people considered that rather "long in the tooth" for an unmarried lady. These thoughts were brought to an abrupt stop as they rounded a curve and the house loomed immediately ahead. It was beautiful though in need of paint as most everything was after the war. Like an aristocratic lady in a shabby gown, Anne thought. Several people were milling around on the balcony and in the yard. Whoops and yells of welcome broke out as people ran toward the carriage.

Anne finished putting away the last of her belongings. A young black woman named Sara, had helped her shake out the worst of the wrinkles in her clothes, and assured her they would be "ironed real good" by tonight. She tried to give Sara some money but was met with a smile and a shake of her head. "I is a 'contract' person," she said proudly. "Call me with this rope if you needs anything before dressin' time." Sara indicated a length of tapestry near the bed. The woman soundlessly slipped out with Anne's clothes over her arm, and Anne was finally alone. That answered a question Anne had wondered about. Since the war what were the arrangements with former slaves? Anne had heard that workers were now contract labor and paid a certain amount a month. This sometimes included living quarters.

She washed her face and unbraided her long blonde hair. Closing her eyes she brushed until her arms ached pleasantly. Dinner to celebrate Emma's return and Anne's visit would be at 7:00, with dancing to follow. She really should rest. Too excited to lie down, she pulled out a book and read until Sara returned. With her help she was quickly dressed and still had plenty of time before dinner. Sara left for other chores, and Anne slipped out on her small private balcony to see if she could really see the river. It was already dusk but she could see the moon highlight laps and small waves. She thought about Emma's family that had greeted her so warmly. They truly seemed "absolutely thrilled" to meet her. Emma's brother, Jon Rue, was to be her escort and apparently relished his role as a harmless rake. He was about the same age as Anne and seemed carefree. He was tall and good looking, and chattered in a delightful complimentary way. A good diversion. Emma's father, Zack, was heavy set and kind looking with snow white hair and vivid blue eyes. Emma's mother had died several years before. There was an older brother, but apparently he was not in from the fields when they arrived.

At that moment a commotion broke out below, with much skittering of horses' hooves and a thin voice apparently trying to be quiet calling, "Cap'n, wait."

Her balcony was in complete darkness now and she looked down just as a figure reined his horse to a stop and sputtered, "Dammit Tib, you startled my horse!"

"I'm sorry Cap'n, but I gots to tell you, Miss Emma is home with her visitor, and they have dinner ready."

"Dammit!" again from the figure. Anne smiled. Apparently "everyone was not absolutely thrilled about her visit." She must have moved as the figure below suddenly looked up and then dismounted, giving the reins to the unfortunate Tib.

Dinner was low key but beautiful. Lovely old china and crystal served simple but delicious food from the kitchen's garden and local wood fowl. The crawfish soup was especially well done with a more delicate flavor than the usual lobster. Dessert was Bilboquet fritters that had to be the lightest she had ever tasted. The wine cellar had been exhausted during the war when the house was a field hospital. Emma's father mentioned this in apology for lack of wine and did not notice the brief paleness of his daughter's guest at mention of the hospital. There was some port served during dessert. Table linens were exquisite but replete with tiny, expert darning. Candles gave the room a splendor that even peeling paint couldn't dim.

Emma's older brother was on time for dinner and was introduced as Jacob. Anne smiled sweetly and secretly nicknamed him "Dammit." He was heavy set like his father with the same vivid blue eyes, but sandy hair fell over his forehead and brushed his collar. He was polite, but not the entertaining charmer that was Jon Rue. Several neighbor families had been invited, and when some talented 'contract' musicians began violin music, everyone assembled in the slightly shabby ballroom for dancing.

Jon Rue as Anne's designated escort led her to the floor for the first dance, and she danced with several of the neighbors. Even Jacob asked her to dance toward the end of the evening. The heat had become close and oppressive, and her long day was beginning to catch up to her. As the dance ended, she looked up at Jacob and asked if they could get some air on the verandah. She guessed he would be relieved to get away from all of them. He apparently had noticed her pallor and gently escorted her into the cool night. The river was noisy now. The wind had picked up and a storm seemed close. She and Jacob stood looking at the tossing water that could now be seen over the levee. "It almost seems like it could come over the top," she said and was surprised at how faint her voice sounded.

"But it can't," Jacob assured her. "The levee's been here fifty years and never been breached. The water is much lower a mile or so away. This is the only stretch like this. You can't usually see the water this high unless there's a storm brewing."

Anne stirred. "I feel much better. We can go in now. Thanks for helping me out. I was more tired than I thought."

Jacob did not move. "There's no hurry."

"This may not be your favorite pastime, entertaining your sister's friends from school," Anne ventured.

Jacob looked at her, his eyes twinkling, "So you were on the balcony. I apologize for my language. I had forgotten about Emma's party."

The storm broke in the early hours of the morning. It raged and lashed at the windows, and lightening flashed through Anne's room over and over. As suddenly as it had begun it was over. Soon she could hear the night sounds again and fell asleep just as dawn was breaking.

Emma insisted that she wanted to show Anne the walking paths near the river right after breakfast. Jon Rue was the only other member of the family present for breakfast. Apparently Zack and Jacob were always long gone by this time. Anne was not sure what Jon Rue's role was or whether or not he had a Job.

The morning was beautiful. The heavy air had vanished with the storm, and the sky was the bluest she had ever seen. The levee walking paths were everything Emma had promised. The river spread out before them as smooth as glass. Red mud stirred up from the night before showed how the mighty "Red" got its name.

Emma nodded as Anne commented on the color of the water. "After a dry spell, it's almost clear as a spring, and then it rains and turns Red. People say the river bleeds when it rains."

"I would love to see it first thing, just at sunrise," Anne said wrapping her skirt around her as she sat down on a large rock.

"You will have to wake up by 5:00 in the morning then," Emma shuddered. "That is awful early."

Emma was right, 5:00 in the morning was "awful early," Anne thought to herself the next morning, as she softly descended the stairs and walked toward the levee. The sky was just beginning to lighten. She took her sketchpad and quickly staked out a small outlook about a mile from the house. The crooked old Cyprus tree that had caught her eye the day before kept her engrossed. A sound further down the path startled her, and looking up she was surprised to see Jacob coming toward her.

"You're out early," he called out.

She smiled. "Yes, but it is the most beautiful time."

"Have you had anything to eat?" he asked.

"No, and I'm very hungry," Anne stood up and realized her stomach was making protesting noises.

Jacob looked in a bag he was carrying. "There is one quoisant left. If I known you would be here I would have asked Auralee to make breakfast for two." He handed her the still warm sweet roll. She munched hungrily. He handed over a small container of warm strong coffee.

"This is wonderful," Anne said. "Do you often come early to the levee?"
He stood looking at the river. "Every day unless it's raining."

Anne looked at him. "I plan to come every day too. Do you mind company?"

Jacob sat down on the rocky ledge. "Of course not. That would be just fine. We'll have breakfast out here." He looked at Anne and grinned, "Emma will think you've lost your mind."

"She knows I always go somewhere by myself early to sketch and," Anne hesitated "and meditate."

The next morning Anne and Jacob had breakfast on the levee. She discovered that the river was as much a part of Jacob as his Irish heritage and blue eyes. It was almost his lifeblood. The river carried the produce of the plantation to and from markets, north and south. Since most of the state's railroads had been destroyed during the war, it was the only means of transportation, not just for crops, but for people too. But it was more than practical matters that tied Jacob and his family to the restless ribbon of red, sometimes clear, waters. Their souls seemed to throb with the ebb and flow of her. Some would even argue that the river tried to help in the Civil War, when suddenly the water level dropped and stranded General Bank's armada at Alexandria. The end of the war brought an even closer tie to this most basic of nature's gifts. Her waters were still pushing at the banks, pulsating with life, calling her people to do the same. Red River was a symbol of hope in the midst of despair and a reminder that they could go on.

Anne learned more about Jacob every day. Though basically reticent, she was able to draw him out and discovered a well read, articulate, and gentle man. She sensed an innate loneliness about him, despite his poised exterior. Once in a casual conversation, he had mentioned his mother and seemed almost overcome at the thought of her. He had described a vibrant and beautiful woman who energized all who knew her. Anne realized he still missed her deeply. Was that part of his loneliness? She could understand that, as she still felt the void left by her father. Soon she found herself telling him things about her life she would not have dreamed of sharing with anyone before. Something about the solitude and atmosphere of the river levee and the feeling that she was safe with Jacob had Anne confiding her most secret self to this man she had only known a few weeks. She found out his vision for the plantation and the plans he and the family had developed together.

Jacob saw the day when all the farmhands would not just be sharecroppers but would ultimately "own" their piece of land. He was open to new ways of farming and explained that Jon Rue was in charge of the development and business end of that venture.

As Jacob learned more about Anne, he was entranced that this delicate, blonde creature harbored a keen intelligence. Yet what he was most attracted to was her sweet nature and what he perceived as a loving heart. She asked questions about the plantation, but he could see she was most interested in the well being of the former slaves, especially the children. He looked forward more and more to their private time each morning. He began to feel more complete when he was with Anne, almost as if she filled up a corner of his soul that had been empty. Jacob would save little tidbits from his day to share, not at the supper table, but with Anne at breakfast on the levee.

The next few weeks, Anne and Jacob continued their early morning levee breakfasts. The days were filled with Emma's friends, Jon Rue and his diversions and small family suppers. Anne felt reborn. She no longer had the tired, oppressed feeling she had struggled with since her father had died.

Early one morning, Jacob, Zack, and Jon Rue left on a business trip for a few days and time itself seemed to hang languid and suspended in the hot air. Anne went to the levee each morning, but without Jacob it seemed a lonely place.

Then influenza or what Emma called "summer flu" took hold and spread among the field workers. So many were sick they could not take care of each other. Emma asked Anne if she would go with her and the household help to nurse them. Anne struggled with the familiar tightening in her throat. But she was strong now. This was the time to face down those particular demons.

As part of their preparation, Emma explained, they would need to take a good supply of 'fever water.' Emma led the way to the kitchen house. As with most large plantations in the south, the kitchen was in a separate building to reduce the risk of fire.

As they entered the large room, Anne was struck by the size of the cooking hearth. It was huge with the typical iron swinging crane that handled with ease the heavy kettle and any number of pots and pans that needed to be over the fire at the same time. She was also impressed with the chain and turn wheel that rotated the spit. Several small storage cupboards housed other utensils and dishes.

Emma reached up over the fireplace and brought down a mortar and pestle and a small pouch of carduus seeds.

"Auralee keeps them on the mantel shelf so they'll stay dry," she explained as she set everything on the big work table that sat about six feet from the fireplace.

Auralee had picked the Marigold Flowers they would need for the remedy earlier in the day, and they lay in a pan of water rather than a vase.

"Putting the whole flower and stem in the basin keeps them fresher, and the stronger they are the more powerful the effect," Emma explained.

Going to one of the cupboards, she pulled out a bowl of unshelled walnuts.

"These are still green. We always try to keep a bowl of walnuts just off the tree for this purpose," she continued.

Next to the walnuts was a covered beaker, which Emma brought over to the table with the bowl of walnuts.

"This is carduus and poppy water. After we grind the seeds, nuts and flowers, we'll put them in the water and add a little treacle to taste and there you have the receipt for 'fever water,'" Emma finished with a flourish of the pestle like a music conductor.

Each day, the two women left the house at daybreak and worked into the night returning home exhausted. There was not much time for conversation and Emma was not prepared for what was to come.

Zack and Jacob were almost home. Jon Rue would follow in a few days. It was late and they were tired but happy. The loans were almost paid off and they would be able to do some much-needed repairs around the place. They would even be able to help Jon Rue with his newest idea for the plantation. As they approached the curve before the house the figure of Tib ran toward their carriage.

"Cap'n! I thought I heard the wheels. Miss Anne not home yet and we can't get her home and we don know what to do!"

"What do you mean she's not home yet? It's almost midnight! Where is she?" Jacob yelled.

"She at Henry's place".

Henry was the black overseer who lived in one of the field houses.

"Dey was sick and now deys better, but she don know it," this last from Tib, as tears began making trenches down his dirty cheeks. Tib had been with Jacob all through the Civil War. He was only thirty, but seemed much older. Small, with a crippled leg, he had attached himself to the Captain from the beginning. He was a great scout and spy and could move back and forth between Confederate and Union lines with the quiet of an Indian. He had seen the worst there was to see; the battlefields after a battle; but much worse were the field hospitals. Much worse because the victims were alive. He closed his eyes against the memories, the blood, and the screams of boys and dying men. And always the women, quiet, moving among the soldiers, soothing, petting, cleaning the awful wounds, crying themselves until all their tears were gone. And then sometimes they could not bear it and would keep nursing the same soldier long after he was dead. They had to be pulled away. He never knew what happened to those women. And now Miss Anne...

Jacob yelled at him. "Tib! Get me a fresh horse ready and I'll go tell Emma what we need. Do you know where Martha is?"

Martha, was now, because of age and infirmity, 'retired'.

"She be here soon. I's already sent word," Tib wiped his nose on his sleeve. A new wave of terror seized him then and he began to shake, "Cap'n, she is wahshocked ain't she?" Tib used the term from the war for people that had such vivid flashbacks of war; they were temporarily or permanently out of touch with reality.

"I expect so," Jacob said heading to the house.

Emma met him at the door. "I didn't know, Jake. I didn't know," she sobbed into her brother's shoulder. "She was teaching and I didn't think about her being in the hospitals during the war. She never said anything about it."

Jacob said tiredly, "I know. I know." He patted his little sister. She had been young and staying with relatives during most of the war and knew nothing of the awful field hospitals.

"Martha's on her way. She'll know what to do. I'm going to bring Anne back." He turned and plunged back into the night.

The night was the deep dark of total cloud cover. Jacob's horse stumbled and almost fell. He slowed down. It would do no one any good to cripple the horse. Sweat poured from his body and his stomach was in knots. Jacob had thought he was over the war, but fear and revulsion coursed through his body like strings of fire. Images he thought were buried came flooding back. He could smell the smoke from the battlefield on a black night just such as this...when he found the young soldier sitting up against a tree. Jacob thought he was just resting, but then he touched him and he fell over, rigid and cold. His eyes were open and staring in surprise. Jacob had looked in his shirt pocket to see who he was and found the letter, wrinkled and soaked with blood. It began, "Dear momma,"...

Jacob wiped his forehead with his sleeve. Sweat immediately drenched him again and he gasped for air.

Suddenly the farmhouses loomed ahead. One small square of pale light shone. It must be Henry's house. Several figures were standing on the porch. They recognized him as he dismounted. From the window he saw Anne.

Someone came close and touched her shoulder. She seemed to stagger and then straightened up.

"How long has she been here?" he asked of no one in particular.

"She been here since daylight, Mistah Jacob," Henry's mother spoke from a makeshift bed the porch.

Jacob entered the small house and put his hand on Anne's shoulder. She started and turned to look at him.

His blood froze. Her eyes were blank and showed no recognition. "We're leaving now Anne. Henry's okay." Jacob said the words slowly and firmly. He forcefully pulled her hands from a frightened Henry.

"They're all dying, all of them! Can't you see, they're all dying!" This last dissolved into wracking sobs.

Jacob lifted her up and headed for his horse. She was shaking so hard he had to ask two of the men to help lift her to him in the saddle. Her wracking sobs continued.

He had to go slow. It took every ounce of strength he had to hold her still enough to see around her in the blackness. After a while the sobs became deep shudders. As the horse plodded steadily onward into the night, Jacob realized this was the first time he had held Anne in his arms. When he had realized she was in trouble, Jacob had hardly been able to bear the thought that something might happen to his lady. He startled himself with the thought. For the first time in his life, a woman seemed to belong to him. A great ache rose up in his chest. The ache had been there since his mother had died. No one had been able to ease the empty place in his heart. Not River Rose nor even his devoted family. The war had left him scarred but a part of him was untouched. Until now. He urged his horse on. Anne had to be all right!

Finally he saw the light through the woods and knew the house was around the corner. Tib, Emma and Martha were waiting. They lifted her down and Zack helped him carry her up to her room. Martha shooed everyone out but Emma. The men were left to prowl the darkened halls.

Finally Emma was touching Jacob's arm. "Martha says she has done everything she can do, but Anne can't be left alone. She must not be allowed up and has to be restrained. It take a man's strength," this last with muffled sobs.

Jacob went back in the room. Everything was quiet. Martha looked at him and shook her head. Jacob gripped her arm and she shushed him. "Quiet!" she motioned to the hall. He followed her out.

"How is she?" he demanded. Martha looked at him steadily. "I don know yet but she can't be allowed up until we suhe she huhself." She looked down at her hands and clasped them together. "I have seen em…try to go back."

Martha put her hand on Jacob's shoulder. "She a beautiful young lady. Is she yoh young lady Mistah Jake?"

Anne was back in the makeshift field hospital. It was filled with the sounds of pain and smells of death. The sounds of moaning and crying washed over her. A surgeon, with his arms bloody below his elbows, knelt by a wounded soldier. "I've given him morphine, but it won't be enough. Help me hold him down." The doctor swabbed the wound but the blood kept coming and all at once it splashed all over her and the walls and streamed down her face...

Anne swirled in a golden mist. It clung to her hair and clothes. Fingers of it tried to hold her down. Then the fingers turned to arms and hands and blood and they were everywhere! She tried to scream, but no sounds came. Then she was wrapped in a blanket of gossamer. Flimsy, but strong. Struggling was useless. The fear became less. She could breathe again. After a long time, there was light in her eyes. She opened them and saw a man slumped in a chair. Who was he? He was unshaven and his hair was disheveled. He seemed familiar. One arm hung down over the arm of a chair. His hand was gossamer, the gossamer that was part of the blanket. That could not be right. He seemed to be sleeping and sighed softly.

"Jacob," she spoke clearly, surprised that she knew his name.

He started up out of the chair. He looked exhausted.

"Jacob," she said again.

"Anne," he was hoarse with sleep. "Do you know me?"

She smiled. Then she understood.

It took several days for Anne to completely shake the terrors. But since she had awakened a great peace had enveloped her. Everyone waited on her hand and foot. She was especially grateful for Martha. Someone had decided Martha should 'be with her awhile'.

Jacob and Martha discussed Anne's condition the day after she recovered. Martha was amazed. "I soh thout yo young lady wouldn't come back Mistah Jake. I has nevah seen one so bad, come back so quick." She cocked her head to one side. "I think she was cuahed by good nursin'. Mine and yos."

Jacob looked at her. "What do you mean? I didn't do any nursing."

Martha smiled. "Deys nursin' and den deys nursin.'"

Martha assured Jacob and the family that Anne was indeed 'cured'. "I think I stay with her for awhile to make sure you peoples don aggravate her." Everyone agreed this was a good idea.

Chapter XXIX

Spring 1868
Red River, 10 miles north of Opelousas. Louisiana
Steamboat *Magnolia*

In the middle of my life, I had lost my way and found myself alone in a dark wood

Dante

The steamboat slowly chugged along, occasionally sending a spray of water toward the lower decks.

Jon Rue McLoed had just completed a very successful negotiating session with two bankers in his role as River Rose factor and was feeling tired but content. He stood looking out over the railing, enjoying the cool droplets after the smothering warmth of the observation deck. As usual the boat was overloaded and the crush of people made the trip a trial of stamina and strength. He felt especially sorry for the ladies who had braved what was an arduous journey from New Orleans to Baton Rouge. Their heavy skirts must be doubly cumbersome with the humidity and heat that was now palpable. He was surprised some of them were not on the outside deck seeking relief. As he finished the thought, two figures detached themselves from the shadows and came toward the railing. Though daylight was dripping away in the mist, he could make out the shape of a man and the slim form of a girl. They had not yet noticed him and were moving his way. The lantern swinging from the overhead beam momentarily lighted the girl's face. Jon Rue caught his breath as her eyes looked straight into his. Green lights sparkled, and he was lost in their depths. She smiled slightly and turned back to her companion. Now he could see the man clearly. He was much older than the girl was and elegantly dressed. Taking her arm with a proprietary air, he nodded briefly to acknowledge Jon's presence and guided her toward the deck door. They disappeared inside.

The feeling that somehow he was bereft stayed with Jon Rue the rest of the evening. Even sharing a game of cards with an especially pretty lady did little to cheer him up. He went to his stateroom early. Giving up trying to sleep, he sat looking out at the dark river and its banks of dripping mosses trailing like elegant tentacles in the water. Jon Rue tried to think back to what caused his successful trip to suddenly turn sour. The green eyes came back to haunt him. Who was she? Was she married to the older man?

Many young women had married older men after the war simply because there were not many young men left. What was wrong with him? There were plenty of beautiful ladies in the world, and he was very good at charming all of them. *"Probably my greatest talent,"* he thought glumly. Though he was on the verge of beginning a new business venture for the plantation as a result of his trip, he really had accomplished nothing after the war other than mesmerize ladies all over Louisiana.

Suddenly all the beauties he had courted seemed pale and uninteresting. Though the war had left him feeling older than his years, this was not what weighed on him. He had been lucky in many ways. His father and brother had suffered through many more battles than he had. After a particularly bloody encounter, he had come to a life changing realization. He had always thought of himself as brave because he had no personal fear. Fear for others, yes, fear for his little sister back home and his brother and father in the war, but no personal fear.

He remembered his first battle of the war. Late in the afternoon he had looked out at a meadow that had been bright with spring flowers in the morning and now stood awash in the smell of gunpowder and smoke. He thought he was a coward. A brave man would not have spilled the blood that was soaking into the ground. A brave man would not have fought in aggression or self defense, but would have thrown his body in front of bullets and mortar fire and saved another's life. A brave man would have let himself be killed rather than slice and thrust a sword until only bloody flesh remained. Darkness that day brought some relief as he tried to block out the sights and sounds of the murderous assault and the equally ferocious response. Countrymen against countrymen. This duel of kindred souls was surely an unholy action that must not only blister the land but also leave tracks of despair on the very fabric of men's souls. It was then that he had volunteered to be a courier. He had become a special assistant to General Beaurgard himself and spent most of the war assisting with maps and carrying secret orders through enemy lines. His amazing skill at moving silently and invisibly through all kinds of terrain, especially bayou country, had been honed hunting, during his young years in this same bayou country. There had been a couple of narrow escapes and though he had resorted to the special training "couriers" received, it was in self-defense and he felt no guilt. Since the war was over a kind of malaise had hung over everything and everybody, including himself. It was as if everyone were sleeping and waiting for some word to come back to life. That at least was his excuse to himself for going from one romantic *attachment'* to the other.

He fell into a fitful sleep but came suddenly awake as the boat jerked under him. The paddlewheel must have hit a submerged log. Stories abounded about the dangers of riverboat travel! Thoughts of the Steamboat Sultana, loaded with Union prisoners of war, exploding at Memphis, with the resulting loss of 1700 men, raced through his mind! Groggy, he groped for the door, which gave easily. He reeled as smoke and fire shot past him. He heard screams and could feel the boat lurching and groaning. Upper deck...he had to reach the upper deck!

"Help me please!" A girl's voice cried over the noise.

It was dark and he could hardly breathe through the fumes. He stumbled toward the sound and found the owner of the voice struggling with a man who was barely conscious. Blood was streaming down his head from a deep gash over his left eye. Lifting the man, they tried to carry him between them, but he was too heavy for the girl, and she slipped and fell. At that moment the overhead beam came crashing down on all of them.

Jon Rue lay still in shock, and then tried to raise his head. Water was pouring over him. He had to keep his head above water! The beam had glanced off his head but had crushed the man he was carrying. Where was the girl? He couldn't see anything and began floundering in the water.

"Here I am," the girl's voice led him to her. "I think he's dead," her voice choked with tears. She was pinned under the beam in some way. The water was rising, and the smoke seared his lungs. He tried to lift the beam.

"I'll count to three. When I lift, see if you can wiggle out," he was shouting now over the increasing noise. "One, two, three, move!"

He noticed slight movement but not enough.

"Are you hurt? Can you move? We have to get out of here!" The boat lurched again and the beam moved slightly on its own.

"My skirts are so full of water I cannot move," she coughed as water rushed over them again.

Jon Rue pulled out his knife. Struggling through the rising water he put the knife in her hand. "Cut them off, hurry!"

Cutting and tearing, the girl frantically pulled away from her billowing skirts. They reached the deck in time to jump overboard as fire, smoke, and screaming people whirled about them.

The shock of the chilly water revived him, and he looked for the girl. She came up for air, and Jon Rue grabbed her shoulders. "We have to get as far away from the boat as possible, it might explode"...his words were cut off as a giant waterspout poured over the struggling people in the water. His left side felt like it was ripped open, and he tasted blood.

He was floating and trying to swim to shore. Had to somehow find...blackness swirled over him.

There was a gauzy canopy over his head. And soft rustling, then a breeze. Jon Rue was fighting to get out of the water; had to get out of the water...it was going to explode! Something was holding him down. He struggled up, then stabbing pain shot through his side, and he fainted.

The old doctor closed his worn black bag and looked at Esme. "He's young and strong. Just give him a few days. I stitched up his side. You can give him this for the pain. I will be back tonight. Now you get some rest."

Esme motioned to a cot near the window. "I will. I nap during the day. But he keeps trying to get up. He thinks he's still in the water. I cannot leave him," she said in her soft Creole accent.

"He's lucky this happened in 1868, otherwise it would be unseemly to have a young woman in the same room with him, much less nursing him."

"After what we did during the war, this kind of nursing is really nothing much." Esme looked sad at the memories. "At least he will recover."

"Give him this," he handed her a small bottle. "It will keep him quiet for awhile. If he's not easy by tonight, I'll sit up with him. Have you heard from his family?" This as the doctor opened the door.

"Yes, his brother came looking for him and they sent him here. I'm to let them know when he can travel."

The doctor looked back at his patient. Jon Rue was black and blue all down the side of his face and body which had taken the brunt of the explosion. *He must be in terrible pain when conscious*, the doctor thought. *Better to keep him sedated at least one more day to give the wound a chance to begin healing.*

Looking at Esme, he was concerned about how tired and thin she looked. "You have to rest too. You lost your uncle that terrible day."

Esme sat down as tears began, "Only twenty of us made it out alive. Why did he have to die?"

Chapter XXX

It was another hot day and the lacy curtains only barely moved. Esme studied her patient as she had for three days. The terrible bruises on his face, neck, and side had lightened, but she knew the pain from his side wound was terrible. He was tall, and his feet hung over the end of the bed. She would never know how she managed to get him close to the shore. He was unconscious and the whirling water had slowed their progress, until finally they fell into the arms of rescuers, who pulled them the rest of the way to the bank. Her aunt's family arrived soon after and brought them both here. They had not yet found her uncle.

Jon Rue tried to sit up, and Esme struggled to drag him back down. He was still flailing his arms and trying to swim. "Have to find her," he mumbled, and then the pain drove him back down. Esme realized he was still looking for her in the water. She would have to have help to get him to take laudanum. She opened the door and called for her aunt.

Jacob arrived that night and sat with her until morning. He was coming back today, but Jon Rue was still not aware of anything.

Suddenly, around mid-day he sat up in bed, and then groaned in pain from his wounded side. She ran over and helped him lie back down. He looked confused.

"Where am I?" he asked.

Esme tried to look stern. "You are in my bed, and you have not been a very good patient!"

Jon Rue realized this was the first time he had heard her voice when she was not screaming. He looked up at the green eyes.

"I saw you on the lower deck the night before with that man. I'm sorry I couldn't get him out," Jon Rue watched her expression carefully.

"You did everything you could. You saved my life." Though she was choked up she smiled at him. "My uncle was escorting me home from school. I have lived with my Aunt and Uncle since my parents died."

"Are you sure you didn't save my life? I don't remember much after the explosion."

Esme hesitated, to even think about the terror of those moments made her shiver. The blood all over Jon Rue...she had thought he was dead.

"I am a good swimmer, and you were limp. People waded out to help us," she reached for her handkerchief and wiped her face. "Let us not talk about that now."

When she looked back, he was already asleep, still weak from loss of blood. *But now when he wakes up, he will be able to eat, and he will get better,* she thought. She realized the thought of him leaving was unbearable. Esme shook herself. Several friends had already stopped by when they found out who her patient was. Apparently he was considered quite the ladies man, and they were quick to tell her about his many dalliances. Yet something about him denied the shallowness of his reputation. She had watched him for three days and he...had such a good face.

The shadows deepened and Jon Rue stirred again. Esme pulled her chair over to the bed so she could keep him from moving and hurting his side. He turned his head and watched as she settled down in the little chair.

"What is your name?" He asked.

"I am Esme Tremoulet," she replied. She looked down at him, then picked up a cloth on a little table next to the bed and dipped it in some water, squeezed it out and wiped the sweat from his forehead.

"Smells good...the water or something," he said.

"It is a special mixture my family has always used for washing. It is magnolia, sweet olive, and vetivert. It is also soothing, very medicinal. You look like you feel much stronger. Are you hungry?"

"I'm starving," Jon Rue was surprised that he was hungry. It seemed like years since he had looked out of the window on the steamboat at the dark river. Though the experience of the exploding boat had been a frightening and life threatening ordeal, it was almost worth it to be here with the girl that had taken control of his heart from the moment she looked at him. She was gone now to fix him something to eat. What would she think if she knew how he felt? Esme would not appreciate his almost being glad about the accident. Her dear Uncle had after all died. "Esme, Esme," he said the name over and over to himself.

"My aunt makes the best chicken gumbo in the world. I will have to spoon feed you. Do not try to sit up." Esme set the bowl of delicious smelling food on the little table and spread a clean cloth over Jon Rue's shoulder to catch any dripping.

He had to agree this was the best gumbo he had ever tasted. It wasn't just the food though. It was the person holding the spoon and carefully ladling it into his mouth. He started to cough and grimaced in pain. He lay back and tried to take some deep breaths. He was covered in sweat.

Alarmed, Esme moved the bowl away and gave him some water. "I think that is enough for now. You cannot run the risk of opening those stitches."

Jon Rue breathed slowly, trying to control his pain. "How is it you don't look like a Creole but you have that beautiful name and accent?"

"My father was French but my mother was from Ireland. He met her in New York at a Christmas Party at some friend's house. *Papá* says the moment he saw her he knew she would be his wife. She felt the same, and soon they were married. Do you not think that is very romantic?" Esme asked.

"Yes," he murmured softly, "very romantic."

Someone knocked gently at the door. An older woman, followed by Jacob, came in.

"Your brother's here to see about you, Jon Rue. I am Esme's Aunt Jolie. Esme tells me you are able to eat a little, so I know you will be up to a short visit with him. We will leave you alone."

Esme and her aunt moved out of the room and Jacob sat down next to the bed.

"How are you really? You look like you've lost weight, but you don't look as battered as you did the first day I saw you." Jacob looked worriedly at his younger brother. "Emma is beside herself. She wanted to come with me but of course I would not hear of it. I have to go back at once with word on your condition."

"I wish you had not interrupted my nurse," Jon Rue grinned.

"I might have known. No matter what your condition, you always manage to have the prettiest girls worrying themselves over you. I have to admit she does have beautiful red hair."

"She has red hair?" Jon Rue sighed, "I only know about her eyes. And this one is not like the others. I just wish I knew how she felt about me."

Jacob looked surprised. "That is different. You always assumed every female you met was head over heels, and they always were."

Jon Rue looked up as the door opened and Esme entered again. "Yes, very different," this was under his breath.

"I am sorry to interrupt, but the doctor is here and wants to speak to you, Jacob."

Esme came back and sat down next to the bed. "You are looking tired again, maybe you better rest some more."

"I'll rest, if you promise not to move from that chair," Jon Rue said.

Word that Jon Rue's boat bringing him home had exploded had reached the family early one morning. The friend who brought the news had said Jon Rue was alive but seriously hurt and was being tended by a family in Baton Rouge. Jacob had left at once while the family waited fearfully. Emma had been distraught and was thankful that Anne was with her.

Jacob returned with the good news that Jon Rue was being very well cared for and though battered and wounded, the doctor said he would recover. Jacob did not describe how terrible his brother looked but assured everyone that he would be brought home as soon as possible.

The flatbed carriage was not the most comfortable way to travel, but it was the only way they could transport Jon Rue lying down. Jacob and Tib drove as easily as they could. Esme hàd agreed to let him go home, but she would travel with him to make sure he didn't reopen his side. She would spend some time with her cousins who lived a short distance from the McLoeds. The doctor had convinced her she needed a change of scene after the death of her uncle and the traumatic experience in the exploding boat.

The constant movement of the carriage was taking its toll on Jon Rue. Her heart constricted as she watched him suffer stoically. Finally when he was soaked in sweat and so pale she was afraid he would loose consciousness again, she had called to Jacob to halt. She had him help make Jon Rue take the pain mixture the doctor had sent. He lay quietly now, but still bore the marks of the battering down one side of his face and neck. She thought again about the warnings of her friends about "charming Jon Rue," but she could not forget that he tried to save her uncle and rescued her from drowning under the beam in the hideous smoke and darkness. One of her friends in particular described a young man that, so far, Esme had not seen. Jon Rue was quiet and courteous and it was not just the pain and weakness. One day when she roused up off the cot at dawn, he was watching her with a look of wonder on his face.

As they slowly made their way down the last few miles, he touched Esme's hand.

"Yes, Jon Rue. What is it?"

He looked into the green eyes, "I love you Esme. When will you marry me?"

Jon Rue and Esme were still holding hands when the carriage reached the house.

Jacob sent Tib for more help to get his brother into the house. He was worried about Jon Rue. Not just from his injuries. He had never seen him so quiet. But as he watched the two in the flatbed, oblivious to the world, he grinned.

Well, that explains that, he thought.

Chapter XXXI

Love is the beginning, the middle,
and the end of everything
Lacordaire

Jacob had now experienced his own heart being captured. Somehow, he was not sure exactly how or when it happened; it had become known that Anne was "Mistah Jake's young lady." This was especially unusual because the serious-minded Jake had never really courted any young ladies. It was taken for granted that Anne would sit by Jacob at meals, he was her designated escort for dancing, and it was smilingly noted that her eyes lit up when he entered the room. Levee breakfasts continued, and Emma noted that Anne was the first person Jake looked for when he came home. Jacob was in a happy fog. Never having been remotely in love before, he had not exactly put a name to it. Anne was firm in her mind. This was the love of her life. She wondered when Jacob would realize what had happened, but she was content to let him stumble along with a bemused look in his eyes whenever she looked at him.

As Jon Rue recovered from his ordeal, he thought the whole thing with Jacob and Anne very amusing. He could hardly stand it that his brother had finally been tripped up with hardly a whimper. Jon Rue himself, totally besotted with Esme, could understand the feeling, but Jake of all people. Jon Rue now spent all his free time with Esme. She was staying with relatives nearby and once he was up and about, he was hardly ever home, and it was thought there would be an announcement soon.

Summer was almost over when disaster struck this happy group.

One evening Jacob told the family at supper that he had to go to Baton Rouge for a few days. This was not an earthshaking announcement in itself. The ramifications were not felt until after the family left the table and were visiting with their neighbors from the next parish that had stopped by for coffee. The men had adjourned to the verandah to smoke cigars and the ladies were chatting around some card tables that had been set up for games later. One of the daughters of a neighbor, not being aware of the ground she was treading on, opined that she was glad to see Jacob getting out in the world and wondered if he was still enamored of the lovely Tillie from Baton Rouge that he used to visit.

Everyone did not hear this comment. Unfortunately the only person who actually heard it from the little group was Anne. A small spasm gripped her heart, but she shook it off.

The men returned from the verandah and they were reminded that the family's harvest ball was in five days, and everyone had to be there. It was hinted there would be some announcements. Jon Rue grinned and thought of his sweet, red-haired Esme. He would definitely have an announcement. This whole comment flew over Jacob's head. Emma smiled at Jake and Anne, sure they would have an announcement too. Jacob, still oblivious, smiled his dazed smile at Anne, while she looked at him wonderingly. Would he ever speak? The connection between Baton Rouge and "announcements" worried Anne. Had she misread something? She would have to speak to him no later than tomorrow at their levee breakfast.

The next morning Anne arrived at the levee but Jacob did not. After pacing back and forth, she went to see the cook and asked if she had seen him. Auralee looked surprised, "why yes missus, he say he goin to Baton Rouge and would not need anythin today."

Anne sat down. The breath was knocked out of her lungs. Auralee was alarmed. "Are you all right Miss?"

"Yes, I'm fine." Anne sat for a moment, then wobbled to her feet and trudged off.

The next few days passed in a blur for Anne. The house was in a fever of preparations for the Harvest Ball. Emma was excited over a new dress and a new beau. No one really noticed Anne was quieter than usual and hardly ate anything. No one that is except Martha.

"Miss Anne why you quit eating? Mistah Jake will only be gone three days. You can last three days." Anne would look at her in an unfocused way and eat a few more bites, then get up and walk away. The day Jake was due to return, Martha went to Emma.

"Something not right with Miss Anne. Is there something wrong between she and Mistah Jake?" Martha demanded.

Emma stared at her. "Why, not that I know of. Why do you ask?"

"She don eat. She just sits and don't talk. It's like…she grieve'n or somethin," Martha said.

Emma felt a pang of guilt. She had been so caught up in her own affairs she really had not paid any attention to her friend. Quickly going upstairs she knocked tentatively on Anne's door. There was no answer. She turned the knob and entered the room. It was empty. She ran down to the levee. Anne was sitting on the ledge she and Jacob always shared when they had breakfast. She was staring out at the river lapping over the levee.

"Anne, have you got your dress ready for the ball tonight?" Emma pretended this was her reason for seeking her out.

Anne gave her a confused look. "Ball? Oh yes, I will just wear something I wore last spring. It's ready."

Emma looked closely at her friend. She was definitely paler and thinner. Circles under her eyes showed some sleepless nights. What had Jake done? Emma felt frustration building. If he had done something to hurt this sweet girl…her fingers longed to reach around his neck….

Evening of Harvest Ball…

The family was ready to ride to the pavilion they always used for the Harvest Ball. Carriages were brought up. Jon Rue and Esme were in the first carriage, followed by Emma and her new beau, then Zack and a widow from the neighborhood. The carriage for Jacob and Anne completed the entourage. So far there was no sign of Jake and Anne was in despair. It was getting late, so Emma and Jon Rue decided to go on. Zack would wait with Anne and her carriage. Almost as soon as the others pulled away, horse's hoofs could be heard.

"There he is now Anne. We'll see you at the ball." Zack and his companion plowed on ahead. The hoof beats got nearer.

Martha stood on the gallery. She was going to give Mistah Jake a piece of her mind before he left for the ball. Coming in all hot and sweaty. Leaving Miss Anne to fret and worry.

Jacob was not the rider of the horse. Tib pulled up by Anne's carriage with a sheepish look on his face. "Cap'n sent me on ahead cause he was de-tained," he enunciated this last carefully. He had practiced all the way home. "He'll be coming soon." Tib looked hopefully at Anne. "Cap'n says I can drive you to the ball, and he'll get there as soon as he can." To his horror Anne burst into tears and ran to Martha.

Martha puffed up to her full size and, as he told it later, "Cap'n, I thought I was a dead man!" She blasted the skinny little scout. "You tell yo Cap'n we don need no puny scrubs to take his place," and with that swept Anne into the house.

Jacob was having a terrible time. He hated leaving Anne without telling her goodbye. A special messenger had arrived late at night telling him he had to leave immediately, and he had no chance to even meet her for breakfast. It wasn't until he was almost to Baton Rouge that he realized he should have left her a note. His inexperience with matters of the heart was a challenge. Serious problems regarding the plantation awaited him in the city. After three days of fierce negotiations, he was able to renew what he and his father thought they had renewed during their last trip. But the time was slipping away, and he knew he could not get back in time to make the beginning of the ball. In desperation he had sent Tib ahead with the message to go ahead, and he would catch up. He knew nothing about a girl named Tillie.

Jacob was riding much too fast, but he finally made it to the pavilion. He looked for the carriage and finally found Tib at the edge of the carriage way.

"Where's Miss Anne?" he asked.

Tib looked mournful in his scratched down dress gray.

"Cap'n…" he stopped. "She wouldn't come," was all he could think of to say.

A blind rage, mixed with exhaustion came over Jacob. He looked at the pitiful little scout….

"What do you mean, she **wouldn't come**?"

Jacob didn't let Tib answer. "You weren't fancy enough for her?" Jacob spat out the words and whirled on his horse and headed for the house. He didn't hear Tib's answer, "It weren't like that, Cap'n…"

Anne sat on the gallery and watched the top of the levee. She thought, "*That water could come over and drown us all.*" She cried for awhile, but then sent Martha inside. She needed to be by herself and think. What possessed her to think a man like Jacob was in love with her, when he had never said anything? She had it wrong all along. He was just too polite. She was his sister's guest; what could he do? He had to go all the way to Baton Rouge to visit any lady friends he might have. She had been so sure the night she was sick. It seemed he was the one that pulled her back from the pit through the sheer force of his will and caring. Her heart felt heavy in her chest. A light rain began to fall. Suddenly she heard horse's hoofs and Jacob rounded the corner and jumped from his horse.

He ran up the steps and stormed over to where Anne was sitting.

"What do you mean not going with Tib," he yelled. Jacob's face was red and the veins stood out in his neck! Anne stumbled to her feet. She had never seen such fury! Her heart felt like it crumbled in her chest. She turned and ran blindly, sobbing into the night.

As quickly as the rage had come, Jacob's anger was gone. He stood stunned and then tore after Anne shouting, "Don't go that way, it's the rock pit…" his words were lost in the wind, rain, and dark.

He ran like a mad man. Several rock pits near the house were hidden by underbrush, and Jacob knew Anne would have no idea where they were. The soft autumn rain made everything stick together, the brush and trees and mud. Jacob slid down the embankment near the first pit, then stopped to listen. He heard some movement and then a soft noise. It seemed like it was to the left. It sounded like a faint cry, then nothing. Blackness swirled around him. He knew one misstep and he would plunge twenty feet into the first rock pit. God! What if Anne was at the bottom of the pit!

Cautiously he began to explore the surrounding lip of the crevasse with his boot. His foot felt something. He reached down and felt the wet, soft muslin of Anne's dress. She was lying very still, and his fingers could feel the sickening, sticky blood coursing down the side of her face. Jake thought his heart would stop in his chest! If she's dead…there was a flutter of breath. He picked her up and scrambled and clawed his way to the top of the pit and sprinted for the house.

Martha hit the front door like a bomb.

One look at the limp, bloody form and Jake thought Martha would kill him.

"What has you done? You has her cryin' all night and then you come chaghing in like a bull and scah her to death? Is you crazy?"

Jacob dropped his head in despair. "Yes, I scared her, and I've killed her I think. Please help me Martha, please."

Martha's anger and rage deflated as quickly as Jake's had, and she cried softly. "Bring her upstaihs."

Martha washed Anne's blood soaked head and face and put dry clothes on her. She wrapped her in a warm blanket and forced brandy down her lips. Jacob paced back and forth with his back to her, his head in his hands as she finished her ministrations. Once Anne was settled in bed she moved away and said, "I've done all I know to do"

Jake fell to his knees by the bed and alternated between crying and begging Anne not to die. Martha could do nothing to assuage his grief. She finally gave up and sat in a nearby chair, wiping her face with her handkerchief and watching the sad little scene.

Anne had a raging headache, and she could not understand where she was. Something big and heavy was pressing on her chest. She could hardly breathe. Opening her eyes she saw Jake's head and heard his sobs. She put out her hand and touched his face. He gulped and began kissing her all over her face and telling her now much he loved her.

Martha quietly slipped out of the room.

Autumn 1868

The countryside had talked of nothing for weeks except the upcoming double wedding at the River Rose Plantation. All neighbors and any relatives ever known to the family were invited. The day dawned with the special brightness that comes just before the long dreary days of winter. The house was full of food and company. Neighbors had been pressed into service to house extra guests. This was the first full-scale celebration in the area since the end of the war, and everyone wanted to be a part of it.

"Miss Anne, you are a beautiful bride. I am so proud of you and Mr. Jake," Martha finished adjusting the snowy veil trimmed in seed pearls.

"Martha I can't thank you enough for your help. I had dreaded the day I would be preparing for my wedding, having my mother and father both gone. I thought it would be too sad. But you remind me so much of my mother, and Zack is going to stand in for my father," Anne's eyes were swimming in tears. She wiped her eyes and smiled at Martha.

The elegant straight line of Anne's white satin gown draped gently at the waist and was pulled back to form the bustle and then the lengthy train. Seed pearls were entwined through Anne's long braided hair and secured her veil. Lily of the valley blossoms cascaded from a small white bible that had belonged to her mother. She took a deep breath.

"I'm ready," she whispered to Martha.

Sara finished pulling out the ruffles surrounding the round neckline that set off Esme's white silk wedding gown. The bodice was fitted and came to a point in front making her small waist look even smaller. White lace cascaded over the front of the gown and then served as a band of ribbon to bring the bustle over the silk train in the back. Her veil was draped simply from her hair, which she wore in coils around her head with a few curls in the front. Each bride's gown expressed her own individuality and enhanced their unique beauty.

Esme and Anne met in the grand hall and went down the wide staircase together.

Seth and Clarisa's little three year old daughter, Lorraine, was the flower girl and threw rose petals with typical Delmonde abandon. LoriDel, as she was called, had Clarisa's pale blond hair, but it was her sparkling black Delmonde eyes that never failed to catch at Zack's heart. He was thrilled when Clarisa and Seth asked if they could name their first born after Zack's wife. Lorraine Delmonde Jamison not only shared her cousin's black eyes, but seemed to have inherited her spirited personality and she spent a lot of time with her "Unca" Zack. She loved to ride ponies and her bright presence was a source of great joy to Zack.

The servants all stood in a line at the foot of the stairs and wished then well with their shy waves and smiles. Sara and Martha each carefully held the trains and would travel in the separate carriages with the brides. Any last minute arranging of hair or clothes was their responsibility. The guests had all gone on to the church so the brides made up the last carriages to arrive. They were going to be married at St. Angeline's and return for dancing and feasting at the Pavilion.

No one returned home before dawn and everyone agreed it was the most beautiful service and celebration they had ever seen.

The happy couples moved through the festivities in a glow and some people said, "Maybe this means all our bad days are gone. Maybe we will soon be like before. Before the darkness of the awful war."

On their way home in the wee hours of the morning, Seth, though tired, was in a thoughtful mood as the carriage rocked gently on the old road. Clarisa and LoriDel were both asleep; the little girl snuggled up to her mother. Seth smiled at the picture they made. LoriDel was the image of Clarisa until she opened her eyes. Then she bore a startling resemblance to her namesake, Clarisa's dead cousin. Seth knew he had only begun to live four years ago when he and Clarisa fell in love and got married. He adored Clarisa and despite his initial misgivings, he had had the good fortune to find a wife who truly loved him for who he was.

Clarisa had inherited all of the Delmonde land and despite the ravages of war, Seth had been able to sell several hundred acres and build a house for his young family. The Delmonde mansion was no more, but Seth was proud of their home. He had built the house with some help, but mainly with his own hands. The land was gradually being reclaimed and using contract labor, the Jamisons had produced a sugar cane crop for the last two years.

Day by day, month by month, the people of Louisiana were reclaiming their land and lives as best they could. The grandeur of a by gone era was no more, but something more important was immerging. The strength and spirit, the soul of Louisiana was once again rising above the rubble and taking hold to build a modern land. The many dialects and cultures, exotic cuisine and way of life unique to this small land area, would remain intact for future generations to admire and enjoy. Louisiana would never become homogenized. She would always have a flavor and texture like no other.

Chapter XXXII

Summer 1869

"1647. Aug 8: There hath suddenlie come among vs a companie of strange people, wch bee neither Indjan nor Christian. And wee know not what to liken them vnto. Some will have it yt they bee Egyptians or Jypsjes, wandering thieves, jugglers and beggars...Never hearing yt any such people were in ye Dutch settlements or Virginia, I surmised yt hee did mean yt they came from ye Spanish settlements, thougsands of leagues awaie...They doe use palmistry and other devilish arts and witchcrafts..."

Jewels of the Third Plantation,
Obadiah Oldpath, Lynn, Massachusetts:
Thomas Herbert and James M. Munroe, 1862

The itchy burlap cloth caused the little girl to jerk awake. She couldn't figure out where she was and then the odd smell told her. This afternoon Unca Zack had taken LoriDel fishing, and while he dozed in the summer shade of a big oak tree, she moved slowly along the bayou, much farther than she usually ventured. A rustling noise caught her attention, and she looked to see if she could see a squirrel or rabbit. Maybe it was Unca Zack coming to scold her for wandering off and telling her it was time for supper. But nothing was there. She turned back to her little doodlebugs that she had lined up in a row. They were her favorite bugs. They felt so tickly on her hand when they opened up.

All at once a sack was thrown over her head and someone was carrying her. She tried to scream but a hand shoved the old sack into her mouth and she tasted nastiness and almost choked. In panic the girl gasped for breath but soon she seemed to be going to sleep. Her struggles ceased.

The Gypsy man named Rau carried his now quiet bundle through the woods. He hurried to the campsite and came around the back of the last wagon. He carefully stowed the sack in the wagon under a pile of rags. He knew she would be quiet for some hours from the sleeping potion he had spread over the sack. He had to keep her quiet. Rom baro would banish him if he were caught stealing another child.

Rom baro was the hereditary chief of the extended family to which Rau belonged and Rau hated him. It wasn't fair that you should be the chief just because of your birth. Rom baro was also handsome; his black eyes seemed to captivate any woman he met. Rom baro had captured the heart of Tshaya, the most beautiful Gypsy girl in the camp and more importantly he had the money to pay the *daro*. Tshaya had said she would marry Rom baro and Rau could not forgive Rom for this. Rau thought that if he could get enough money he could change both Tshaya and her father's mind. She loved pretty beads and bangles. Rau would buy her gold bracelets and red glass beads and her own pony. Rau would offer so much money Tshaya's father would not be able to refuse. Rau would sell the beautiful girl child with the long blonde hair for a lot of money. He had heard of men on the riverboat who would buy girl children for a handsome price. All he had to do was keep her quiet until the caravan got to the river. The caravan would reach the river by sundown tomorrow and then he would be rich!

Zack woke from his nap and was surprised to find LoriDel no where in sight. He called out to her several times. He stepped to the edge of the bayou and looked down at its still surface. Zack called out again. No answer. Just the stillness of a summer afternoon. This was unusual. LoriDel had never strayed this far before. He walked along the quiet water, green and yellow in some places, undisturbed except for the giant dragonflies and occasional bullfrogs. Shadows were deepening when he came upon the little basket. LoriDel carried the basket with her whenever she went walking to capture "roly-poly" bugs to take home. She let them go eventually, but could sit and watch them curl and uncurl for hours. He turned the basket over and the little gray bugs rolled around for awhile and then crawled slowly off. But where was LoriDel? Zack was beginning to get a bad feeling. He turned toward home and then stopped and fired two shots in the air from the pistol he always carried. This was the plantation signal for trouble. In a few moments he heard the answering two shots that meant help was on the way.

Jon Rue came running with Seth coming up behind limping as fast as he could.

"What's the matter?" Jon Rue asked, out of breath.

"I can't find LoriDel and she left her basket. She would never do that. I think something's happened to her," Zack said shakily.

"Do you think she fell in the bayou?" Jon Rue asked. As soon as he asked this he knew this wasn't right.

Seth came struggling up the muddy rise by the bayou in time to hear this exchange.

"LoriDel can swim. She would've been able to get out. It's not even that deep around here," Seth said.

Jon Rue began pacing. "Someone has been here besides LoriDel," he said. "I can smell him."

Zack and Seth looked at him in surprise.

"Are there any strangers in the neighborhood? It doesn't smell like anyone I know," Jon Rue continued.

Seth looked uneasy.

"There's a band of gypsies camped out about a mile from here. They're a group we know and have never caused any trouble before," Seth said.

"Wasn't there some rumor last year about a child being stolen in Alexandria by gypsies?" Zack asked.

"That's what was thought at first, but the head man of the gypsies brought the child in to the sheriff and said she had been found on the road," Seth offered.

Jon Rue looked at Zack.

"Papa, we need to go get LoriDel. I can lead you."

The Gypsy camp had settled down for the night. LoriDel kept waking up and dozing off. She couldn't seem to stay awake. She hated the rough sack that kept scratching her arms and legs and the awful smell. Finally, she woke up enough to sit up and wriggle out of the sack. Looking around she could see she was in a wagon with clothes, blankets, and rags piled around. A small figure rose up from one of the piles. In the darkness LoriDel thought he was a boy. He had long hair tied with a piece of cloth around his head. The boy made a shushing sound and shook his head. He spoke words she did not understand. Pushing her aside, he piled some blankets into the old sack where she had lain so that it looked like she was still there. Then he motioned her to follow him.

Tall wooden wagons made a semi-circle around the camp, except for one tent where a Gypsy woman was laboring to give birth. She had been in labor three days and was growing weaker by the hour. The woman's husband began to howl and dance around the tent. He waved smoking sticks and shook them and shouted Romany curses at the *tsinivari* thought to be lurking nearby in times of trouble. Gradually other Gypsies, men and women, joined him screaming and shaking their fists. A few of the women began to shake their skirts in the direction of the tent.

The boy leading LoriDel away from the wagon stopped behind some bushes and tried to explain what was happening. LoriDel could not understand his words but when he made a cradle in his arms she nodded her head.

"Is she having a baby?" LoriDel asked. The boy shrugged and then nodded. LoriDel pointed to herself and said, "I am LoriDel, who are you?"

The light from the campfires was enough for her to see him smile, showing beautiful white teeth against his dark skin.

"Nanosh," he said, and then grinned broadly. He pointed at her. "Gajo," he said, then pointed at himself and said, "Rom." LoriDel did not understand any of this, but thought Nanosh must be his name.

He gestured for her to follow him and they plunged into the dark wood. Nanosh ran quickly, sometimes getting so far ahead of LoriDel she thought he had lost her. But he would reappear and urge her on. Finally, exhausted, LoriDel stumbled and fell. She began to cry with tiredness and frustration. Nanosh came back and helped her to her feet. LoriDel couldn't understand why they were in such a hurry. She didn't think anyone had seen them leave the wagon.

Rau grew tired of the dancing around the tent and went back to check on his prize. He glanced in the wagon and was pleased to see no movement coming from the sack. The sleeping smell potion had worked better this time. Rummaging through an abandoned army camp a couple of years ago, he had found a vial of something that smelled funny. He had tested it on one of the old dogs in the camp and saw that it had a "sleeping draught" effect. The first child he had tried it on, he had been timid and only used a small amount. Waking up after only an hour the girl had caused him to almost be banished from the *kumpania*. *Rom baro* had warned him that if he ever stole another child he would be subject to a formal *kris* which would carry the penalty of *marime*. Rau looked in once more and realized the form under the sack was almost too still. What if he had killed the little Gajo? He pulled back the sack and saw the pile of blankets and swore under his breath. She had escaped. But where…then he remembered he had not seen Nanosh all evening. That little devil. Rau suspected he had helped the first child escape. But this time Nanosh would not succeed.

The black stillness seemed to cover the children. In the quiet she could hear a noise close by. Someone was following them! Nanosh grabbed her hand and they ran blindly, falling over sticks and holes left by small animals. The thing following them was closer now and louder. They could hear bushes crackling and small branches breaking. Suddenly they were up against a large rock. Nanosh scampered up the side of the rock clinging to tiny niches with his small nimble fingers. He then reached down and pulled LoriDel up into a hole, a crevice that was barely big enough for them both. Their hands and knees were smeared with blood from scraping along the rock. They waited, scarcely breathing for the thing to catch up with them. Suddenly the noise of horses and shouts of men burst through the vines and scrubs.

"LoriDel, can you hear me?" Seth called out.

"Papa," LoriDel screamed. "Here we are."

Both children peered out from their hiding place on the scene below. Seth was reaching up to help them down. Zack and Jon Rue were holding one of the Gypsy men.

"Oh papa," LoriDel sobbed as her father gathered her in his arms.

Zack, Seth, and Jon Rue rode slowly into the Gypsy camp. The campfires had burned low, almost out, so that all you could see were shadows standing near the tall wooden wagons. One shadow disengaged itself and came forward.

"I am Rom baro." The tall shadow gestured to one campfire now being rekindled by one of the other shadows. "Come sit and tell me what has happened." Rom baro waved to two others who had joined him. He spoke in a strange language. Two of the shadows moved toward the man the River Rose men had captured. "We will take him for now."

Zack nodded at his men and they let the man go with the two Gypsies.

Zack, Seth, Jon Rue, and the two children sat down near the now blazing fire. A woman came forward with coffee for the men and warm milk for the children.

"I'm Zack McLoed. This is my son Jon Rue, my cousin's husband, Seth Jamison and his little daughter LoriDel. It seems that one of your people kidnapped my cousin's daughter this afternoon from my place. This lad apparently tried to help her escape."

"His name is Nanosh," LoriDel offered.

Nonosh ducked his head in embarrassment.

"We found the man we brought back here, chasing them in the woods. The children had managed to climb up into a small crevice about two miles from here. My son, Jon Rue is an excellent tracker, and we found them before the man had harmed them. I believe this has happened before."

Rom baro stood up and gestured to the men holding Rau to bring him forward.

"What do you have to say for yourself?" Rom baro growled angrily.

Rau looked at Rom baro with hatred. He spoke in Romany and spat out the strange words.

Rom baro spoke to the men holding him in words the River Rose people could not understand and they took him away, though he still yelled angrily.

"I ask your pardon for his despicable behavior. He will be dealt with and you will have no more trouble I assure you."

Zack looked troubled. "What about notifying the authorities?"

"I can understand your concern. We will take him to the sheriff ourselves tomorrow. Let us handle this in our own way." Rom baro stood. "I will get back to you tomorrow and tell you what has happened in his case."

Next day...

Fifteen colorful wagons lined the road to River Rose. Rom baro had arrived at River Rose with Sheriff Dickerson in the early afternoon. Zack, Jon Rue, Seth and Jacob, who had just returned from Baton Rouge, gathered in the plantation office to hear what Rom baro and the Sheriff had to say.

The men drank coffee and listened to Dickerson as he explained Louisiana law and traditional Gypsy law or *Romani*.

"We try to work together in situations like this. Cooperation seems to work to everyone's advantage." Dickerson rubbed his hand over his chin and sighed. "According to Gypsy law, this man, Rau, should be tried by a *Romani kris* and punishment meted out according to their justice system. However, in the case of kidnapping, I operate under special constraints, especially as it involves a child. I will allow Rau to be kept in the custody of the Gypsies for their formal *kris*. They will try him; meet out whatever punishment they deem appropriate and then turn him over to me. He will also be tried in a Louisiana court and sentenced according to our guidelines as well. This is where the difficulty lies. According to *Ramani,* our law has no jurisdiction in a Gypsy case."

Rom baro set his coffee cup down and looked at each man in the room. "I am the chief of the *kumpania.* My responsibilities include interpretation and enforcement of *Ramani.* Rau not only committed a crime against our *kumpania* but against your community. He was warned previously about this type of activity in the past. Because of this crime he has made the entire *kumpania* unwelcome in this community. Therefore, I rule that he not only will be subject to *Ramni* justice, but also to your justice. As soon as our *kris* is complete, he will be turned over to you. I ask that our punishment be coexistent with yours."

"I am in agreement with your decision," said Dickerson. "You will bring him to our facility as the conclusion of your *kris*."

All the men stood and shook hands, Rom baro, the small boy, and two Gypsies, who had accompanied him, walked out to the caravan waiting on the River Road.

The River Rose men watched as the tall, colorful, wooden wagons slowly made their way down the road.

"Do you think they will bring him back?" Seth asked Dickerson.

"Gypsies always keep their word." The sheriff put on his hat. "They have to if they want to come back."

Chapter XXXIII

April 1870

Anne closed the last schoolbook and began dusting the chalkboard. She had been teaching the local children for six months and was thrilled to see their progress. They were all ages, sizes and colors. The war had disrupted so many things, schooling included. When she first mentioned her idea for starting the little school to Jacob, he was surprised and then delighted. Everyone pitched in to try and refurbish the little schoolhouse that had set idle for almost nine years. Thesues had managed to keep the school going during the first year of the war, but then in the winter of 1862, he had succumbed to an influenza outbreak that swept through the area.

In the two years since they had married brothers, Esme and Anne had become very close. Anne helped Esme finish her studies, and she now assisted in the teaching. On this late afternoon day, Esme had gone on ahead as Jon Rue was returning from a business trip. Jacob would come back with the carriage soon.

Anne suddenly realized it was getting very late. She lit one of the lanterns and wrapped her shawl closer around her shoulders. As she started to move the lantern closer to a book she was reading, she thought she heard a scraping noise. Someone or something had brushed up against the side of the little house. She thought how alone she was, a mile or more from River Rose. Darkness had come on all at once. Where was Jacob?

The schoolroom door burst open, and two little girls came running in. A large dirty man came right after them. Two of Anne's littlest, poorest and surely the skinniest pupils threw themselves at her. They clung to her skirt and when she tried to stand, they clasped their tiny arms around her waist.

The older girl, began shrieking, "Don let Da git us! He's kilt mamma! Please hep us Miz Anne!"

The huge man towered over all of them and reeked of sweat, liquor, and filth. His face was what shocked Anne. His brow bone curved over a forehead that looked like some pictures she had seen of prehistoric man. Under these overhanging brows were eyes that showed no humanity but glittered with hate. Overall the impression was of a dark-complexioned man, yet there were places on his face and arms that looked like the skin had been peeled off.

"Gimme my kin back! Yu guls comin' with me. Git out uf the way woman!" He slapped Anne so hard she fell off the chair, and the wriggling, crying girls fell on top of her.

Anne was terrified. Blood spurted from her mouth and frightened the two little girls.

"He's killin her, too," Mary sobbed and both girls struggled to their feet as their father unsuccessfully tried to grab both at once. They ran out through the open door and right into the path of the carriage barreling down the road.

It took both Tib and Jacob to stop the horses from running down the screaming children.

"Da's killin' Miz Anne just like he done kilt our momma!" Mary screamed, as both men grabbed at the small girls floundering on the ground.

Jake charged into the schoolhouse in time to see a bloody Anne dragging herself to her feet. The girls "Da" was much less fearsome when he had to face a large, angry man who immediately began to pummel him with his fists. He soon was crying and begging Jake to stop. However Jake was in a crazed state, and though Tib tried to pull him off of the man, he was no match for his enraged Cap'n.

"Jacob'! Jacob! Stop! Please, I'm all right!" Anne was screaming now, too, afraid he would kill the man cowering on the floor. She grabbed at his arms, and finally, Jake became aware of Anne's pleading and slumped back against her desk. Tib found a rag and wet it in the school bucket. He helped Anne wipe the blood from her face while Jake, still panting, glared at the miserable wreck on the floor.

"We have to go see about their momma, Jacob," Anne whispered. The little girls hung damply from her waist, afraid to get out of her reach.

Suddenly the man on the floor rolled away from Jake and shot out the door.

"Let's go, Tib. The girls will have to show us the way. We won't worry about him for now," said Jake.

The carriage rolled precariously over the rutted excuse for a road. The two girls were now rolled up in Anne's skirts, snuffling quietly. The pale moon was barely enough for them to see between the trees. The brush and vines were getting so thick Jacob was almost ready to turn the carriage around. Then Mary piped up.

"Ther tis. Is ours house," she pointed at a small dark shape. No light showed from the windows. They could barely make out a sagging porch.

"Tib, stay with Anne, just in case he's in there." Jacob spoke softly as he quietly started toward the little shack.

In a few moments they saw a feeble light. Jacob had found a lantern. He came back holding the light high.

"Be careful. This is the only light," he said, helping Anne and the girls scramble down out of the carriage.

Jacob led Anne and the two girls cautiously up the rickety steps with Tib uneasily trailing behind.

"These folks out here has guns, Cap'n. We need to be careful," Tib's voice was quivery. Though brave in war, sneaking around in these Louisiana woods at night with a drunken maniac, mad as he could be, possibly right this moment with his rifle cocked…his thoughts were interrupted by Jacob.

"You're right, Tib. But I have my gun in my boot. Come on in and close the door. Prop a chair under the knob."

Jacob set the lantern on a small table in the middle of the room. This left all the corners in shadow.

Anne stood close to Jacob and whispered. "There's no one here. Where is she?"

Jacob shook his head. He had expected to see a bruised and beaten woman and had hoped Mary's description of their mother "being kilt" was the result of seeing a bloody nose or lip. But not this. No sign of anything.

"Let's search the house as much as we can tonight. Then I'm taking you home, Anne." Jacob's jaw tightened. "Your face is swelling fast and it must be hurting bad." He gently touched her check.

She winced and nodded. Now that the shock of the last few minutes was wearing off, her cut lip was excruciating.

"We'll spread out from the table and see if there is anything we should look at. I'll bring the lantern over."

Anne looked down at Mary and her sister. "Jacob and Tib, this is Mary and Ora Durin."

Both girls shyly buried their faces in Anne's skirt.

"We are counting on both of you now," she paused, "show us where your momma keeps her clothes."

Mary and Ora looked at each other with puzzled looks.

"Dresses, shoes, anything like that," Anne prompted.

Mary seemed to be the spokesperson for the duo. In fact, Anne realized she could not remember ever hearing Ora say more than her name and a mumbled "yessum" in the few weeks she had known the girls.

"She has her clothes on her, Miz Anne." Mary glanced at Ora as if to say, 'did they think their momma went outside without any clothes on?'

"Where did she put her clothes that were waiting to be washed, not the ones she had on at the time she left," Anne patiently continued.

"Oer clothes is jest on us, Miz Anne, and that's the truth." Mary felt bad. She just could not get the answer right.

Jacob motioned Anne close enough to his side to whisper; "It's probably true. They may not have clothes other than what they are wearing." Anne looked shocked.

Mary picked up the conversation, still trying to help her teacher understand how it was. "Tha's how come I han't been to school regular. My 'wearin' shoes jest kept gettin holes in the bottom. A church lady and her husband left some things at the stone and that's how'n I come by these." She looked down at her current 'wearin' shoes. They were very old brown sandals that were so big for her feet, they flopped when she walked. "They'll fit me soon," she explained proudly.

"What's the 'stone' Jacob?" Anne asked totally mystified.

He answered in a low voice. "No one goes in this bayou as far back as the Durin's house unless they're related by blood. Mary and her kin are part of the Redbone population. All of them are desperately poor, so when kind-hearted folks want to help out they leave things by that boulder at the head of Bayou Chatis not far from the house."

Mary and Ora watched the whispered exchange. Had they said something wrong? Mary shifted nervously from one foot to the other.

"That's all right. Mr. Jacob explained everything to me," Anne said, seeing the child's discomfort.

"Show me where you keep your things. Toys, books anything like that," she asked. Mary looked down at her newly shod feet. "None left," she admitted sadly.

Anne felt like she had been suddenly dropped into a foreign country where they spoke English, but all the meanings of the words were different.

Tib spoke up, "You mean you had some toys and they broke or got lost?"

Ora's big eyes in her little face filled with tears. "'I'm a bad'un,' Da said. I was caus us loosin our'n things. Even my baby doll." This last was too much for Ora and she started crying.

"What she done wer'n so bad," Mary attempted to console her sister. "Ora forgot to close the gate in the back and we lost one of our'n chickens." Mary looked pityingly at Ora. "Da burned her dollbaby and then burned Ora."

Jacob, Anne and Tib stood like statues, a cold fear engulfing them.

"Where," Jacob had to clear his throat. "Where did your Da burn you Ora?"

The little girl looked stricken. "Da says if'n I ever says a word...." She trailed off and tears started again. Her right hand stayed firmly behind her back.

Something clicked in Anne's brain. Though Ora used her left hand to write, her handwriting was hardly legible. Instead of the large, fat penmanship that marks a young student, hers was loose and uncontrolled. Maybe she was not naturally left-handed. Anne reached down and tried to pry Ora's hand from behind her back.

Mary suddenly took control of the situation. "Show'em Ora, maybe they can help."

Ora slowly brought her hand around and held it up for all to see. This was too much for Anne. She sat down in a chair and covered her face with her handkerchief.

Jacob brought his fist down on the table and it wobbled precariously. He caught himself in time and didn't swear. Tib turned away for awhile so no one could see his face.

The two little girls watched fearfully.

Mary and Ora were tucked in bed with Emma. No one thought they should spend the night alone because of the ordeal they had been through. Anne had to go to bed with cold compresses, as her face continued to be painful and the swelling showed no sign of easing.

Zack had confirmed that the girls' "Da" was a notorious Redbone named "Pog" Durin.

Before he went back downstairs, Jacob tried to explain the Redbone phenomena to Anne.

"They keep to themselves and don't trust 'outsiders'. 'Outsiders' being anyone not related to them in some way. Most of them live far enough back in the swamps and woods that no one ever sees them. Somehow they manage to eke out an existence with vegetables they grow or chickens they keep and birds or animals they hunt or trap. Because the mistrust is so deep they only marry within the small circle of people that make up their group. As a result of the inbreeding some are terribly deformed, both in body and mind. Some are even Albinos. Pog Durin has some of that. You saw the skin splotches. They have their own code. They don't come out and bother anyone and they

don't tolerate anyone coming into their area. But this has become personal."
Jacob felt the anger rising within him again.

Anne took his hand. "Please don't become involved. Let the Sheriff handle this. I couldn't bear it if you were hurt or...worse," this last was strangled as she buried her face in his shoulder.

"Our so-called carpet bagging Sheriff that we have now is a joke. I wouldn't be surprised if ole Pog isn't hiding out at his house right now." Jacob bent down and kissed his wife's head. "But I promise I'll be careful. Now please try to rest."

Jacob slowly went down the stairs. Anne was right. This was a dangerous situation. But even if he didn't seek revenge, what about poor little Ora? Her hand was an abomination! He tried not to think of the agony she must have suffered. Ora's little fingers were like tiny claws, the skin taut and bright red. She probably had received no treatment. Ora's mother was the next part of the equation. Was she dead or being hidden somewhere back in the woods, possibly hurt?

He rejoined the group in the sitting room.

Jacob, Jon Rue, Esme and Zack sat in the parlor and took turns staring at the floor and each other. The brutality of what had been done to Ora and Anne almost made them embarrassed to belong to the same species as Pog Durin. As Jacob had said, he was part of a Redbone family and a particularly malicious family at that.

They were in a quandary. Jacob was convinced he could find some clue as to the whereabouts of the girl's mother if he could go back and search the cabin in daylight. However if Durin was back he certainly would not let him in and could even claim trespass and have Jacob arrested.

Tib suddenly appeared at the door. "I think you all need to come look at this," he motioned to them to follow him.

On the verandah he pointed back toward the general area of the Durin house. Flames could be seen lighting up the sky.

"I'll bet that's not a forest fire," Jon Rue muttered.

"Tib and I'll go look." Jacob gestured to Tib to get their horses. "Jon Rue and Papa, I think you should stay here and make sure no one gets near the house."

Quietly, Jacob and Tib approached the cabin, going the last few yards on foot. The heat from the structure was already setting twigs and brush on fire. It was the cabin and it was fully ablaze.

"Let's go. Any evidence here is gone." Jacob mounted his horse and he and Tib headed back.

Jacob thought out loud as they rode along. "I think there should be a guard around River Rose for the next few nights, Tib. Pick some hands that you think are dependable. Spend some time with them, teach them to move quietly, not like a herd of cattle." He looked at Tib. "I don't really think Pog will do anything. I think he just wanted to make sure we didn't search the cabin. But we can't take a risk."

Tib said, "No one will get near the house; you can count on that."

"If you accidentally happen to find someone snooping around, bring them to me, even if they have no known connection to Durin."

No one had left the sitting room when Jacob returned.

"Was it the cabin?" Zack asked knowing the answer.

"Yes, looks like somebody set a good fire and destroyed everything." Jacob disgustedly threw down his hat and paced back and forth.

"Looks like we need to bring in reinforcements," Zack said. "Some real lawmen and maybe even a judge or two."

"I agree, Papa," Jacob nodded. "We not only have a missing woman and suspected arson, but also a child that can't possibly go back home. Actually two children," he said as an afterthought.

Zack went to his desk. "I'm sending word to Judge Wright in Baton Rouge asking him to come for a 'visit'. It's almost hunting season. I would imagine he has a few marshals who wouldn't mind having some time off too." He turned and looked at his sons. "Jon Rue, I think either you or Jake should be with the crew guarding the house at all times. You all can split it up like you want. There may have to be some important decisions made quickly and I want one of you to be there if that happens."

"I'll take the first shift. Let me go tell Esme." Jon Rue headed upstairs.

"I guess I better sleep fast. Daylight will be here soon," Jake agreed, following on his heels.

By the next day guards were conspicuously posted all around the place and Zack personally visited all the farmhands and made sure they had firearms. As he told them, "you may need a gun to save your house."

He promised them that he was bringing in extra hands and would try to have help for them, so that every corner of the plantation would be patrolled. They knew the danger of Redbones and did not have to be told twice the seriousness of the situation.

By dusk the second day after the Durin house went up in flames, three carriages had arrived at River Rose. Judge Morgan Wright and eight U. S. Marshals had decided they needed a vacation. They especially needed to stay at the McLoed home because the hunting on River Rose was so exceptional. Two marshals in farmhand clothes would be at the main house at all times. The other six would rotate with Zack, Jon Rue and Jake and the three plantation overseers. Everything seemed tied down and all contingencies covered.

While seeming to go about their regular routine, the marshals and the three overseers were gradually closing in around the cabin and the area where it was known several of Durin's relatives lived. They were searching, looking for any trace of Durin or…freshly turned earth. Before dawn on the morning of the third day after the fire, several figures crept toward the burned out cabin. They were acting on information given to them by Tib who had managed in his usual way to infiltrate even this tightest of groups. He let them know that the first night there were people picking up certain things from the dirt floor of the burned out cabin.

At dawn a tight circle of men in clothing that blended in with the trees moved toward the shell of the cabin. Shadowy figures were again moving around inside intent on their search. They did not notice the circle being drawn around them, until a burly figure shouted, "Halt! You're under arrest! Put up your hands." The marshal hardly got the words out when guns blazed from the shadowy figures. The marshals had anticipated this reaction and while they were dodging behind trees they were also letting loose a barrage of bullets at the cabin. Figures toppled over, then a voice shouted. "Stop. We'n won't shoot no more!"

The marshals quickly handcuffed the group, dragged out three wounded men and put them in two wagons they had brought and hidden earlier. Judge Wright approached the wagons.

"Which one of you is Pog Durin?" he demanded. Silence. "He's wanted on suspicion of murder, arson and child cruelty. Either you give him up or all of you will be arrested on those same charges for aiding and abetting." Judge Wright's voice boomed out in the darkness. "I don't think you want to risk hanging for something you did not do."

Silence. "That's fine. I need some prisoners in my jail anyway. I hate an empty jail. Course you know I also hate trials, so I put them off as long as I can. And there is nothing I hate worse than a murderer, especially of a woman. I hate people who set things on fire and I really hate people who hurt little children!"

This last was delivered in the booming voice of doom that Judge Wright was famous for.

"But this will be good. My hangman hasn't been getting enough practice. He's getting sloppy. It took him 30 minutes the other day to finally get old Jasper Willet to quit jerking. Yes, you bunch will give him plenty of practice. Oh, by the way. I am authorized to offer $100 to anybody surrendering Pog Durin into my custody tonight. Bring 'em on boys. Let's head for Baton Rouge," the Judge started to get in his carriage.

"Wait," a thin voice called out. "Let's give 'em up. We'n can split that there money and be rid of a no account varmint too."

One of the figures detached himself from the group and started to climb out of the wagon. A shot rang out and he fell over the side.

"Everybody down," the chief marshal yelled.

For a moment there was a brief flurry of noise as many men scrambled in the dirt and leaves. Now there was dead silence. Even the normal night sounds were gone, as small animals and even the insect hum were momentarily quiet.

After a few minutes, the marshals slowly crept forward toward the wagon. Nothing moved. Little shafts of early morning sunlight began to creep through the tangle of cypress and underbrush like skinny fingers bringing unwelcome illumination to men crouched in the wagons and behind trees.

The chief marshal gave the order to "group and shoot." At the prearranged signal the marshals ringed the area and sent a fusillade of gunshots in the general direction of the rifle shot that had toppled the man in the wagon. The shooters then dropped to the ground and waited for a response. The silence was total again.

"All you men head out and search every inch of this area," the chief marshal gave the order.

Though the men searched well into the morning, the Louisiana swamp failed to yield any human prey. It was as though Pog Durin had melted into the very fabric of the trees, bushes, and ground cover. "Melting away" was a skill his kind possessed above all others. This was how they survived. Periodically authorities would attempt to follow up on a complaint that starved looking children and bruised women had appeared on roads or in fields. It was always noted they wore ragged clothes and no shoes. They gave the appearance of hunted animals, casting furtive looks over their shoulders. The few times anyone heard them speak it was with the barely understandable dialect of people totally unschooled.

Occasionally a bearded, unkempt man would turn up at a rural store to buy flour or coffee, but this was rare and communication consisted of the minimum words necessary to complete the transaction. One young girl described such a man who had visited her father's store on the edge of Alexandria.

"He had wall eyes and they were sunk back in his head. His hair had dirt and twigs and leaves in it like he had been sleeping on the ground." The girl paused for a moment. "He was speckled like. Almost like spots on a dog." Then she shivered at the memory. "The way he looked at me scared me to death. I had a nightmare that night that he tried to come steal me out of my bed and I woke up yelling!"

Finally convinced of the futility of their search, the men headed back to River Rose. The chief Deputy reported to the Judge that they were sure Pog was no longer in the area. They were also convinced the little girls' mother had been killed, but finding a body in the swamp without someone leading the way was next to impossible.

After breakfast the law enforcement contingent headed back to Baton Rouge. Judge Wright left two marshals to guard the plantation for the next few weeks.

Within a few days, the grandparents of the two little girls came forward to take them home. They related a story of a daughter who somehow became involved with Pog Durin against their wishes. Hearing nothing from her for several years they had resigned themselves to the idea that she might be dead. In fact she was living only a few miles away, but trapped and apparently unable to escape because of what she feared might happen to her girls. This latter was pieced together by scrapes of information from little Mary. Now at least they would be safe and able to lead normal lives.

Chapter XXXIV

Jacob still was troubled at how close he had come to killing a man with his bare hands. He was certain that if Anne had not intervened, Pog Durin would have died in the Schoolhouse. The hold his wife had on his heart and soul was revealed to him in those moments when he and Durin struggled that night. It was as the full realization of what she meant to him grew in his heart that she approached him and suggested a picnic in the middle of the week. He thought about it later and smiled at how a year ago he would have thought that was ridiculous, and now, whatever made Anne happy seemed what he wanted to do.

They selected the grassy outcropping that was their favorite place on the levee. Anne spread the cloth out and settled her skirts as Jacob lifted the picnic basket down. "Ceil must think you need fattening up. This thing is heavy as lead." he said.

"Come sit down here and let's just talk for awhile." Anne indicated the place next to her.

Jacob leaned back against Anne's favorite old cyprus tree and looked at his wife. She seemed even more beautiful than ever, almost like she was glowing.

"I wanted to be where we wouldn't be disturbed when I told you this," she looked deep into his eyes. "Jacob, we are going to have a baby!"

The world tilted. "Are you sure?" was all Jacob could manage.

"I am positive," Anne reached up and kissed him.

Suddenly a thought stuck him. "You didn't hurt yourself when Durin struck you in the Schoolhouse?"

Anne smiled. "No, it happened after that. In fact, I know exactly when," She at least had the good grace to blush.

Then she was in his arms, held as tightly as he had ever held her.

The following month Jon Rue and Esme announced they too were expecting a baby. Happiness seemed to permeate River Rose.

Conversations regarding names and how to decorate nurseries preoccupied the family. Then came the inevitable guessing as to whether there would be a boy or a girl. Anne was sure she would have a boy just like Jacob. Esme declared she would be happy with either, but Jon Rue was insistent on a girl. Ceil cooked all the special and even peculiar dishes mothers-to-be sometimes want and everyone hovered over Anne and Esme as if "they were the first to ever have babies" according to Martha, who was the biggest hoverer of all. Even terrible war memories were pushed aside in this euphoria.

Then Zack received news of a surprise visit from an old friend.

Chapter XXXV

November 1870

Zack reread the letter that had come in the morning post. His excitement mounted! Pierre was coming in three days! His soldier's soul swept him to his feet, and he began to pace. He was back presenting a battle plan in a hot tent in the middle of the war. General Beauregard would be listening carefully as always and watching his every move. Zack knew Beauregard had a theory that great officers had to feel their ideas in every fiber of their being. Body language and timbre of voice all communicated to him the soundness and "commitment of the man to the plan." This was only one of the many strengths of leadership Zack saw evidenced by this great General.

This reverie was interrupted by a commotion outside his window and he watched as his daughters-in-law were helped into the carriages taking them to a planned picnic. Emma was included as usual, but he felt a pang as he saw his only daughter settle herself between her "sisters." Though Emma had many beaus, there had not so far been that special one that she wanted to spend her life with. It was surprising to Zack that she would be the last to be married as she was in his view, more beautiful than any of her contemporaries. The porcelain skin and black eyes set off by black curls were stunning. Young men swarmed around her, but she seemed to be picky and always found something wrong with them. *Sort of like her mother,* he thought smiling. He remembered conversations with his wife's father as he bemoaned the fact that she laughed at all the young men asking for her hand. Emma was still young. But occasionally he caught her looking wistful as Anne and Esme enjoyed their full lives with husbands they adored and babies on the way.

"Ah, well," he mused. "I must start making plans for Pierre's arrival." General P.G.T. Beauregard and Colonel Zackary Patrick McLoed had been friends since West Point. Zack and both sons had served under the General that most Louisianaians considered the greatest commander of the Civil War. And now he would be able to entertain him in his home! Of course Beauregard had open invitations in all of his men's homes, but this was the first time he had heard from his friend since the surrender. According to his letter he had some important business to discuss and asked specifically if Jon Rue and Esme could be present. It should be a very interesting visit.

As the carriage pulled to a stop in front of the house, Zack, Jon Rue and Jacob stood as excited as small boys in front of the verandah. They did not have to wait long to get their first glimpse of their hero. The door opened and Pierre was out and hugging everyone in a flash. They stood back in the way of men and looked at each other. Beauregard looked different in his civilian clothes, though very smart. A little older, the black hair streaked with white, but ramrod straight and still possessed of the incredible energy that drew people to him and made him seem larger than life.

"My compliments. You all look very fit. Civilian life is agreeing with you," the dark eyes sparkled. "I want to introduce you to my colleague, Mr. Robert Casey. He is engaged on a special assignment that we will be talking about later."

"I am very happy to meet you. General Beauregard has told me a lot about you and your great services to 'the cause.'" Casey had an easy manner that belied the quick perusal of the blue eyes that seemed to bore into each person he met. He was tall with brown wavy hair and dark skin that looked a result of exposure to sun rather than heredity.

The men moved toward the house and as they ascended the steps to the balcony the three ladies of the house emerged. Introductions were made all around and Zack was surprised to see Emma blushing slightly at some remark from Casey as he bowed to greet her. Emma never blushed! Maybe this was a good sign. Zack was immediately caught up in the conversations and everyone moved into the house for dinner and he forgot about this moment.

Dinner was gumbo, roast chicken, and vegetables from the garden and blancmange. Though considered a "light" dinner everyone was ready for a sleepy afternoon respite, especially the travelers who had been on the road since before dawn. It was announced that coffee would be at four on the south balcony and supper would be at seven.

Mr. Robert Casey was glad to be able to wash up completely and change clothes. Though he had washed face and hands before dinner, there had not been time for the complete wash-up needed after long hours in a dusty carriage. He lay down under the netting as the heat seemed to settle into every corner of the spacious room. Closing his eyes he again saw the lovely face of

Emma smiling up at him, slightly rosy from his compliments when they were introduced. She had charmingly thanked him but was not overwhelmed, as many women seemed to be in meeting him for the first time. Casey had no idea why he had this effect. It was just something he had felt over the years. Emma was young, but with her beauty must have been accustomed to all sorts of compliments from various suitors, though she did not appear to take any of it too seriously. Holding her own in a conversation about the strategies of different battles in the war, let him know she had actually listened to what must have been constant "battle talk" around the family table. He sighed. It didn't matter what he thought of the delightful Miss McLoed. What was in store for him precluded any attachments of the heart for a long time.

Emma brushed out her hair; the hundred strokes could wait until last thing at night. She lazily finished her toilet and stretched her self out under the netting, turned on her side and looked out at the huge magnolia that was taller than her bedroom window. Mr. Robert Casey was a surprise. She had not been aware that anyone was accompanying General Beauregard especially someone like Mr. Casey. Emma stopped. What did she mean "like Mr. Casey"? He was undeniably handsome and well spoken, but then so were most of the young men she knew. That was it! He was not very young. Not yet thirty, but close, she guessed. And what in the world was he involved in with the General? She sleepily considered the fact that this would probably be the only time she would every see Robert Casey. This thought suddenly was unbearable. Sleep was no longer an option. Emma reached over and withdrew her journal from the night table drawer and began an entry.

Coffee was pleasant and conversation centered on reconstruction and the grumbling over "carpetbag" government. Everyone seemed to realize the real discussions and explanations for General Beauregard's visit would take place this evening.

Supper was over and the family was gathered in the drawing room. Surprisingly, Pierre asked that the large double doors be locked so no one could interrupt or be privy to their conversation. The family sat expectantly.

"First I must ask your total agreement that nothing discussed in this room will ever leave it. It is not only confidential. It is top secret to the government." He looked around the room for acknowledgment. "I've wanted to spend some time with Zack and all of his family for a long time. One of the main reasons is to clarify and give recognition to a young man that was not able to have the usual accolades of war resulting from bravery and dedication to a cause."

Beauregard shifted in his seat so he could make eye contact with Jon Rue.

"Many of you know Jon Rue was on special assignment throughout the war and because of that had no rank. He also was awarded no medals or even publicly shown any appreciation of the difficulties he faced. I cannot of course tell you the most secret of his missions, but I can assure you he would not be in this room today, alive, if he had not been the best. The reason for that is not that he was fortunate and did not get wounded. The reason he is alive is, he did not get captured." The general looked around at the intent faces.

"Now you are thinking, the prisoner of war camps were bad but some did survive. Jon Rue would have never been interred in a prisoner of war camp. If Jon Rue had been captured…" he paused for effect looking at each person, "he would have been executed on the spot."

There was a gasp from the women, but not the men. Apparently these former soldiers knew.

"You see, the so called "couriers" were more than mere bearers of messages in the strict sense of the word. They were scouts, and the information they carried had to get through. It meant life or death to hundreds of men and in many cases effected the course of a battle. They had special training, and they were sworn to do anything necessary to get their information through. Anything." General Beauregard sat back in his chair and looked at Jon Rue. Esme was holding his hand. Jon Rue looked steadily at his old commander and said nothing.

"Jon Rue, I cede you the floor. Do you wish to make any comments?"

"No, sir, I think you have explained everything in the clearest manner possible." He still sat impassively

"We are forming a "Courier in Action" corps, a civilian counterpart to our military couriers. I cannot give any details, however Mr. Robert Casey is director of the Louisiana unit. As was the case with Jon Rue, he is not able to discuss with anyone his activities. I have asked Jon Rue to spend some time with Robert sharing his experiences and expertise. That is why he is with me on this visit."

General Beauregard stood and nodded to Robert and Emma. "I am going to ask you both to take your leave of us because after I arrived, I saw that I could share some experience and information with Jacob, Jon Rue and their wives and" he nodded at Zack, "you can contribute to this also.'"

Surprised, Robert and Emma left the room to the remaining family and Pierre.

"It's cooler on the verandah. I will have some lemonade brought out." Emma indicated the wide French doors just off the dining room.

Robert walked over to the railing and looked out into the Louisiana evening. He was anxious to spend time with Jon Rue. One of the very few surviving Civil War "couriers", he could give him valuable insights into the twilight world he had entered.

"So you will be just like Jon Rue, only it won't end at the end of a war?" Emma asked in a stilted voice.

"Yes, it will be my permanent job unless or when I become compromised." He accepted the cool drink and sipped appreciatively.

"What does "become compromised" mean?"

"It means someone finds out who I am when I am on assignment," Robert watched Emma's profile in the semi-darkness of the balcony. She swallowed. "Do you know where you will be on assignment?"

"Yes, and that will be secret too."

Emma turned and looked at him, "What a shame. I probably won't ever see you again."

For the first time, Robert felt a twinge of regret at his choice of careers. Having no close family to speak of, it had seemed the perfect choice. But now…

After having obviously made some sort of decision, Emma spent the next hour showing Robert the house and explaining some of the customs and legends surrounding her part of Louisiana. For his part, he also held up his part of the bargain and betrayed no hint of the regret he felt at not being in a different position.

Meanwhile in their private meeting, General Beauregard was sharing personal tragedies with the two young couples and suggesting a way to prevent the same thing happening to their families. Pierre had lost his wife and sister in childbirth and strongly urged the family to seek the services of a woman physician from New Orleans who had made a name for herself in helping women survive this ordeal. He knew her personally and assured them she was a well respected and sought after doctor.

The next morning, the director of the Civilians in Action spent several hours with Jon Rue behind closed doors, while Pierre and Zack went riding and renewed their old friendship.

After dinner, the family wished Beauregard and Casey well and watched the carriage disappear around the curve taking them back to New Orleans.

Chapter XXXVI

November 1870

Jacob and Anne talked into the night about Beauregard's concerns. "I'm going to New Orleans Friday and bring Dr. LeSeur back for consultation. I can't run the risk that what happened to the General's wife and sister would happen to you. It is 1870 and these advances in knowledge about childbirth mean that help is available."

Jacob was adamant and Anne had to agree. She was very heavy now. Her wish for a boy like Jacob looked like it was coming true. Though Jacob's mother had no trouble having her children, she was a much larger woman, "almost as tall as papa," Jon Rue remarked.

Esme was still relatively small and it looked like Jon's wish for a girl would probably come true for them. But even so, there were things that could go wrong and Jon was anxious to meet with the esteemed doctor as well.

The carriage with Jacob and Dr. Isobelle LeSeur rounded the corner and stopped in front of the house.

Anne watched as the tiny woman in black traveling clothes was helped from the carriage.

"Doctor, this is my wife, Anne. Anne this is Dr. Isobell LeSeur."

"Madam, it is so good of you to come," Anne greeted the small figure.

"It is my pleasure Mrs. McLoed, especially to assist such an enlightened family"; her dark eyes sparkled with intelligence and interest. "Many people still will not let doctors near their women at this most important time".

Dr. LeSour was warmly welcomed by the rest of the family and soon comfortably settled in her room. Dr. LeSour's credentials, as General Beaurgard had indicated, were impeccable. A graduate of The Medical College of Louisiana she was one of the first women in Louisiana to graduate with a degree in medicine. She had several letters of recommendation not only from medical societies but also from prominent patients whom she had attended in and around the New Orleans area.

She exuded confidence and calm. After dinner, she sat with both couples in the drawing room and explained her approach to the "birthing" process.

"Mrs. Jacob McLoed will be first of course and I will use several different protocols to make sure we have a healthy baby and mother."

Dr. LeSour indicated she would finalize her plans after she had examined each woman. Examination would take place the following morning and she would have information for them the next day. "I will need to depart on Tuesday afternoon as I have another family to see in Baton Rouge. I think when we have thoroughly reviewed all the procedures and you have been given the instructions I will leave with you, everyone will feel much better."

December 14th dawned dark and rainy. The windows and eves over the balconies dripped with heavy winter moisture.

Anne felt the first twinges of pain at supper and a courier was dispatched at once to New Orleans.

Daylight had just begun to color the sky with a weak, pale yellow as if the rain had faded all the color from the sun, when Dr. LeSeur's carriage pulled up in front of the house. People, who had been waiting, immediately began unloading the large portmanteaus she brought with her. She gave brisk orders as to their disposition and quickly went to Anne who was now in the throes of hard labor. A midwife and several helpers, all previously requested by Dr. LeSeur during her earlier visit were assisting Anne. A special mixture the doctor had directed to be prepared had been given sparingly given to Anne to ease her pain.

After examining her patient, Dr. LeSeur came into the hall to speak to a pacing Jacob.

"She has suffered all night,—how much longer will it be?" he asked.

Dr. LeSeur took him by the arm and started down the stairs.

"Are you leaving her—where are you going?" Jacob was beside himself.

"Mr. McLoed, your wife is progressing nicely and I have increased the pain mixture. We will start birthing in about two hours. Right now," she hesitated in pity as she looked at the haggard, frightened man, "we must tend to you. Later you will need to play a most important role."

Anne was nearly exhausted. Dr. LeSeur had increased the pain mixture but these last two waves of pain were terrible.

Dr. LeSeur and Jacob entered the room. The doctor looked at Jacob. "Can you do this? You can't grow faint hearted on me now. I thought I gave you enough," she hesitated "stimulant…."

Actually the "stimulant" Jacob had gulped down, was three shots of Irish Whiskey. "I'm fine," he said shakily.

The midwife moved away to let the now white clad doctor take her place. "Jacob, wipe her face and talk to her for a moment."

The doctor gave the midwife the ether mask.

"As soon as I look up, put it on. Not before."

Dr. LeSeur performed some slight surgery that caused Anne to scream and then the baby crowned and the birth was over in minutes. The midwife immediately put the mask over Anne' face and Dr. LeSeur handed the baby to a helper to clean up.

Jacob had noticed none of this. He was so shaken by his wife's screams that tears were running down his face. When the ether did its work and she closed her eyes, he once again wiped her face with the special water the doctor had given him.

"Mr. McLoed, you have a fine healthy son." Dr. LeSour's words penetrated Jacobs mind as the midwife handed him Jacob Patrick McLoed, Jr.

Jacob looked stunned! His son. This baby calmly looked at his father, then began chewing on a chubby fist.

"Get the wet nurse" the midwife ordered. "He's already hungry."

"How are you papa? Holding up?" the doctor asked. She was quickly preparing her special procedure. This was the procedure that would save Anne from the fate of so many mothers. This would keep her from bleeding to death. "Now is when I need you the most."

"Yes, I'm fine." Anne was resting now and he wiped his face on his sleeve. Jacob was told to continue to bath Anne's face with the special relaxing herbal water mixture and to keep talking quietly to her.

"I will direct some small amount of ether, but she has lost some blood and I do not want to overload her heart. There will be some pain that she will feel, but nothing compared to that last. As soon as she is awake, I want you to show her the baby, can you do that?"

Jacob nodded.

"Jake. Jake," a groggy Anne moaned softly.

Jacob was startled.

"Yes, darling, I'm here."

He looked at her as she nodded off again. "She has never called me Jake, never!"

Dr. LeSeur smiled. "She calls you that in her heart, Mr. McLoed."

The doctor and the new father looked at each other. "At times like these, the heart speaks its own language." She went back to her work and Jacob was left to ponder another mystery in this day of mysteries.

Anne was beginning to rouse up again. The midwife handed Jacob his son again. He awkwardly held the baby down close to Anne's face.

"Here's our baby. Can you see him?"

"Oh yes," she reached weakly for the infant. "Oh! Oh!" she cooed and then a spasm of pain interrupted. Jacob returned the baby to the midwife. He continued talking softly to Anne. "Dr LeSeur says it will not be as bad as before and will be over soon," he said, bathing her face again.

Mother and child were sleeping as the soft evening descended on the home place.

The family and doctor were gathered once again in the drawing room.

"She will be fine. I will be back in five days. I have left instructions with the aides. They know what to do. My special mixture for building blood is to be given in specific doses every three hours during the day. They also know all about this. Mr. Jacob McLoed, you have a strong healthy son and a brave wife."

As the doctor predicted, mother and son flourished and Anne had no complications. Christmas was an especially joyful occasion with Jacob and Anne's new son named Patrick, and prospects of Jon Rue and Esme's child to come soon.

Chapter XXXVII

January 1871

The Angel of death has been abroad throughout the land; you may almost hear the beating of his wings.
John Bright, Speech, House of Comm

February 23, 1855.

Sara, Esme's personal maid, softly opened the door and entered Jon Rue and Esme's bedroom. She was surprised to see Esme still sleeping. Esme had wanted to be ready when Jon Rue came home. It was almost dark and still the figure on the bed seemed to be sound asleep! Seemed to be asleep until the little maid saw the handle of the crude knife sticking up at an angle out of Mis Esme's chest and the blood…she screamed in one long scream that seemed it would never stop!

From the River Road Jon Rue heard Sara's hideous screams. He spurred his horse into a frenzied gallop as a cold terror gripped his chest. Horse and rider skidded to a stop in a whirl of dust and grass. Jon Rue dismounted and crossed the verandah in two strides. The screams kept coming, now and then muffled as Sara strangled on tears and then resumed the soul searing sounds.

Reaching the top of the stairs, Jon Rue stopped. Just outside the door to his bedroom Sara was collapsing in the arms of Martha. Anne, pale and gasping, was leaning against the door with Jake holding her up. His father stood with his hands at his sides looking at him, tears streaming down his face. Zack would occasionally shudder, and a deep grinding moan would rise from his throat.

Jon Rue still stood motionless. If he just did not move, maybe this nightmare would stop. If he just did not go in that room, maybe…suddenly he heard a sound like none he had ever heard and realized it was coming from deep within his chest. His chest was on fire! Then his eyes were on fire! His whole body was burning up with the blistering fire of unshed tears. He was running now, into the room. Falling to his knees beside Esme, he hesitated. She was only asleep—why was everyone crying? She was only asleep.

Small wisps of red curls lay across Esme's pale face. The coverlet as always was neat and unruffled. Esme never moved once she was asleep. Could they not see she was only asleep?

The knife was the only thing out of place…a knife! A knife had pierced his darling Esme and their child; had cut away his heart, but he was still alive! He breathed deep ragged breaths and moaned in torment. Each beat of his heart seemed ready to pound the blood from his chest. The awful knife was cutting him in two! Only this pain would never stop. As long as he lived, some portion of this would remain a scar on his soul.

His father and Jacob lifted Jon Rue to his feet and took him into Zack's room. Someone handed him brandy, and he sank down in a chair.

Shock, horror, and grief descended on River Rose. After a while, Jon Rue came and knelt by his dead wife and child and didn't move or make a sound.

Jake figured the killer had entered through the balcony, the heavy vines on the side of the house acting as a perfect ladder. The ground below was trampled and muddy, matching exactly the mud on the balcony. Could it be Pog Durin? Jacob wished for the hundredth time that afternoon he had killed him when he had the chance. He went over to his kneeling brother. "Do you think it was Durin?"

Jon Rue got to his feet. "I know who it was. I just don't know his name."

"What do you mean?" Jacob looked as Jon Rue carefully pulled the covers over the body that still looked peaceful as if asleep.

"I can smell him. I'll be leaving as soon as I get ready. I'll meet you at the edge of the back clearing in about thirty minutes." Jon Rue started changing clothes.

"Leaving? Where are you going?"

"Do you remember when the General talked about what I did in the war? Well, this is war and I am 'going under.' I'll see you at the clearing."

Jacob left him alone and went out to find Zack. He wanted all vines cut and guards posted around the clock until the killer was caught. Zack had already handled the posting of guards.

"How is Jon Rue?" Zack asked his son.

"I don't know, papa. He says he is 'going under.' He says this is war. I think he's going to look for the killer!" Jacob stood looking at his father.

"If what Pierre says is true, and I have no reason to think otherwise, he will probably find him."

"And when he finds him, what then?" This was not a question that Zack even considered answering.

It was totally dark when Jacob went to meet his brother. He would never have seen him had he not moved out from the trees and spoken softly. Jon Rue was scarcely visible. All skin was covered with what Jacob assumed was mud. His clothes, too, seemed slimy with the stuff.

"I will not be gone long. Wait for me here before daylight tomorrow." Jon Rue started to move soundlessly away.

"Wait. How do you know how long you will be?" Jacob put out his hand to restrain his brother.

"Don't touch me!" Jon hissed. "You'll contaminate the scent." He stopped for a moment and explained patiently. "I know he's not far. I smell him. I will be here before dawn."

"Won't you need help bringing him back?"

"I won't be bringing anyone back." This last was whispered over his shoulder as he vanished into the night.

The smell of his prey was so strong that Jon Rue could hardly breathe. No one seemed to understand that once he 'had prey,' there was a scent so overpowering he had to find it. Then and only then did he have peace. Silently he moved, scarcely disturbing the rain soaked bog. His special booties and years of scouting enabled him to virtually skim the ground. There was no chance of leaving a track. Jon Rue became a blurry thing. Only occasionally would anyone have even seen a contour or a movement, so well did he blend into the environment. The scent of his prey was strong now, its sickening sweetness washing over him. The blurry, not quite seen thing stopped by a pirogue where a man huddled sleeping. The slumbering figure was suddenly pulled upright, like a puppet on a string, head back, and arms grasping at something around his neck. Only garbled choking sounds came now as two figures stole through the turgid, dark water and slime. The strange procession of invisible puppet master and struggling puppet went on for a mile then abruptly the puppet was dropped into the heavy, dank water. It roused up sputtering and crying. "She's here, under this here log, now leave me be," the puppet squealed, looking all around franticly searching for the puppet master. A knife flashed even in the dimness and the puppet's head fell to one side, a bloody grimace, before the water closed over it.

All was quite now, the blurry thing was gone. The swamp pond was placid; the surface of green mold was as if it had never been disturbed.

Zack and Jacob stared sightlessly into the fire as the clock ticked toward midnight.

"What will happen to Jon Rue when he comes back and has to face the funeral and the rest of his life?" Jacob simply could not comprehend the extent of the agony his brother must be going through.

Zack looked up. "As soon as the funeral is over I'll be going to New Orleans." He stopped and wiped his eyes. "One stop will be to Dr. LeSeur to tell her we won't be needing her services. The next stop will be Pierre. Maybe he can think of some work for Jon Rue that will take him away from here."

Just before time to meet Jon Rue, Jacob once more looked in on his sleeping wife and baby. Was the fact that their room was not near the back of the house and had no balcony what had saved them? He shuddered.

It was the time just before dawn breaks. The Louisiana marsh was quiet before first light. Jacob thought he heard a noise and stepped back into the cover near the clearing's edge. He had confidence in Jon Rue, but with a maniac like Durin loose it would pay to be careful. Not a sound could be heard.

When Jon Rue touched his brother's shoulder, Jacob almost collapsed. "God! Jon Rue you almost gave me a heart attack!"

"I found the little girl's mother." Jon Rue motioned to Jacob to follow as he headed toward the house.

"Where did you find her? Is she alive?"

"Durin led me to her. No, she is not alive. Neither is Durin. It's over." Jon Rue silently went past the back door sentry who stared in surprise but recognized Jacob and let them in.

Three days later

Everyone for miles around attended the funeral for Esme Tremolet McLoed and her unborn child. The shock and grief for the family and Jon Rue washed over the mourners. Death of such a young woman in such a brutal fashion was terrible enough, but the fact that it also took an innocent baby touched the very essence of one's soul. A funeral mass was celebrated at St. Angeline's, and the family cemetery at River Rose added one more grave. The day after the funeral, Zack left for New Orleans along with Jon Rue who did not want to stay on the site of his heartbreak another day.

Zack and Jon Rue knocked on the door of General Beauregard's office in New Orleans late in the afternoon. A young man ushered them into a small foyer and asked them to be seated.

"The General has gone for the day but the Director, Mr.Casey is in."

In a moment Robert Casey was striding down the hall toward them. "What a great surprise! I hope nothing is wrong." He looked from one to the other.

"Can we go somewhere private?" asked Zack.

"Of course. Come back to my office."

They followed Casey into a small plain office, and he motioned them to sit on a couch. Instead, Jon Rue walked to the window and stood with his back to the room.

Apparently word had not reached Beauregard about the murder.

Zack gave Casey the awful news.

Casey went white. "What about the rest of the family? Are they in danger? Are they guarded?"

Jon Rue turned. "The killer has been taken care of. They're in no more peril. Robert, I would like to come back into the corps. Do you think you have a place for me?"

"Of course. You would be a great asset. You have more actual experience than anyone."

"I'd like to go ahead and stay in New Orleans. Do you have someone who could ride back with papa and get the rest of my things?"

"We can arrange for all of that. How is the rest of the family, Zack? This must have been a terrible shock!"

Zack stood up and, like Jon Rue, walked to the window. "It's hardest for Emma. Anne and Jake have each other and Patrick. Emma can't seem to accept Esme and the baby both being gone. She is devastated. She seems almost unreachable."

The three men had dinner with Beauregard that evening, and Casey volunteered to go back with Zack for Jon Rue's personal effects and extend Beauregard's personal condolences.

Early the next morning they set out for River Rose. Beauregard was already setting up plans for Jon Rue to resume his career.

As the carriage rumbled along, Casey commented, "It's too bad Emma is so affected by this. I can see how that could be. She is very young, isn't she?"

"She's eighteen and always thought she should look after Jon Rue. When Esme found out she was going to have a baby, Emma could hardly wait. And she dotes on Patrick, of course. It is just too much. The baby and Esme, and Jon Rue so wounded," he trailed off.

Both men were preoccupied with their own thoughts and continued the journey in silence.

Robert Casey had spent a sleepless night. The shock of thinking of some harm coming to Emma had jolted him to his core. His brilliant career in the CIA no longer seemed as important as getting to River Rose and seeing for himself that Emma was truly safe. But if he left again how could he ever be sure she was safe? Toward dawn he made a decision. He would go to Emma and…what? If he gave up his position, how would he take care of her? Robert remembered Emma telling him about a plantation adjoining River Rose that had been destroyed during the war. Zack and Jacob were thinking of buying it and making it a part of River Rose. Robert had saved the money from his family's farm, which he had sold, when he joined the couriers. Maybe he could become a partner in that venture. He put his head back in the carriage and closed his eyes. But what if the lovely Emma was not in love with him? He thought she seemed to share the same feelings, but had he crushed that out of her with his talk of his secret work?

Zack was exhausted, physically and emotionally. He was relieved that Jon Rue had found some salvation with Beauregard in work he loved. But what about Emma? The shock of losing Esme, the baby and now even her beloved Jon Rue would be almost too much for her to bear. He dozed fitfully, not really resting. If only Lori were still alive. She would know exactly what to say and do. Zack never went through a day that he did not miss her smiling black eyes and generous heart. Emma was so like her. He put his handkerchief over his eyes.

"Are you all right sir?" Robert asked in concern.

"I am thinking of Emma. She was very close to Jon Rue. She loves Jake and Anne of course and the baby, but…it's very hard." He choked up and could not continue.

They finished the ride in the silence of shared grief and concern.

Shadows mixed with shafts of sun worked their way across the gazebo's floor, but Emma did not notice. She sat in the center chair quietly now. Tears had come and gone, and though her handkerchief was still damp, it seemed there could be no more tears. It was as if her heart was being squeezed, and she had trouble breathing. Footsteps sounded gently coming toward the small enclosure, but she did not hear anything. It wasn't until he stood in front of her, reaching down to clasp her hands that she even realized someone was there.

"Emma. I am so sorry...," He did not get the chance to finish.

"Robert! Robert! Oh, Robert!" Emma fell in his arms sobbing in deep gulping sobs. He led her over to one of the side settee. She continued weeping. He held her tightly.

Because of his conversation with Zack, as soon as he had greeted the family, Robert had immediately gone to the gazebo where Jacob said Emma had been all day.

They sat motionless for awhile. Each came to the realization of what had happened and was afraid to move.

Emma stirred and softly whispered, "I'm so glad you came. You are the only one who could help. I don't know why. I can't bear to be around anyone. But when I saw it was you...," she looked up into his face.

Robert was ruined at this point. All of his meticulous and carefully laid out career plans seemed like ashes when he held Emma and looked into her tear-stained face.

He traced a tear down her cheek with his finger. "Well, we are in a predicament, aren't we?"

Throwing caution to the winds, Robert kissed her and held her gently.

"Robert, what about never seeing you again?" She sounded tremulous, and he was afraid tears were beginning again.

"Forget about all that. Right now you need to come back to the house and eat and be cared for." Robert tucked her arm in his, and together they walked slowly back to the house.

Zack looked up as they entered the balcony and one look told him all he needed to know.

Six months later...

The stone with the two small angels, a slender woman and a small child, had been put in place at Jon Rue's direction and inscribed as he wished.

This was his first visit back to River Rose since Esme's death. It was just dawn when he arrived. He didn't wake the family but left his horse and walked quietly to the family plot in back of the big house. Jon Rue wanted to be alone with his thoughts. He knelt in the still dewy grass and read the words he had found that so described his love.

Esme and Unborn Angel
April 15, 1850 ~ January 25, 1871
Beloved Wife and Child of Jon Rue McLoed
There is no shadow where my love is laid;
For (ever thus I fancy in my dream
That wakes with me and wakes my sleep), some gleam
Of sunlight, thrusting through the poplar shade,
His requiem for the Day, one stray sunbeam,
Pale as the palest moonlight glimmers seem,
Keeps sentinel for her till starlight fade.
And I, remaining here and waiting long,
And all enfolded in my sorrow's night,
Who not on earth again her face may see,
For even Memory does her likeness wrong,
Am blind and hopeless, only for this light
This light, this light, through all the years to be.

Jon Rue began to shiver. It was summer but he could not get warm. He had been cold since he killed Pog Durin in the frigid waters of the swamp. He pulled a flask from his pocket and drank deeply. The whiskey failed to warm him. Nothing warmed him anymore. As he rode to River Rose he had hoped the sight of Esme's grave would give him peace. He had killed a murderer; a double murderer. But there was no peace. His choice of career as a courier during the war was because he could not bear to take another life. But he had killed Durin with no compunction. He had even felt justified. But in his soul there was now a stain. A stain whiskey could not obliterate. He rose and stumbled toward the plantation house kitchen.

Jon Rue was a haunted man.

Author's Notes

Arpent: This was a French unit of land measure that was employed throughout lower Louisiana in the 18th century. Forty arpents was standard plantation **depth.** (Deep enough to provide fire wood and construction materials from forested swamps and fronted on the river or bayou.) **Width** depended on the resources of the planter. Plantations were referred to by width since arpents were fixed. (An 18 arpent plantation was 3,456 feet wide as each arpent equaled 192 feet. Normally this would enclose 610 acres.)

Balance'ment: Loosely based on Angela Ridgway's Dressage Philosophy of horse training. Because of setting I have given it a French context.

Batture: Sandbar, gravel, or mud deposit (on the inward side of a river bend).

Bousillage construction: The insulation used in buildings in the 1700s. (Parlange Plantation in New Roads, Louisiana, built in 1750, the model for River Rose, used bousillage construction.) It consisted of moss, deer hair, and dried mud overlaid with a thin layer of mud and then paint and supported by brick pillars.

Creole: "...the white descendants of the early French and Spanish immigrants born in the New World." From "The Creoles of Louisiana," by George Washington Cable.

Fiñe: Baptiste's nickname for Jon Rue; means slender or delicate.

Louisiana Gypsies: By the mid 1800s Gypsies were well established in Louisiana moving from place to place as the seasonality of work dictated.
Terms: *daro*: bride price; *gaje*: (Plural)non-Gypsies; *gajo*: (Singular)non-Gypsies; *kris*: A Gypsy court; *kampania:* A group of extended families

living, working, and traveling within the same geographic territory; *marime*: Impure or shameful; *Rom*: Refers to the Gypsy people; also the term used for a Gypsy man and husband; *Rom* baro: "Big Man"; chief of a Gypsy *kumpania; Romany*: Name of the Gypsy language; *tsinivari*: Evil spirits that inhabit the night fog.

Hectic: A fluctuating or persistent fever, usually involving the lungs.

Hogsheads: The barrels used to hang sugar that was still being "purged" so it could drip into pans for later use as molasses. These barrels would hang from rafters in the aptly named "purgery." The hogshead barrels were about twice as large as regular barrels of the time, holding from 1,000 to 1,200 pounds. They were also used as containers to ship the final product to market.

Hurricanes: No major hurricanes struck Louisiana in 1853. I have used as my model the hurricane called "Racer's Storm" that struck the Louisiana coast just east of Cameron on October 6-7, 1837. The storm caused a surge of water 8 feet above high tide on Lake Pontchartrain. All wharves along the Mississippi coast were washed away with the tide. The storm caused widespread flooding and considerable damage to shipping; all boats, including four steamboats, perished in the storms. Lower portions of New Orleans were submerged. Crops were seriously damaged along both sides of the Mississippi. Six lives were lost.

In Louisiana, lunch is referred to as dinner and dinner is called supper.

Mattressing or wind-rowing sugar cane: This process consists of laying the cane, unstripped of leaves, in "mattresses," or "mats," and covering it with earth to protect it from cold weather.

Medical College of Louisiana: Established in 1834, was the precursor of Tulane University Medical School

Preceptorship: A medical student's training in 1860 consisted of his three year preceptorship under the direction of a practicing physician and his attendance at two courses of lectures of at least sixteen weeks each. In 1861, in anticipation of the medical needs of the Civil War, the curriculum included a one month course on military surgery, dissection, and clinical instruction on the wards.

Santerian ritual: Santeria is a syncretistic religion whose origins date back to the slave trade when Yoruba natives were forcibly transported from Africa to the Caribbean. God is worshipped as the creator of heaven and earth and of guardians called Orisha. Ritual Sacrifices believed to make the saints (Orisha) happy, are animal's blood, usually chickens. Dancing and chants during these rituals are believed to cause the particular Orisha invoked to take over the spirit and body of the person, who then acts and talks like the Orisha.

Storm Riders: This is strictly an invention of the author. The storm rider would be dispatched to warn areas of the state that could be impacted by storms from the Gulf of Mexico.

The U. S. Military Academy: West Point

"The Old Bank of the United States," located at 343 Royal Street is the oldest building used as a bank in New Orleans." (New Orleans French Quarter History, Architecture and Pictures)

The country's money and credit problems intensified during the Civil War. In 1863, President Abraham Lincoln, urged by Salmon Chase, the secretary of the treasury, signed the National Bank Act to help solve the nation's money problems. The act established a national banking system and a uniform national currency to be issued by new "national" banks. From 1863 to 1877, national bank notes were issued privately by the national banks.

Bibliography

A Catalog complementing the Pictorial Exhibit, **Green Fields, Two Hundred Years of Louisiana Sugar,** Prepared Under the Auspices of The Center for Louisiana Studies, University of Southwestern Louisiana, 1980, Published by The Center for Louisiana Studies, University of Southwestern Louisiana

Aïde, Charles Hamilton, French-English musician, composer, dramatist, and novelist (1826-1906)

Alexandria Daily Town Talk*, Centennial Edition, March 18, 1983, "The Burning of Alexandria," on May 13, 1864

Bartlett, John, **Familiar Quotations**, Little, Brown and Company, Boston, Toronto, 1968

Bailey Lee, **Southern Food & Plantation Houses**, Clarkson N Potter, Inc., 1990

Botkin, B. A. , edited by, **Lay My Burden Down,** A Folk History of Slavery

Brasher, Mabel, **Louisiana,** A Study of the State, Johnson Publishing Company, Copyright, 1929 by Louisiana Teacher's Association

Brown, John, **Slave Life in Georgia: A narrative**, 1854, Edited by F. N. Boney, Savannah Behive Press, 1972

Bunner, H.C., **The Light** from "the Century Illustrated Monthly Magazine, November 1887, Vol XXV #1 poem on Esme's gravestone.

Cassin-Scott, Jack, **The Illustrated Encyclopaedia of Costume & Fashion from 1066 to the Present,** Crane, Stephen, **The Red Badge of Courage**, first published, 1895, now Bantam Books, New York. Edition: 4th enlarged edition, Studion Vista, 1994

Foote, Shelby, **The Civil War, A Narrative** (Red River to Appomattox),Vintage Books, A Division of Random House, New York, 1986

Frazier, Charles, **Cold Mountain**, 1997, The Atlantic Monthly Press, 841 Broadway, New York, NY 10003

Freeman, Douglas Southall, **Lee's Lieutenants, Vol. I, Manassas to Malvern Hill,** 1971, Charles Scribner's Sons, Macmillan Purblishing Co., New York, N.

Glausiusz, Josie, **Otizi's Boots Were Made for Walking,** Discover Magazine, January, 2004

Hancock, Ian, **We are the Romani people,** University of Hertfordshire Press, College Lane, Hatfield, Hertfordshire AL 10 9AB

Henry, Joanne Landers, **Robert Fulton, Steamboat Builder,** Illustrated by Tram Mawicke, Edition: 1rst Chelsea House, New York, Chelsea Jrs. 1991

Henry, Robert Selph, **The Story of the Mexican War,** Da Capo Press, Inc., A Subsidiary of Plenum Publishing Corporation, Indianapolis, 1950

Hurmence, Belinda, **Slavery Time When I Was Chillum,** G. P. Putnam's sons, New York,1997

Kemble, Frances Anne, **Journal of A Residence on a Georgian Plantation in 1838-1839,** Afro-Am Press, Division of Afro-Am – Books, Inc., Chicago, 1969

Keyes, Frances Parkinson, **Madame Castel's Lodger**, Farrar, Straus and Company, New York, 1962

King, Wilma, edited by**, A Northern Woman in the Plantation South** (Letters of Tryphena Blance Holder Fox, 1856-1876

Kirchberger, Joe H. **The Civil War and Reconstruction: an eyewitness history**, New York, Facts on File, 1991

Library of Congress, Geography and Map Division, **Civil War Maps: an annotated list of maps and atlases in the Library of Congress,** 2nd edition, Washington: Library of Congress, 1989

Lane, Miles, **Architecture of the Old South**, A Beehive Press Book, Abbeville Press, Publishers, New York, London, Paris, 1993

Lester, Julius, **To Be A Slave, Scholastic Inc.,** New York, N.Y.,by arrangement with Dial Books for Young Readers, a division of E.P. Dutton, Inc.

Linley, John, **Architecture of Middle Georgia** (The Oconee Area) University of Georgia Press, 1972

Medical Training in 1860, **sls.downstate.edu/student affairs/history.html**

Microsoft **ENCARTA** Reference Suite 2000

Mitchell, William R. Jr., **Classic New Orleans**, Martin-St. Martin Publishing Co.,1993

McPherson, James M, **Ordeal by Fire: The Civil War & Reconstruction**, New York: Knopf, Distributed by: Random House 1982

National Georgraphic Magazine 1990, **Battlefields of the Civil War,** (U.S. – History Civil War 1861-1865

Nichols, William, Edited by, **Words To Live By**, J. G. Ferguson Publishing Co., Chicago 1967

Oates, Stephen, **The Approaching Fury, Voices of the Storm, 1820-1861,** Harper Collins Publishers, Inc., 10 East 53rd Street, New York NY 10022

Plante, Ellen M., **The American Kitchen, 1700 to Present: from Hearth to Highrise,** N. Y., N. Y.: Facts on File, 1995

Ridgway, Angela, Dressage – Philosophy- **"Balance in Movement"** see internet resource section

Rowland, Charles P., **Louisiana Sugar Plantations During The American Civil War,** Leiden, E. J. Brile, 1957

Savas P. Theodore, map of **The Battle of Yellow Bayou**, Wharton vs. Mower, May 18, 1864, (Early afternoon phase), *Civil War Regiments*, from "War Along the Bayous, William Riley Brooksher

Severa, Joan, **Dressed for the Photographer**, (Ordinary Americans & Fashion), 1840-1900, The Kent State University Press, Kent, Ohio & London, England 1995

Shakespeare, William, **A Midsummer Night's Dream,** Act 3, Scene I, Titania, Airmont Publishing Co., New York, N.Y.

Shakespeare, William, **Julius Caesar,** Adapted from the Wood and Syms-Wood "Oxford and Cambridge Edition" by F. A. Purcell, D.D and L. M. Somers, M.A., Scott, Foresman and Company, Chicago, Atlanta, New York, 1916

Silterson, J. Carlyle, Pub., The University of Kentucky, **Sugar Country, The Cane Sugar Industry in the South, 1753-1950**

Sway, Marlene, **Familiar Strangers,** 1988 by the Board of Trustees of the University of Illinois

Taylor, Joe Gray, **Louisiana A History**, W. W. Norton & Company, Inc. New York, New York, 1976

Taggart, W. G. & Simon, E. C., **A Brief Discussion of the History of Sugar Cane, It's Culture, Breeding, Harvesting, Manufacturing & Products,** The Louisiana State Department of Agriculture & Immigration, Baton Rouge, La., 1956

Walker, Lester, Preface by Charles Moore, **American Shelter,** Overbrook Press, Woodstock, New York, 1981

Whitman, Walt, **Leaves of Grass,** Prometheus Books, 59 John Glenn Drive, Amherst, New York 14228-2197

Whitman, Walt, **Whitman, selected poems,** by Peter Washington, by David Campbell publisher's Ltd, 1994

Winters, John D., **The Civil War in Louisiana**, Louisiana State University Press, Copyright, 1963

Worrell, Estelle Ansley, **American Costume 1840-1920,** Stackpole Books,1979
From the private collection of David B. Stewart, Alma Plantation, Lakeland, La:
  The Century Illustrated Monthly Magazine, November 1887; Alma Plantation-A History by William D. Reeves, May, 1999; E. A. Maier's Story of Sugar Cane Machinery, Copyright 1952, American Printing Co., New Orleans, La.; "Every Saturday" magazine, May 20, 1871 issue; "Hearth & Home", Nov. 11, 1871 & Nov. 25 1871 issues; "The New South", Supplement to "Harper's Weekly", Aug 13, 1887; "Leslie's Weekly", March 22, 1906.

Williams, T. Harry, **P. G. T. Beauregard, Napoleon In Gray**, Louisiana State University Press, 1965
Yoors, Jan, **The Gypsies,** Waveland Press, Inc.,Long Grove, IL 60047-9580m Reissued 1987
Internet Resources:
 http ://www.anglefire.com/ky/LeCorde/cajunes.html, **Louisiana Creole Vocabulary and Louisiana Creole common Expressions**
http://www. Capeandislandscigars.com/cigars.htm, **A Brief Lesson in Cigars**
http://www.frbsf.org/currency/industrial/legal/516.html, **Legal Tender Notes, 1862**
http://history.latech.edu/publications, **Louisiana Railroads**
http://www.inetours.com/New_Orleans/French_Quarter_History.html, **Old Bank of New Orleans**
http://www.kitchenhaircut.com/megazine/clasic_lit/emmancipation.htmlj, **Emmancipation Proclamation**
http://pubweb.acns.nwu.edu/~baa328/project/hurricane.html **Hurricanes in New Orleans History**
http://www.religioustolerance.orgl/santeri.htm, **Santeria, A syncretistic Caribbean religion**
http://home.comcast.net/~angela.ridgway/Philosophy.html **Balance in Movement: Angela Ridgway Dressage - Philosophy**
http://www.tomtom.co.uk/ciga/ciga2a.htm, **The History of Cigars**
http://www.50 states.com/louisiana.htm, **Flags of U.S.**
h ttp://www.noaa./gov/stories/evolut.html **NOAA History**
http://www.venangoil.com/bridgesplankroad.html **Plank Road Pony Truss Bridge Over Little sugar Creek, Crawford County, Pennsylvania**
http://www.virginiaplaces.orgl/cave/, **Caves and Springs in Virginia**
*Now known as The Daily Town Talk